"Kessler's debut novel will captivate fans of Sherrilyn Kenyon and Laurell K. Hamilton from the very first page. The novel is steamy, humorous . . . take it to a deep . . . New . . . s."

"Ms. Kessler has hit the jackpot with this debut novel of dark fantasy. *Hell's Belles* offers something for everyone; devilishly witty humor, a sassy heroine, a hunky hero and demonic creatures; what more could a reader ask for? Don't miss it!"—*PNR Reviews*

"Had me hooked from the first sentence . . . I'll be reading this one again and again."
——MaryJanice Davidson, *New York Times* bestselling author

"With characters that are intriguing and fully developed and a plot that's out of this world, this is a fabulous start to the 'Hell on Earth' series. *Hell's Belles* will enchant paranormal fans."—*Romance Reviews Today*

"As sinful and decadent as melted chocolate on skin. A dazzling debut!"
——Cathy Clamp, co-author of *Hunter's Moon*

"Wicked, sexy, and delightfully funny, *Hell's Belles* is hot stuff. I'm burning to get my hands on the sequel."

——J.A. Konrath, author of *Whiskey Sour*

Praise for *The Road to Hell*

"This is writing of blistering splendor: Kessler's acid wit and wry style make for damn fine reading. Trust me, the seven deadly sins have never had it so good!"—Cornelia Read, author of *A Field of Darkness*

"A deliciously wicked story that mixes romance and humor with dark urban fantasy."—*Romantic Times*

"Jezebel is a refreshingly angst-free character, cheerfully libidinous and very, very funny. This fun, fast-paced series works as urban fantasy or paranormal romance. There's some great world-building here and an intriguingly subversive mythology, served up with a breezy tone that fits the heroine perfectly.
——Elaine Cunningham, author of *Shadows in the Starlight*

"A wicked, deliciously inventive treat. This book thoroughly seduced me. It'd be a sin to miss it!"—Rachel Caine, author of *Midnight Alley*

"Sizzling . . . Kessler's raunchy blend of heaven, hell and eros makes for a wild thriller ride, and hot, tough-talking Jesse has gumption and sass."—*Publishers Weekly*

Books by Jackie Kessler

HELL'S BELLES

THE ROAD TO HELL

HOTTER THAN HELL

Published by Zebra Books

HOTTER THAN HELL

JACKIE KESSLER

ZEBRA BOOKS
KENSINGTON PUBLISHING CORP.
http://www.kensingtonbooks.com

ZEBRA BOOKS are published by

Kensington Publishing Corp.
850 Third Avenue
New York, NY 10022

All Kensington titles, imprints and distributed lines are available at special quantity discounts for bulk purchases for sales promotion, premiums, fund-raising, educational or institutional use.

Special book excerpts or customized printings can also be created to fit specific needs. For details, write or phone the office of the Kensington Special Sales Manager: Kensington Publishing Corp., 850 Third Avenue, New York, NY 10022. Attn. Special Sales Department. Phone: 1-800-221-2647.

Zebra and the Z logo Reg. U.S. Pat. & TM Off.

ISBN-13: 978-0-8217-8104-3
ISBN-10: 0-8217-8104-9

First Zebra Trade Paperback Printing: August 2008
10 9 8 7 6 5 4 3 2 1

Printed in the United States of America

For Brett. Always.

Acknowledgments

My heartfelt thanks to . . .

John Scognamiglio, the rest of the Zebra gang, and Ethan Ellenberg, for making this book possible.

Miriam Kriss, for your unbridled enthusiasm.

Eileen Cruz Coleman, Vibekke Courtney and Dream Forge Media, Magee King, Marie Lu, Diane Nudelman and the Advance Promotions team, and the incredible staff of the Delmar P.O., for their support when I decided to Hit the ROAD.

Backspace and the CR-RWA, for being terrific author communities.

Jaci Burton, Rachel Caine, Cathy Clamp, Elaine Cunningham, MaryJanice Davidson, Joe Konrath, Cheyenne McCray, Michelle Rowen, Martha O'Connor, Cornelia Read, and Gena Showalter, for their love of all things Hell.

Caitlin Kittredge and Richelle Mead, for keeping me sane.

Renee Barr, who goes above and beyond.

Heather Brewer, the best critique partner an author could ever hope for.

Mom and Dad, for cheering me on.

Ryan and Mason, for being who they are.

And Brett, who should get a medal for putting up with my *mishegas*.

PART I

THE ASSIGNMENT

Chapter 1

Coitus Interruptus

Anyone in my position would've thought the buzzing in my head was anticipation. Five minutes to go, then the client would be eating from my hand. Literally. I had the grapes ready and waiting in the ice bucket, chilling. She liked it when I let the cluster dangle over her lips—she'd poke out her tongue, sinewy and slick against the ripe fruit, darting pink flesh over purple. Sweetness on sweetness, both begging to be sucked. Plucked. My blood pounded through me, boom *boom*, boom *boom*, sending happy signals to my brain and my balls, getting my body primed. T-minus five minutes, and counting. Small talk until then—light touches here, knowing smiles there, lying about her job and mine. Thinking about sex. Killing time.

So it sort of wasn't my fault that I didn't sense the demon approaching.

The client had moved some things around in the bedroom since my last visit. Now her wedding photo was missing ("Getting it reframed") and the threadbare pink comforter had been replaced with one that was red and advertised sin. We sprawled on the bed, clothing still on, intentions thick in the air. She was decked out in a white silk sheath and pearls and lacy thigh highs. I was a study of blacks. A bit cliché, but Tall, Dark, and Handsome was all the rage. She liked it, and I aimed to please.

"I got a new perfume," my client said. "Envy Me."

"I'd prefer to ravish you."

Her smile pulled into a grin—white teeth flashing in a lip-stick sea of red. "The perfume, I mean. It's Gucci." She leaned forward, offering me her neck as she pressed her breasts against my chest, rubbed. Looking for a quick feel through the silk. My kind of woman. She purred, "Like it, baby?"

Inhaling deeply, I took in the peony and jasmine and other scents blending together with her eager sweat, her underlying smell of female in heat. "Nice," I lied. Me, I preferred the musk of her sex alone, without the cloying flowery scent over it. "You smell good enough to eat." No lie there.

"Yeah?" She was playful, almost kittenish. "You going to . . . eat me?"

Heh. Sex kittenish. "Oh, yeah, doll. Eat you alive." Among other things.

"My big bad wolf."

That made me chuckle. Brushing her hair away from her face, I asked, "You my Little Red Riding Hood?"

"Depends, baby. You want me to ride you?"

I smiled, wistful. "Like you would not believe."

My head buzzed, hummed as she oozed sex, her body prac-tically begging me to climb on top of her. Soon, doll. Soon. She jiggled against me once more, reached her hand out to-ward my thigh—stroked once, lushly, then pulled back. She knew the dance by now: only teasing at first, quick-fingered taunts. Nothing overt. Not yet.

Seduction, after all, had its rules. Date Number One had been all about getting her to kiss me. Number Two had been pleasing her like no other man or woman ever had before. Three had been making her want me more than anything else. (One thing about us Seducers: we always put our clients' de-sires ahead of our own. If not for the rules, I would've fucked her silly after I introduced myself.)

Here we were at Date Number Four: D-day, the Big One. Otherwise known as The Payoff. It set my blood to boil just thinking about it.

But first things first: I had to get her revving—ready, steady, go—on the first real touch. Thus a five-minute warm-up of sexual tension. Seduction 101. Child's play. And never mind how that single stroke of hers on my leg had rippled up my back, settled into my stomach. I shifted; the front of my pants was too damn tight.

Sometimes the rules really sucked.

"Don," she said, her voice a low purr that went straight to my crotch. That's all she said: my name, or her version of my name. That's all she needed to say. Her hand again, now on my stomach. I wagged a no-no-no with my finger as I grinned, thinking about how she'd taste like candy. Thinking about how she'd call my name.

Mmm. Shivers.

"I've been waiting for this all week," she whispered.

"Me too."

"I couldn't stop thinking about you." She dropped her gaze to my fly, where she saw just how much I was thinking about her. Her desire filled the air, thick and pungent, as she begged me, "Come on, baby, let's get started already."

But damn, how I wanted to. Oh, the things I wanted to do. Would do. Four minutes—no, less now. Three and counting. I said her name, put just the right amount of foreplay into my voice.

She looked up at me through her makeup-crusted lashes, slowly ran her tongue over her fuck-me lips. Bedroom eyes; blowjob mouth. Intoxicating. Boom *boom*, boom *boom*.

"Now, baby," she said, her voice a throaty growl. The woman was giving way to the animal, to the instinct that tingled deep inside her. Giving way to lust. And all with no nudging from me. Sweet. She said again: "Now." Insistent. Demanding.

A hum again, this time strong enough to make me sit up. Frowning, I felt the buzz resonate through me, pitched high in warning. No, this wasn't just anticipation. This was—

—her mouth on mine, her tongue jabbing through my lips and running against my teeth. My momentary caution faded into bemused surprise. She usually wasn't so direct, but who gave a damn? Screw the countdown to bliss. She was ready. Steady.

Go.

Heat rolled over me, bathed me in fire from head to toe. I opened my mouth to hers, pushed that heat into her. She said, "*Mmmmmm*," melted into the kiss like chocolate over flame. I washed my hands over the silk of her body, and the buzzing in my head sputtered, died.

Oh, doll, how I'm going to make you scream . . .

She groaned against me, and my tongue lapped up the sound. I left her mouth to kiss up her jaw, now playing by the lobe of her ear. She squirmed against me, all soft and delicious, delectable, making contented sounds that told me I hit one of her sweet spots. Her hand clenched on my shoulder, then pushed. With a hungry *rrrr* she rolled me onto my back, straddled my hips. The hem of her dress rode up, exposing the fullness of her upper thighs, the flash of white satin panties.

Boom *boom*.

"This is different," I murmured, my hands on her waist.

"You're always so good to me, baby." Her voice was thick with need, her eyes dark and brimming. Leaning down, she poured herself over me to whisper in my ear, "I want to ride you. Now."

Maybe I ditched the countdown, but other rules had to stay in place. Clients first, even on D-day. That was ever the rule. So I ignored the ache in my groin and said, "Ladies first, doll."

"Don . . ."

"Maybe I'll take the grapes, run them over your naked body. Nibble them off your skin."

"I don't want grapes. I want you."

"You got me."

"No, I don't. You never let me do you, bring you there." She gyrated over my crotch, a slow dry hump that did maddening things to me. "It's always been about me."

"I'm a giving sort of guy," I said, my voice husky.

"Your turn, baby," she said, punctuating her promise with wet kisses down my neck. Her fingers played by my crotch, and over the buzzing in my head and the pounding of my heart, I heard her unzip my fly. "I'm going to love you so fine," she said, "you're going to sing my name. I'm going to make you explode."

Down she kissed, down my chest, my stomach, my—

Wa-*hoo*.

Okay, maybe the customer was always right . . .

In the midst of mind-blowing pleasure, a deafening crash, followed by a man's shout: "What the fuck are you doing with my wife?"

Uh-oh.

Louder than the man's words, the buzzing screamed its warning in my head.

Shit.

Getting interrupted in the middle of sex is bad enough. Worse is when the cause of *coitus interruptus* is a demon.

A glance told me all I needed to know: he was obscenely muscled, and his eyes glowed with malefic presence. Definitely not a Seducer; I would've felt the psychic connection. Sloth was out of the question. Pride, maybe, or Envy . . .

Between my legs, the client was still going to town. Side effect of entrancing the clientele over the course of four Dates: they wound up being a bit one-track minded. Usually it was anything but a problem; at the moment, though, the pleasure was a tad . . . distracting. Not that I was complaining.

Because my client didn't seem to be one to talk with her mouth full, I put on my charming face and said to her husband, "Your wife's told me so much about you."

He roared, a wordless cry of pure rage. Terrific—one of the Berserkers was riding his body. They weren't exactly known for their reasoning skills. How was I supposed to convince a demon of Wrath that the client was mine? Hell knew I had all the paperwork to prove it . . .

The husband cocked back a fist. The flesh burned red, and energy sizzled off his skin.

Whoops. I grabbed my client by her shoulders and pulled her off of me, then rolled with her to the floor. She landed on top of me, her mouth working like a landed fish. Sandwiched between the wall and the bed, we were trapped. Last Stand at the Sealy Corral.

From the other side of the bed: "I'll kill the both of you!"

The haze of passion began to clear from my client's eyes. Before the fear took hold, I ran a finger over her brow, pushing a command into her mind. She crumpled on my chest, dead asleep. I nudged her to the ground. Back in a second, doll.

Far over my head, a bolt of magic slammed into the wall. Smoking plaster fluttered down, singeing my face with tiny kisses. Maybe the man was possessed, but he was also a lousy shot.

He bellowed, "Think you can sleep with my wife?"

"Actually," I called back, "sleeping wasn't what I had in mind."

He screamed his fury, then the wall behind me exploded. I threw myself over the unconscious woman, shielding her from the smoking debris. I'd be blessed if I let another demon claim her. I'd been on her case for a month; she didn't die until I said so.

Sometimes, I was as possessive as a Coveter.

Pieces of the ruined wall crashed on me and around me, covered me in filth and soot. Dust made me sneeze, and sneezing during a fight was both dangerous and rather lame, so I stopped breathing. The stench of smoke lingered in my nostrils. Nice. Reminded me of home. Not including the part about getting buried by a falling wall. The wreckage hadn't killed me—when I was on a collection, the only thing human about me was my appearance—but getting slammed with it hurt like a bastard. My own fault; I should have known better than to taunt a Berserker.

Over the sound of the settling rubble, he shouted, "You dead yet, asshole?"

"Hate to break it to you, chuckles, but you missed."

Couldn't help it. For demons, Berserkers were just so fucking stupid.

"Seducer!" The man's voice deepened to that of a consti-pated buffalo's bellow. "I'm going to rip you apart!"

"Some nefarious just talk, talk, talk." I shot my arm out and leveled a blast overhead. The light fixture overhead shattered, crashed down to the floor. I heard the man jump clear and land heavily in the far end of the room. Recharging my power as the man regained his footing, I reviewed the possibilities. It came down to three options.

One: I could kill the possessed human.

No, the paperwork involved in the accidental slaying of a mortal would kill my sex drive for the better part of a decade.

Two: I could run.

Hah, as if.

Three: I could banish the demon, leave the human alive.

Ding, ding, ding, we have a winner. Banishing, *sans* killing. That meant attacking him directly with my magic was out. And *that* meant I had to figure out what its weakness was and kick-start the exorcism.

It occurred to me that priests had other uses besides between-meal snacks. Live and learn.

The sound of clumping footfalls, along with labored breath-ing. Some mortals just couldn't take a hint. I scrambled to the foot of the bed and yanked on the baseboard until I pried the wood free. Shouting to do the banshees proud, I leapt up and hurled the makeshift weapon at the human.

And . . . bull's-eye! The wood splintered against his torso with a satisfying crack. He staggered back three steps, blinked stupidly at the slivers embedded in his flesh. Then he snarled something about my parentage and aimed another blast my way. I hit the carpet two seconds before it rained plaster again.

Wood was a big no. What else? I didn't have any iron on hand . . .

He shouted, "Come out and fight like a man!"

"I'm not a man." I reached out blindly, found the ice bucket, heavy with grapes and melted ice. The rim and handle on the black lacquered wood gleamed with a silver sheen. Yes, maybe silver would do the trick. Come a little closer, chuckles. Give me a hug.

"Fight me!" Two voices spoke the same command—the mortal's ire blending with the demon's innate wrath.

I gripped the bucket, getting ready for the windup. "Don't you think two on one is a bit unfair?"

"*Fight me!*"

"Come here and make me."

He shrieked his unholy rage, and then I heard him stomp toward me. Charge of the Dark Brigade. I popped up and pitched the ice bucket at the ballistic human, catching him full in the face. The silver handle bonked him about a second before the melted ice and chilled fruit splattered on his skin . . . skin that immediately bubbled and smoked. He roared in either fury or agony, and then he swatted madly at his face.

Gotcha.

I took a moment to zip up my fly. Then I stepped around the wreckage strewn almost artfully through the ruins of the bedroom to approach the wounded demon. Under my feet, a collage of shattered glass sparkled amidst the chunks of smoking plaster and plywood. Love really was a battlefield.

The man had fallen to the floor, clutching at his steaming face and gibbering in pain. Interesting. The silver handle was nowhere near him, yet he was still reacting so strongly . . . Ah. Smiling, I scooped up a handful of stray ice cubes. Allergic to water, my, my. If I had any feelings, I would have felt sorry for the creature; having such an elemental sensitivity would crimp any demon's style. But I've never been accused of being compassionate.

Water pooling in my hand, I squatted over the squirming form. "Need a towel?"

Beneath his clawed fingers, the flesh of the man's face looked rather spongy. Hmm. Hope that's not permanent. I didn't think the human would be long on the mortal coil with his face slipping off his skull. The thought of all the red tape associated with accidental slaughter made my stomach roil. Damned bureaucracy would be the death of me.

He snarled, "Bless yourself, asshole!"

"Don't suppose it'll help to tell you there's been a mix-up," I said, juggling the ice from hand to hand.

Lowering his fingers, the Berserker glared up at me through the human's red-rimmed eyes. "No mix-up, whoremaster."

"That's 'Mister Whoremaster' to you."

He spat at me, but the thick glob sizzled and vanished before it touched my skin. Company perk: adjustable heat aura.

"Bastard!"

"Now, now," I said, dangling a sweating cube over his face. "Play nice, kitty, or you get a bath. What do you mean, no mix-up?"

For a long moment, he stared his hatred at me, charged the air with fury so brutally raw that my flesh should have been flayed from my bones. Finally he said, "I was sent on purpose."

"A snafu, then. I've got all the paperwork. She's mine, chuckles."

"No snafu."

Oh, really? "Explain yourself."

"Killers, the man and woman both."

I'd known about the woman; there was a reason she was a client, after all. The man, though, was a surprise. Then again, I hadn't bothered to research him. He wasn't the one I was supposed to fuck to death. "What, they get off on the murder?"

"Thrill of the bloodshed." His eyes gleamed, and a smile unfurled on his softening face. "The gospel of butchery. The ecstasy of violence."

"Uh-huh." I'd heard the Wrath party line before. "That's lovely. But she's still mine."

"No, whoremonger." He bared his teeth in a parody of a grin. "The flesh puppets, they were to kill you."

Jaw clenched, I asked, "Kill *me?*" Humans, attacking a demon? Outside of some wildly popular television shows, that was unheard of. There had to have been a mistake.

"They were to bathe in your blood," he said with a sigh of pleasure. "Then I was to slit their throats, claim them both for Wrath."

Blinking, I repeated, "For *Wrath?*"

"Want I should speak in smaller words, rake?"

I didn't know which was more insulting: that the humans had wanted to kill me, or that a Berserker was insinuating that I was stupid. A snarl on my lips, I crushed the ice in one of my hands and wiped it over the remains of his forehead. His squeal of pain was almost worth the mess of melted flesh on my fingers.

After his screeching faded, I asked, "Why me?"

Arms wrapped over his head, I almost didn't hear his muffled reply. "Would be telling."

I still couldn't grasp that the mortals had wanted to slice and dice me. *Me.* That wasn't in the Demon Playbook. Not that we had a playbook, but still . . . "She was *my* target," I insisted.

"Murder is murder. The more, the better." Panting, he peered out from his barricade of arms. "Kill two humans, kill one Seducer. All the same to Wrath. But destroying you, that would have given me pleasure." He chuckled wetly. "You understand pleasure, no?"

I sat heavily on my haunches. Well, this just sucked angel feathers. Where did humans get off, thinking they could actually take down a demon? Next thing you knew, they'd be shooting me with silver bullets and flinging holy water on me. Idiots.

No, my client couldn't have known I was a demon. To her and her husband—before he'd been possessed—I'd been just another flesh puppet, one whom they could play with and prey on. No more.

The man's breathing took on a burbling sound. I asked, "You dying on me, chuckles?"

"You Seducers . . . all the same," the demon whispered. "Clap-carrying . . . sluts . . . suck the fight . . . out of a body."

Could I help it if I was a lover, not a fighter?

"Paperwork . . . keep you bound . . . for eons."

"Ah, go to Hell." I dropped the rest of the melting ice on him.

* * *

"**O**pen your eyes, doll."

My client's eyelids fluttered, then opened. The confusion I saw staring back at me was like a shot of whiskey burning the back of my throat. Mmm. Straddling her hips, I rubbed against her, just once, just enough to send her body signals that her brain was still too fuzzy to interpret. Beneath us, the ruined bed protested but still held. I was planning on breaking it within ten minutes. Anticipation . . .

She blinked, tried to open her mouth. Then she tried to move her body. No dice; she was frozen on her back, her arms by her sides, her virginal white silk dress covering her from knockers to knees. Confusion sparked into fear. I inhaled deeply, took in the scent of her growing terror.

Boom *boom*.

"You're wondering why you can't move." I smiled, picturing all the things I was about to do to her. "You're wondering what happened. I'll recap."

I stretched over her, ran my hand from her cheek down to her chin, her neck, her breast, her belly. "You were going down on me when your loving husband came tearing into the room." I reached behind me until my hand found her crotch. Sliding between her legs, I ran two fingers over the whisper softness of her satin panties, felt the lips of her vulva quiver. "He was going to kill me, with help from you."

She stiffened beneath me.

Grinning, I said, "That's him on the floor. Had the audacity to die and not remove himself after. I'm afraid he's going to stink up the place in another day or so."

Her eyes slipped closed, and tears leaked through her lids. How touching. I pushed her underwear to the side and stroked my fingers over her clitoral hood, then pressed gently. Stroke, press.

"No worries, doll," I said. "You won't miss him for long."

Stroke. I heard her breath catch in her throat, and I grinned as I pressed, lingering. Now her inner muscles tensed with my touch, seemed to reach for my fingers as I moved them away.

Passion in the depths of despair. Sin at its sweetest. The smell of her fear was now spiced with desire. Demonic aromatherapy.

"I have a question for you. It'll go easier on you if you tell me the truth. And believe me, I can smell the truth on you." I rubbed her sex harder. "You do believe me, don't you? Go ahead, doll. Speak."

"Yes," she said thickly.

"Good. Now then, tell me why you and Loving Husband didn't try to kill me on our first Date."

Shuddering from my touch, she said, "You were a surprise. We always pick our takes together. But you, you came on to me. He was out of town, and you picked me up . . ." Her voice turned into a moan as I reached inside her, nudging her toward bliss.

"So your man was away, and you decided to play?"

"You kissed me," she breathed, "and nothing else mattered . . ."

Have to love the demon gigolo mojo. Gigolojo at its best.

"Actually, doll, you kissed me." I slid my fingers out of her, then moved my hand up and down her inner thigh, tickling her flesh with her own wetness. She reeked of passion and panic. Mmm. Soon, soon, soon. "That's how it works. You kiss me willingly, and then boom. Magic. But the fun starts when you call my name."

She opened her eyes, looked at me as those fat tears kept winding down her cheeks. "Please," she said. "I wasn't going to hurt you, not you . . ."

"Uh, uh, uh. That's a lie. Shame. Here you were doing so well until now." I pressed the nails of my fingers harder against her plump thigh. "You and hubby, you were going to kill me good and dead, then do whatever it is serial killers do to celebrate. Champagne, maybe? A bloodbath? Tell me true."

"Sex," she whispered. "We have sex. We're already sticky with your blood, and we kiss, tasting you on us . . ."

"Why, doll, that's positively perverted. How impressive!" With my other hand, I cupped her full breast, feeling the hardness of her nipple poking through the silk of her dress. "How many have you killed? I'm just curious."

"Seven . . ."

"A powerful number. So they say." Now I had her other breast in hand, rolling the mound in my fingers, teasing her until the nipple was fully erect, begging me to have a taste.

"Please . . . Why can't I move?"

I leaned down to whisper in her ear. "That would be because I commanded you not to move. Boom. Magic."

She bit her lip—a nervous tic that reminded me of someone else. "You a magician?"

A quick suck on her earlobe, then a sharp nip. "I eat magicians for breakfast."

She squeaked: a tiny, terrified sound. I nearly exploded in my pants.

"I'm an incubus," I said, stretching the last *s*. "And do you know what an incubus does to fragile human dolls like you?"

Stinking of terror, she whispered, "No . . ."

I leaned over her until my mouth was barely inches away from hers. "An incubus sucks the life from you. An incubus fucks you and kills you, then takes your soul to Hell."

"*No* . . ."

A quick kiss on her dry lips, wetting her mouth with mine. "So here's where we are, doll. Your man is dead. Your life was already forfeited. Now it's going to happen a bit sooner than I'd planned."

"Please . . ."

I loved it when they begged. "Tell you what, my little murderess. I'll give you a chance. All you have to do is not call my full name when I make you climax. If you can do that, I won't fuck you to death." I'd break her neck. But what was the point of telling her that? "What do you think? Tell me true."

"I . . ." She swallowed, said, "I don't know your full name."

"But you do." I licked the hollow of her throat, kissed the sensitive flesh. "In their souls, all humans know the nefarious. What do you say, doll? I'll screw you so hard you'll see stars." Between her legs, my fingers danced over her slit. She groaned, tried to move, groaned harder when I pressed down. "Think you can keep from calling my name when you come?"

Gasping, she said, "Yes."

"Wonderful." I kissed her neck, worked my way down to her breast. Debated whether I should let her move beneath me. I gave her fifty-fifty on being able not to call my name. She was evil down to the core; I had to admire that in a human.

She was mine three minutes and forty-nine seconds later.

Chapter 2

Stalling

"I'm dead."

Bloody Hell. For the umpteenth time, I said, "I know."

"I'm dead."

"I still know."

"I'm dead."

My client was also a buzzkill, so I ordered another shot of Jager. On the other side of the ebony bar, Randolph acknowledged my request and made with the pouring. I didn't know why a nonmagical human mixed drinks at the most popular interplaneary pub this side of the Astral Plane, and I didn't care. So what if he always wore an expression of wide-eyed terror and his mouth was set in a frozen scream? As long as he didn't spill the booze when he poured, Randolph was all right in my book.

And he was eye candy, in an androgynous, Goth kind of way. Me, I'll always prefer the ladies. But in my line of work, the lads are also fair game. I'm an equal-opportunity sort of Seducer. I'll happily flirt with any mortal, especially one who looked like Randolph. His mop of black hair was set off by ghostly skin, which was slightly marred by a prominent blue vein snaking over his nose. His face was delicate-jawed and clean-shaven; his body was slender, yet it managed to fill out his black T-shirt with the Voodoo Café logo emblazoned on its front. Attractive. And so damn young, practically overflowing with potential.

I could suck him dry in a New York minute. I bet he'd taste like saltwater taffy.

Maybe he saw something in my gaze, something in the curve of my lips as I watched him, because his eyes widened until a ring of white surrounded the chocolate brown of his irises, and a tic danced along his jaw. I caught the scent of his fear—tangy, like grapefruits—before it wafted away, blending with the other bar-heavy smells of cigars, booze and sweat. And brimstone, of course. Where there be demons, there be the stench of rotten eggs.

I grinned big, let my teeth slip into fangs as I inhaled the fading odor of Randolph's terror. Mmm.

Swallowing audibly, he slid the full cup over to me, the glass making that distinct wet scrape against the countertop, the sound of an object rubbing suggestively against another. Ah, how I loved friction. "Six dollars," he said, his voice pleasantly deep and cracking on the last word.

I softened my grin into a winning smile as I pulled out my wallet and produced an American ten-dollar bill. "For you," I said, offering him the money with a flick of my fingers. "Keep the change."

As he took the ten, I scraped the nail of my middle finger against the meat of his palm and *pushed*. Just a whisper of power, a hint of lust. Sweat popped on his brow as a wave of desire broke over him, flushing his face and glazing his eyes.

Heh.

I don't shit where I eat, so I let him go. Besides, he wasn't a client, and I wasn't allowed to tempt him. The rules are damn clear on who's a target and who's not. Randolph literally served evil. As long as he worked at the Voodoo Café, he was off limits.

Randolph blinked twice, then flashed me a nervous grin before he scuttled off to the far end of the bar to wait on other patrons. Swim away, little fishie. Swim away.

I grabbed the drink and knocked it back, relishing how the

back of my throat caught fire. Just knowing that Randolph would be mine if I ever really wanted him was enough to satisfy me. For now. Already I felt the fire rekindling inside of me, a slow honing of my senses to better experience desire whether through smell or sight or sound, a whetting of sexual appetite that heated my blood and stirred my cock.

Mortal men say they always think about sex. Hah. They should be in my pants for one night. A perpetual state of horniness goes with the demonic package.

And I wouldn't have it any other way.

"I'm dead."

My good mood evaporated, and my fangs shrank back to human teeth as I snorted my frustration. The damned sure as Hell were self-centered. Didn't my client know she'd have the better part of eternity to mull over her fate?

I glanced over my shoulder to see her hovering just behind me, her soul a thing of pulsing blacks and reds, like a charbroiled heart seeping blood. Her weakness for sex and violence stained her spirit, highlighted how her internal berserker and seducer warred for dominance over her immortal soul. Very nice.

"I'm dead."

"Tell me something I don't know, doll." A serial killer was always a toss-up between Lust and Wrath—desire for slaughter is still desire, but the rage that fuels murder scores for the Berserkers. My client's ultimate punishment would be determined by which aspect of evil weighed the heaviest in her core. If I was a betting sort of entity, I would have laid odds on Lust. But that judgment wouldn't happen until after I brought her to Hell—and I'd be blessed if I was going there any time soon. I'd just slaughtered a nefarious *and* a human (granted, wearing the same body) without a permit. I was seriously fucked, and not in the way we incubi prefer. The heaps of paperwork that I'd have to fill out . . . Just thinking about it made my eyeballs throb.

I pressed my fingers against the bridge of my nose and closed my eyes, but that did nothing to kill my headache. Fucking red tape was going to tie me up for a human's age. Maybe I couldn't escape it, but I sure as Hell could delay it. At the very least, I was going to get plastered before I ventured down Below. And based on the way my metabolism burned off alcohol, I'd be holed up at the bar for at least three weeks before I had anything close to a steady buzz.

"I'm dead."

Then again, three weeks of incessant whining from my client might feel more like an eternity than it would filling out miles of Wrongful Termination forms.

A scent of lilacs tinged with winter frost, just before delicate fingers brushed over my shoulder. A feminine voice asked, "Why so glum?"

I opened my eyes and turned to see a stunning blonde smiling at me like a televangelist eager to get with the hallelujahs. Mmm. Look at her, with hair so golden that Rumpelstiltskin would have creamed his leggings—eyes so blue, the Almighty must have had that color in mind when He painted the sky. Porcelain skin, and a lean body wrapped in a white evening dress that emphasized the swells of her breasts.

Helloooo, sexy.

Her smile was good; it would have been terrific if not for the slight tremble in her full lips. She was nervous. And based on the stink of chilly goodness that wafted around her, I understood why. I peered through her mortal costume and grinned as I recognized her true form. For a moment, I wondered who'd told her about the Voodoo Café; her kind didn't deign to mingle with creatures of clay or coal. But what the Hell—she was here, apparently looking for action. And I was pretty sure she didn't recognize me for who I really was.

Excellent. Just what I needed: a little fun to cheer me up.

"My client's a bummer," I said, flashing a disarming smile at my new companion. A slit ran down the right side of her dress, starting just beneath her hip and extending all the way down, teasing me with a glimpse of pale thigh. I wondered if she'd squeeze those thighs around me as I pounded her, or if she'd spread them wide as I dove into her secret waters. "All she can think about is her new antilife status. It's getting me down."

As if on cue, my client chimed in: "I'm dead."

The blonde's slender fingers pressed down on my shoulder, working the muscle. She was getting bolder. Nice. She said, "Your client seems to be in denial."

"Yup."

"Why haven't you brought her to the Abyss?"

"I'm extending the torture."

Her fingers paused, then continued their dance over the black material of my shirt. "How thoughtful."

"I'm a caring sort of demon. So what are you doing here, sweetness?" I ate her with my eyes, relishing how my heated gaze brought a blush to her cheeks. "Don't you have mortals to tempt?"

"I'd rather be here, with you."

Heh. That wasn't quite a lie, but it wasn't the full truth. Working for the Pit has been rubbing off on her. I arched a brow. "Really. And what would you rather be doing with me?"

Her smile faltered. After a pause, an idea lit her eyes. Her voice low and laden with meaning, she said, "Maybe you could buy me a drink, and we could talk about that."

"A *drink?*" A chuckle burst out of my mouth. Couldn't help it; she was like something out of A Beginner's Guide to Seduction, without the obligatory illustrations. "*Talk* about what we could do? You're acting like I'm one of your marks. And a stupid one, at that. What am I, sweetness—target practice for your turn with the flesh puppets?"

My laughter obliterated her smile. She straightened her spine and looked down at me, dispassionate. Cold. Her kind always masked their discomfort with disdain. Frigid bitches, the lot of them. She sniffed, this cute little sound of derision. "I've been told that practice makes perfect."

"Good advice." Still chuckling, I reached over and encircled her waist in my hands, then pulled her onto my lap.

"What are you—"

"Like you said, sweetness, practice makes perfect." She gasped as I rubbed my crotch against hers. "Time to practice."

She spluttered, "We're in *public.*"

Damn, she was adorable when she was flustered. "I'm sorry, I thought you were a Seducer. My mistake."

"No, I *am* . . ." She took a shaky breath. "I *am* a Seducer."

"You sure? You're acting prissy enough to be one of the Arrogant."

"I'm dead."

Fuck me raw. I glared at my client and snarled, "You: shut up."

She shut up.

"Much better." I turned my attention back to the blonde, who tensed as I cupped her ass. My voice a purr, I said, "You're so anxious, sweetness. You'd think you haven't flirted with anyone before."

Her cheeks flamed. "That's not true . . ."

I nuzzled my face between her breasts, took in her odor of flowers and spice—no perfume here, no false scent covering her core. This was all her. "You'd think," I said, kissing the curve of her left mound, "you'd never been touched before."

"I . . ."

My mouth found her nipple, which was tenting the white silk of her dress. She let out a startled squeak when I kissed it, sounding like a mouse cornered by a tomcat.

Boom *boom*.

I trailed my tongue over the nub, teasing it with my lips and teeth until she groaned—a full-throated sound, caught between a whimper and a growl. Mmm. I sucked her nipple, and with a cry she leaned back, pushing her flesh against my face, begging me with her body to do more. I squeezed her bottom, then ran my fingers up over her back, her neck, her ear. As she quivered against me, I kissed my way up the swell of her breast, her throat, then slowly licked the line of her jaw.

She was moaning now, her hips dancing in circles over my groin. Going with the moment. Losing herself. Sweet. I nipped her earlobe, then lapped away the sting with my tongue. My fingers left her ear to trail along her neck, her collarbone, then dipped lower to brush over the swells of her breasts just as I kissed the hollow of her throat.

A sudden burst of peppermint overrode the stink of lilacs, and I knew I had her.

Heh.

I whispered in her ear, "You'd think you were an angel pretending to be a succubus."

She froze.

"And based on how you're reacting, you'd think you've never been fucked. Angels don't fuck, do they?"

Her quick intake of breath told me my words had touched a nerve. Or maybe that was from me fondling her.

"So what are you, sweetness? An angel playing the part? Or a succubus looking to score? Is your snatch holy, or hungry?" I thrusted against her, dry humping, my rod nearly bursting out of my pants. I'd been told that cherubs taste like gold. I wondered whether her molten gold would rush down my throat, or if I'd have to coax it out of her. Tease her. Tempt it out of her.

"I'm a Seducer," she stammered. "As the King of Hell decreed."

"Right, the King." I kissed her neck, relishing how she squirmed in my lap—she was turned on, on, on, and she was so very afraid. Positively intoxicating. "Brilliant move, replacing all the succubi with one-time angels. Like you could do anything better than a real succubus."

She tried to wiggle out of my embrace, but I locked my arms around her waist. I said, "Of course, fucking something as holy as you would probably freeze my dick off."

"You can't speak to me that way," she said, shooting me with a glare that was supposed to remind me she had once walked close to God. As if I cared.

"I can do whatever I want to you, Feathers." I allowed my true form to radiate through my mortal shell for a moment— but that moment was all it took. Her eyes widened as she glimpsed my horns, my eyes, my fangs. The real me. "I'm a first-level incubus. And you're just a fallen angel with her legs locked at her knees."

"My lord Daunuan. I . . ." She took a deep breath, then

smoothed her features until she wore a mask of perfect cold-ness. "I didn't recognize you, my lord."

"Never would have guessed. You need to work on your act-ing, Feathers. Not to mention your pickup lines."

She sniffed again, a tiny sound brimming with contempt. Im-pressive. She said, "Don't call me that."

"No? Why not?"

"Because it insults me."

"Aw, poor little cherub. I've singed your tail feathers." I massaged her bottom, squeezing her cheeks, enjoying how firm she was in my hands and how she acted like I'd just stuck a hot poker up her ass. "I'll rub it and make it feel better."

Her face could have been chiseled from ice, except for her eyes—they flashed a heat that bordered on hatred. Not that her kind could feel something so negative. The cherubim were all about forgiveness and love. Puke. Who needed love when there was passion?

"Pissed off, Feathers? Sweet." I moved my hand beneath the curve of her ass, stretched my fingers between her legs, probed. "Let's have angry sex."

Her jaw clenched. "My lord. Don't."

"Don't?"

"Please."

"So polite, she is. So easy for her to beg." I winked at her, let my grin stretch wider than my human-seeming mouth should have allowed. Between her thighs, my fingers glided over the silk of her dress, barely touching, only hinting at what I could do, how I could make her feel. "You don't want me touching you, Feathers?"

"No, my lord."

"You didn't seem to mind before, when you were shoving your tit in my mouth."

She swallowed thickly, turned her head away. Her flaxen hair spilled over her shoulder, winking in the light of the bar, begging me to run my hands through it. Her voice a whisper, she said, "I didn't know it was you, my lord."

The poor thing sounded like she was going to cry. One could

only hope. My fingers pressed harder, stroked her, stroked until she let out a shuddering gasp. Oh, sweetness, the sounds you'd make if I fucked you . . .

"Please, my lord. Stop."

I stopped, but kept my hand between her legs, waiting. "So I was good enough for you before, but not now?"

"You will never be good enough for me, my lord." The angel lifted her chin, then turned to look me in the eye. Her baby blues sparkled with enough pride to make the Arrogant whistle in appreciation. "You can't be good. It's not in your nature."

"You sweet-talker, you. Bet you say that to all the demons. Or maybe you're just being nice to me." I grinned, flashing my fangs. "I think you like me."

"I *don't* like you, my lord."

"You like everyone, sweetness. That's in *your* nature. And I think you like me more than you care to admit. I think you want me. What do you say? Want me to pop your celestial cherry?"

"No." She added a belated, "My lord."

I laughed softly, enjoying the picture of her holy indignity. "Get off your high horse, Feathers. You work for Hell now. Sooner or later, you're going to have to spread your legs and bring in a client. You haven't yet, have you?"

She swallowed, said nothing.

"You're still virginal. Pure," I said, stretching the word, turning it into something wicked. "Take it from me, the lower-downs aren't too keen on poor performers. The consequences are pretty steep."

"I am well aware of my situation, my lord."

"You should take me up on my offer. A little pain, a lot of pleasure. Once I break in that tight body of yours, the mortals won't be able to restrain themselves. They'll be begging you to fuck them and take them to the Pit." Oh, to bed an angel, to seduce one who used to bask in the light of Heaven . . .

Shivers.

I nibbled on the shell of her ear, and she shuddered against me—I felt her nipples harden, smelled the desire burst through her body in a peppermint splash. "I'd go slow with you, sweetness. I'd make your first time unforgettable." I nudged my hand away from her slit, trailed it over the curve of her waist, the top of her breast, up farther until I cupped her chin. Looking her in the eye, I said, "Let me make a succubus out of you."

Something in her gaze shifted, softened. But I'd never know what she was going to say, because at that moment, a voice boomed in my mind:

DAUN, GET YOUR ASS DOWN HERE.

Shit.

Before I could voice a proper response, the mental connection broke.

So much for my goal of a three-week buzz before going Downstairs. When one of Hell's elite wanted you, you didn't stall, not if you wanted to avoid a dip into the Lake of Fire.

On my lap, the angel squirmed. "My lord? Are you all right?"

Look at that: she cared, despite all her protests. Or maybe that really was her celestial essence shining through. "Got to go, Feathers. Pan wants a word with me. Think about my offer."

She sniffed again. I decided it was sexy—sort of her version of foreplay. "There's nothing to think about, my lord. I will never make love to you."

"Love? I'm talking about good old-fashioned fornication. Making the beast with two backs. Having sex. *Fucking.*"

She shuddered delicately. Poor thing's sensibilities were offended. Heh.

"Come here, you." I pulled her to me and kissed her roughly, bruising her lips with mine. She squealed into my mouth, and my blood boiled from the sound of her fear laced with desire. My tongue pried its way between her lips, ran over her teeth, prodded. The angel gasped and tried to break the kiss, but I fused my mouth to hers.

Don't fight me, sweetness.

Either we had our own connection or she just decided to surrender, because her protests died and she went limp in my arms and opened her mouth to mine. Her taste flooded my mouth: gold, mingled with peppermint. Very nice. I *pushed*, drenched the cherub with my power . . . and then transferred my client's soul into her. As the angel absorbed the spiritual bond, she let out a long, delicious moan.

Boom *boom*.

When I couldn't feel the murderess's soul on my tongue any longer, I ended the kiss, pulled away. The cherub's eyes were closed, a look of bliss stamped onto her face.

Fuck me, she was so damn beautiful.

"There you go, Feathers. Your very first soul claim. Don't say I never did anything for you."

She opened her eyes, which were glazed from the joy of tasting her first human soul. "My lord? Why did you—"

"I'm dead."

The angel stiffened, turned to look at the red-and-black form of the dead woman's spirit, which now hovered to her right.

"Enjoy the company, Feathers."

"Oh . . . damn me."

I loved it when she cursed. With a parting wink, I let my power wash over me and take me to Hell.

Chapter 3

Panic

The first thing to hit me when I stepped out of the nothingness between realities and into Pan's antechamber was the smell of trapped sweat and deep earth. Any incubus worth his horns could distinguish the kinds of sweat—the citrus tang of fear, the pumpkin spice of sex. Me, I could assign a body part to the sweat, and what position (or instrument) was used to set the mood.

Hmmm. Cat-o'-nine-tails . . . across the back of the thighs. Pan must be in a BDSM phase.

Beneath the heavy odors of flesh and loam, a pungent scent beckoned—a heady bouquet, like truffles, that awoke every nerve in my body. It was the raw smell of unbridled desire. Animal passion. *Grrrrrowl.*

I breathed in and held it, let the musky aroma tickle my nostrils and dangle by the back of my throat until it faded like a dying scream, leaving my mouth parched and my lips tingling with blood. The smell sent "fuck now" signals to my brain, and my body practically vibrated with need. Hellooo, erection. I didn't bother trying to adjust myself; meeting Pan with a raging hard-on was par for the course. Arousal was to the god of carnality and sensuality what belching was after a particularly fine meal: a sign of appreciation and respect. And unless you wanted to insult the King of Lust, you showed your respect. (In my case, thirteen inches of respect.)

After the smell and the mad urge to copulate with the nearest creature washed over me, I took in the utter darkness—obsidian so complete that the concept of light seemed like a bad dream. In the maw of Pan's stronghold, there was no color but a suffocating black. And with it, a patient silence. Cave darkness, cave quietude; the stillness of impending madness. A perfect waiting room for the creature who inspires panic. Me, I like the dark. It makes me horny.

The solitude heightened my senses, turned up my heartbeat until it rivaled the gunshot sound of an orchestra pit's bass drum—boom *BOOM!!!* boom *BOOM!!!* My blood thrummed, making its own melody as it crashed through me, heated me, revved me until I was ready, steady, go. Caught in the backbeat of my body, I remembered green eyes and an eager smile, imagined curly black hair that no brush could tame. And then I pictured her: short but far from small, moving her lithe body in time to music, dancing more seductively than Salome with all her seven veils.

I love him, Daun.

Him.

The flesh puppet with the stupidly big shoulders. Him, named after the prude Apostle who claimed it was better to marry than to be set aflame with passion.

What could a mortal like him know of lust?

Her voice insisted: *I love him.*

Love? Demons don't love, babes. Whatever you think you're feeling, you're just fooling yourself.

So what if I wasn't really talking to her? The message still worked: the memory of her voice faded, blended into the complete silence of Pan's antechamber. It took another moment to banish her face from my mind; even after her words stretched into empty ghost whispers, the image of her dazzling eyes, gemstone eyes, winked at me—the deep green of emeralds, vitreous, sparkling with mirth.

Damned flirt. I poked those eyes with mental fingers. *Get out of here, babes. You're not welcome.* Before my treacherous memory could toy with me further, I announced: *I'm here.*

ABOUT FUCKING TIME.

I rolled my eyes. Pan was a master of bitching and moaning. If he'd really wanted me that badly, he could have just summoned me directly into his receiving room. But if it wasn't urgent, then the King of Lust obeyed our Sin's unwritten rule: give a Seducer a time to complete current business. To creatures like us, clients came first. Always. Pan had given me time to finish up with the angel; therefore, his summons was merely important, not life-threatening.

The flesh puppets, they were to kill you.

I shrugged away the Berserker's words. Humans can't kill demons, not without a lot of help. Good thing I'd destroyed that particular demon of Wrath; he'd been too stupid to live.

Through the psychic link that connected all Seducers, I said to Pan, *I got here as soon as I could.*

WHATEVER. GET IN HERE.

Sure thing. Where's the door?

NEVER MIND. I'LL SHOW YOU IN.

Strips of nothingness wrapped around me, papered me like a mummy and hefted me up. Oh, fuck me, I hate this part . . .

I tumbled backward as invisible hands scooped me up, spun me in a windup. All I could do was snarl and bear it. But flashing my fangs did little good; now I was careening through the darkness, flying like a demonic fastball. Sensations battered me as I tore through the boundary of Pan's antechamber: the stench of sewage and charred meat coated my nostrils; damp coldness smothered me, drowned me in brackish water. A crushing weight splintered my ribs, squeezed my heart until it was a pulpy liquid mass in my chest. From the blackness around me, a low rumble sounded, growling, stretching into a hungry snarl.

He's such a Goddamn showoff.

I landed in an unceremonious heap on the ground, only slightly buffered by a thick rug—wool, still holding the stink of the sheep from which it had been shorn. I spat the fabric from my mouth and sat up, only to be assaulted by an over-powering stench of greenery and woods. *Pfaugh!*

My eyes watered, and I waved a hand in front of my nose. No luck—the thick smells of foliage and fertile soil coated the roof of my mouth. Not breathing did nothing to dissipate the smell. If I hadn't known better, I'd swear that I'd materialized into the heart of some Athenian nighttime paradise. I snorted, expelling the odors of cedar and pine. It fucking reeked of for-est. I half-expected to see a cartoon deer with obscenely huge eyes come traipsing out, swishing its obnoxiously cute tail like it was cruising for a piece of ass.

But as I looked around, no woodland scene unfolded before me. Just a freakishly huge bed—far past king size; this was god size—atop a stone altar, surrounded by various short tables that overflowed with incense, lava lamps, and bowls of jelly beans. (Pan insisted that the candy was an aphrodisiac. I'll stick with oysters and all-consuming fear.) The room was lit by multi-colored spotlights from somewhere up on high. All it needed to complete the mood was a soul man crooning in the back-ground about getting some sweet lovin'. This definitely wasn't what I'd expected from Pan, who was known across the Heart-lands for his penchant for duct tape and ball gags.

"Finally, he arrives."

The deep voice of my liege-lord reverberated through the room. I looked up at the gigantic bed, saw humped shapes lolling beneath the vomit-green cover and at least seven women, all naked and unconscious, sprawled atop the blanket. If there were any less than a dozen people in that bed, I'd eat a horseshoe. And the horse still attached to it.

The source of the voice was farther back, reclining against a small mountain of pillows by the headboard. Curly brown hair, from the top of his head down to the goatee on his chin, framed a face of leather and hasty seams, a tribute to ugliness that even the gorgons would have appreciated. Ice-blue eyes regarded me, their pupils elongated, rectangular. Goat's eyes. He smiled, tight-lipped, and settled back on his throne of pillows. Watching me. His chest gleamed with sweat or oil; tawny curls covered the expanse of his torso, led the eye down the plane of his stomach, down to the thick mass of hair that started just over his hips. His erection was a thing of epic poetry—grotesquely huge, ready to be sheathed in the nearest available flesh.

With at least a dozen juicy women around me, I'd have a huge boner too.

One bulky leg, swathed in a curly pelt, lounged insolently over a feminine shape beneath the blanket; his other leg was shrouded from hoof to thigh by the bedcover. His sinewy arms splayed out to either side of his body, his right hand cupping the breast of a nude woman, his left stroking another woman's inner thigh. Neither lover responded to his touches, but that didn't halt his caresses.

Behold, the great god Pan, original party animal and current Lord of Lust, answerable only to the King of Hell. Wonder of wonders, gigolo of gigolos.

Pan grinned hugely, slicing his face in two. "The incubus Daunuan is come. Can you give me a hallelujah?"

I'd never understand his humor. Bowing low, I touched my forehead to the carpet. "Sire."

A pause, then he asked, "Who're you supposed to be? Johnny Cash?"

"Last client was into it, Sire."

"Taking the Tall, Dark, and Handsome thing literally, huh? Still, worlds better than the pastel shit that was all the rage a few years back."

Decades, but whatever. Time tends to blur for creatures like Pan.

"Oh, get up already. We go back way too far for all this bowing shit."

I unfolded my body and rose to my feet, sure to remain at a respectful distance from the bed. We did go back a ways; Pan had been my contemporary for most of my existence. Recent events (known far and wide as the King of Hell's poor temper control) had placed him as a Principal of Lust, but that was a thing of the past; just two weeks ago, he'd been tapped to be the new dread ruler of the Seducers. Not too shabby for an entity that used to entertain himself by scaring the piss out of shepherds and then fucking all the sheep.

Snorting out fumes of pine, I said, "Love what you've done with the place, Sire."

"Yeah?" He stroked his goatee as he glanced around the room. "I'm thinking of going S&M once I'm done auditioning the girlies. It's been forever since I was into the nature scene, but they seem to like it. Makes them think of cute and fluffy bunnies frolicking in the meadows, or some shit like that. I say fuck the meadows, give me the masochism."

Eloquent, as usual. "Auditioning? What for, Sire?"

"I need me a new Queen of Lust. Our esteemed leader went and destroyed the last one."

Couldn't help it: I shuddered. Even Lillith, bitch that she was, hadn't deserved such an indignant end. "So you put out a casting call?"

"More like a cattle call." He smacked the closest rump, belonging to the sacked-out female on his left. She didn't respond. Definitely dazed or dead—the latter being quite the trick, considering we were in Hell. Pan chortled, slapped his palm against the woman's bottom hard enough that the *CRACK!* resonated through the room. "Fuck me, these cows here are quite the slice of Heaven."

I peered closer at his companions. "Angels?"

"Yep. Got me a halo of them, all for my very own playthings." His grin was sharp enough to slice off his pointed ears. "Whatever else our dread ruler's shortcomings, Him declaring that cherubs were the new succubi was a thing of genius. I've wanted to bang a celestial since the Beginning. And now I can, whenever I want."

The closest of his fuckbunnies was in sorry shape: bloody and bruised . . . and, based on the teeth marks on her body, it looked like Pan had a habit of snacking in bed. And she was the least damaged of those I saw. Me, I preferred giving my lovers a different kind of love bite. "Getting your fill of angel food cake, Sire?"

His grin stretched wide. "And then some. At this rate, I'll be palling around with the Gluttons."

I couldn't smell the telltale odor of anything good—that chilly, snow-sky smell of arctic purity—but that could have been due to the nauseating incense clouding up the room. I squinted, tried to look past the women's outer forms. Nothing. All I got were their human shells; if there was anything deeper to them, it had been warped far past my ability to sense. No, that wasn't quite accurate; there was something there at their cores, something vague and sickly, that filled their otherwise empty forms. It was like they'd been scooped out, then inflated with poisoned air.

Frowning, I said, "They don't register as angels."

"Maybe that's because they're full of dark meat now." Pan chuckled, a vicious sound. "Not that any of them knew what to do with me. Boring lays, the halo of them. I need me some maenads. Fuck, even a water nymph'd be more responsive."

If these women really had been angels once, there was no way to tell. Pan had slaughtered them with his own brand of lust. I wondered if they had at least experienced pleasure before their existences had been snuffed out. "How'd you seduce them? The angels I've seen are so frigid, they consider the South Pole a nude beach."

"Daun." He shook his head like I'd disappointed him. "I'm their King now. They can't tell me no. They can't run from me. And they come when I call—whether they want to or not." Eyes gleaming, he said, "Angels, reduced to the playthings of Lust. I do so love the cosmic irony."

I hid my distaste by grinning. I wasn't into rape. I liked my lovers to come willingly—literally as well as figuratively. Sure, my power helped them relax their inhibitions, let them acknowledge the passion they tried to keep under lock and key. But not once in all of my existence had I ever forced myself on anyone, client or no. I'm evil, yes. And the best way to be evil is to encourage and entice others to follow suit. Why steal the milk when the cow would follow willingly?

I love him, Daun.

The memory of my own words whispered in my mind: *If I gave you the choice, right now, would you stay with me? Answer me true.*

And her reply, as final as Atropos cutting someone's lifeline short: *No.*

This was bullshit. I refused to think about a former succubus who'd willingly gone the way of flesh and decay. I cleared my throat, then said to Pan: "Looks like you broke some of your toys, Sire."

"Yeah." He snorted. "You'd think they'd be tougher."

"Why? How hard is it, flying around with the clouds and the birds?"

"You've got a point." He poked the grounded angel to his left, and her head rolled to the side. Pan said, "These must've been bottom of the barrel. I'll have to get me some new ones."

"I have to admit, Sire, I'm surprised you want an angel to rule by your side."

"Someone's got to keep the new succubi in line, and it sure as Hell won't be me. I'm not into all that female girly-girl shit." Pan wiped his hand on the fallen angel's arm, then shrugged. "Besides, the new Queen of Lust doesn't have to be a cherub. I just thought I'd start there. I've still got me tons of minor goddesses and a handful of demons eager to slide down my pole. Nothing I haven't done before, but who knows? Maybe one of them'll feel right."

"A little bit of lubrication will do wonders."

"Screw that. If they can't juice up to handle all of me, they're not meant to be my Queen. Maybe I'll try something different, audition some of the damned. Get me a mortal mortem piece of flesh."

"Creative." Stupid, too, but I didn't say that. What would a one-time human know about ruling the succubi? And then there was Pan's godly stamina to consider. Unless said humans had been porn stars in life, I didn't think they'd stand a chance. Whatever. Not my problem.

"See, this is why you're going to be a great principal. You're open to possibilities that others don't even consider."

The grin slid off my face. "Principal?"

"Specifically, my number one."

Fuck. I sucked in a breath of pine-tinted air, wondering how to talk my way out of this.

There are two ways that demons descend to the ranks of the lower-downs. The most common is to hoard power. Mortals claim that power corrupts. In the Pit, the saying is different: Corruption empowers. The better you are at your affiliated Sin, the stronger you become. And once you're strong enough, you leave the ranks of the lesser demons and become one of the elite: Hell's barons, dukes, marquises . . . and principals. The other way the nefarious get promoted is to be appointed by one of the Kings. That's how Pan had taken over as Lord of Lust.

And now it looked like that was how I'd become a principal. And not just any principal; I'd be the Prince of Lust, First of Principals.

Problem was, I didn't want to be one of Hell's elite. Sure, there were upsides. Who didn't like a title change after working at a company for a long time? And along with the title would come the increased benefits: the raw power, the respect from the greater demons and minor gods, the fear from the lesser demons. The downside? The elite were all assholes, no matter what their affiliated Sin. That included Pan, who at least knew how to have a good time. I still don't know where it's written that the more evil you get, the more of a jackass you become, but that's a rule the elite seem to have taken to heart.

Worse, being Prince meant going to Court and dealing with our sovereign ruler, the dread Lord of the Abyss. And He was certifiably insane. Lucifer, for all of His faults, had been a fine King. But the current Overlord of the Underworld was destroying Hell piece by piece: changing our Rules, softening the boundaries between the Lands of Sin, nearly provoking the nefarious into open warfare against one another. He destroyed all who offended Him, or annoyed Him, or looked at Him the wrong way. Or, for that matter, the right way.

Bishop's balls, I didn't want to be a principal, let alone the Prince.

I realized that Pan was waiting for a response. "I'm . . . flattered, Sire."

"As well you should be. I've passed over Callistus and the others to give you this honor."

"You shouldn't have." He really, *really* shouldn't have.

"No?" He smiled thinly as he looked at me, his goat's eyes glinting. "You're one of the best Seducers I've ever known. Who better to be my go-to guy?"

Think, incubus, think. Put your tongue to better use than licking a lover to orgasm. What could talk Pan out of this idiotic "honor"? Stalling, I said, "Cal will have a fit when he hears."

"He did. Who gives a shit? Callistus can go fuck himself until his cock falls off. If he were half the demon you are, he'd be the one standing here now."

I hissed a surprised breath, shattering my demonic stoicism. "He knows? You told him?"

"Of course. There's a certain decorum to be followed." Pan's teeth shone wetly in the spotlight. "I've already made my choice known to all the elite, across the Sins and Land. All the lower-downs of Hell know that the King of Lust wants the incubus Daunuan to be his Prince, First of Principals."

In other words, there was no way I could turn down the so-called honor. My head throbbed, and a high-pitched whine buzzed in my ears as I fought to disguise my horror. This truly sucked angel feathers. "Thank you, Sire."

"All you have to do is prove yourself. And then the rank, and the power that goes with it, are yours."

Knowing the answer, I still had to ask, "And if I don't adequately prove myself?"

"Then you'll be destroyed," Pan said, bored. "Can't have a mistake wandering around the Heartlands, reminding the nefarious that I'd been wrong to have selected you."

Nothing like a little pressure.

He chuckled softly, the seams of his face creaking like old leather. "No worries, Daun. I'm confident you'll do well. And if you screw up and don't pass the test, I'll make sure your death is quick."

I bared my teeth in a false smile. "You're too kind, Sire."

"Don't tell anyone. That'll fuck up my rep."

Not bloody likely. This fit right in with Pan being a sadistic son of a nymph. "So how am I supposed to prove my mettle, Sire?"

"All you have to do is lure a pure soul into an act of lust."

"Terrific," I muttered, "another game of Tempt the Nun." Boring, boring, boring. The clergy is the one loophole about not seducing the innocent; any human who insists on flaunting his purity is fair game. It falls under the "no light without darkness" category—if people of the cloth successfully resist temptation from one of the nefarious, then Heaven can have them, with our infernal blessings. Lucky for Hell, many so-called men and women of God were easy to lure Downstairs, especially when it came to lust. Take nuns: dress yourself up like their idea of Jesus, boom, they're putty in your claws. Amazing how quickly those brides of Christ learned to go from tight end to wide receiver. Yawn.

"Nothing like that," Pan said. "I've got something special for you."

Lucky me.

"Until now, your clients have all been marked for Hell—evil people who you killed and brought to the Abyss for damnation. Easy shit. This will be different. I want you to tempt someone meant for Heaven, a truly good person, into committing an act of lust. One big enough to damn her to Hell."

"In other words," I said, "she needs to fuck a Seducer." That's one offense Heaven would never overlook. Willingly screwing a demon was an automatic sentence to Hell.

"Think of it as just another client run," Pan said. "With a few strings attached."

Uh-huh. "Such as?"

"She needs to spread her legs for you, not for some possessed meat she knows. And no morphing into a familiar mortal shape, for the same reason." He smiled toothily. "She's got to give herself to you, Daunuan, and know what you are when she does so. She's got to call your name knowing you're going to suck her soul and spit it out in the Bonfire of the Heartlands."

Just another client run, he said. Hah.

But still . . . Part of me hungered for the challenge. Seducing corrupt humans is always fun, but that usually requires creativity, not effort. And even the creativity gets easy after thousands of years. Pan's assignment promised to make me work for the prize.

Thinking how sweet that would be, I nearly salivated. I hadn't known how much I'd been hungering for such a challenge. I grinned, imagined the taste of purity on my tongue. Yes: definitely sweet. Sweet enough that I didn't bother worrying about the possibility of failure. No human—no normal, born-to-skin human—could resist me, not when I set my mind to my job. I was better than damn good at my role; I was one of the best. I'd bet my libido on it. Hell, Pan had already bet my existence on it. If I had any doubts at all, I'd be sweating. One thing about being a creature of the Abyss: we don't sweat easily.

Yes, this little test was just what I needed. And maybe being the Prince wouldn't be all that nasty. Maybe being royalty had its privileges. Like concubines. I thought of green eyes, of achingly soft flesh. Yes, I bet she'd go gaga over Prince Daun. "So who's the mark?"

Pan's smile stretched into something obscene. "I have just the person for you."

The city block we materialized onto glittered with people moving from place to place—some rushing, most strolling, all catching the gleam of the full moon and the illumination of streetlights reflecting their clothing, their hair, their eyes. Their desires. The mortals ignored Pan and me as they walked, laughed, lived. No surprise there; it was only the rare human who could perceive the nefarious when we chose not to be noticed. Wind brushed my hair, danced with the hem of my trench coat. Cold night, but the temperature didn't touch me. If I was riding a mortal body, I'd be able to smell the people and their city the way they did, would feel the bite of the wind on my face. But barring possession, my senses on the mortal coil were dulled. Limited.

That would change as soon as Pan showed me my intended. Once I focused on a client and marked her (or him), no matter what form I selected, I'd sense my target, bask in the glorious aromas she took for granted, taste sweetness when our tongues met . . .

. . . sweetness spiced with hints of the soul within the mortal shell . . .

Mmm.

I took a shuddering breath, forced my body to relax. No sense in getting all revved up before I met the one who'd make me Prince Daun. Plenty of time for that.

"Let's get this party started," Pan said. He pointed with his goateed chin to a pub across the street. "Your lady's in there. You sticking with the Johnny Cash look?"

I glanced down at my raincoat. While it had been suitable for a Seattle evening with my former client, it was out of place for a mid-December night in Saratoga Springs, New York. And I had to dress to impress. I could wait to fashion my costume until I saw my intended, but after eons of working with Pan, I knew his style: he wanted me to put on my work clothes before starting the job. "You giving me anything to go on?"

"Not a maiden, not a crone."

"A mother?"

"Minus the children."

Translation: a woman of childbearing age who'd given her virginity to another. These days, that narrowed it down to a female between the ages of twelve and fifty-one. Based on my intended being in a bar in the United States, I tightened the range to between sixteen and forty-five. No, she was a pure soul; a fake ID wasn't in the picture. Make that between twenty-one and forty-five. "Race?"

"Human."

Funny guy. "More specific."

"Caucasian."

"Anything else?"

"You want it easy? Go to a cathouse. You got to work for this one, Daunuan. No more hints."

Without any more information on what would Hook the client, I needed to outfit myself in something conservative. Not a problem. Time to get dressed for work.

Power washed over me, whisked away the Tall, Dark, and Handsome shell my previous client had found so enthralling and replaced it with Former High School Football Hero: well built, blond and blue, clean-shaven, screamingly white teeth. Over the cake came the icing: thin-striped white shirt, charcoal slacks, black toggle coat. Leather gloves, leather boots. Cover-model perfection.

Pan's eyes gleamed, reflected the false light of the street lamps. "White Bread, huh?"

Everyone's a critic. "Give me more to go on, I'll change."

"What are you, a girl?"

I spread my arms wide. "Why? Does this outfit make me look fat?"

"Wiseass. Come on, let's go."

We marched across the street, ignoring the oncoming traffic. Around us, cars swerved and halted, their drivers reacting to something they felt but couldn't see. Being evil has its privileges; in this case, Malefic Presence. Unless we choose to hide our auras, most humans automatically avoid us. Helpful when you don't want to wait for a traffic light. Getting hit by a car wouldn't kill me, but it would still hurt like a bastard. As we crossed, drivers cursed at one another, flinging profanities and insulting at least two major deities. Words blended, weaving a tune of threats and promises. Buzz, buzz. A screeching of tires, then a thump announced a minor crash. The stench of fury, smoky and sharp. I inhaled, relished the smells of such primal human emotion. Desire was best, and fear a close second, but I would happily take the aroma of rage.

Call it what you want, anger was still a form of passion. And that always put a shit-eating grin on my face.

We trotted up the stairs to enter the pub. Inside, the sounds and smells of humanity hit me in waves—first the day's grime, then the night's desire; an undertow of promises and words as solid as the alcohol fumes that rode the air. I pushed my way in, glanced around. Decently packed for a weeknight: enough people to drown out the music playing in the background, not so many that it was impossible to hear individual conversations when I concentrated. Talk of stocks, of the latest war, of disappointments and triumphs that all balanced out in the end.

Boring. These people needed an enema.

As I passed a particularly uptight pretty, I let my fingers brush her rump, *pushed*. She swayed, then let out a drunken giggle before she launched herself into the arms of the nearest man. He might have done the decent thing, except I touched him, too, as I walked; leering, he scooped the woman into his arms and sucked away her lips.

Much better.

Pan steered me through the crowd, and I left a trail of sex-happy humans behind us. At the back of the long room, we turned left to enter a small lounge laden with the faux-elegant trappings of mahogany and leather. Clusters of patrons were sprinkled liberally in the small room, squished onto sofas, overflowing the plush chairs. Lamps on end tables cast a warm glow around them, unlike the dead fireplace in the far wall that slummed as a chintzy stonework decoration. A cigar room, without the pleasure of cigars. I rolled my eyes at the idiocy behind the intent. It was like trying to seduce someone without foreplay. I swear, I will never understand humans, not in a million years.

A puff of musk and goat: Pan's breath in my ear. "Your dolly is in the corner over there."

I glanced over to where he motioned. Seated around a square table, four women were chatting in the overly animated way of the drunk and the desperate. Two blondes (one natural, one bottled); two brunettes, one of whom had her back to me. "Which one?"

"The short one, with the curly ebony locks." Pan chuckled softly, the inhuman sound very distinct amidst the mortal chatter. "I know how you like the type."

The one whose face I couldn't see. Of course.

Approaching slowly, I worked my way around the other patrons so I could get a better look at my intended. Thick black hair, masses of curls spilling over her shoulders, down her back. A glimpse of pale skin—full cheeks, a pointed chin. Heart-shaped.

Familiar.

I heard myself gasp, and the sound filled the room, muffled everything save the wild thumping of my heart. Even before I caught her profile, I knew I'd see wide eyes framed in sooty lashes, eyes the dazzling green of emeralds.

My voice strangling in my throat, I whispered her name. "Jezebel."

Pan chortled, and for a moment I considered ripping out his larynx. Then self-preservation kicked in. Tuning out the King of Lust, I watched her as she laughed with her companions, a rich melody of amusement. No—it wasn't Jezebel, not even in her current form as the mortal Jesse Harris. On second (or third) glance, I saw the differences: this woman was shorter, plumper, older than Jezzie's mortal self. Maybe thirty-five. More naturally beautiful. This woman wore no cosmetics that I could see; the sheen on her lips was from alcohol, not lipstick.

Not Jezebel, no . . . but the similarity couldn't have been a coincidence.

Pan snorted laughter. "Have fun, Daun."

A pop, a flash of burning sulfur, and he was gone, leaving

me to stare at the woman I needed to seduce, the woman who looked so much like the succubus who'd chosen to stay with the prude Apostle of Shoulders.

I felt a grin slash across my face as I thought of Jezebel.

Oh, babes. You don't know just how big a mistake you made. But you'll learn.

Because once I'm done with your poor-man's doppelganger here and I'm the Prince of Lust, I'm coming for you.

Chapter 4

And the Holy Kept Rolling In

Los Angeles, April 1906

"This?" I glanced at the decrepit warehouse across the street, took in its slipshod paint and sagging wood, its air of decay and neglect. "This ramshackle building houses base delights?"

"Yep."

"Interesting. From how you described it, I expected the harem of the Topkapi Palace."

A low chuckle, throaty and distinctly feminine. "You, Daunuan? Judging by outward appearances?"

"Me? Never. But admittedly, it lacks a certain razzmatazz."

At my side, Jezebel pursed her lips at me, inviting me to watch them sparkle with her saliva. I did so, hearing my heartbeat quicken as I yearned to taste those lips again, to feel her tongue duel with mine. And then she blew out a raspberry.

"Such a mouth on you," I said with a grin. "I can think of other things you should be doing with it."

I wrapped my arm around her waist, pulled her body closer to mine. Her ample curves mocked me, even as they flaunted the latest fashion: an embroidered blouse that fit snugly around her torso and emphasized her bosom (albeit a mono-bosom, as if individual breasts were something unseemly); a voluminous skirt with a tiny waistline that displayed her hourglass figure to full effect; a lace collar that swathed her long neck right up to the chin, drawing my gaze up past her face to the chestnut hair piled magically atop her head in a mountain of curls; kid gloves and boots wrapped around her impossibly small hands and feet. Dressed to the nines. It was a look that mortal women attempted to achieve through a painstaking process involving a multitude of boned bodices and corsets that were, in turn, lost in a sea of hooks and wires. They were also a blasted pain to remove, especially in the heat of passion. Luckily (for me), they were easy to tear. Or burn.

The humans responsible for such damnable mortal fashion would easily find a place amongst Hell's elite—and they'd possess the best-dressed entourage in all the Abyss.

Jezebel smiled pertly at me, nothing like the aloof Gibson Girl she otherwise embodied. How I longed to shred the fabric from her human form, run my hands along every exposed feminine swell, explore deep within her most intimate crevices. No matter what guise she wore over the millennia, I was constantly confounded by her beauty, and by my own ceaseless hunger for her. She was the finest opium, the meanest drink; like all of her ilk, she oozed sex and scandal.

My sweet succubus, dolled up like a flesh puppet. As was I, at her insistence. Clad in a dark overcoat and pants, clutching a silver walking stick in one gloved hand, I stood with a bowler hat perched upon my head, a high collar and bow tie wrapped around my throat, and too-tight boots upon my feet. To say nothing of the pants. Obscured by my coat, my erection throbbed, pushed against its confinement. Just being near Jezebel did that to me. All I wanted to do was throw her in the bushes for a quick dog's match. Or two.

She must have felt her effect on me, even buffered by the layers of all our clothing. Her lips parted in a wet smile—bemused, sardonic. "Patience, sweetie. First things first."

"Ladies first," I said, breathing in her exquisite smell of brimstone and sex. "I promise, ladies first. As always."

"I'm no lady."

"You're still first." I reached out, *pressed*, and she fluttered in my arms, a delighted gasp emanating from those wet, wet lips.

"Later, incubus," she said, breathy. "Later."

"Babes, what could be more important than the business? Our bodies spooning, our hips bucking . . ."

"That's what I mean to show you," she said, untangling herself from my arms. "It's past time for us to get some religion."

"Religion? Can't we get perpendicular instead?"

"We will, we will." She chuckled, a sound filled with delight and devilishness. "Come, let me show you." She entwined her fingers around mine, led me like a dog. I spied block letters painted onto the side of the edifice, forming the words APOSTOLIC FAITH GOSPEL MISSION.

"Religion," I moaned aloud. "She's preaching the Word instead of the business. She's forsaken her hooves."

"Daunuan, would I ever do that to you?"

Damnation, how my name on her lips set fire to my blood! "That's a halo your hair is hiding. You're leading me to salvation instead of temptation."

"I promise, sweetie, in this instance, the one leads to the other."

"Truly?" Walking toward the two-story structure, I openly scoffed. "Perhaps you're keen on bestiality. I still smell the livestock that once were housed here. Or maybe that's the stench of humans packed too tightly."

"It's the smell of opportunity."

"For what? Switching to the other side? That's why we're in the City of Angels, isn't it?"

She chuckled but said nothing. The doorway loomed large as we approached.

Religion. Ridiculous. "We're on a schedule, babes. San Francisco, in three days."

"This is worth the detour." She regarded me over her shoulder, her hair anchored in place by feats of magic I could never hope to accomplish. "Do you know why we're supposed to go there? I was rather enjoying Naples."

I shrugged. If the King of Lust had bothered explaining to any of his entourage why we were to be in that particular city in a few days' time—we, and the bulk of the nefarious, from what I'd gathered—then none of the elite had seen fit to share that information with a mere third-level Seducer. "Heard things. Rumors. Maybe it will be something on the scale of Vesuvius."

Jezebel dimpled a smile, and I saw wicked thoughts sparkling in her eyes. "That was delicious. All of that lava. All of those souls."

"I love eating Italian."

"A saucy people. Wish we could have stayed longer."

"Vesuvius," I said again, rolling the mountain's name. "Temperamental. Nothing like what it did to Pompeii, but still quite the spectacle." Even with a demon's love for destruction, all my talents couldn't come close to one sweep of God's hand. The Almighty breathed; the volcano erupted. More than a hundred died, and quite gruesomely, for reasons only He would know.

At times, I wondered whether the Almighty had shaped the nefarious to mirror the worst in Him. But those thoughts I kept quite silent. A demon didn't think about God. And if he did, the demon certainly did not admit such a thing. It wasn't healthy.

"All of that lava," Jezebel repeated, her voice a low purr. She always did have a weakness for heat. "But I prefer our chosen method of collection. What's the sport in taking spirits from already deceased shells of wicked people?"

I squeezed her hand. "Ours not to reason why."

"Ah, Lord Tennyson. There was a man who understood the importance of lust. 'Better to have love and lust than never to have lust at all.'"

"You're mangling his words even more than I do."

"Poetry is best when left open for interpretation. Here we are."

From the other side of the door, muffled sounds spilled out into the street: a man's booming voice, heralded and followed by the bleating of the masses, insisting on praising their Savior and amening themselves and everyone within the city limits to death.

Demons, about to saunter into a holy place.

I sighed, resigned. The things I do for her.

Opening the door, I motioned for her to enter. Ladies first, after all. Inside, cold air clogged my nose; I frowned, then snorted out the frigid chill of good. *Pfaugh!* But even more palpable than the cold was the sense of building energy, soft and low, yet growing all the same. It was an orchestra's hum, a thing of oboes and violas, of bass drums, rumbling, gaining in volume, in intensity. In power.

"There's a magus here," I said, my voice pitched too low for human ears to catch.

"They call him pastor. His name is Seymour."

"I'd think it would be Simon."

Her lips stretched into a knowing smile, glistening. "Watch. The people are getting saved."

We hovered in the back of the small room, for all intents invisible to the mortals. Minor precaution. One never knew if a magus could determine our true natures; dimming ourselves to human perception nearly guaranteed we would be unnoticed. Boring, really, but Jezzie didn't seem to want to cause a scene. I'd never understand her. I folded my arms across my chest, prepared myself for much eye rolling.

The better part of two hundred people gathered in the round, sitting and standing in prayer. Dressed in rags and riches, in working clothes and their Sunday best, the congregation was caught in a spell of salvation as they clapped gloved hands and stomped booted feet. In the center of the room, a lone man stood at a pulpit, delivering his message to eager listeners. He seemed to quiver as he preached, his voice filled with a passion deeper than mere words. Surrounded by his followers, he alternately trembled like the meek and thundered like the mighty. He was speaking of allowing the Holy Spirit to fill them, to surrender themselves completely to God.

Satan spare me.

"Look at them, Daun," Jezebel murmured. "What do you see?"

"Lunch."

She pinched my arm. "I mean it. Look. Look at their colors."

"Humans all look the same to me."

"Their skins are dark and light and all shades in between. There's no segregation here. They've come together, here in their house of God. The color line, washed away by holy water."

"So?"

"It's not like them to overlook their differences. White and black, mixed in religious frenzy. And more than that. Seymour has white men under his authority." She grinned, her teeth small and perfect. "Some would call that miraculous."

"The only miracle is that we're here in this holy place and not vomiting all over our shoes. Look, they're jerking." I watched a great number of the humans shake and tremble as if they'd been stricken with palsy. "I think they're breaking."

"They're overcome."

"By what? A plague?"

Her grin stretched wide, and for a moment I glimpsed the fangs beneath her false human teeth. "The Word, Daunuan. The Word."

"The Word causes fits and spasms?"

"They believe so."

The preacher's voice burst forth, suddenly volcanic in its intensity. " 'And they were all filled with the Holy Ghost, and began to speak with other tongues, as the Spirit gave them utterance.'" He paused, seemed to measure the adoring looks of his followers. "'They denounce us for our holy baptism, my brothers and sisters. They say we spew a weird babble. They call us fanatics. But they are wrong. It is our mission to displace such wild fanaticism with a living, breathing Christianity.'"

Yawn.

He rolled on, preaching his message amid a hundred hallelujahs, saying that the only true sign of a second Grace was when God Himself entered your body and allowed you to speak in a tongue that the Almighty Himself understands. Et cetera. He called for testimony, and soon the humans were standing, decrying their sins, begging forgiveness and for the power of the Almighty to wash them clean. More clapping, more shouting from the congregation.

Yawn, again.

"Aren't they fascinating?"

I arched a brow at Jezebel, whose face was entranced as she watched the humans make fools of themselves. "They're idiots, being led by a half-blind religious faker."

"You're so certain he's a charlatan?"

"He's a magus," I said, shrugging. No more needed to be said. Magicians were shifty, and they tasted like mildew. "His power over these mortals has nothing to do with religion. It's all hypnosis. Suggestion."

"It's amusing. Listen—that one's speaking in tongues."

I listened. A dowdy woman spewed utter gibberish, shaking as if she were falling apart. "That's chatter and clicks. That's no language at all."

Next to me, Jezebel sighed, petulant. "You're ruining my fun."

"Babes," I said, stroking the swell of her ass, "you know what I consider fun."

She turned to regard me, and I saw something delicious and altogether evil dance in her eyes. Her lips pulled into a smile filled with promise. "Yes. Yes, I do."

Oh-ho. I cocked my head, waited to see what she'd do next.

She turned her attention to the crowd, and I watched her blow out a breath, a puff of power, watched that bit of magic float over the room and slowly settle on a handful of people. They shuddered, then as one they let out peals of laughter. One elder fell to the floor, his ancient body riddled with spasms as the laughter tore through him.

"Not usually the sound I aim for," I said.

Jezebel smiled, all innocence. "A little tickle before the slap. Your turn. Try to be subtle."

Subtle? Where was the fun in that?

More of the humans slowly fell sway under Jezebel's power, their giggles and chortles and guffaws riding the air along with the praises to the Lord and the declarations of their sin being washed away.

Their leader banged his fist on the pulpit, pronounced their delight a sign of "holy laughter" and commanded his congregation not to resist the power. "It will go through you like a wave of electricity. And when you feel it, give way! Surrender yourselves to the power! Let His power fill you, thrill you!"

Well, who was I to pass up such an invitation? I spread my arms wide and *pushed*.

As my power touched them, the mortals shivered, *ahhed*. Some it passed over completely; those people were the truly good, the humans slated for Heaven—ones even the promise of lust could not tempt. Alas. Those frigid mortals watched their brethren succumb to fleshly excitement, and they covered their mouths and widened their eyes as they beheld the physical joy denied them. Poor fools. One could only hope that one day their innate passion would melt the ice around their heart. And then they would dance in the Bonfire of the Heartlands. For now, they watched, they whispered. And the seeds of temptation were planted.

As for the ones who held some evil in their souls, they felt my touches, my caresses, and they threw their heads back and cried out in glee, their huzzahs and shouts like music; they swayed and staggered and hiccupped with giggles, inebriated with the power of lust; they dropped to the floor and bucked and kicked, fornicating with lovers only they could see and feel; they leapt up and danced in wanton abandon. With every moan of ecstasy, every delighted gasp that relished the pleasure I bestowed upon them, I tasted them—just a lick, a little nibble of their souls.

Mmm. They were delicious. Amazing. Orgasmic.

"Just like a man," Jezebel said. "Getting them tanked up before going for what's in their pants."

"Who, me? Would I do that?"

"I'd suggested subtle. Look at them. They're loaded."

"Drunk in the Holy Spirit."

"You."

We turned to see the magus standing before us, his one good eye fierce with righteous ire and holy thunder. He pointed a finger at us and bellowed, "What are you, you who stand here in this place of God?"

Fuck. I hate the magi.

Jezebel stepped forward, first one delicate foot and then the other, running her gloved hands over the abundant curves of her torso, the swells of her hips. "I? I'm but a painted Jezebel, come to witness the saving of souls. Are you saving them, Preacher?"

I bit back a laugh. Damnation, how I adored her . . .

"You have no place here, demon spawn!" The magus barely stammered. If I cared at all, I would have respected that. He shouted, "Get you gone!"

"Oh, but Preacher," I said, "your congregation needs you. Look at them, lost little lambs, waiting for their shepherd to lead them home. So many things could happen to lost lambs, Preacher. So many things to tempt them off the path." I grinned, big big big, allowed my fangs to flash in a moment of clarity.

The magus trembled, but his feet remained rooted to the floor. Either foolhardy, or too terrified to move. Either was fine with me. "Get thee behind me, Satan!"

"We're not that one," I said. "And from where I'm standing, you don't seem to have anyone on your side, Preacher. It's just you, and us two."

I spoke truly (which I did not make a custom of); none of the humans had come to his side to stand with him as he faced off the minions of Hell. No, those godly people were too busy feeling the throes of ecstasy (or standing agog as they watched the fully clothed orgy around them) to notice our holy showdown. As far as we were concerned, it was just Seymour and we two Seducers.

If he wasn't a magus, I'd have eaten him for brunch. But I preferred sweeter tastes on my tongue.

"You're strong enough to resist temptation," Jezebel purred, her hand reaching out, now touching the mortal's thigh. "Aren't you? You're strong enough to lead them to the Light."

His voice strangled, the magus intoned, "I shall fear no evil."

"As you say, sweetie." Jezebel leaned forward to whisper in his ear, words that I heard clearly, even over the din of copulation and salvation: "Why don't you scuttle back to your altar, Preacher, and determine how to turn this to your advantage? Unless you want it known that your entire flock fell under a power quite different than your so-called baptism."

He paled, and sweat beaded on his brow.

"Go on now," Jezebel said, planting a kiss on his gray cheek. "You've got work to do."

She released him, and he staggered backward, his good eye glassy and fearful, his mouth agape. Then he turned and ran to his pulpit, which he clutched as if it could shield him. Taking in the scene around him, he blew out a breath, then a second, and finally drew himself high.

"You feel it, don't you?" he asked, addressing his followers. "Waves of power, overwhelming you. That's a foretaste of Heaven!"

Heh. Really? Jezebel and I exchanged a bemused look.

He declared: "You've given yourself to the power of the Holy Spirit! Don't resist the power of the Lord! Let it fill you! Let your bodies sway and faint, let your hearts leap in joyful response! Ring the air with loud laughter! Be drunk in the Holy Spirit!"

"Hey," I said, affronted. "That's *my* line."

Jezebel's hand snaked around my waist, pulled me close. "Perhaps you should consider switching to the other side."

I laughed, wrapping my arms around my little succubus. "I do seem to enjoy getting religion. But you know what would make this even more fun?"

"What?"

"A holy fuck."

"Why, Daunuan," Jezebel declared, batting her eyelashes, "you sure know how to sweet-talk a girl."

"One of my many talents." Then I sealed our lips in a burning kiss, and we fell to the floor in our own religious ecstasy.

Hours later, we made a Pit stop. Jezebel had insisted: she wanted to start the paperwork on the group of mortals we'd encouraged to reach new heights of passion. Looked like she was angling for a promotion. I didn't have it in me to tell her not to bother; her bitch Queen would never see fit to advance my little succubus to the place she deserved. Jezebel had said on many occasions that Lillith despised her, and I had to agree. What I couldn't fathom was why. Not that it mattered; it wasn't my concern.

After a lingering, groping kiss—and a quick clutching of breasts and balls—Jezebel turned away from me to saunter into Pandemonium, promising to be just a few hours. "All I need is to hand in the names," she said, her voice almost lost amid the cacophony of wails and screeches of the damned. "I'll be done in plenty of time for us to get to San Francisco."

"You have two days," I said. "Then I'm leaving without you."

"Duly noted. I'll call you when I'm free."

With that, she walked toward the mountain complex that housed the demons and offices of Hell. Standing at the boundary of the Heartlands and Pandemonium, I watched her move, fascinated by her every step. As always. I didn't understand what it was about Jezebel that affected me so; other succubi were just as sexy, just as talented between the sheets. But none compared to her. And—bless me for even thinking it—it wasn't just about the sex.

It was something that was uniquely her. Something I couldn't put my finger on (or in), yet it was there all the same, in everything she did, everything she said, every motion of her body. It was infuriating and intoxicating. And I couldn't put a name to it.

Not true. It had a name.

Jezebel.

A pop of burning sulfur, almost undetectable here in the Abyss. Then, in my ear, Pan's voice: "You know, you get this look in your eyes after you get bacchanalian with her. And I swear, your horns are three inches bigger."

"There's something about her," I said, watching where she'd been just a moment before. "She's different from the others."

"Fuck that," Pan said. "One hole's as good as the next."

"Right," I agreed, knowing that was sheer bunk.

Whatever else she was, Jezebel was one of a kind. And I meant to find out why.

Until then, I meant to screw her senseless every chance we had.

Chapter 5

Hey, Baby—Come Here Often?

Pushing aside memories of Jezebel, I ambled past the table where my intended sat. Grinning broadly, I shrugged my way through the crowded lounge, all swagger and confidence. A ladies' man. Well, one lady's man.

Finding a free spot near the fireplace, I leaned against the wall, took in the crowd—just another guy scanning the room, hunting for Ms. Right Now. Blending. Invisible, without having to pull magical strings. Around me, the throng of humans vied for attention, *anyone's* attention, begging to be noticed, to be heard, to be held. To be stroked. Sucked. Fucked. Begging to feel like their lives mattered, even just for a moment. Screaming in their laughter, desperate for connection.

Sometimes, humans made it so easy.

Twenty feet away, my target sat with her companions. I studied her, drank in her face, even with it partially hidden by her curtain of curly black hair; I let my gaze roam over her torso, enjoyed the fullness of her breasts that neither her overly large sweater nor her crossed arms could camouflage. I watched, focused, *flexed* . . . marked her with my psychic signature as property of Daunuan.

Mine.

With that declaration, smells flooded over me, through me, connecting my prey to me—chocolate, jasmine, blackberries, musk. Her unique aroma, branded on my senses. It made me think of satin sheets, of bodies sliding together. My muscles tightened as I held her scent, imagined her in my arms and me in her, pictured how she'd shiver as I showered her body with new sensations.

Mine.

I've got you, doll.

She was laughing again, but now I heard the undercurrent to the mirth: the laughter of her companions was alcohol-inspired and carefree, but hers was a polite copy, guarded. And her bright green eyes sparkled only partially with amusement; there was something deeper there, something I couldn't place. Yet.

Her eyes shine with passion and sorrow and rage as she begs me to kill her so she can save her man's soul.

I snorted, batting away the image of Jezebel's human face. For fuck's sake, stop thinking about her. She made her choice. Focus now on your intended.

Yes, look at her: a half step behind her companions, the smile a touch too late to be spontaneous—see the way she's sitting with her arms folded and her legs crossed and her shoulders so slightly hunched, all but screaming "keep your distance," even though she's out with friends and pretending to enjoy herself.

Why the mixed signals, doll?

I tuned out the rest of the sounds, the smells, of the other humans in the cigar lounge that boasted no cigars. Honing in on my target's table, I *listened*, the buzz of the small group's conversation filling my ears. The true blonde was in the middle of a passionate declaration, insisting: ". . . best movie I've ever seen!"

The bottled blonde clucked her tongue. "Come off it, Ter. You know the only reason you love it is because Matt Damon's in it. He could be in the most boring film ever, and you'd love it because he's in it."

"If Matt was in it, it wouldn't be boring."

"Right, because you'd be too busy lusting after him to actually pay attention to the movie!" This burst of wit from the straight-haired brunette.

Blondie turned to my intended. "Back me up here, Vee. Am I really a fool for all things Matt Damon, or am I a grown-up who simply admires an amazing actor?"

" 'Admires'?" Bottled giggled. "Is that another word for 'Lusts after and wants to have his babies'?"

My intended—Vee?—cleared her throat, smiled (but so very tightly, as if the movement pained her) and said, "Matt Damon is a fine actor."

Blondie grinned in triumph.

Then Vee added, "But you know as well as I do, if Matt Damon ever spoke to you, you'd spontaneously combust from the rush of hormones. Or you'd drop dead on the spot."

The other women broke up with laughter, and my target took a careful sip of the contents in her glass. A sharp tongue on her, tempered with humor. I smiled, already wondering what that tongue would feel like as it dueled with mine. Would she be commanding in bed, insisting on the position and dictating the terms of the sex? Or would she be more yielding? Did she just need the right one to tame her? Either way was fine with me. Already my cock throbbed for her. Hungered for her.

"Busted," Bottled said. "Terri is so busted!"

The other brunette said, "Virginia, anyone who tells Terri like it is, is officially okay in my book. You've got to hang with us more often."

Ah. Not Vee. Virginia. My smile stretched into a grin. Was she like Gloriana, the so-called virgin queen who claimed to see and keep silent? Perhaps she was moody, turbulent, like the suicidal Bloomsbury writer. Or maybe something between the two—a quiet passion. No matter. Whatever she'd been before this moment, all she was now was my target. My intended. My ticket to First Principal. Mine.

Virginia.

I relished the taste of her name on my tongue.

At the table, Blondie laughed. "Please, I'm just glad that I finally got Vee out to play." She lifted her glass, saluted. "Girl, you've been solitary far too long."

My target smiled, smiled hard and tight and said nothing as she sipped her drink.

So cold, Virginia. So aloof. I have just the thing to penetrate that coldness, doll, right here in my pants. I'm going to melt you, make you so hot you're going to boil over . . .

I spied a harried waitress making the rounds. Telling my dick to settle down, I flagged the server. She trotted over while precariously balancing a tray full of used glasses. Sounding pissed off and put out, she barely looked at me as she asked, "Get you anything?"

You can get less uptight, for one thing.

Pursing my lips as if I meant to kiss her, I *pushed*. She gasped as my power licked her, tickled her sweet spot. She staggered, and I helped her steady her tray. When my fingers brushed hers, she let out an *ooooh*.

Heh.

As she swayed against me, I murmured in her ear: "See the woman sitting there? The brunette with long, curly hair? Send her a Sex on the Beach, with my compliments." I *pushed* again, and the waitress came in her panties—a splash of spice and cotton. Mmm. "Got it, doll?"

Her voice a squeak, she said, "Yes, sir." Then she oozed away.

Grinning, I watched Virginia as she continued her charade. The other women prattled on, filling the space between them with inane chatter. All through it, Virginia smiled, and sipped, and laughed. The pretense loomed over her like a death shroud.

I'll strip away your cover, Virginia. I'll thaw your body and find your core. I'll make you call my name like it could save your soul.

Yes, doll. You're mine. You just don't know it.

I watched as the waitress arrived at the group's table, a solitary drink on her tray. She settled the full glass down in front of Virginia, said something to her, then motioned my way. Five sets of eyes locked onto me.

Helloooo, ladies.

I turned on the charm and grinned—nothing too cocky, just enough playfulness to hint at mischief, to whisper of sex. Four of the women looked intrigued, and two of them licked their lips. But the one who mattered looked surprised . . . and annoyed.

Annoyed? Well, that'll change.

The waitress slid away, leaving Virginia and her companions to stare at me. Unabashed, I stared back, focused on my intended. After thousands of years tempting mortals, I knew the game well, had memorized its complex rules. Now's the part where the others will leave us alone . . .

"I have to powder my nose," Blondie said. "Who's coming?"

Bottled and Brunette stood quickly, and even Virginia scraped her chair back, but Blondie shook her head. "No way, Vee. You stay. Guard the table from the vultures. And the foxes." She paused long enough to send me a lusty look, then turned back to Virginia. "Enjoy your drink."

"But—"

"Get his phone number," Bottled said.

"Find out if he has a friend," Brunette added, slyly glancing my way.

I would have winked at her, but I didn't want her to think she had a chance with me. I had eyes only for my Virginia.

"Terri, don't you dare leave me!" She sounded on the verge of panic. Sweet.

Blondie smiled at her, a look filled with sympathy and barely contained glee. "Nature calls. Come on, girls!" The three strutted away, giggling, leaving my intended alone.

Virginia lowered her head so that her thick curls hid her face. Her shoulders bobbed in a deep sigh—she was either resigned or vexed. That's something I planned to change; soon she'd be sighing with pleasure. Anticipation.

Boom *boom*.

My blood humming with her name, I sauntered over to my

intended. My lady. Wrapped in her overlarge sweater and hidden by her hair, she seemed to seek invisibility. Why so nervous, doll? Why hide your juicy body, your porcelain face?

Start with the direct approach. That should get her to open up, just a little—just enough to talk. Yes, Virginia. I'll talk to you for a few minutes, feel you out before I know what Hook I need to feel you up. What'll tickle your fancy, Virginia? Will a glimpse of my body make your heartbeat quicken? If my gaze hits you like a laser beam, smoldering with intention, will your reservations burn away? Will it be the casual touch of my hand on yours?

Every mortal has a Hook, Virginia. What's yours?

"Hope you like Sex on the Beach," I said as a greeting.

She peeked up at me, shook her hair away from her face. Her eyes telegraphed her unease; her smile was forced, and fragile, and so fucking delicious to look at that I wanted to eat her lips.

"Thank you," she said, striving for Miss Manners. "I'm flattered. But I'm not interested."

Ooh, hard to get. I softened my smile, put a chuckle in my voice as I said, "In the drink or the activity?"

"Neither."

"You accepted the drink."

She sighed again, this time a sound of frustration. "The waitress walked away before I could say no thanks." She spoke with infinite patience. "So really, thanks, but no thanks."

"You didn't exactly try to stop her."

Her smile slipped. "Look, you seem like a nice guy."

Heh. Her intuition sucked. "But?"

"But the only reason I'm even out tonight is to do my friend a favor. I'm not looking to get picked up. So thank you for the drink, but really, I'm not interested."

I straddled the chair to her left, sat and hunkered over the backrest so that my coat gaped open. All the better to let her envision the sculpted muscles beneath my shirt. Except she didn't even meet my gaze, let alone stare at my body. Instead, she played with her drink—the one she'd been working on before I'd ordered her another—swirling the ice cubes almost violently.

"I think you're interested," I said with a smile. "More than you know."

She stopped toying with her drink. Still not meeting my eyes, she said, "I think you don't know me at all."

Whoops. Deflect the damage. Grin on, full strength. "But I'd like to."

That got her to look at me. Her green eyes shone with emotions I couldn't place. Why did mortals have to complicate everything with stupid feelings?

She asked, "Why? Just because I'm sitting here, in a bar, that means I'm looking to hook up?"

"No. But you not saying no to a drink says you're looking for something."

She pushed the full glass to me. "There. Happy?"

Far from it. Still didn't know how to Hook her. "Come on, doll. Let's not be so hasty."

"Hasty? Hasty would be me saying 'go away.' I haven't said that yet."

"Yet?"

"I'm trying to be polite."

"Yeah, I see that." I leaned over, invaded her personal space until my mouth was barely inches away from hers. "I've been watching you trying to have a good time. Pretending you're enjoying yourself."

Virginia shied away from me, but not before I saw the indignity on her face. Apparently, she didn't like hearing the truth. Humans rarely did.

Turning to the wall, she said, "Now it's time for you to go away."

"Oh, Virginia, I haven't even started yet. Don't I get to at least do a decent pickup line before you break my heart?"

A pause. Then: "How do you know my name?"

"I listen. I watch." I smiled my good intentions.

"Great. Now you're a stalker."

"Nope. Just a horny little devil."

She turned to look at me over her shoulder. "*Excuse* me?"

"I'm a regular demon of love." Even though I wasn't supposed to, I *pushed*, just a little, just enough to make her knees unlock and loosen the stick so firmly rammed up her ass. But instead of an *ohhhh* or a parting of her lips or even a slight widening of her eyes, she looked even more frigid.

Shit, that's right—humans meant for Heaven aren't affected by the nefarious. Unless she kissed me willingly to kick-start my gigolojo, she'd be completely unaffected by my demonic charm.

Well, so what? I've been doing this routine for Hell only knows how long. Flirting with mortals is as easy as a starving whore. Who needed magic when you had the moves? "Come on, doll. Let's talk some, see if we click." I patted my thigh. "Why don't you sit on my lap, see what pops up."

"Does that shtick actually work on real women? Or has all your experience been with the plastic variety?"

"Kiss me," I purred, "and I'll show you what you've been waiting for all your prim and proper life."

Her jaw clenched before she turned away again. "Trust me, you're not the one I'm waiting for." She folded in on herself—shoulders hunched, head lowered, hair hanging. "You're nothing like him. Go away. Please."

Nothing like her ultimate lover? I do believe that I'm insulted. "Doll, you're so frigid, the ice caps are jealous."

She stiffened. Then she turned to face me again, slowly, a beatific smile on her kissable face. Did my quip Hook her? Didn't feel right, but who was I to look a gift horse in the mouth? I returned the smile, winked. Virginia reached for the drink I'd ordered for her, lifted it up in a toast—and threw the contents in my face.

"I've returned your drink," she said sweetly.

That could have gone better.

Outside the bar, I zapped the dripping mess off of me; with the right amount of heat aura in place, alcohol evaporates pretty damn quickly. Did nothing for the smell, though—I was drowning in cranberries, grapefruits, schnapps and vodka. Fuck me, I stank like a coed on Spring Break. Minus the sex. All thanks to my intended, who had the gall to toss her drink in my face. Who didn't find me remotely appealing. Who dared suggest I wasn't even close to being her fantasy lover.

Unholy Hell, what a woman. I couldn't wait to taste her soul.

Grinning through the stink of fruit juice, I willed my form to dim, fade into nighttime shadow. Invisible, reeking of inebriation, I waited for my lady. I reached out, felt my mark on her. Sensed her talking to someone she held close, a good friend. Listened as Virginia said . . .

". . . he was an asshole. He deserved it."

"Jesus, Vee, a guy shows some interest, what do you do? You give him a beer shampoo."

"It was a Sex on the Beach."

"Honey, there are better things to do with a Sex on the Beach than spill it over some guy's head. Especially a hottie like that."

A whiff of frustration before Virginia spoke again. "I'm leaving. Talk to you tomorrow."

"Aw, Vee, don't be like that."

"Look, I appreciate what you're doing and all, but it's time for me to go home."

"Why? So you can mope?"

A strained pause, filled with tension and bitterness. "Don't go there, Terri."

No, Terri. Go there.

Stretching away from Virginia for a moment, I let my power brush over her friend's presence, encouraged her to lower her inhibitions. That's right, Terri. Feel the alcohol coursing through you, relaxing you, loosening your tongue, allowing you to say . . .

"I'm the only one who will, you know. Everyone else tap dances around it, like just talking about Chris is going to break you into pieces. But you're stronger than that. How long're you going to be a martyr?"

A flash of pain so raw, it stole my breath.

"You're only thirty-five, Vee. That's too young to stop living your life."

I felt Virginia's pain crack, then shatter in a sea of ice. Felt her heart freeze, her face settle into a tight, emotionless mask.

What had hurt you so brutally, Virginia?

And how could I use that to my advantage?

She sniffed, a sound of derision that would do any angel proud. She said, "I'm going home now. To mope."

"Oh, come on, Vee! Virginia, I'm sorry! Come back!"

Too late—my lady was storming out of the bar. Obviously tortured. Probably needed a strong shoulder to cry on. No worries, doll. I've got the strongest shoulders this side of Creation.

She breezed out, booted feet tripping down the steps. An enormous winter coat disguised her curves, buried those magnificent breasts in layers of padding and synthetic fibers. Her thick curls were momentarily tamed, tucked into a hood. With every layer of clothing she begged not to be noticed. I wondered about the shape of her legs, how they'd look stripped from those loose pants . . . how they'd feel as I ran my hands between her thighs.

The wind kicked up, and she ducked her head as she marched past me, leaving me with a vague impression of cold fury—a blaze of green eyes, a slash of pale lips.

Damn, there's nothing like a woman when she's angry.

Your emotions are sky-high, aren't they, doll? Bet you'd be more receptive now to certain . . . suggestions. Going home, are you? Well then, I'll just have to make sure you get there safe and sound. I left my post by the stairs and started walking after her. Stalking her.

Thinking about what line to use to Hook her interest, I trailed my intended, weaving around the handful of stray mortals between me and her. Three blocks down, Virginia walked into a public parking lot. I followed, watched her duck between aisles until she stopped in front of a blue-gray car. As she fumbled in her shoulder bag, I noted her vehicle's make and the license plate. Nondescript, like how she tried to be—

between my knuckles. I growled, deep and low, as rage tore through me.

With her free hand, Uvall plunged the teeth of another silver comb deep into my chest. I barely noticed the new hole in my body; my neck stung, and my fucking hand was on fire.

She smiled, a triumphant look etched onto her human host's face. Then I grabbed her other wrist, and her triumph was replaced with confusion. And a hint of fear.

"I got your heart," she said. "You should be on the ground, in agony. Dying slow."

"Want me on the ground, bitch? You bet." I slammed my forehead into hers, then shoved her to the ground. She landed flat on her back, stunned. I pounced on her—straddled her hips and pinned her arms.

Bishop's balls, I was hurting. My cheek and nose throbbed; if I were mortal, the bones would have been fractured, the flesh swollen. A flash of heat aura evaporated the pieces of comb stuck in my neck and chest, replacing that pressure with an unpleasant numbness. The scratch on my throat burned, but that was already fading. Worst of all was my left hand—it was bleeding steadily, made the woman's wrist slick beneath my grasp.

"Silver," she said, her voice slow, thick. Uvall clearly wasn't long for the human body. "Combs . . . are silver."

"I noticed."

"Should be dying."

I leaned over her, whispered: "Newsflash, Haughty: silver isn't my weakness."

She let out a sound, half-growl, half-whimper.

"You know," I said, "after attacking me without cause, I could lay claim on this human, steal her soul away from Pride. And when all the paperwork comes in, the story would spread how Uvall, Duke of Hell, had attacked the incubus Daunuan . . . and lost. Bet that would bite you on the ass, wouldn't it?"

She bucked beneath me, tried to shake me off. But I wasn't going anywhere. Neither was she. I blew her a kiss. "You'll be a laughingstock."

"Kill you!"

"Why? What'd I do to you?"

Her eyes gleamed with malice and secrets. "You'll never know."

Screw me, what was it with demons wanting to kill me tonight?

In my mind, the Berserker's taunting voice: *Would be telling*.

Shit. My stomach clenched as I realized there was something brewing, something big. "You were told to attack me. You and the Berserker both."

She said nothing, watched me as I tried to piece it together. "What's going on, Uvall?"

"Piss off, dog. I don't answer to you."

"Tell me, or I'll let the Pridelands know about your *failure*." I made sure to drawl the word. The only thing worse than an eternity of agony to one of the Proud was owning up to failure.

The demon grinned. "I know something you don't know."

Fuck this.

I released one of her arms to grab her by the top of her head, tangling her blond hair in my fingers. With a growl, I raised her head up, then slammed it down. A delicious *crunch* as the back of her head connected hard with the ground. Her eyes rolled up, and her body went limp beneath mine. Lights out, doll. She was still breathing; I'd pulled back at the last second to keep from shattering her skull. If I can't kill a woman with lust, it's not worth my time.

In a pop of burning sulfur, Uvall exited the host body.

Silver. I shook my head, snorted my disgust. Where'd the Haughty get such shoddy information? I practically flossed with silver.

The fading roar of a car's motor told me Virginia had just left. And I had no idea where she was going—where she lived, what her last name was. Nothing.

Bloody fucking Hell.

Maybe her friends were still at the bar; one of them would have information on my intended. Information that I needed. Badly. But the way tonight was going, they'd be long gone before I got back to the pub.

The Amazon lay on the ground, dead to the world. Lucky bitch. If I didn't loathe paperwork, she'd be dead, period. I stared at her face, debated whether I should slice off her nose, just for spite. The air crackled with the stink of spent magic and burning blood.

Ah, let it go. Uvall can have her. I wasn't one for sloppy seconds.

I stood up, shook out my limbs. My hand was still bleeding, but the flow had slowed to a trickle. It would stop soon enough. My face, neck and chest were already mostly healed; in a few more minutes, they'd be perfect. But my hand would be sore for the better part of a day. I flexed my fingers, winced. Glancing at the diamond ring on the Amazon's hand, I realized just how bad it could have been.

Uvall's attack meant one thing. What happened earlier tonight, at my client's house, had been no accident.

If it had been other Seducers trying for a piece of me, I would've shrugged that off as Callistus being pissed off at getting passed over for Prince of Lust. But whatever was happening was big enough to score a demon from Wrath and an elite from Pride, set them after me with murder on their minds. They wouldn't help one of Lust's scorned principals; if anything, Wrath and Pride would get a huge chuckle seeing dissention in the Heartlands.

No, whatever was happening, it was bigger than Callistus trying to pull a Machiavelli.

Someone in Hell had set me up.

And fuck me, I had no idea who . . . or why.

Chapter 6

A Bit of Spice

Midnight in New York City. The witching hour, so they say. Me, I think it's more like happy hour. Especially when I'm in a strip club, waiting on my favorite dancer. Just the thought of watching her peel away clothing in time to music is a particularly heady torture. I've never been good at looking without touching.

Music flirted with my heartbeat as it thrummed along my skin: the song was loud and lusty, the kind of tune that snakes up your body and entices your limbs until they're moving with a will of their own. I drummed my fingers on the small round table in front of me, adding my soft beat to the growing spell of seduction playing in the sexually charged air. The red plush chair I sat on was a thing of upholstered sin, decadent and soft. The other two seats around my table were empty, even though the club was crowded; at least fifty customers talked and drank and fantasized about the lovely ladies overflowing with womanly charms. Guess I radiated something that told men to stay away.

Well, most men. One of the bouncers had been giving me the eye for the better part of ten minutes. I would have noted his name for a future visit, except he stank of goodness. Figured. Most of the gay ones were good.

Onstage, a platinum-haired piece of temptation danced, her lithe body illuminated with yellow and red spotlights as she enticed the audience with her movements. Faith, according to the DJ. Cute. So was she. But she wasn't who I was here for. Who I needed.

Who could tell me how to seduce someone meant for Heaven.

Faith's set finished to thunderous applause and a shower of money. As she exited the stage, the music tempo shifted— faster, a heavy percussion with a dark undertone, a beat that swept through the club, filled the room with anticipation. The DJ said something about every businessman's fantasy, but I stopped listening to him because I saw *her*, standing at the back of the stage, one hand on her hip and the other by her collar, fingers tapping to the music, hinting at wickedness. Black-framed glasses masked her eyes, and her thick curls were corralled into a sloppy bun at the back of her head. A black suit jacket hugged her torso, and a matching skirt flowed over her hips. Her nylons gleamed, translucent, emphasizing her strong, sleek legs, and her feet were tucked into black stilettos, the toes of the shoes pointy enough to serve as weapons. The spotlight transformed her dark hair into satin, her pale skin into porcelain; her lips, plush and red, were parted in a knowing smile.

Jezebel.

She strutted forward, confident, her steps sure and her hips swaying to the music. The smile gave way to a huge grin as she pranced across the stage. Look at her, reveling in the spotlight, relishing the attention. Every businessman's fantasy, indeed— smart and sexy, strong and slutty. Powerful and passionate. Turning her back to the audience, she planted her feet wide apart, crouched down fast and rose up slow, teased us with a glimpse of the lacey tops to her thigh-high stockings. Her hands traveled up the curves of her body, lingered over her breasts as she looked over her shoulder—right at me.

Boom *boom*.

She whipped off her glasses and tucked them into her jacket pocket as she danced. Some strippers need to get the feel of the beat before they know how to work their bodies for maximum effect. Not her. She owned the sound, was in complete control and was obviously having the time of her life. Caressing her face, she trailed her fingers over her chin, her cheeks, back farther until her hands were buried in her hair. With a flick of her wrists, her makeshift bun exploded in a shower of ebony curls. Freed, her hair cascaded down her shoulders and back, bounced with her every move. Hands spread on her thighs, she rocked her hips, gyrating sensually. Luxuriantly. She danced like she was fucking the music itself.

My body tightened as I lounged in my comfortable chair. I wanted to leap up onto the stage and pin her down, thrust my tongue inside her mouth and kiss her until my teeth grazed her soul. I wanted to feel her around me and in me, hear her delirious gasps as I made her come.

I wanted *her*.

The music kicked up, overrode my heartbeat as it pounded erratically in my chest, drowned out the sounds of the other men in the audience as they fantasized and drooled. She stripped off her jacket and dropped it to the floor, revealing a white shirt buttoned up to just below the mounds of her breasts. After a jiggling turn, she ran one hand down her inner thigh as she unfastened her blouse with the other hand, slowly, fondling each button with deft fingers until I fought a maddening urge to rip the material from her body. With a smile that promised wicked things, she discarded the shirt. Her cleavage beckoned, glistening, sheathed in a black lace bra. Her skirt rode low on her hips; the tops of her panties peeked out, winking in the spotlight.

Again, she looked right at me. Never mind that she was making eye contact with every man in the room—she was looking at *me*, as if she saw through my mortal shell, recognized the demon within. She winked at me before dancing to the other side of the stage. Damned flirt.

Gritting my teeth, I forced myself to sit, relax. My cock hated me for it—I felt like my dick was a bull in a china doll shop. My balls threatened to implode. Bloody Hell, incubi weren't built for such restraint.

I watched as she shimmied to the brass pole at the front of the stage, watched her reach up high, clasp it with both hands, squeeze. Oh, to be that pole . . . She pulled herself up, and up, and up, stretching like a jungle cat as she climbed. She wrapped those strong legs around the pole, held on tight as she slowly swung her way down. Still twirling, she dipped her head back so that her hair brushed the stage floor. Her tits defied gravity as she spun around, the music propelling her on, on, on. The drums boomed out and she launched her legs up, turned up-side down. Eyes closed, a look of sheer pleasure on her face, she hung suspended as the music pulsed.

Rrrrr.

She righted herself, all in time to the beat. Sinfully graceful. Feet once again on the floor, she paused long enough to run one hand up the length of her body, seductive, taunting. Her hand trailed up her hair, over her head, then she pushed her-self away from the pole. Dancing across the stage, she saun-tered as if her five-inch heels were soft as angel's wings. The music took on a harder edge—playfulness gave way to some-thing more primal. More urgent. With a yank, her skirt tore free. A black G-string caressed the swells of her hips; a match-ing garter hugged her thigh, demanding to be filled with money.

Like Pavlov's dogs, men responded to that garter, leapt out of their seats to stand by the tip rail, clamoring for her atten-tion. Smiling, sassy, she peeled off her bra and dropped to the floor, stretching out long and slithering her way to the front. By the brass rail, she pulled herself up to her knees, thrust her tits in front of one guy's sweaty face. He stared at her pearled nipples for a moment, hypnotized. She touched herself, smil-ing, squeezed those ripe melons as she said something I couldn't hear. With a groan, the man delicately tucked a folded bill into her garter. She winked her thanks, moved on, worked her way down the line—enticing the customers with her body, letting them touch her, trace their fingers on her. Caress her. Sample her.

I was on my feet before I knew what I was doing, striding toward the stage. I wanted to take her, make her see stars as I pounded her, filled her. Thrilled her.

My little succubus.

Her eyes shine with passion and sorrow and rage as she begs me to kill her so she can save her man's soul.

Jezebel.

For one crystalline moment, I explode within her, remember how perfect she feels wrapped around me. And then she screams like her body is on fire, scorching her slowly from the inside out, and I steal her pain.

What was it about her that called to me?

She dies in my arms, my mouth on hers.

Why couldn't I stop thinking about her?

Approaching the rail, I reached into my back pocket and pulled out a twenty-dollar bill I'd just magicked up. The humans parted for me, innately sensing the unholy power beneath my mortal costume and shying away from it, giving me plenty of elbow room. Jezebel hovered over me, her eyes twinkling, her lipsticked mouth shining in the spotlight. She brushed her fingers languidly down her leg, offered her garter as if for worship. Her skin gleamed with sweat; her thighs begged me to lap their salty moisture, to find the liquid heat between them.

I flashed her the twenty folded between my fingers.

Her dark brows arched, surprised or bemused, and she turned her back on me, presented me with her rump. Wiggled. Flipped her curtain of curls over her shoulder as she turned to regard me, lips pulled into a sly smile, fingers dancing along the line of her G-string. Daring me.

Mmm. Shivers.

I reached up, skimmed the folded edge of the money along the back of her thigh, over the heart-shaped swell of her ass. With a smile of my own, I tucked the tip of the bill into her panties.

You don't recognize me, do you, babes?

She bent over her right leg to face me. "Thanks, sweetie."

"Maybe you and I can get some quality time," I said over the music, wanting to run my hand up her leg again. "Just you and me?"

"Love to." Jezebel dimpled a smile at me. "I'll find you after my set's done."

I tore myself away from her, made my way back to my table. Waited for her.

My Jezzie.

The spotlights shimmered over her, transformed her into an organic prism as she danced. Watching those colors play on her body, I frowned, remembered when I'd killed her (as she'd begged me to do, anything to save her prude apostle), remembered her dying in my arms and—

Her soul flies, and there's a moment that's an eternity as she slips away from me, lost . . .

—remembered how something . . . odd . . . had happened as I bonded her soul, and—

. . . and then I feel her again and pull her from the ether, save her from oblivion and bond her to me, forever, and I look at her and truly see her, for the first time really see her . . .

—remembered how her essence hadn't reflected only the colors of her own spirit—

. . . a thing of such beauty unholy Hell such grace and power and damn me the light and oh oh Jezebel don't you see?

—no, it was something else, something that was blurry and infuriating and right there in front of my face and damn it all to Hell why couldn't I remember?

I closed my eyes, remembered saying . . .

"You. You're—"

The angel's voice cuts in, slices my words. "Never going to blend in Hell, looking like that. Your soul is clean. You'll stand out like—"

"Like an angel among the demons."

A sudden pain stabbed me between my eyes, and the memory shattered in the wake of a savage headache. Growling, I pressed my fingers against the bridge of my nose. Just my luck. All out of nefarious-strength aspirin. Whatever I'd been thinking about unraveled in spools of pain. I frowned, not liking how easy it was for me to lose my train of thought.

Ah, fuck it. If it was important, it'd come back to me.

Onstage, Jezebel danced.

"Thanks, sweetie," Jezebel said as I handed her a glass filled with bubbly booze. I figured it was called the Champagne Room for a reason; therefore, I'd ordered a bottle of the stuff. Frankly, I thought champagne tasted like angel piss. But when in Rome, and all that. Her fingers brushed against mine as she took the drink, setting my blood on fire with that soft touch. Something flashed in her eyes, then her gaze settled back to its green wickedness.

She'd felt it too.

We still have a connection, don't we, babes?

She took a small sip, and her mouth sparkled with the wet shine of alcohol. I wanted those glistening lips on mine. Now. My cock pressed against my pants, demanded to be unleashed. Boom *BOOM*.

Down, boy. I'm here for information, not fornication. Although that would be a fabulous perk . . .

I knocked back my drink, tried to drown my arousal in sparkling wine. *Pfaugh!* Angel piss would have been preferable.

"Slow down, sailor." Jezebel's eyes sparkled with mirth. "Better ways to get a buzz, if that's your pleasure."

"You're my pleasure," I said, feasting on her form. She was inclining on the leather sofa, her red gown so tight she must have poured it on. Propped up on one elbow, she rested her head in one hand as the other held her champagne flute, her full breasts almost spilling out of the dress. A lazy smile played on her face, framed by those wet lips, her mouth painted blow-job red. Her black curly hair was tousled, wild, looking as if she'd been right and properly fucked. One leg draped over the other, her nylons gleaming through a slit in the material of her gown, her high heels sharp and shapely and so damn sexy that I almost came in my pants. Sitting next to her was maddening; I wanted to be on top of her. In her. "You make all the other women here look like amateurs."

She chuckled, low and lush. "I've been doing this for a while."

"I'm sure." I reached over, tucked one of her curls behind her ear, caressed her cheek. Her flesh was warm beneath my fingers, and as I traced the line of her jaw, I saw a shiver ripple over her.

Maybe she didn't recognize my current form, but her body knew me. Remembered me.

My Jezebel.

"Sweetie," she breathed, "you're not supposed to touch."

"No?" Locking my gaze onto hers, I slowly dropped my hand, let it linger down her neck, dust ever so lightly over the mound of her left breast. She gasped, a sound of surprise tinged with pleasure.

But she didn't tell me to stop.

My thumb spiraled her nipple, teased the sensitive spot until it was plump and firm and begging me to taste it.

"You can't do this," she said, either to me or to herself. Her voice was thick, brimming with desire. "This is bad."

"I'm a bad boy." I leaned closer to her, inhaled her intoxicating scent as I kept rolling her nipple between my fingers. "Maybe you should spank me."

I nuzzled my face in her neck, kissed the hollow of her throat. Her breath erupted in quick bursts by my ear, goaded me on. The muscles in her neck and shoulder almost sang with sexual tension. My kiss became hungry and I scraped her flesh with my teeth, lapped her skin with my tongue. Sucked.

She froze beneath me.

Whoops.

Jezebel shrugged away from me, slapped a hand over the reddening spot on her neck. Eyes narrowed, she glared at me, stabbed me with that green gaze. Touchy, touchy. I glanced at the champagne flute in her hand, wondered if she'd mimic Virginia and toss her drink in my face. Instead, she slammed the glass down on the coffee table.

Her voice clipped, she asked, "What do you think you're doing?"

"Giving you a hickey."

"You want a fuckbunny, go to a massage parlor. I don't do that." She didn't add the "anymore," but the implication hung in the air.

So angry, Jezzie—at me? Or at yourself for reacting to my touch? "I don't want a fuckbunny. I want you."

"Sorry. You're cut off."

She's so cute when she's indignant.

I held up my palms in a gesture of compliance. "Got it. No touching. I'll keep my hands where you can see them."

"Touching, nothing. You need a muzzle. Time for you to leave."

"I haven't even gotten my private dance yet."

"Complain to the management. Don't let the door hit your ass on the way out."

"But I want to talk to you."

"Here: sign language." She flipped me off.

Heh.

"How about body language?" I reached out with my power, *nudged* her sweet spot without physically touching her. I was nothing if not a demon of my word. (When I chose not to lie, that is.) I nudged again, tickled her between her thighs.

Her gaze darkened, those cherry-red lips parted as she asked, "What . . . ?"

"Like I said. Body language."

I leaned back on the sofa, smiled at how she tried not to be aroused. She bit her lip, worried it between her teeth. But that couldn't muffle her groan of pleasure. Pressing harder with my magic, I stroked her vulva, slow and firm.

She gasped, closed her eyes as her body shuddered. The gasp turned into a long moan as invisible fingers flicked her clit. Pressed.

A burst of hot wetness, a splash of cinnamon and pumpkin spice.

Gotcha.

I licked my finger. *Mmm.* "You know, babes, even after all this time, you still taste like a succubus."

Her breath hitched. When she opened her eyes, they were glazed with lust, sprinkled with panic. Talk about eye candy . . .

Staring at me, she asked, "Daun?"

"In the flesh."

"I shouldn't be surprised." She tried to keep her voice steady, but I felt her desire, smelled the sudden fear exuding from her pores. Heard her heart pounding in her chest.

Growwwl.

She rubbed her neck like she could wipe away my mark. "What do you want?"

"You."

"Not interested."

I smiled. "Liar."

She bit her lip before she turned away. "Not available."

"Oh, that's right. You're in love. *L'amour.* You know," I said, my words slow and steady, "considering how in love you are with your meat pie, you still have no problem with me getting you all hot and bothered."

Jezebel wrapped her arms around herself as if she were cold. "Go away, Daun. Leave me alone."

"Don't be too hard on yourself, babes. You can't help but want me."

"You're so full of yourself, you should be one of the Arrogant."

"Ooh, I hit a nerve. Just like I hit your sweet spot a moment ago."

"Bastard."

"Flatterer."

"What do you want, Daun?"

"You, Jezzie. You." My voice was a rolling purr, sensual, tailor-made for verbal foreplay. "We've been so good together for so long. Our bodies belong together, whatever form they wear."

"Stop. Just stop." She turned to face me, her eyes gleaming like moonlight on a blade. "That's not who I am anymore. You even said it yourself. Remember? Said I was too human for you."

I let her gaze stab me, relished the raw emotion on her face. "Demons lie."

"Go fuck yourself."

"I'd rather fuck you."

"In your dreams, incubus." But I heard the quaver in her voice, saw the shine of fear and longing in her eyes.

You're mine, Jezebel. Even if you won't admit it.

"Tell you what," I said. "You help me with something, I'll leave you alone." For now.

She frowned. Considered. Finally asked, "Help you with what?"

"Figure out how I can seduce a mortal woman meant for Heaven." Her eyes widened, and I added, "Don't flatter yourself, Jezebel. I'm not talking about you."

Silence hung between us, thick and laden with words unspoken. I waited. After thousands of years, I've gotten damn good at waiting.

Finally, she nodded to herself and reached for her drink. "Seducing someone good, huh? That's different. The new succubi rubbing off on you?"

"Please. There's only one way those wannabes could rub off on me, and that involves my dick."

"Nice. Bet your good girl will melt, hearing you say such sweet things."

"I can be a silver-tongued devil if I want."

"Uh-huh." She took a sip, frowned at me. "Why someone good? Don't you have enough on your plate, what with the nefarious actively influencing people to sin?"

"Latest assignment," I said, shrugging. I wasn't about to tell her the full truth—that went directly against my demonic nature—but giving her small pieces would mollify her enough to let down her guard, give me what I needed. "The King of Lust tells me to tempt one particular human meant for heaven, and I say, 'Yes, Sire.' Ours not to reason why."

A smile played on her lips. "Ours but to do; they die."

We shared a quiet laugh. The sound was like music.

My Jezebel.

I said, "You always did have a tendency to mangle Tennyson."

"Poetry's best left open to interpretation." Her gaze softened, and she leaned back against the cushions. Relaxed. Sipped her drink. "All right. You're supposed to what, exactly? Tempt her how?"

"Get her to commit an act of lust big enough to damn her."

"Seducing her's enough to do that?"

"Once I get her to fuck me willingly, boom. Ticket to Hell. Nonstop. One way."

She looked down at her glass. "You're wrong, you know."

"Really?"

"I fucked you willingly, but that didn't condemn me. The King couldn't keep me in the Pit."

"You're different, babes. You didn't beg me to ball you for lust's sake. You did it out of some stupid, self-sacrificing notion of love."

That scored me a glare. "Love isn't stupid."

"It's just another four-letter word."

"You have no idea what you're talking about."

"What, about *love?*" I couldn't hide my disgust. "Babes, I don't need to know about it. Demons don't have feelings. You mortal types, though, you let your feelings rule you. They make you do stupid shit."

"I thought it goes, 'The Devil made me do it.'"

"The Devil sure as Sin didn't make you go back to Hell to save your meat pie. That was all you, Jezebel. All you and your fucked up notion of love."

Shouting. Why am I shouting?

I lowered my voice, said, "When you threw yourself at my hooves, told me to have at it, it wasn't because you wanted nothing more than to be with me forever. If you had, then we'd be in the Red Light District even now, screwing each other's brains out."

"*Daun* . . ."

"No, you were all about pulling an Orpheus. How is Shoulders, by the way? Coping well, knowing that his sexpot's fucked more humans than his tiny mind could ever comprehend?"

Her eyes narrowed. "Leave Paul out of this."

"Believe me, I'd like nothing more."

"*Daun* . . ."

"Hey, you chose to stay with Shoulders. And say what you will about me, but I always respect your choices."

"And ignore them, when you see fit."

"Babes, I'm a demon, not a saint." I paused. "Unlike my latest intended. You should see her. She's prettier than you. And her tits are exquisite."

"Congratulations."

"When she calls my name, with no other motive than because she wants me to fuck her silly until Salvation Day, that's one for Lust. No pardons for her. Even love won't save her."

Jezebel stared at me, her thoughts hidden, her face unreadable. "Sounds like you've got it all figured out. Why do you need my help?"

"Because you managed to wrap your meat pie around your finger using only what's between your legs. You didn't use any magic to make Shoulders fall head over heels for you. I need to know how you did that. I can't use my magic on my intended. My power doesn't work on her."

"Of course it doesn't. She's meant for Heaven. Your magic can't touch her, not if it's with malice aforethought."

I smiled tightly. "Someone's fucked one too many lawyers in her time . . ."

"You're not exactly winning me over with your wit."

"But I can win you over in other ways. And none of them involve talking." I rubbed my fingers together, slowly, told her with that small movement exactly what I could do to her. Wanted to do to her.

She paled, but two hectic spots sizzled on her cheeks.

The only thing sexier than her face right after she climaxed was her face at this moment: caught between desire and terror.

My body trembled with raw need, and I clenched my teeth, forced myself to ignore the almost overwhelming urge to throw her down and lick every inch of her body until she screamed with pleasure. "Tell me what I want to know, or I'll pick up where we left off."

"Thought you're not into power games."

"This isn't a game, babes." Rough words, raw voice. Bridled passion. "You seduced your meat pie without magic. Tell me how you did it."

Emotions played on her face, warred in her eyes. Then she took a deep breath, blew it out. "I didn't seduce him. It just happened."

"Really."

"Bless me, Daun, the last thing I'd wanted was to fall in love. I didn't plan it. Paul and I just . . . I don't know, we connected."

"Before or after you fucked him?"

"Before. Way before."

Shit.

I sank back on the sofa, rubbed the bridge of my nose. I'd been sure there was a technique she'd used, hopefully involving a variant of sixty-nine. What was I supposed to do now?

Her hand brushed over mine. Hello. That was a surprise.

"You need to stop thinking about how to seduce your good girl," she said, her voice soft. "You can't bedazzle her. And she won't welcome you to her bed, not when you're a stranger. So you're going to have to get to know her."

"How?" I pulled my hand away from hers, stood up and began to pace. "She's not slated for the Abyss, so Pandemonium won't have any records on her. I don't know anything about her."

"Do it the old-fashioned way. Strike up a conversation."

"Talk? Without angling to get in her pants? Spare me."

"Daun, don't be such a *guy*."

"I don't even know how to find her," I said, crossing the room and back again.

"Ask your King."

I barked out a laugh. "As if."

"Okay. So what do you have on her?"

"Her scent and her first name. Fuck me, maybe she doesn't even live near where I saw her tonight. Maybe she's in another city. Another *state*."

"Sounds like you're going to be doing a lot of walking, sweetie."

"Fucking humans. Why couldn't they all stay in caves?"

"Times change. Come on, Daun. Think. You said you saw her tonight. Did you get anything else about her? Any hints about how to find her?"

I stopped pacing, turned to look at Jezebel. "I know her car and license plate."

"Then for fuck's sake, Daun, just Google her."

"Sounds kinky."

She rolled her eyes. "No, you dumb demon. Do a search on the Internet."

"Yeah, I'll have to get me one of those Internet things."

"Fine, scratch that. Possess someone, go to the DMV and get her record. That'll give you her home address, at least."

Ah. It was something. A start. And a whole lot better than wandering the streets of Saratoga Springs, my nose in the wind, desperate for the barest hint of chocolate and jasmine, of blackberries and musk. "Jezebel, you're a regular fount of information."

"No, sweetie. You're just a Luddite." She stood, placed her empty glass on the table. "I've got to get back to work. Because unless I'm mistaken, you're not about to give me two-fifty for our time here."

Grinning, I ravished her body with my gaze. "I could give you something else."

"Appreciate the sentiment," she said, heading for the door. "But no thanks."

I could have pushed. Part of me wanted to. But she'd helped me, and I'd promised to leave her alone.

For now.

Chapter 7

Stalker Time, Infernal Style

I decided to start in the last place I'd seen Virginia: Saratoga Springs. Even if I didn't know exactly where she lived, I was willing to bet it wasn't in New York City.

Besides, there wasn't anything for me in the Big Apple. Not for the moment, anyway.

A burst of magic transported me Upstate. Infernal locomotion, brimstone optional. Back outside the wine bar. I had hours to kill before business would open for the day and I could get the information I needed. That meant one thing: happy hour. Normally, I would have popped over to the Voodoo Café to fill my thirst, but thanks to the nefarious looking to get in some target practice on everyone's favorite incubus, that particular haunt didn't bode so well. So drinks were limited to the mortal coil. Hell knows, there are worse things in life, after- or otherwise.

I hit a couple bars on Caroline Street, hung with the college kids and the twentysomethings who stayed up all night knowing they'd head to work bleary-eyed and nursing headaches. And I had me a rocking good time. I flirted with the humans, and they with me; I caressed sweet flesh and sampled secret waters; I inhaled their intoxication and exhaled my desire. A little drinking, a lot of lusting. Only a few were beyond my grasp—genuinely good souls, slumming with the sinners. But the others were fair game.

I know, I shouldn't play with my food.

Morning eventually rolled around, and with it came the opening of various shops. The aromas of baking bread and fresh coffee teased the crisp December air, acting like a magnet for the mortals. I loitered outside a coffee shop, invisible. Watching. Waiting.

Here, people, people, people. Feel the lure of caffeine and carbohydrates. I'm waiting. Come to me.

And people came, dressed in their grown-up clothes of business and stress, bound by their daily ritual of breakfast. Some yawned, some smiled; some stared, blank-faced and half-asleep. Most moved like they'd rather be in bed. Couldn't fault them on that point. Of course, to me, bed was just to set the mood. I reached out, sampled their souls one by one. So far, only the good showed up. Probably because they weren't out drinking until the wee hours of the morning.

The real reason vampires didn't come out until dark? They had to sleep away their hangovers.

Soon enough, a Young Turk approached, his coat open enough to flash his power suit. His dark hair was slicked back, not a lock out of place; his face was clean-shaven without a nick or a whisper of stubble. Sunglasses shielded his eyes. His shoes gleamed with polish. No one looked that perfect this early unless their soul held a little evil. I sniffed him as he ambled by me to enter the coffee shop. Yep, I should have guessed. The guy was greedy enough to make Midas look like a saint. The guy radiated easy money.

And that meant easy target.

A few minutes later he left the shop, a steaming cup of liquid nutrition in his hand. I followed. Halfway down the block, he stopped by a silver car that must have cost more than some European countries. After he unlocked his door, I shrugged off my invisibility and tapped him on the shoulder. He turned to look at me, and I reached out with my magic.

Contact.

His jaw dropped; his shoulders slumped. He lowered his arm, and coffee leaked from his cup onto his shoe. He didn't notice. My power held his mind enthralled, captivated, as it relaxed his body, lowered his innate psychic shields. Most humans have a basic mental defense against the nefarious; it's part of the "hear no evil, see no evil" mindset that had kept their race safe from bored demons millennia ago, before we had our Rules. Now we weren't allowed to possess humans unless they openly courted evil—murderers, drug addicts, politicians, that sort of thing. Which meant that first, I had to find an acceptable flesh puppet before I borrowed a body, and second, after I targeted said puppet, I had to encourage its mind to let me in.

Piece of cake.

I felt the last of the human's shielding slip away, and with a grin I switched from invisible to incorporeal and entered his body.

A moment of dizziness washed over me as I adjusted to the shorter frame, felt the weight of gravity hit my human limbs. Whoa. Head rush. Possessing mortals always felt like swimming through congealed blood. And it was just as sweet. I relished the tastes and smells and textures this particular mortal took for granted—the way the warm Styrofoam cup was just south of uncomfortable in his (my) hand, the leftover sleep fuzz on his/my tongue, the bite of the cold on my cheeks, the way my heart pounded in my chest as I breathed deeply and drank the wind. I threw my head back and laughed, thrilled in the feeling of that laughter bubbling from my throat. Unholy Hell, nothing felt as real as when I rode a human body. Except when I rode a human between the sheets. But even that, sometimes, paled compared with stealing flesh. Possession was a perpetual state of pleasure—orgasm experienced from the outside. Utter fucking bliss.

I settled back, allowed the puppet—

. . . *joe my name is joe* . . .

—to float to the surface, reclaim his body. To a degree. Nestled deeply within him, I still influenced his thoughts, his movements. Told him to drive to the Department of Motor Vehicles. He frowned as we got into the car—

. . . don't have to go to motor vehicles why'm i going there . . . ?

—but he didn't fight me as we started the engine, drove off. Ten minutes later, he parked outside of a shopping mall. I reminded him we needed to get to Motor Vehicles, not do his holiday shopping.

. . . this is the dmv it's inside the mall . . .

Okay then. Let's go.

We marched in, strode over to the large directory of stores, scanned the list. He pointed to a listing down near the bottom: Saratoga County DMV.

Really?

. . . dmv is department of motor vehicles . . .

Excellent.

We walked down the hallway, passed countless stores offering services and goods ranging from clothing to shoes to food to entertainment. It was a major change from the intricate labyrinths within the heart of Pandemonium, with its bare walls and ammonia smells that killed even the richest scent of deep earth. However long it would take at the DMV, I was positive it wouldn't hold a femur to the Abyss, where the wait to fill out vastly detailed paperwork was enough to kill some minor demons out of sheer boredom. Humans didn't like to be bored (granted, neither did demons, but humans could choose to do something to assuage that boredom), so they opted for distractions that led them away from their goal of completing required forms and tempted them instead to spend their hard-earned money on things they didn't need. Fairly insidious. Rather impressive. Small wonder the Nameless Evil had Its eye on the mortal coil instead of in the depths of the Pit: these humans were ingenious when it came to distracting themselves from inconvenient truths.

At the DMV, we could have waited on line and let the other mortals go first. Yeah, right. We walked to the front desk, where a mountain of a woman typed furiously on her computer. Without looking up, she hollered, "Wait in line."

I love it when they play hard to get.

Lowering the Turk's eyewear, I smiled, asked, "You see that?"

She glanced up, her broad face screwed into a furious scowl. "See what?"

"Me."

Contact.

My power caressed her, seduced her. Her eyes glazed and her mouth opened, and a little sound like an *oooh* escaped her. Barely any shielding to her; with a whisper of magic, she was mine.

I leapt out of the Young Turk and into Miss Congeniality. Her essence grabbed me, pulled me down, battered me with her misery.

. . . *fucking hate this job it sucks my life sucks no one listens to me no one needs me i'm worthless and hate everyone everything* . . .

Whoa. I told her: ***Deep breath, doll. I need you.***

She was so lost in her bitterness that she didn't hear me. I said it again, made my tone compelling. Flattering. ***I need you.***

This time she heard me.

. . . *needed i'm needed tell me what what what tell me i'll do anything to be wanted not like they ever appreciate me here assholes i hate them all they don't deserve what they've got* . . .

Definitely marked for Envy. I would have felt sorry for her, except demons don't feel stupid things like pity. She'd get what she deserved when her time came. That was the way of it.

"What the hell . . . ?"

On the other side of the counter, the Young Turk shook his head, looked around. "Where am I?"

"DMV," one of the other customers snapped. "Where there's a line of people here before you."

"But—"

"Wait your turn."

As the guy tried to figure out how he'd gotten from Broadway to the Wilton Mall without remembering it, I gave my new host a job: I told her Virginia's license plate number, commanded her to scare up an address. She worked her own magic on her computer. I watched, fascinated. One of these years, I'd have to take some time off to get up to speed on the latest technologies. Damn problem was that for the past five decades, there'd been so many changes so fast that a working demon like me barely had time to note major cultural influences, let alone the latest and greatest way that humans amused themselves. Once I was Prince of Lust, that would be the first thing I'd do: get a crash course on new media. Until then, I'd deal with influencing mortals to get what I needed.

. . . here it's here . . .

There it was, on the small computer screen: my intended's information. Full name: Virginia Heather Reed. Pretty. More stuff—an address, her phone number. And other information I didn't care about.

Come on, doll. Let's go for a ride.

"I'm on break," my puppet bellowed.

The customers in line all groaned, and some let out a few choice curses. One of her coworkers tried to discourage her from leaving, but I was a demon on a mission, so my host grabbed a coat and a purse, then took off. Having her walk out on the job might get her fired. Well, that'd be one more thing for her to be bitter about. Outside, she unlocked a car that redefined "piece of shit," and we were on our way.

We drove to Virginia's house, somewhere in a rural part of Wilton, New York. Lots of dead trees and frozen grass, all captured in winter splendor. My intended's home was at the end of a long driveway, the house set back far from the road. Liked her privacy. Good to know. Before I exited my host's body, I gave her a tiny orgasm; my way of saying thanks for the lift. As she squealed her bliss, I morphed out of her and the car, let her come to in private. Ta, doll.

I ghosted to Virginia's door and slid my way inside her home. And proceeded to be less than impressed with the small house.

First stop beyond the front door: a living room, complete with overstuffed sofas and chairs, short table with magazines and books, potted plants, woven rug that looked like it had never been used to cushion someone's bare bottom as their lover took them on the floor. All tans and creams, cautious neutrals. Tastefully boring. Next.

Straight ahead: a big kitchen with a large wooden table and tons of counter space; lots of cabinets; black dishwasher and matching stove with pans on the range top. Resting on the back edge of the range was a ceramic cup, painted blue and hugely cracked. More ovens, both of the toasting and nuking variety. A big wooden block filled with knives stood sentry off to the left of the stove; to the right were roughly a million cooking utensils and gadgets stuffed into holders and lined up in neat rows. Lining the back of one counter were cookbooks, two rows high. Even with all the telltale signs of someone who enjoyed cooking, I noted the dust on the books, the unused look to the stove. A check of her fridge showed take-out cartons, soda cans, a bottle of white wine. On the wall closest to the living room hung a corkboard and calendar. I thumbed through the various notes on the board and scanned the rest of December to get a sense of her plans. Easy: none. Not even on the 31st, a biggie for most mortals in the Western part of the globe. Barring some appointments—hair, car, doctor—Virginia didn't get out much. Or if she did, she didn't advertise it. Based on what I was picking up, the only spice she got in her little life was the stuff that grew in gardens.

The door to the right of the kitchen led to her garage. Empty, except for outdoor tools hanging neatly on hooks or leaning in the corners. Behind the garage was a tiny patio, which opened to a snow-covered fenced backyard.

Yawn. Bring on the bedroom.

Off the kitchen to the left stretched a long hallway. Bathroom and a guest bedroom on the right; a plain room filled with about a thousand boxes and stuffed bags on the left. And, finally, the master bedroom. Which was just as vanilla as the rest of the house: a full-sized bed with an afterthought for a headboard—and no footboard; shit, there went the possibility of bondage—two pillows and a washed-out blue comforter. Perfunctory furniture of dark brown completed the set, with a large television and other electronics resting on top of the dresser. The only mirror was mounted behind the door. Same style of rug here as the one in the living room.

No pictures. Anywhere.

I could have ransacked her house to find more evidence of who Virginia really was—hints of her likes, flashes of her past. But I preferred to wait for my intended to come on home and then observe directly. So what to do until she arrived? I spied three remote controls on her nightstand. Practically a sign from Below. Settling back onto the bed, I picked up one of the remotes, aimed it at the television screen, and clicked the POWER button. Nothing happened. Ditto with the other two controls.

Fucking technology.

Grumbling, I summoned a lick of power and zapped the tube. It flickered onto a news channel. One of the anchors was breathlessly explaining how we were a hair's width away from starting World War Three.

Cool. I could use a little comedy while I waited.

At seven fifty-two, post meridiem, I heard the garage door open, then close. Time to be unseemly. Or at least unseen. I switched off the television, snapped myself invisible, and crept out to welcome Virginia home.

From the hallway I had a clear view of the kitchen. Virginia was standing there, throwing down her purse and shrugging out of her large coat. I watched her untangle herself from its embrace, marveled in the form of her body as it emerged from its cocoon of black wool. She tried to disguise her allure with a baggy sweater and pants, but I saw the way her full breasts molded against her shirt, the swell of her hips poking out from the bulky material. No bone-thin fragile doll was my Virginia; here was a woman lush with curves, plump with femininity. I inhaled her scent, tasted blackberries and jasmine.

Mmm.

She draped her coat over a kitchen chair, then tipped her head back and worked out a kink in her neck. Her hand came up, pressed onto her shoulder and kneaded. As her fingers danced, I saw the gleam of gold.

Oh-ho. What's this?

Letting out a huge sigh, she rolled her shoulder twice and moved toward the refrigerator. Come on, doll. Let's see that hand . . . She rummaged for food, pulled out a plastic container with what looked like intestines squished inside. Carrying it to the table, I saw her left hand very clearly: on the fourth finger was a golden band.

A wedding ring.

I grinned as she got the rest of her meal ready. Well, that should certainly make this assignment more interesting.

She ate the noodles cold, straight out of the container, and chased it with a can of soda while she pored through her mail— bills, ads, and catalogues (sadly, nothing involving lingerie). Then she rinsed the container and the soda can, put the plastic in the dishwasher and the empty can into a bin beneath the sink. She tossed her opened envelopes into the trash, put the bills into a counter drawer and the catalogues into another bin by her garage steps. She performed all of these actions with the look of someone who was asleep on her feet—her mind obviously was elsewhere as her body enacted a routine. She hung up her jacket in a closet and wiped down the kitchen table. Even her motions with the cleaning rag were methodical. She glanced at her phone before she turned off the kitchen light and walked down the hall to the bathroom.

I blew out a sigh. Bishop's balls, were all good people this freaking dull? Maybe once her husband came home, I'd see what made Virginia tick. I hoped he'd get here soon, because at this rate, my brain was going to putrefy from ennui.

She left the bathroom and headed toward her bedroom. Yeah, that's more like it. With a big smile on my face, I followed.

Would her body be similar to Jezebel's? Or did the familiarity end with the face?

One way to find out.

Next to her bed, Virginia stood poised on one foot, bent

over as she stripped off her boot. Nice balance. And—hey, flexible. Very good. She dropped the boot to the floor, switched feet. Her nyloned toes looked small and crushed as she stood on the banded rug. I wanted to suck every digit until she squealed. Soon, soon . . .

Crossing her arms, she pulled her sweater up and over her head. She stretched out for one glorious moment, long and enticing—her breasts lifted and her back arched as if she were caught in the throes of pleasure. My entire body clenched as I watched her, breathed her. Wanted her.

Virginia.

Then the shirt was discarded and the spell broke; she shrouded her face with her hair, bowed her shoulders and shrank within herself, careful to reveal only heavy arms, an unflattering bra, a rounded belly. She unfastened her pants and jiggled them over the bulge of her large thighs. Such beautiful thighs. Fuck me, I wanted those thighs around my ears. Would her legs feel soft when I ran my fingers up them? Or would they be toned beneath the padding? Her underwear, I noted, didn't match her bra. Simple cotton. No frills. Unmade-up.

Like her.

She scooped up her clothing and dropped the pile into a wicker basket by the corner of the room, then opened a drawer and pulled out a long T-shirt. She unhooked her bra, and my dick roared to life as I beheld her bare breasts. Unholy Hell, they were magnificent: full and ripe, their nipples seductively pink, the areoles without a hint of the tan that forever marks a mother. I wanted to feel her in my hands, capture one of those succulent nipples in my mouth and tease it with lips and teeth and tongue it until it was swollen and she was raw and aching . . .

Boom *boom*.

Then she put on her T-shirt, which swam over her frame and draped down to her knees. Once again camouflaged in plainness, she put away her bra. She turned on the television set and turned off the overhead light, and at eight fifty-six PM, Virginia climbed into bed. Exhaustion and something else weighed down her features; there was a glazed look about her that could have been sadness. Or loneliness. The television cast a gray pallor over her, turned her gold band to a drab olive. Muted the vibrant green of her eyes.

Still no husband by her side.

She pressed buttons on her remote control, and soon she was watching a show about people living on an island.

And I was watching her.

Are you lost, Virginia?

No worries, doll. Soon I'll find you—the real you. I'll find you and seduce you and make you mine.

And then I'll take you to Hell.

Outside of Virginia's house, I breathed the crisp December air to clear my head of blackberries and jasmine, of chocolate and musk. Stalking Virginia for the past three days was boring as Heaven, but intoxicating as Hell. I inhaled deeply, smelled snow. And not a dusting, either; soon a fresh blanket of crystalline white would cover the driveway. I wondered whether Virginia would shovel, or if she'd hire some young buck to do the deed for her. Maybe her husband would return home in time to plow.

I doubted it.

You're only thirty-five, Vee, her friend had said that night in the bar. *That's too young to stop living your life.*

An absentee husband; a lonely wife. A perfect setup for seduction. Except my intended was good. She didn't give in to temptation. Not then at the bar, and not today. An hour ago, Virginia had ordered a pizza. The delivery guy turned out to be this kid straight out of a frustrated housewife's raunchiest dream, so I'd decided to go the porn star route and ring her doorbell dressed only in a cardboard pizza box and wicked intentions. And in a model-class human. He was a pothead, which had made the possession fast and sweet. Sure, Pan had said no riding a mortal to ride Virginia and steal her soul. But I figured I could at least loosen her up a bit that way before I sailed in and took her away to the Lake of Fire.

Besides, after three days of watching her sleepwalk her way through her life, I had to shake things up a bit. For my sanity, if not hers. In sum, Virginia's workday was wake, shower, dress, leave for work, get to work, do work, leave work, come home, eat dinner, get undressed and ready for bed, and watch television until falling asleep. Yawn.

Maybe her husband wasn't on a trip. Maybe he'd left her for someone more exciting. Fuck me speechless, even a corpse would be more lively than Virginia was.

And a zombie would have more ambition. Virginia worked in Albany, which was a fifty-minute drive from her home. From what I gathered, she was an assistant of some sort, doing administrative work for a group of business people who dressed sharp enough to make your eyes bleed. But Virginia was more than just the scheduler and planner and coffee-fetcher; I'd watched her pitch ideas and suggestions to one of her bosses, who'd then pitched them as his own . . . and then received full credit for the ideas. Virginia, apparently, didn't care. She certainly hadn't fought for the recognition she deserved. She seemed used to the notion of being the behind-the-scenes player.

Pan must really want me dead. Because stalking Virginia was seriously going to kill me out of sheer tedium.

When I'd opted for Pizza Guy Daun earlier tonight, I'd hoped that would at least shock her awake. No such luck. Virginia had opened the door, and I'd cut loose with a wave of raw sexuality, hitting her with enough desire that even Mother Teresa would've creamed her panties. But all Virginia had done was sneeze, apologize for spraying me with her germs, and pay for the food. As I had Pizza Guy take her money, I'd worked his mouth and asked Virginia out on a mortal date. "You know, like, go somewhere. Have some fun." Frustrating rule of possession: unless the puppet was asleep or unconscious, the invading demon was stuck speaking in the puppet's manner.

She'd smiled—such a sad, sweet smile—and mentioned something about her husband, which she and I both knew was a crock of shit.

"Aw, you're breaking my heart," I made Pizza Guy say.

"You're a sweetie."

Jezebel's words, Virginia's voice. My throat tightened, closed, leaving me gaping like a suffocating fish.

She slipped something into my hand, and I breathed in her heady scent, all berries and chocolate. My head had spun, making me feel as stoned as my human host was. I gasped out a "Whoa."

"Thanks for the pizza," she said, smiling. "And the flattery."

With that, she'd closed the door, leaving me with a possessed delivery guy and an eight-dollar tip for a twelve-dollar meal. I let the kid go; he was so out of it that he didn't even notice he'd grayed out on this last delivery. Humming off-key, he climbed into his truck and motored away.

I'd been standing outside of Virginia's house for the past fifteen minutes, trying to clear her smell from my nose, wondering how in Hell I was supposed to spark her interest. Her husband was away, didn't even call her—or she him—didn't seem to give her a second thought. Why wasn't she at least tempted with the possibility of a fling? Of fun?

Why did the thought of desire make her so sad?

I took a deep breath of snow-tinted air, and my nostrils flared as oxygen suddenly gave way to sulfur. I tensed, but only for a heartbeat; I had nothing to worry about from this particular demon. I would've known who it was even without the psychic connection that all creatures of Lust shared. He wore enough cologne to fell an elephant at a hundred paces.

From behind me, a snort. "You're supposed to fuck her, not stalk her."

I turned, casual and slow, hands in my jacket pockets. "Thought it was you. Either that, or a madame from a French cathouse."

Callistus snorted again. He hadn't dressed for mortal eyes— he stood in his natural form, from goat's horns to hooves, his pale human torso covered in a thick pelt of black hair. Pan preferred satyrs in his entourage, which was why Cal was his number two. It sure wasn't due to Cal's intelligence. Or his dick size. He rumbled, "The sluts in France don't wear Drakkar Noir."

"No one wears Drakkar Noir."

His eyes gleamed red in the shadows of his white face, rubies and ebony in a bed of snow. "I like it. Reminds me of the Inquisition."

"Everything reminds you of the Inquisition."

A flash of fangs in the night as he grinned, deadly and quick. "Those were good times. Screams and sex and blood . . ."

"You wanted something, Cal?"

The smile tightened. "Want? I want to be Prince. But you went and fucked that up for me, didn't you?"

I shrugged. "Unintentional."

"I'm sure." His goat's eyes shone brightly, promising murder. If he wasn't a Seducer, I would have pegged him as the one orchestrating the attacks against me. But he, like all creatures of Lust, preferred the direct approach; if he wanted me out of the way, he'd challenge me openly. Stepping closer, he asked, "You think you can rule us, Daunuan?"

"Pan rules us."

"For now."

Interesting. "Already planning a revolution, are you?"

"Just asking a question," he said. "You think you can keep the incubi in line?"

I arched an eyebrow at his bravado. His back was definitely up. Callistus wasn't one to buck authority, or to question the status quo. Then again, things had been changing in the Abyss on a level the nefarious had never known. The boundaries between Sin and Land were blurring more and more with every passing day. Infernal hostilities blazed hotter than ever. And the standing of the elite was never more ephemeral; I'd lost count of how many lower-downs had been destroyed in a burst of whimsy from the King of Hell.

Looking at Callistus now, watching his hands glow with power, I had a very unsettling thought: The King's madness was spreading. Maybe Cal really was a threat.

My voice whisper-soft, I asked, "You challenging me?"

The Seducer stood silent, his hands clenching, unclenching, wringing out magic and letting the untapped energy wisp away in the nighttime sky as he stared at me, his face unreadable, his thoughts shielded. A minute ticked by. Demonic testosterone filled the air; tension hummed across my skin, rippled through my muscles. I wanted to cut loose, release the frustration that had been building for days. But only if Cal made the first move, used his magic against me. I'd be blessed if I'd end up filing more paperwork just because I was impatient.

Finally, Callistus opened his hands, spread them, palms up. Energy wafted up, dispersed. "No challenge, Daun." He didn't have to add the "yet"; the word was all too clear in his bloody eyes, his tight-lipped smile. "For now, just a message. The Boss thinks you're taking too long to do your job."

"He didn't mention anything about a time limit to me when he gave me the assignment."

"Maybe that's because he thought you'd be done by now."

Was he baiting me? I couldn't tell if he was lying about Pan, and that pissed me off more than the thought of Cal challenging me. "What's the rush? We give our clients three Dates before we fuck them as a grand finale."

"But you haven't even scored one Date with your latest, have you?"

Jaw clenched, I said, "Working on it."

Cal chuffed laughter, his shoulders bobbing. "Hardly. All you've been doing is watching her. Satan knows I've nearly died out of boredom, watching you watch her."

Terrific—the stalker was being stalked. "Figuring out my best means of attack."

"It's the part that you point with," he said, glancing at my crotch.

Asshole. "Thanks for the tip."

"Got lots of them."

"You should be a mohel."

The ruby of his eyes shone, red and wet against the ghostly white of his face, spilled blood on snow. "I prefer foreplay to foreskin. I gave you the message, Daun. What you do with it is up to you. My job's done." He smiled then, and his eyes lit with hunger. "Me, I say take your time. You pissing off the Boss makes it that much more fun for me."

A blink and he was gone, only a puff of smoke and brimstone marking where he'd been. That, and the lingering odor of a tomcat in heat. I waved away Cal's stink, peered through the window to see Virginia getting a glass of water before heading toward her bedroom.

Callistus hadn't challenged me—but then again, he didn't have to. If Pan really was losing patience with me, then I was running out of time. I had no desire to be annihilated, especially in the name of Pan's ambition.

I grinned. Time to kick things up.

Chapter 8

Wet Dream

Most humans relax when they sleep. They can't help it—with the loss of consciousness comes a sort of mental and emotional freedom: their shields crack, their careful layers of deception and protection slip away, their minds unshackle. The only exceptions are those who choose to guard their dreams, like practitioners of the magical arts, or those who have been so emotionally scarred that they can't bring themselves to ever lower their defenses, not even when sleeping.

Virginia was the latter.

I watched her as she slept, her face hidden by her curtain of thick hair. She lay on her stomach, her pillow on the floor, her head turned to the side. She'd gone back and forth with propping her head, sleeping on her side, her back, her side again, finally tossing the pillow to the ground and settling prone, mouth open, limbs wide as if making an offering to a god. The past two nights had been similar; whatever she wrestled with in her mind played itself out in her bed. Nice to see the mattress getting some action, but I could think of better uses.

I listened to her breathing, tried to puzzle her out. The only way my magic would work on her was if she kissed me, willingly. Preferably with tongue. And especially with Pan's restriction on me assuming a pleasing shape that she knew, I had to manipulate her into kissing me. And that meant I needed to understand her more. Or at all.

The first step to penetrating her mind was to work on her body's defenses. It would be so much easier if I could just get her to relax. Her back rose and fell with her breathing, rippling her long black curls. Look at how her head is twisted away from her body—how could she possibly be sleeping like that? It looked like someone had broken her neck. My lips twitched from the thought; it'd be just my luck for her to accidentally kill herself before I seduced her.

I watched her.

She'd have an unpleasant crick in the morning. I thought of how she tended to massage her left shoulder, rotate it in its socket as if it constantly pained her. That wasn't just from how she slept; there was something deeper there. She'd been hurt—physically? emotionally?—and her body told the story of her scars.

If only I could touch her, soothe her with my power. Cajole those tense muscles into unwinding, relaxing. Give her some release.

I debated doing just that: straddling her and working her body with my fingers until she was pliable, limp. Receptive. Except she would have woken, and screamed. A lot. Probably would have a heart attack and die. Which, at this point, did me no good at all.

You're not the one I'm waiting for, Virginia had insisted. *You're nothing like him.*

Who, then? Who was it that had captured your heart and refused to release it? Certainly not the missing husband, no matter what the ring on her finger suggested. A man who cared about his woman didn't ignore her for days on end, not in this age of instantaneous communication.

What sort of man makes your heartbeat quicken, Virginia?

Your magic can't touch her, Jezzie had said, *not if it's with malice aforethought.*

But what if it had nothing to do with malice? Intentions

mattered for humans. Were demons subject to the same rules? If I truly didn't mean her any harm—no plotting to seduce her soul away, just something to help relax her—would that be enough to make her susceptible to my magic?

I ignored the taunting question of how Virginia would taste, her body slick with want, her soul just out of reach. Instead, I thought of how tense she was, how she couldn't relax even when slumbering. How her shoulder and neck pained her. I thought of the hurt and sadness that made her green eyes bright with sorrow. Let me take that hurt away, Virginia. At least for tonight.

Summoning my power, I sent out a silent command, couched in a plea: *Let me in.*

I exhaled, blowing my magic over her, washing her body in lust. Still sleeping, her breath caught in her throat. Then she let out a sigh, the barest hint of a moan.

Yes.

Dream of the one you're waiting for, Virginia. I nudged the command into her mind, soft as a caress. *Show me the one you want.*

She rolled onto her side, her back, tossed one arm over her head and murmured something—a name.

Chris.

Focusing on that name, I reached out, let my fingers penetrate her mind, her dream.

And I shifted.

The restaurant isn't too crowded—a smattering of patrons at various tables, a handful of waiters doing their penguin impressions, the occasional busboy filling water glasses, a host dressed to the nines and wearing a mask of sycophancy. Smells waft in the air, mostly garlic and frying oil. Italian food. My lips twitch in unexpected mirth, and I'm inexplicably thinking of Mount Vesuvius. I hear *her* voice, rich with laughter as she speaks of lava and Naples.

I push away the memory; I'm not here for that one. I scan

the room until, sequestered in a corner, I see my lady. And her man.

Virginia lounges in her seat, at ease, her attire incongruous with the pseudofinery of the restaurant. Over her torso is a ripped gray sweatshirt, the neck wide and hanging over one shoulder, the sleeves torn off. Baggy flannel pajama pants cinch tight at her waist. Instead of shoes, she wears fuzzy tan slippers, one dangling precariously off of a foot as she swings that leg, lazily, the material of her pants bunching around her knee, flashing glimpses of her bare calf. She's younger now, maybe twenty-two, and about twenty pounds lighter. I prefer her with more flesh; with less weight on it, her face now is almost gaunt.

The man sitting across from her, tearing chunks of bread with his large hands, is good looking, but far from cover-model features: short black hair on the brink of thinning; light chocolate eyes that crinkle in the corners; broad face with a strong jaw, softened with extra pounds and a five o'clock shadow. His skin is more olive than Virginia's, hinting at Mediterranean ancestry. Thick neck; shoulders broad enough to make Jezebel's meat pie look like a wimp. Like Virginia, he's dressed more for sleep than for dining out: he's wearing a faded white T-shirt, dark sweatpants. His big feet are bare. Hairy toes.

A waiter bustles past me, interrupting my view of the Couple of the Moment. Just as well; I'm out of place here, even in my human costume. She'll notice some guy watching her, listening in on a private conversation. In a dream, the sleeper makes the rules; even if I ghost, she may see me. Better for me to blend than attempt invisibility. With a thought, I'm dressed in a black suit, holding a bottle of wine.

I glide up to Virginia's table, refill her glass. She gives me a winning smile and thanks me, and it's all I can do to keep from sucking her face. Look at her: the smile comes so naturally, is set on a face accustomed to laughter. This is the real Virginia, not the fragile shell of a human who sleepwalks through the world. This is a woman who *feels*. Mmm. A glance at the man's glass shows his own wine untouched. With a smile of a job well done, I step back, fade away in the manner of servants across the ages: visible, but not truly seen.

Virginia picks up her wineglass, swirls the liquid. "God, I do so love Santa Margherita." She sips, delights in the taste; her smile lights up her eyes, emeralds glinting in the softly lit room.

A grin eats half his face, the teeth revealing a smoker's history. "Really? Couldn't tell." He booms his words, and they resonate with mirth and something else, something thicker that I can't place. Popping bread into his mouth, he chews, winks. "You're sure we're here for your birthday? There's no Guinness."

"Not just my birthday."

"No?" Eagerness in her voice. Anticipation. "What else?"

He lifts his cup and reaches over to clink glasses. "We're celebrating your first A."

Virginia's smile falters, but she recovers with a sip of wine. "Thanks." Her cheeks flush from alcohol and embarrassment.

"I'm so proud of you, honey."

"Oh, it's just studio art." Her shoulder rises and falls in an offhand shrug. "Not exactly brain surgery."

"It's a grad school A. Which is at least double the value of an undergrad A. Proves you're a damn fine artist."

She chuckles, the sound melodious and rich. "More like it proves I can clean brushes with the best of them."

"A for effort?"

"Something like that." She waits, searching his face. He's good—he obviously knows something she doesn't, based on the mischievous glint in his eyes. And he's enjoying watching her squirm. *My kind of guy.* Virginia asks, "That's really why we're out tonight? Your birthday, my grade?"

All innocence, he bats his lashes. "You thought there'd be another reason?"

"Oh hell, Chris," she laughs, balling up her napkin and making as if to throw it at him. "Don't make me say it!"

"Say what?"

She blows out an exasperated breath, drops the cloth to the table. "When're you going to propose already?"

"Propose?" He pats his pockets, grins sheepishly. "Damn. Left the ring in my other pants."

She rolls her eyes, but her laugh ruins the effect. "Funny guy."

"See, you think I'm funny. That's it—you're doomed. Nothing good will come of it once you like my sense of humor."

Virginia frowns, a sudden thought flashing behind her eyes. She looks down at her drink, studies the contents. "This is when we have dinner," she says, not to him. "The overpriced veal that melts like butter. Gorging on garlic bread while we wait. Drinking wine."

He smiles, slow on the uptake—he doesn't get that she's somewhere else. "Hey, I'm just trying to get you drunk. I want to have my wicked way with you later. Ravish you properly."

"Yeah . . ."

Now he senses something's off; he shrugs, nonchalant. "Is it the place? You want, we can go somewhere else."

"No, this is great," she says, her voice flat. "I love Italian."

"Especially sausage." He waggles his brows, but she's not looking at him. "Vee?" She turns to him, and he looks deeply into her eyes. "Honey, what's wrong?"

The humor's bled from her face, leaving it pale. Haunted. "This is how it happens. We'll eat, and you'll pay. You'll take me back to your place, tell me you want to show me one of your birthday presents."

He nods, his gaze intent on hers. "Yes."

"And we'll get there, and there'll be a small stuffed animal on the kitchen chair. A white kitten."

"With a red heart around its neck." He smiles, his eyes thoughtful as he looks at her. "And a ring around its tail."

"And a note that says, 'To Vee, for the rest of my life.'" Her breath hitches, and she puts down her glass. Wine sloshes over the rim, laps at her fingers, but she doesn't notice. "And then you come up from behind me, reach around my waist, turn the cat around . . ."

"And then you see the ring. And I ask if you'll marry me."

Her eyes shimmer with tears. "And I say, 'Oh my God, oh my God, oh my God, *yes*, oh my God.'"

He laughs gently, takes her wine-wet hand. "You left out an 'oh my God.' You say it five times, with the 'yes' in the middle. Why're you crying, honey?"

"Because this is how it happens, how it starts."

"Yes."

She dabs her eyes with her napkin. "And then we get married."

"Yes."

"And then you leave me."

His face contorts, stricken. "Honey . . ."

"You told me you'd be with me *forever*." She spits out the word like it's poison. "You promised."

"I tried, Vee."

"You promised!"

He sighs. "I lied."

She pulls her hand away, lowers her head so that her wild hair covers her face, hides the tears streaking down her cheeks. Now he's behind her, massaging her shoulders, and she's leaning into his touch. The restaurant melts away around them, and now she's sitting on a rumpled bed, the alcove dark and cramped, and his arms are wrapped around her like he's never going to let her go. But they both know that's a lie.

"Vee. Oh, Vee." He's whispering into her ear, but I hear him clearly. "I didn't mean to hurt you."

Her laugh is harsh, brittle. "Hurt me? You ripped out my heart."

"I know." His hands travel up, press on her shoulders, start to massage them. She melts, just a little, just enough to lower her head and go with the movement. He says again, "I know."

His fingers must work magic, because she says, "I love you so much . . ."

"And I you," he whispers, his hands pressing. Stroking.

"I won't marry you, Chris. I'm not doing it."

He kisses the curve of her neck, says, "It's already done. I'm so sorry, Vee."

"You're going to leave me."

"I know." Now he's in front of her, cupping her chin. Looking in her eyes. Brushing away her tears. "I swear, I didn't mean to hurt you. I love you, Virginia. I love you."

"You have a hell of a way of showing it."

"I love you." He kisses her lips, softly, as if he's afraid of bruising her. "I'll always love you." He kisses her cheeks, her chin, and her tears flow around his mouth. "I'm so sorry, honey." His lips on her jaw, her neck, the ridge of her collarbone. She tilts her head up, exposes the pale silk of her throat as she looks to Heaven for an answer to a question she won't voice. His words like a prayer, he says again, "I'm sorry."

"Don't tell me you're sorry," she whispers, her voice rasping like sandpaper. "Don't."

"Vee . . ."

"Don't tell me." Her eyes close. "Show me."

He opens his mouth wide and kisses her neck, works his way up, his lips forging a trail to her ear. His tongue flicks out to her lobe, and she lets out a mewling sound as he tastes her. He moves his hands slowly, slides them down her neck, her shoulders, now over her breasts, cupping them. Caressing them. Her breathing quickens, encourages him as his fingers splay, his thumbs reaching up to brush over her nipples.

"Show me," she says again, voice thick with sorrow, heavy with arousal. "Make me believe you."

He leans down to kiss her breast, and she arches against him, moaning low and lush. Their sounds fill the alcove: her moans, his suckles, their breathing intertwined in a lover's knot. He teases her with lips and hands . . . no, not teases; this is no prelude of desire, no roadmap to pleasure—he attends her body, worships her with every stroke of his fingers, every lick of his tongue. He showers her with adoration, and beneath his touch of springtime rain, her body blooms.

"Chris . . ."

"Vee."

Opening her eyes, she clasps his hands, brings them together and presses them to her chest, over her heart. Her eyes are bright with passion and despair. "You're going to leave me."

"But not tonight," he says.

"Not tonight," she agrees, then seals her lips on his and kisses him hard.

I watch their jaws move, hear their tongues roll together as they devour each other. I'm out of place here even more than at the restaurant, but they don't notice me—they wouldn't notice the Apocalypse annihilating the world around them. His hands are on the hem of her shirt, now pulling the clothing up, and Virginia breaks away from him as he yanks the sweatshirt over her head. He drops the shirt and takes in her bare torso, as do I: her shoulders are pale against the inky hair that cascades down her back, and gooseflesh pebbles her arms, dots her full breasts, belies the heat in her eyes.

"You're so beautiful," he says, his voice husky.

She is. Oh, she is.

Virginia opens her mouth, perhaps to protest, but he cuts her words short by cupping her breasts and squeezing them gently together, his mouth working on one nipple and then the other. Her breath catches, and she groans when his tongue flicks over her sensitive flesh, gasps as his teeth nip a taut peak. He licks away any pain and hums against her skin, the sound mingling with her ragged breathing. With his tongue he outlines the underswell of her bosom, runs within the valley between her breasts; with his hands he sketches her curves.

"Please," she says, throwing her head back, giving him more of herself to suckle, to shape between his fingers. He drinks her slowly, and she arches against him, says once again, "Please."

Smiling as he laps her nipple, he reaches behind her body until he cradles her back. Leaning forward, he guides her down his until she's lying on the bed, looking up at him with heavily lidded eyes, her lips parted, face flushed.

"This?" He straddles her hips, rocks over her sex, slowly, rubbing his length against her. "This, Vee?"

"Please . . ."

He sits up tall to strip off his shirt, revealing a barrel chest, a belly thick with muscles and fat. Her hands reach up to glide over the expanse of his skin, playing with the hair on his chest, tracing the line of black curls that leads over his round stomach and disappears in the waistband of his sweatpants.

I watch her fingers skim the bulk of his erection, watch as she teases him with featherlight touches, and my cock thrums with need. I watch, wanting her hands on my shaft, wanting her moving beneath me and staring at me with lust in her eyes. Wanting her nails grazing my balls, relieving the throbbing ache she's causing with her wicked hands, her suck-me tits. Wanting *her*. I growl, deep in my throat, watching them as her name and her scent fill my mind.

Virginia.

He's kissing his way down her stomach, one hand running up her thigh, the other propping himself over her body. She shivers from his touch, his lips, grinds her hips and tells him with her body that she's ready, steady, go. His fingers dance between her legs and back up to the concave plane of her stomach, drum on the curve of her abdomen before dipping down. He pauses in his kisses to ask, "This, Vee? This what you want?"

"Please . . ."

He circles her navel with his tongue just before his hand plunges beneath the waistband of her flannel pants.

"God, yes," she pants as his fingers probe inside of her.

He slides her pants and underwear down her thighs, peppers her legs with wet kisses. She shudders with every press of his lips, whimpers as he works his way up her calves, past her knees, tauntingly slow. He pauses over her mound, says her name gruffly. "Tell me what you want, Vee."

Groaning, she reaches out to clasp his head, fisting her hands in his hair. Pushes down.

With a grin, he buries his face between her thighs.

She bucks, thrashes her head and digs her nails into the bed, panting from his attention. A lingering stroke, and again, slower now, and she cries out a sound of pure joy. He kisses her, teasing and tasting her. Fucking her with his tongue. Coaxing her with lips on lips. Her breath catches, her head rocks back, and she's saying "there there yes there God there" and her hips arch up, up, up. She screams his name as she comes, and he laps her juices, drinks her sweetness.

A sting in my palm. I unclench my fist, ignore the slashes where my nails—my talons—have cut through my flesh. Instead, I watch the aftershocks ripple over her, see him shucking his sweatpants and briefs. My heart's racing, my blood's pounding in my head, my cock, as she lies sated beneath him and he positions himself over her.

My name, Virginia. It will be *my* name you call, my touch you crave.

He enters her smoothly as he lets out an *uhmmm*, and she takes him in with a satisfied sigh, hooking her legs around his waist.

How I want to hear your voice sing my name, your lips speaking the one word that will forever brand your soul. It will be sweeter than song.

Her nails score his shoulders as he pumps inside of her. Hip to hip, breath to breath, they move with the fluid ease of longtime lovers, their bodies speaking a language that needs no words. Still they make sounds—the animal grunts, the ragged pants that are evicted through clenched teeth.

"Love you," he says thickly, and then he thrusts deep. Shudders wrack his sweat-slick body, and when he finishes he collapses over her, still inside of her, bearing the brunt of his weight with his arms, his thighs. Wrapping her in his arms, he rolls over so that she's lying on him, her curly hair matted around her face, his chest. He grins, content; she smiles, more reserved. Guarded. Bittersweet.

I promise you, Virginia, I'll make you forget he ever existed.

They lie together like that for a time: her head on his chest, their limbs entangled, their breathing and eyelids heavy, saying nothing as their bodies relax and their sweat slowly dries. He strokes her with thick fingers, makes lazy patterns on her back.

"I love you," she says into his chest.

"Me too."

"Please don't go."

"Oh, honey," he says, voice cracking.

A whisper: "Please."

"Don't do this, Vee. Let's have this moment. Let's be right now, together, with a little piece of forever."

"Please don't leave me again."

He must feel her tears pooling on his chest, blending with his sweat. He must hear her breathing hitch in her throat as she tries to control her sobs. He must know how much he's hurting her. But all he says is, "I have to."

A pause, and then she replies, "I wish I could hate you."

"I know, Vee." His voice is like a sigh. "I'm so sorry."

They say nothing more as he holds her and she sobs quietly. Shift.

I shook my head as I watched Virginia sleep. The tears had dried on her face; when she woke in the morning, she'd have to scrape off the gluey remnants of stale sorrow. How could she still care so deeply for a man that had abandoned her?

Talk about fucked up.

I love him, Daun.

You know, babes, you and Virginia here share more than physical traits. You're both incredibly stupid when it comes to human men.

You have no idea what you're talking about, the memory of Jezebel's voice replied.

I walked out of Virginia's room, out of her house, as I debated what to do next. The only thing I knew for sure was that whether they were mortal or supernatural, I would never understand women.

Chapter 9

Jealous, Much?

San Jose, California, wasn't much warmer than Saratoga Springs, New York. Then again, given my infernal thermostat, there's just not much difference between the mid-thirties and the high-fifties. Flip the switch to broil, and then maybe I'd feel a temperature change.

I leaned back in the plush seat, admired the excellent acoustics, the intoxicating nearness of the stage and the performers, of my fellow patrons. The California Theatre had changed much since I'd last visited; uprooted from its vaudeville origins, it served now as an opera house. Intimate, too; maybe there were a thousand seats in the entire auditorium. Me, I liked intimate. Especially when it involved music—and this opera in particular. Mozart's best. Onstage, a baritone strutted, proclaiming to be the miscreant Don Giovanni: the legendary seducer who slept with thousands of women.

I wasn't a creature of Pride, but damn, it's nice to be made immortal.

Besides, I had a lot of thinking to do, and I thought best when I was in the presence of beauty, whether physical or spiritual. And to say that Mozart's music was beautiful was like saying that sinners were damned. *Don Giovanni* was his most magnificent—witty and dark, unforgiving. Lyrical. Lustful. Groundbreaking.

In my mind, a young man's breathy promise: *I will write you an opera like none has ever heard before.*

Ah, Wolfgangerl. You would have made a fine Seducer, if that had been the way of things . . .

The woman seated to my left darted a glance to the aisle, then again, and finally murmured an apology before she quickly exited over the grumblings and toes of those of us in her row. I rolled my eyes. Humans. So fucking easily distracted. But my annoyance soon gave way to admiration as onstage, the Don's much-beleaguered servant consoled the obsessed Donna Elvira—whom Giovanni had loved and then left—by reciting the comprehensive list of his master's conquests. Two thousand sixty-five names. Impressive. A little black book, à la opera. Even though Elvira swears vengeance against him, she adores him still. Don Giovanni had ruined her for all other men. Now *that's* a Seducer.

You're not the one I'm waiting for.

Was that what your husband did to you, Virginia? Was his touch so magical that your body can't imagine another's hands traversing its planes, tracing its curves?

How can I get you to lower your guard? To trust me?

A buzzing in my head overrode the group of villagers on-stage, singing robustly about the upcoming wedding of the peasants Zerlina and Masetto. My nostrils flared from the faint hint of sulfur skimming the surface of the sea of human odors. Demon—not a creature of Lust. One of the elite. Drawing close, based on the humming in my ears.

Fuck. Can't I at least finish the opera before I have to fight for my life?

I glanced to my right to see a woman traipsing in front of seated patrons, slowly picking her way toward me—not the same one from before. She wasn't cutting through the mortals, nor making them recoil in terror. Not one of Wrath or Pride, then. And though she was big, she was no Glutton. No imme-diate threat of being skewered, sliced or sat upon. Small favors. A moment later, I pinpointed her affiliated Sin: Envy.

I turned back to the stage, watching peripherally as the

demon approached, wearing a human skin. Large as a mezzo-soprano, the bulk of her form was swathed in a low-cut dress of raw silk, pitch-black. Around her neck hung a citrine pendant so gaudy it had to be worth a small fortune. Her hair, a thing of burnished gold, was pinned back into an elaborate coil, the likes of which I hadn't seen in a human's age; the majority of women today were more about convenience than about style. The smile on her thick face was thin-lipped, and lipsticked to scarlet perfection. And bitter, of course. Unless they grinned in triumph, her kind could smile only out of bitterness. Her small green eyes shone darkly when her gaze found mine, made me think of starving birds. And then I placed her.

Bishop's balls, what was *she* doing here?

She dropped into the seat to my left and arranged her black wrap over her shoulders with a finicky precision. Smoothing her gown, she murmured, "Fancy meeting you here, Daunuan."

I inclined my head. "Eris."

"No title, incubus?" Her eyes lit with jade fire. "You presume too much."

"We're equals now, Princess. But if you prefer, I'll call you Lady Envy. Wouldn't want you to think I'd stolen your honorific." I flashed her a smile, a hint of fangs. "Certainly not after you stole the mortal's seat. What, no orchestra seating available?"

"Nothing that I could touch so easily," she said, shrugging. "Your neighbor had a sudden desire to make sure no one had stolen her car." Catching my gaze, she smiled wetly. "You can understand desire in this context, can't you?"

"Depends. What sort of car?"

"A Lamborghini Gallardo."

"Sweet. Maybe I'll steal her car after the performance."

"Alas," Eris said, "she's long gone. The trouble with possessing something that everyone envies, you find yourself unable to think of anything else for very long." She played with her necklace, the amber of her nail polish winking as she fiddled. For one of the Envious, Eris was all right. Well, at least she was tolerable, whereas most of her ilk were insufferable. I never did have much patience for the Jealous. She leaned toward me, rewarding my glance with her plunging neckline. Her current form certainly had some impressive assets. "Tell me, Lord Libertine," she said, her voice a throaty purr, "what brings you to watch the Opera San Jose? Don't tell me you're fucking the soprano . . ."

I smiled at the thought. "Nothing like that."

"Good. I enjoy her voice. Would hate to see such a promising career cut short." She listened to the bass, sniffed her derision. "But you can take the one playing Leporello. He's murdering the role."

"I'm not here for him."

"No? Then who?"

"No one here."

"Of course not," she said, her mouth twisting into a snarl before she smoothed it back into indifference.

I'd touched a nerve. Not my problem. I turned my attention back to the stage. "Believe me or not, Lady Envy. It makes no difference to me."

She fell silent, but I felt her gaze crawling on my face. No matter; I wasn't here for her amusement but for my own. Onstage, Don Giovanni was coaxing the peasant bride Zerlina away from her groom, offering her pleasure and wealth if she would just allow the Don into her bed. Greedy thing that she was, she considered his offer, even as his arms wrapped around her waist. The baritone's voice was excellent; the music, sublime. Mozart intimately understood that to seduce, you must first be aware of your target's innermost heart, even more aware of that deep desire than the prospective conquest was. Brilliant man, that Mozart. Then again, he'd had an excellent teacher. Smiling as I thought of Venice long gone, I watched the Don ooze charm as he enticed Zerlina to go with him. Finally, smitten with his tender lies, she took his hand. Another belt notch for Don Giovanni.

Through the applause, Eris hissed, "Why are you here, incubus?"

Pushy, wasn't she? "Merely to enjoy and relax," I said. Not

a lie, but not the complete truth. That would prickle under her skin.

"Do tell. The wicked, resting?" She chuckled, the sound lost amid the lively violins. "The first sign of the Apocalypse, surely."

I smiled at her. "What of you, Lady Envy? I never would have pegged you as a music lover. What brings you to the opera?"

"The understudy," she said, motioning in the direction of the stage. "She's longing to perform as Zerlina on a Saturday night, instead of being relegated to Sunday matinees."

"She'll get her chance, if she's patient."

Eris smiled tightly. "Patience may be a virtue, Lord Libertine, but it serves no purpose for vice. All waiting does is allow opportunity to slip through your fingers."

"Spoken like someone scorned."

"Scorned? No. Wronged. But never scorned." Her smile hardened, and something close to glee danced in her eyes. "And all wrongs are eventually made right."

I arched a brow at her. "Doesn't that require patience?"

She laughed quietly, the wrap slipping from her shoulders. "Did you catch me in a lie, Daunuan? Whatever shall I do?"

"Think it over as we watch the rest of the act. Here's where Donna Elvira attempts to persuade the others not to believe Giovanni, that he's a scoundrel."

"And so he is," she murmured, casting me a wicked gaze.

If I didn't know better, I'd have sworn she was flirting with me.

She settled back to observe Don Giovanni smooth talk his way around Donna Elvira's accusations. But the Don spoke too much, and one of the thousands of women he'd wronged recognized his voice as the man who'd murdered her father after trying to rape her.

Eris leaned toward me again, pressed her generous breasts against my arm. I held my breath, heard my heartbeat screaming over the orchestra. Bloody Hell, the Princess of Envy wanted me to cop a feel.

She whispered in my ear, "You know the opera well?"

"My favorite," I said flatly, trying to ignore how my dick

was pushing the material of my pants to the breaking point. "By my favorite composer."

"Oh? And what do you know of Mozart?"

Her breath smelled of burned coffee and freshly cut dandelions. I inhaled deeply, drank her down.

"I know his music," I said, shifting my arm beneath her so that it slowly rubbed against her tits. Oh, how her mounds moved over my skin . . . Encouraged by her sigh of pleasure, I added, "And I knew him." I remembered his body shivering in my embrace, his tortured breath as he begged me for a favor.

She moved against my arm, and I felt her nipples pebble. "Did you, now?"

"Indeed. *Don Giovanni* is my opera," I said, sliding my gaze toward hers. "Mozart wrote it for me, as a tribute." I almost felt the heat behind the jade of her eyes. This was moving beyond whimsical flirtation, meaningless touches. Did Eris really want me to bed her? Or was this one of her games?

"Lord Libertine, you sound almost proud." Her hand dropped to my thigh, squeezed. Any higher up, she'd feel my erection. Not a bad thing—by far—under normal circumstances. But until I knew what Eris wanted, I was much better off keeping my hands out of her cookie jar.

I clenched my teeth in a false grin, forced my body to relax. "Nothing wrong with appreciating a quality gift."

Her mouth twitched, bemused. "As you say." She glanced down at her cleavage and my arm, and seemed surprised at her brazenness. Pushing away from me, she rearranged her wrap over her décolletage. Instead of covering her breasts, the material draped in such a way that it emphasized her lush curves. Demure, she said, "I never would have imagined Mozart belonging to Lust."

"Passion, Lady Envy. Music is passion set to melody." And the man himself had been so beautiful. Fragile. And quite remarkable. Talented to the point of godhood, and troubled to the point of insanity. A heady combination.

"Music is many things. As was Mozart," Eris mused, watching the performers. She placed her hand on the chair's armrest, right next to mine. Her yellow nail polish gleamed as golden as her hair. Beneath that dress, did her pubic hair glitter like stolen gold? Or was her treasure hidden by darker curls? She said, "But being historically accurate was not something he took pains with. He tells a pretty story of seduction and violence in *Don Giovanni*, but it's nothing close to your nature, Daunuan."

I bit back a laugh. What could she possibly know of my nature? Envy and Lust, while not natural enemies, were far from bosom friends. My fingers itched to dance between her legs. I wondered how long it had been since Eris had last had an orgasm.

Bad incubus, I scolded myself. No cookies for you.

She winked at me, and covered my hand with hers.

The island of Anthemusa, a very (very) long time ago

"That one." Pan pointed at a woman sunbathing on a rock, one of her small taloned feet dipping into the sea below her. Her nude torso was feminine perfection—soft, curvy, made for an incubus's hands to wander and touch and grope. Lower, her flesh gave way to feathers, starting just below her stomach. The downy plumes covered her from hip to ankle, hiding her sweetest opening and plumping her thighs. "I want that one."

I snorted laughter. "Good luck to you. That one's Parthenope."

"*Virgin?*" Pan grinned, his fangs gleaming in the bright sunlight. "One of the sirens is named *Virgin?* Now that's funny . . ."

"Claims none have ever touched her." I shrugged. "Probably due to luring sailors to their deaths instead of to her bed."

Pan leered as he watched the siren bask in the sun, and his hand wrapped around his shaft, pumped. "Sounds like she needs someone to give her a new name."

"Your left hand is the only thing that's going to touch you there if you go after her. She's not interested."

"I'll *make* her interested. She won't be able to tell me no."

Pan's ego made his erection look tiny. "Then there's her sisters. That one there's Ligeia. I hear she sings when she comes. And that one." I motioned to a third bird woman, who was splashing in the water. "I'd be happy to pluck the feathers from her—"

"No," he said, his hungry gaze fixed on Parthenope. "I like my first choice. She's succulent. Sweet. And *so* untouchable. I do so love to touch the untouchable ones."

Oh, so he wanted to play hard to get. That was more than fine by me . . . but even though I was staring at the sirens and appreciating how they radiated sensuality, my mind kept picturing another form, of a minor succubus whom I'd bedded and played with, whom I actually spoke with after having sex. Whom I wanted to see again, both in and out of the bedroom. Thinking of Jezebel, I said, "You ask me, one siren's as good as the next."

"I didn't ask."

"I hear they taste like chicken. Me, I prefer a sweeter taste on my tongue." Grinning, I remembered Jezebel's claws raking my back as I made her squeal in pleasure. Yes, I wanted her again. Soon, soon, soon . . .

"Sweet is fine," Pan said. "But bittersweet is better." He slid his gaze to me, and I saw dark ideas swimming in his eyes. "And bitter can be very sweet, if you fuck the right Envious."

My jaw dropped. "You bedded one of the *Jealous?* That must have been fun," I said, barely able to mask my disgust. Fucking one of the Envious held as much appeal to me as rubbing my cock against an iceberg and letting it freeze there.

"Oh, it was fun. I made her body move in ways she'd never known. The only thing she wanted last night was me. And I let her have me." He paused, his goat's eyes gleaming like sapphires. "And in return, she told me so many interesting things."

"A talker," I said, unimpressed. "Wah, wah, wah, I want, I want, I want."

"Nothing like that. She told me things only the Old Ones

know, from the Beginning. And Daun, if she was telling the truth, then I understand why the Old Ones are all insane." A shiver worked up his back.

Interesting. "What did she say?"

He regarded me, a crafty smile on his leathery face. "One thing I'm learning, Daun—you want to live more than a couple centuries, you have to hoard as many secrets as you can. Never know when that information will be useful."

"You're not going to tell me, are you?"

"You want to know? Go find Eris and fuck her. Maybe she'll tell you too."

I felt my eyes widen. "Her? You bedded a duchess? Why in Hell would you do something like that?"

He laughed softly, his shoulders bobbing. "Because she's got a hole between her legs and my cock fits it perfectly. But more to the point, she's no longer a duchess. You can call her princess."

"Really." I whistled my appreciation. Getting a promotion in Hell was a very, very rare occurrence. Usually someone has to die—permanently—for there to be an available opening in the ranks of the elite. "What did she do to earn such an honor?"

"Something about starting a fight among the goddesses, launching a war among the humans."

"Nice," I said. "But you're being stupid with her."

"You think so?"

"She could have hurt you when she was just one of the lesser elite. But as Second for Envy? She can destroy you on a whim."

"I like to live dangerously. Besides," he added, rocking his hips as he worked his hand over his shaft, "she couldn't tell me no. No one can say no to me."

If he did say so himself.

"Be right back," Pan said. "I got me a craving for drumsticks." He leapt off the cliff and dove into the dark water. A moment later, the sirens began to scream.

* * *

During intermission, Eris and I strolled out to the theatre's courtyard and watched the moonlight play against a shimmering fountain wall. The night was kind to the princess—it softened her hair to a touchable gold, gleamed off the raw silk of her gown to swath her figure in liquid shadow. And nighttime transformed her scarlet smile from a raw wound to lips that hinted at mirth, begged to be kissed. The mortals gave us a wide berth; Eris must have been radiating the nefarious "go the fuck away" vibe. Fine by me. We amused ourselves by judging the humans near us and condemning them to Hell.

"That one's haughty," she said, gesturing with a tapered, amber nail.

I glanced at the human she pointed to, a Silicon Valley tycoon out spending his hardly earned fortune. His tuxedo was magnificent. Of course. "Fits the bill. The one on his arm? Greedy."

"No bet," Eris said, all teeth. "She's practically humping his leg, but there are dollar signs in her eyes."

"I thought those were colored contacts."

We shared a laugh. Amazing how bitterness and desire could blend, form a seductive harmony of sound.

"Humans mix so easily," she said, twining her fingers through mine. "Like a flesh cocktail." Her skin was cold, yet I felt the heat pulsing beneath her form. She could wrap herself in human intention as a way to walk the mortal coil, but she couldn't disguise her true self, not completely. Not from me. Eris was a creature of Hell, and she burned as fiercely, as passionately, as any of the elder infernal.

"They don't always mix so well," I said, squeezing her hand. "They have their problems. Racism, for one."

Fingers laced in mine, she pulled the meat of her hand away to trace the blunt edge of her thumbnail over my palm, making intricate patterns that sent clear messages to my cock. Smiling lazily, she gazed up at me through her lashes. "How are they so different from the nefarious in that regard?"

"Not so much," I said, trying to ignore how my blood was

boiling and my muscles were coiled, screaming for me to take her now, here by the fountain wall, fuck her until she screamed my name. "But our animosity is much older than theirs."

"Animosity." She laughed, rubbed her hip against mine, stroking herself over my erection. "Yes, I feel that animosity even now."

I leaned down to touch my lips to the top of her head. Her hair tasted like whiskey. "There's passion, of course. But passion always mixes well."

"If temporarily."

I smiled into her hair. "Indeed."

"Passion is fleeting," she said, working her hand down my leg. "But hatred? Hatred burns hotter—" She traced her fingers over my crotch. "—and longer."

"And thicker," I said. "Whose hatred are we speaking of? Demons? Or humans?"

"Why, ours, of course. Mortal emotion flickers and dies, compared to feelings that build over the centuries. Eons."

"Feelings, Lady Envy? Us?" I laughed, stroked her golden hair as lightly as she brushed my groin. "We don't feel as they do."

"Oh? So you don't feel this?" She moved her fingers and— Wa-*hoo.*

I swallowed, clawed my way through the torrent of passion that threatened to drag me under. "What do you want, Eris?"

"Want? Me?" She laughed silently, her hands moving up to lie flat against my chest. I wrapped my arms around her, enjoyed the fullness of her back. "What I want matters little. Things are different now."

"What things, Princess?"

She paused before whispering, "Below."

I waited.

"He's changed things," she said. "Changing things still more."

I picked my words carefully; no telling whether Eris held the ear of the King of the Pit. Fucking her wouldn't make her my ally, not if she came only when our Supreme Ruler called. "Mortals say that change can be interesting."

"A Chinese curse, that." She sighed, resigned. "We live in interesting times, Lord Libertine."

"Yes." I nodded, thinking about the infernal attacks I'd survived earlier in the week. Was this a sign of change to come? Was the hierarchy in Hell shifting so that only the strong—and cunning—survived? "Things are heating up Below."

I felt her laughter vibrate on my chest. "Amusing."

"But true. Tempers flare hotter than the Lake of Fire. The boundaries between Sin are blurring into nonexistence." I nudged her face up, locked gazes with her. "The barrier separating Envy and Covet is particularly thin, last I saw. It's a breath away from shredding. What then, Princess?"

"War, Daunuan. War." Her eyes were hard as diamond chips. "The Coveters would freeze for eternity, their screams soothing me to sleep . . ." Her lips gleamed crimson promises.

"Why, Eris, you're as bloodthirsty as a Berserker."

She smiled at that, and pinched my arm. "I suppose I am."

Pain sang through my limb, sharp and sweet, and I imagined her in her natural form, razor-tipped talons piercing my back as she writhed beneath me. Mmm. Shivers. "Things will soon explode," I said, the double entendre thick on my tongue. "What will happen then?"

We stared at each other for a moment, then she dropped her gaze to pluck at her wrap. "It's good that demons lie by nature," she said idly, "otherwise some might believe me when I say I could imagine Lust taking the Crown. Imagine, the horde of Hell, caught in a miasma of fornication-induced sweat and blood . . ."

Fuck me, that was it. She thought I meant to take the kingship from Pan, rule the Seducers. She was casting her lot with me.

For a moment, the thought blew enticingly in my mind. King Daunuan. It did have a nice ring to it . . .

Then I remembered that I didn't even want to be a principal, let alone Prince of Lust. I shook my head at her audacity, chuckled. No, I had no intention of challenging Pan; for a liege-lord, he wasn't too hideous. And besides, we'd had some fine adventures before he'd descended to the elite. Too many nymphs to count, scoring the wrath—and envy—of a multitude of deities. No, I'd not willingly destroy him. But there was no need for me to let Eris know that.

"Or maybe the Crown would go to Envy," I said with a grin, tossing the implication back at her. King Mormo ruled the Jealous; was Eris making a play for the head of her Sin? "But that wouldn't bode well," I added playfully. "The nefarious would be so jealous of one another that they'd slay themselves. The trenches outside of Pandemonium would run with ichor and blood. A bitch to clean."

"What of Sloth?" She pillowed her cheek on her hands, feigned sleep. "The Lazy could hold the Crown, and we'd all slumber until Judgment Day."

"Perhaps one of the Coveters would take the Crown," I said, pretending to snatch something out of the air. "Hell knows, it's shiny enough to capture their interest."

Her eyes snapped open, and her mouth tightened. "Your joke goes too far."

Oh-ho, I'd gotten her back up. "You're right," I said, pushing. "Greedy things that they are, the new King of the Abyss would never let any of the demons or damned out of His sight. And then there'd be none left to send evil mortals to the Pit. And Hell would go out of business. Greed? Not so good."

She snarled, and her eyes glowed a poisonous green. "The Coveters should all be stuffed into their gilded pots and boiled in oil until the fat sloughs off their bones!"

"Temper, temper," I said, unable to hide my smile. "You're sounding like you've bought into the Wrath party line. And tone down the infernal glow, or take out a pair of sunglasses. The flesh puppets will notice."

She clutched at her necklace, her fingers stroking the large citrine as if it gave her comfort. The glow to her eyes subsided until they were merely jade. "I'd happily change Sins if it meant the end of that house of evil. Coveters!" she spat. "They're nothing but a plague on the infernal, a disease deep within the bowels of the Earth itself."

I smiled. "A plague o' both your houses."

"A quote or a curse?"

"Which do you prefer?"

"I? I prefer the end of the Coveters." She gritted her teeth and tugged on her pendant, the gold chain biting into the thick flesh of her neck. "They've insulted Envy and have scarred Greed. Bastards of two Sins, deserving of neither!"

As if that made any sense.

"You don't know, do you?"

"Know what?"

She frowned, stared down at either her cleavage or her jewelry. "At first, much before your time, the Coveters were Envious."

Interesting. "You mean they were jealous of something?"

"I mean, Lord of Seduction, that they belonged to Envy."

Most interesting.

"In the old days, it was Avarice that bordered Envy in the south," she said. "The Jealous and the Greedy weren't allies, but neither were we rivals."

"You don't say." Hard to imagine such a time; none loathed each other more than the Envious and the Coveters.

"But then a branch of the Jealous decided to *act* on their envy," she said, her voice a growl. "The Coveters. They took what they wanted."

When she stopped speaking, I asked, "So?"

She stabbed me with her gaze, balled her hands into trembling fists. "So? *So?* The Envious don't *take*. We want what *isn't* ours. That's our nature. If it's ours, then it's not worth having."

And this was why I had little patience for the Jealous. Their Sin made no sense to me.

"The Coveters, with their *action*, weakened the boundary between Envy and Avarice enough that the Sins blurred. And the Coveters crossed over, became demons of Greed."

Impossible. We didn't choose our natures; we were what we were, from the moment of creation. I belonged to Lust; Eris, to Envy. That was the way of things. Uneasy, I said, "Sin cannot be reassigned, reshaped."

"But it can," she insisted with a bitter laugh. "It has been. It can be again."

I felt sickened by the thought. I'd assumed that the worst that would happen when the Sins blurred was that there would be carnage among the infernal—no areas of sanctuary, no respite from hostility. Ongoing warfare. But to actually have one's affiliation, one's very nature, change? Unholy Hell—that was an anathema.

She fussed with her black silk wrap, smoothed it as she spoke. "The original demons of Avarice despise the Coveters almost as much as the Envious do. Thanks to the sheer number of Coveters that had crossed over from Envy, the name of the Land of Greed changed from 'Avarice' to 'Covet.' Imagine the insult, Daunuan. To the original Greedy, those who'd arrived in Hell with the First King, there is nothing more heinous."

My head still spun from her words. Perhaps Eris was lying, trying to force me off-balance. But to what purpose? "Such venom over a name? Insanity."

"Names have power." Eris smirked, warping her smile from bitterness to hatred. "What if I said all of Lust was now part of Envy?"

"Our two Sins are nothing alike."

"No? What is lust, if not envy over another person's sexual prowess?"

That struck me like a blow. To claim that all I was, was jealous over someone's conquests was more offense than I could bear. I snarled, "That's a crock of shit, and you know it."

"Do I, Daunuan?" Her shoulders shook with silent mirth. "I've been around far longer than you. I understand the nature of sin more than you ever will."

"Fine, I'll play your game. Let's say sin is, indeed, malleable. Then envy is nothing more than lust for everything anyone else has," I said, grabbing her by her wrap and pulling her close. "You'd be one of mine."

She smiled at me, her mouth scarlet, mocking. "Possessive, Lord Libertine?"

"Always."

"See?" she asked, laughing. "Envy is greater than lust. Look at the mortal coil: humans kill and die all the time out of envy."

"Read the news," I said as I thought about kissing her neck. "Humans are just as quick to kill and die out of lust. More so."

"They may sin out of lust, but not on the scale that they do out of envy."

"Murders of passion are commonplace, Princess." I breathed in the whiskey scent of her hair as I hugged her, wanted her. "I swear, the humans are far more twisted than the worst of the nefarious when it comes to destroying themselves."

"Passion isn't lust," she said, voice soft. "Passion is born of love. People die for love. And lust may be many things, but it's not love."

Satan spare me, not another entity proclaiming the virtue of love. "People kill out of lust."

"It's not the same," she insisted.

The lighting around the courtyard flickered, warning us there were five minutes left to the intermission. The humans around us put out their cigarettes, finished their conversations, wrapped up their business, worked their way back inside the theatre.

"Envy always triumphs over lust, Daunuan. And love is beyond either of us. It's not in our nature." Eris threaded her arm over mine, smiled up at me. I wondered whether her lips were actually colored from cosmetics, or if she'd simply chosen to make her mouth as bloody as raw meat. If I kissed her, I'd know for sure.

But as tempting as that was—especially with Eris hinting that she'd be open to such a move—it would be a colossal mistake. Bad enough I had to figure out how to woo and win Virginia. Worse would be having Eris on the side . . . and giving her a reason to truly be jealous. Heaven might have no rage like love turned to hatred, but Hell absolutely had no fury like a woman scorned. And considering that I personally knew—and feared—the Furies, that was saying something.

"Believe what you will," I said. "But I'll throw my money on lust over love." And over envy. But that part, I kept to myself.

"Maybe you should see more operas," she said. "Try *Aida*. Lovely little play that ends with the woman choosing to be buried alive with her lover."

"Crushing."

She squeezed my arm. "For love, people make sacrifices. Show me any sacrifices made out of lust."

"As if people make sacrifices out of envy."

"Don't underestimate the power of envy, Lord Libertine. The promise of revenge is a strong one."

"But Princess, isn't revenge an action of pride?"

Eris smiled—bitter, yes, but also hard. Calculating. "And who says that pride isn't simply envy of another's victories?"

She was as self-centered as any of the Arrogant, I'd give her that much.

We returned to our seats for the second act of *Don Giovanni*. And as I watched Leporello threaten to leave his master, Don Giovanni, then be tempted to remain in the Don's service for a purse of gold, I thought of Eris's words. Specifically, about *Aida*.

I smiled, relaxed back in my seat. Lady Envy had given me an idea how to approach the saintly Virginia and lower her guard. Perhaps, when all of this was over, I'd have to come up with a way to thank Eris.

My smile pulled into a grin. I was sure I could think of something.

PART II

THE SEDUCTION

Chapter 10

Incubus Meets Girl

Virginia's office building wasn't impressive, as those things went: it was tall, and red, and across the street from a coffee shop. And that's it. Not an architectural feat by any stretch, like the Taipei Financial Center with its eight tiers of eight stories of steel and glass. No, this particular structure couldn't even properly be called a skyscraper; if it could claim twenty floors, I'd suck an angel feather.

Six eighteen, post meridiem. Almost quitting time for Virginia. After three days of observation, I knew that by now she'd be tired after a long day of being the behind-the-scenes player at the office, weighted down with the knowledge that there was a fifty-minute commute home and only an empty house waiting for her. She was pliable now in a way that she wasn't earlier in the day, when she was pumped full of coffee and so damn cautious in everything that she did. And when she got home, she'd be bone-weary from exhaustion, a zombie barely able to function enough to scrape up her dinner and crawl into bed. Now was when she wasn't quite on autopilot, but also wasn't focused enough to keep her defenses honed to razor precision.

Which meant now was the perfect time for me to make my move.

I practiced my disarming smile as I opened the main door

to the building. No security person by the front station. Guess there's no crime after-hours in this part of Albany. Except for me, the lobby was deserted. No real surprise; the weekend had officially started more than an hour ago. Anyone with anything to do was already doing it, or getting ready to get it done.

Not my lady, of course. The only thing she was getting was a surprise visit. My smile slipped into a hungry grin. After I pressed the call button for the elevator, I adjusted my features to get my costume just right—no cocky smirk for me. To charm Virginia, I needed something much more laid-back. Simple. Honest.

Heh. That was me: unscrupulously honest.

I'd put a lot of thought into how to dress to impress. I didn't want to scare my intended away with dashing good looks; the wine bar the other night proved that she wasn't into blond-and-blue cover-model perfection. So going the Adonis route was out. And while she might possibly be attracted to younger men, she clearly wasn't looking for a surfer-dude pizza guy, no matter what extra toppings he promised. The only other information I had was based on her dream: she seemed to prefer her men on the meaty side. And good with their hands.

So there I was, standing in the ground-floor lobby of her office building, wearing an average form. Fortysomething, shorter side of tall, larger side of bulky. Brown hair, leaning toward chestnut, too long and choppy in the front. Wide hazel eyes, heavy-lidded and sleepy. Roman nose, narrow mouth. Angular face, the rough planes eased with a touch of fat, the hint of stubble along the jaw. Thick neck and shoulders, but nothing too imposing. Strong arms and legs, barrel-chested. Hands callused, fingers long and dexterous. Over a chambray shirt and dark pants I wore a long wool coat, black boots and leather gloves. Reviewing my reflection in the mirrored elevator door, I practiced my smile again. My teeth were off-white, suggesting either a caffeine or nicotine habit.

Not my first choice, Hell knew. But the client was always right. Besides, I'd dressed in worse. And I should be thankful that Virginia wasn't into the ladies; being a male trapped in a lesbian's body would really fuck me up. How would I think properly with only one head?

The elevator dinged and the doors opened. Empty. Fine by me. My name and backstory at the ready, I entered the car, scanned the panel of options. Pressed the button with the number sixteen. Ignoring the temptation to moon the security camera, I reached out with my power, scanned the elevator and lift shaft. A simple mechanism, really: steel ropes attached to the top of the car rolled over a grooved pulley and pulled up the steel box. There was a counterweight and gears and a motor . . . and braking systems near the top and bottom of the elevator shaft. Perfect.

The elevator dinged again. Top floor: home of Morse Consulting. Virginia's office. The doors slid open, and I stepped out into the lobby. Showtime.

I walked down the hall to the main entrance of the office and tried the door. Locked, as expected; Virginia's coworkers weren't married to their jobs. And neither would be Virginia, once she got to know me. I was going to reacquaint her with life, just before I killed her. Really, it was the least I could do.

Thinking about blackberries and jasmine, I pressed the buzzer near the glass door.

A moment later, my lady turned a corner, one arm in her coat, coming to see who was asking for admittance at this hour. Oh, look at her: that wild curly hair, so black against the paleness of her heart-shaped face; those green eyes, like sparkling emeralds, so very different from the spiteful jade of Eris's gaze. Those plump lips, already looking as if I'd attacked them with my mouth, kissed them red and raw until they were swollen, bruised. A bright scarf—cheerfully red, like sin—wrapped around her throat and dangled over her right breast, the tassels mocking me as they outlined her ripe mound. But there her display of sexuality ended: her thick blue sweater hung tentlike to mid-thigh, erased the shape of her belly and hips as much as her loose tan slacks negated the curves of her legs. Even her feet were obscured by oversized work boots.

Taking one last, quick look at her scarf, I snapped my gaze up to her face. As I waited for her, I decided I liked her in red.

She opened the glass door for me. Her smile was warm, but her eyes reflected caution. "Help you?"

Returning the smile—nothing too forward, just an easy movement of lips—I said, "Thanks, I'm here for a six thirty with Mr. Brook." Her boss.

She cocked her head, frowned as she regarded me. "I'm sorry, but he's long gone."

"Really?" I crinkled my brow as I tried to look both annoyed and dismayed. "We'd set this up weeks ago . . ."

That was the right phrase, because her frown melted into a sheepish smile. "I'm sorry," she said. "He does this a lot."

I sagged my shoulders, aiming for disappointment. Shook my head as I blew out a sigh. "Thanks for letting me know."

"He's a good guy," she said, stuffing her other arm into her coat. "Just distracted. He's not usually like this, but he has a new baby. Isn't getting a lot of sleep."

How cute was she, defending her boss? Loyal, even when no one was here to appreciate it. You really are a good girl, aren't you, Virginia?

"Ah." I nodded as if I understood or cared, gave a "what can you do" shrug. "Okay, thanks. I'll call him on Monday, see if he wants to reschedule."

"He usually gets in after ten," she said.

What a helpful person she was, when she wasn't throwing a drink in a guy's face. Where flattery had failed, cluelessness seemed to work. Maybe she liked her men big and dumb.

I smiled, conveyed my appreciation. "Thanks for the tip."

"Wish I could help more," she said, sounding sincere. I could tell she was curious about what sort of appointment her boss had with me, but she was too polite to ask. "Sorry for the inconvenience. I hope you didn't come too far out of your way."

"Not your fault." Turning up the wattage in my smile, I asked, "Want me to hold the elevator for you?"

"Thanks, that would be great. Just have to lock up. Won't take a minute . . ."

"Take your time. I'll wait for you." Trust me, doll. I'll wait.

She beamed at me, then dashed off to get something she'd left behind.

Okay, she liked helping people. I could work with that. Definitely.

At the lobby, I pressed the button to signal the elevator, then rocked back on my heels as I waited. Yes, I could go from clueless to helpless, see if that would Hook her. Not exactly the alpha male that I prefer to be, but I was happy to sacrifice in the name of the job. I had to keep her off balance enough so that she didn't raise her guard, shut me out. A minor emergency should do the trick.

The car arrived just as Virginia was locking up. I was the perfect gentleman, keeping the doors open with the press of a button. She scooted into the elevator, her purse hitched over her shoulder, coat flapping behind her.

Panting, she smiled at me as I let the doors close. "Thanks," she said, breathless. "The elevator takes forever in this place."

"You didn't have to run," I said, admiring the blush in her cheeks. "I said I'd wait."

"It's almost six thirty on a Friday night. I'm sure you've got someplace to be."

"So do you," I said, pressing the button for the ground floor. "What's a few extra seconds, in the scheme of things?"

"Still. I appreciate it."

I threw her an easy smile. "Next time, you can hold the door for me."

She laughed. "Agreed."

It was a good laugh—warm and rich, the kind that went to my chest instead of my crotch. Different, but nice. The sound faded slowly, as if the air in the small car fought to hold on to the laughter. I wanted to hear that sound again. And more: I wanted to know what made her laugh, what she found funny. Sexy. Enjoyable. I wanted to show her pleasure and hear that laugh as I tickled her, ran my fingers up her thighs. I wanted that laugh to catch and ripple into a soft moan as I drifted my hands over that sweet spot between her legs.

Soon.

We rode in silence as the car slowly descended. Fifteen. Fourteen. Twelve. (Bless me to Heaven, I'd never understand human superstition. What in Hell was wrong with the number thirteen?) Eleven.

Next to me, Virginia glanced at her watch, blew out a sigh. In a rush to get home, doll? That was a cue if I'd ever gotten one. Smiling to myself, I reached out with my power, *flexed*, felt the steady motion of the elevator, the heavy movement of the pulley.

And then I hit the brakes. Hard.

The car lurched to a halt. Virginia and I stumbled; I let myself trip and stagger against the wall. Glancing at her, I saw she'd dropped to a crouch, her arms out for balance. Her purse had slipped off her shoulder, dropped onto the floor in a heap of black leather. The lighting in the elevator had dimmed, casting Virginia in soft shadow. Her eyes gleamed in the pale darkness, very wide and exceedingly bright, the whites almost glowing. She must have bitten her bottom lip, because it shone wetly, her saliva and teeth doing what cosmetics could only mimic.

Damn, how I wanted to kiss her.

"You okay?" I put just the right amount of tension and concern into my voice: protective, but not possessive.

Her face was starkly white against her black curls, her large coat. She took a shuddering breath, released it. "Yeah. You?"

"Okay."

We stared at each other for a moment, my uneasy smile mirroring hers. Then I looked pointedly at the digital display that indicated our current floor. Instead of numbers, the read-out showed two red *X*'s.

"Well," I said, "that can't be good."

Her brow creased as she stared at the letters. "Oh, boy."

"Maybe it'll start again in a minute." Not likely, with my magic keeping the car stalled, suspended between the tenth and eleventh floors. But I was going for the hope-springing-eternal thing that mortals seemed to thrive upon.

"Sure," she said, letting out a nervous laugh. She brushed her hair away from her eyes and met my gaze. "This sort of thing happens all the time."

"Absolutely." If a demon was desperate enough, that is.

We waited.

I counted twenty breaths, then said, "It should have started up again by now, don't you think?"

"Uh-huh."

"Time to call for help?"

"Yeah." Scanning the wall panel, she reached out, pressed the call button at the bottom. An annoying buzz, then silence.

We waited again.

"I bet Brian's on a cigarette break," she said. Her arms were wrapped around her torso. Afraid? Frustrated? I couldn't tell. "He'll be back in a minute."

I arched a brow at her. "Brian's the security guy?"

She nodded.

"He wasn't at his station when I entered the building."

A flutter of dismay on her face, then she shrugged. "Okay, that's good." Her voice was soothing, with a touch of strain around the edges. Was she trying to comfort me? Virginia the caregiver? She said, "That probably means he'll be back in a second."

"I'm sure you're right."

I counted sixty seconds, then cleared my throat. "If this is how security works, remind me to switch careers." Glancing at her, I noted the worry in her eyes. She was still hugging herself like she was afraid to let go. Nervous, and practically screaming with tension. Very good. I said, "I could use a job with nice long breaks. Think your building's hiring?"

A smile flitted across her lips. "Based on how long it's taking Brian, I'd say there's going to be an opening pretty soon."

"Maybe I'll apply."

"Sure. But keep in mind the job's not so hot when the gunmen come to rob the place. Security guy's the first to get shot."

I barked out a laugh, honestly surprised by her gallows humor. "You guys get robbed a lot?"

"No. Just speculating." She pressed the button again.

You have a dark side, Virginia, don't you? There's a part of you that's scarred, cynical. I can't wait to see more of it, doll.

More of you.

When there was still no answer from the main lobby, Virginia blew out a sigh. The sound, I was pleased to note, was much closer to aggravation than fear.

Her voice clipped, she said, "Remind me to tell Brian to quit smoking."

I grinned at her. "Tell Brian to quit smoking."

"Thanks." She smiled again, still nervous, but now humor was poking through. "You're very helpful."

"I try."

"Time to send in the reinforcements." She scooped up her purse from the floor. Rummaging through it, she pulled out a slim cell phone. Flipped it open. Pressed a button. Grimaced. "Damn it, can't get a signal. You have a phone?"

I shook my head. At her surprised look, I added, "Left it home by accident."

She blinked, then rewarded me with a rueful smile. "You should know I'm reconsidering the 'helpful' comment."

"When we get out of here, I'll make it up to you." In a very big way.

"Oh, good." She tried more buttons on her cell, sighed. "Really open to suggestions, here."

"Okay," I said, pitching my voice to get the right blend of calm and commanding, without venturing into the realm of arrogance. She was the one calling the shots, even if she didn't realize it. Last thing I wanted was to transform into a hero, only to discover that she considered heroes untouchable. "Okay. Like you said, Brian will be back in a moment. Meanwhile . . ."

I let my voice trail off as I made a show of scanning the wall panel. Call buttons to choose a floor, their text and icons raised, Braille counterparts off to the side. Door OPEN and CLOSE buttons. A STOP switch, requiring a key for access. And an ALARM switch, no key required.

I looked over my shoulder at Virginia, flashed her a smile. "Ready for some noise?"

She smiled grimly, nodded.

I flipped the switch. A bell clanged, shrill and grating in the enclosed space. I didn't mind; after thousands of years listening to the damned scream as demons tortured them, the elevator alarm was barely noticeable to me—just a continuous din, almost like the background noise in a metropolitan city, another siren wailing down another street, off to another emergency. But a human would have been uncomfortable with the harsh sound this close, so I made myself wince and grit my teeth.

I stole a glance at Virginia. She was looking down at her feet. Her black curls had fallen over her face, but I could see enough of the flesh beneath to catch her frown. Loud noises? Not such a turn on for my lady. Rock concerts would be out.

Two minutes later, static burst from the call box, barely audible over the blaring of the alarm. A man's deep voice shouted: "Everyone okay in there?"

I flipped the switch to shut off the alarm. Pressing the intercom button, I said, "Not really. We've been stuck in here for about ten minutes."

"Sorry about that, folks. I'm calling the service right now."

"What, you can't just press a button and get the elevator moving again?" Virginia asked.

"Sorry, ma'am. I'm sure service'll just be a few minutes. They're very responsive. Hang on, all right?"

"Like we could do anything else," Virginia muttered.

I coughed into my hand to hide my smile.

We waited. A minute ticked by. Virginia started tapping her foot, looking at her watch. I kept my hands stuffed in my pockets and stole glances at Virginia. The tail of her red scarf lay snug against her breast, taunting me as it fondled her swell.

"Could be worse," I said to break the tension. When she looked at me, I smiled innocently. "Could be elevator music playing."

She let out a chuckle, then cleared her throat, killed the humor. Aw, don't stop yourself from enjoying the absurdity, doll. Before I could comment, the intercom coughed out a burst of static.

"Folks," Brian said, "I just heard from service. Be about thirty minutes before they arrive."

"Thirty minutes?" Virginia let out a groan.

"Sorry, ma'am. I'll keep you posted."

The static died, leaving Virginia and me alone in the dimly lit, unmoving elevator.

She glanced around at the walls, rubbing her arms. "I hate being stuck."

"We're not completely stuck," I said. "We could try to force open the doors, shimmy down the elevator shaft." If she'd actually go for that option, I'd make sure that my magic kept the doors sealed tight. But she didn't need to know that. At the very least, I thought Virginia would appreciate my ingenuity.

She looked up at me, seemed to read my face. Finally, she brushed her hair away from her eyes, said, "You don't have your cell phone, but you remembered your utility belt?" A sardonic smile played on her lips.

Took me a moment to get the reference; in all my years of service, only three clients had had a thing for Batman. Superman was more of a favorite, for a reason I couldn't fathom. "More of a spy than a superhero," I said.

"So no crawling along the walls for you, either, I suppose." She sighed, wistful. "James Bond has a phone in his shoe . . ."

"And you've got one in your hand. With no signal."

"Which is why I wish you were more of a superhero than a spy. Try attaching to the wall," she said lightly. "Maybe your hands will stick."

"Or maybe I can magic us out of here."

She shrugged. "Sure. Worth a shot, Mr. Potter."

I waggled my fingers. "Hocus pocus!"

We waited a dramatic moment. When nothing happened, she slid a glance at me. "You left your magic wand at home with your cell phone, didn't you?"

"And my utility belt."

"No offense, but I don't think you're cut out to be a spy. Or a superhero."

"Or a magician?"

She laughed softly, her eyes sparkling in the dim light. Yes, I definitely wanted to hear more of her laughter. "Sorry, no."

Time to ease into the backstory. Smiling, I asked, "How about a massage therapist?"

She eyed my gloves—was she thinking about how large my hands were? Wondering what my fingers would feel like on her body? "Sure," she said, "that I could buy."

I extended my hand. "I'm Don."

"Virginia." She touched her hand to mine, and shocks danced over my arm, through my body, set my world ablaze in a sizzle of heat.

Mine, Virginia. You're mine. Soon you'll kiss me, and then . . .

Oh, and then.

I clasped my other hand over hers, trapping her between my palms. "It's a pleasure to meet you," I said.

And I meant every word.

We were both seated on the floor of the elevator, our gloves peeled off, jackets open. Had been that way for about twenty minutes. Passing the time by playing Worst Elevator Trip Ever. I was pretty sure Virginia was telling the truth with all of her stories. Me, I was making it up as I went. The challenge for me wasn't lying, but rather making the lie believable. And amusing.

"I've got one worse than that," Virginia said, mouth set in a huge grin. "Once, I was on an elevator with a kid who growled at everyone."

My shoulders bobbed as I laughed at the image. I loved evil kids. Especially roasted, with a little salt. "Maybe he was rabid."

"Come to think of it, he was biting at his mom's fingers . . ."

Damn, how I enjoyed teasing the laughter out of her. This was its own sort of foreplay, limited to verbal touches, coaxing a response of mirth instead of moans, all while sitting apart, she tailor-style, me crouching back on my heels. Our bodies didn't touch, but I was engulfed in her presence—her unease and exhaustion had given way to a simple pleasure that had nothing to do with sex.

And me? I was slowly getting drunk on her scent: the black-berries cloying, juicy; the chocolate thick and rich . . . the way her jasmine tickled my nose, the musk of her sex making my head swim.

Mmm.

I was slowly doing something else as well: adjusting my heat aura, keeping it tightly focused on my body. My shirt was already sticking to my back, and I felt my hair clinging in damp streaks to my forehead. In another minute, I'd turn up the heat more. I couldn't see my reflection in the elevator mirror without being obvious, but I was sure my cheeks were shiny with perspiration. Dressing like a flesh puppet meant that my outer shell could be sensitive to temperature changes, if I allowed it.

At the moment, I didn't just allow it. I was counting on it. And on Virginia's good nature. She wasn't looking for a hero. Maybe she needed someone to take care of. It was a chance I was willing to take. I could play the hero later, if needed.

"Kids can be such fun," I said, ignoring the trickle of sweat inching down my face. "I saw one licking candy this one time, sticking pieces of it on the walls. And the floor." I grinned. "And on a few passengers. Wonder if anyone ever told them they had gummy worms on their backs."

"Kids and candy," she said with a laugh. "There ought to be a law. Worst I've seen was a little girl pulling out her gum in long strings, then chewing it up again slowly." She mimicked the motion, pretending to stretch something from her mouth, then working her jaw noisily as she reeled it back in. "Nauseating."

"You want nauseating? Kids eating their boogers."

She made a face, then ruined it with a giggle.

We sat in silence for a moment, me listening to the sound of her amusement fade in the stuffy air, her letting her guard down more and more with every laugh. That's right, doll. I'm harmless. Nothing for you to be afraid of. I'm someone you could be yourself with. Someone you could trust.

Up, up, up goes the heat aura.

My cheeks must have flushed, because she cocked her head, stared at my face. Her eyes were intense, and her mouth pulled down into the slightest of frowns.

"Don? You okay?" Her voice was soft. Concerned.

Perfect.

I cleared my throat, said, "Sure. Why?"

"You're sweating."

I smiled to show her that I was fine, but I exhaled a shaky breath to belie the sentiment. "Just a little hot in here."

She gazed at me with those emerald eyes, her thoughts unspoken but very apparent on her face. She knew I was lying. But she wasn't about to embarrass me by pushing. Instead, she got up and pressed the call button.

Brian's voice: "You still okay, Ms. Reed?"

"We're both fine, Brian. Wondering how much longer it's going to be." She smiled at me as she spoke, telling me with her words and body language that everything was going to be all right.

My stomach cramped from that look. She was pitying me.

"I'm guessing another few minutes, ma'am. They'll be here soon."

"Thanks, Brian."

Pitying *me*.

I bared my teeth in a sickly grin to clamp down on the sudden rage that roared through me. Yes, I wanted her affection, her sympathy, but bishop's balls, I didn't want her *pity*.

No, don't smirk at her soothing. Don't mock her attempts to keep me calm. She's supposed to be the caregiver, remember?

Pfaugh. My lips peeled back in a snarl. Wonder how she'd react if I morphed into my natural form? Or if I just pulled her down to me and kissed her, knocked aside her restraint with the power of my mouth, my tongue? My teeth? Would she pity me if I ripped her clothes off her body and stroked her until her blood caught fire?

Daun, a voice whispered, *don't be such a guy*.

Jezebel?

A moment of vertigo—my head spun as I tried to grab that fleeting psychic connection, hungered to hear Jezebel's voice in my mind, even though my heart knew it was just a memory, the ghost of a conversation. I blinked rapidly, then lilted to the left. Smacked the floor with my palm to keep from falling.

Jezebel, you're not really there, are you?

You need to stop thinking about how to seduce your good girl.

Fine, babes. You have a better idea? I'm all ears.

In my mind, Jezebel laughed.

A soft touch on my arm. I glanced up, saw Virginia crouching next to me, pressing on me lightly.

Hel-*lo*.

"Don," she said, "listen to my voice. Take a deep breath."

I stared at Virginia as I tried to figure out how to play this. Let her be in control? Show her my strength? What was I supposed to do?

Stop thinking, Jezebel whispered.

So I did. And I took a deep breath, my gaze locked on Virginia's.

"Good. Hold it for three counts. One. Two. Three. Now let it out slowly."

I exhaled, was shocked by how my breath shook. That hadn't been my intent. What the fuck was happening to me?

"Good," she said again, smiling. Touching me. Encouraging me.

My heartbeat slammed in my chest, and my throat felt too tight as I surrendered to Virginia, waited for her to tell me what to do next.

"Now another one. Deep breath. Hold it. And let it out."

I breathed for her.

"You know," she said, her hand still on my arm, "one time, a guy in an elevator asked each passenger what floor they wanted. So they told him. And he'd press the wrong buttons." She bared her teeth in an evil grin. "The jerk made me late for a meeting."

I let out a strained laugh. And dialed back on my heat aura.

"Think that's bad?" I asked, my voice rasping. "Once there was a guy in a robe, handing out religious tracts to everyone who got into the car."

She smiled at me, for me. And I marveled at her compassion. It was so foreign from what I knew. And so damn compelling.

"Thank you," I said, surprised by my own words. I hadn't meant to thank her. Mortals were gullible; every demon knows that. My enforced crisis was supposed to draw her closer to me, not the other way around.

"You're welcome," she said, her smile big and open and breathtaking.

Basking in that smile, I released my magic. The elevator started again with an electric hiccough.

Virginia and I let out relieved sighs as the elevator descended.

She kept her hand on my arm the entire ride down.

Score one for the demon.

By the time we left the building, it was nearly seven thirty. Long since dark, and the street was close to empty. Virginia, no longer holding my arm, was bundled once again in her concealing winter coat, her long curls tucked into her collar.

I asked, "Which way are you headed?"

Motioning with her chin, she pointed south. "Down three blocks, to the public lot."

"Mind if I walk with you?"

She smiled at me. "I'd like that."

Good. Very good. Step One, getting her to let down her

guard. Complete. Time to move to Step Two: a demonstration of my strength. And that meant I needed a prop.

As we braved the December wind, I reached out with my power, sampled the mortals relatively near us, hunting for a particular type. Here, psycho, psycho, psycho . . . I'm calling you . . .

A presence flared in response—black as a lie, purple as disease. A man, already damned to Hell.

Exactly what I needed. I focused, commanded him: **Come**.

. . . coming i'm coming . . .

Based on his thoughts, he was about three minutes away. Now all I needed to do was stall a bit, make sure Virginia didn't slip away before I could rescue her.

"Hope this didn't royally screw up your plans," I said to her, curbing my longer strides to keep pace with her shorter ones.

She shook her head. "Just getting home later than I'd like. Maybe I'll grab some Mickey D's on the way, eat in the car."

"Long drive?"

She nodded. "Up to Saratoga Springs. You?"

"I'm not that far from here."

"Nice." She glanced at me, seemed to weigh the pros and cons of continuing the conversation.

"I like Saratoga Springs," I ventured. "Fun town."

"It is. I'm actually just off Route 50. In Wilton."

"Quieter there."

"I like quiet." A touch defensive. Careful.

"Me, too. Sometimes, there's nothing better than curling up with a book and reading the night away, or just watching TV until I fall asleep."

"Really?" A tiny smile. "Me too."

"I'll probably follow suit, get some Mickey D's." I stumbled over the name, but she didn't notice. I thought I knew which restaurant she was referring to, but I didn't want to push my luck.

"I don't usually like doing fast food," she said, "but tonight the fast part sounds pretty good. So McDogfood it is."

Ah, *that* restaurant. "Sometimes, fast food is a necessary evil." To say nothing about profiting evil. The Gluttons, in particular, owed much of their recent boom in the Abyss to the glories of trans fats and high cholesterol.

Virginia said, "I'm ruining my diet, all because I was stuck in an elevator." She sighed dramatically, but her eyes sparkled with mirth. "What about you? Did getting stuck somewhere on the tenth floor in a metal box ruin your evening?"

"On the contrary. I think it was the high point of my night."

It took her a moment, then she groaned. "That's a horrible joke."

I chuckled. "So, I'm not cut out to be a superhero, a spy, a magician . . . or a comedian?"

Laughing, she said, "Sorry . . ."

"No, that's okay. My ego can handle it."

Her smile was warm, genuine. "Glad to hear that."

As we crossed the street, I saw him: a big man, bald and bulky, looking like trouble, from his motorcycle jacket to his shit-kicking boots. An abundance of leather and spikes. Bad news waiting to happen. And directly in our path.

Of course, that was because I'd summoned him. Benefit of being a first-level demon: the ability to sense and summon evil humans, no matter what sin damned them. I'd used this particular power only a few times since I'd acquired it. It wasn't as impressive as riding a mortal body, but then again, possession was nine-tenths of the awe.

I altered my psychic message to him, transformed it from a summoning to a compulsion. Specifically, one that had to do with Virginia: *You want the woman.*

. . . woman wrapped in a coat i can peel it off of her see what's inside . . .

I pushed: *First get rid of the man.*

. . . stick him till he bleeds . . .

He'd come at me with a knife. Good to know.

All right, yes, it was cheating. Hey, I'm a demon. I'm supposed to cheat.

"So, no," I said to Virginia as we stepped onto the sidewalk, "getting stuck in a metal box didn't really put a dent into my evening. I really liked the company."

She smiled at me. "Me too."

Maybe she would have said more, perhaps even would have asked me to join her in her McFeast. But the danger sense that all prey has buried deep within their minds must have cried out a warning, because Virginia closed her mouth and glanced around. From the look on her face, she felt something was off. Wrong. Her pace didn't slow, and neither did mine, but her defenses went up, layer by layer. I could see it in the way she carried herself straighter, the way her eyes suddenly seemed hooded. The set of her mouth, once so kissable, now pulled down in a deep frown that on anyone else would have been unattractive.

If this didn't work, the past hour was going to be a complete waste of time. This was my one chance with her—in this form, at any rate. But I had a feeling that Pan wasn't going to give me that much more lead time. I needed to Hook her. Tonight.

Now.

About thirty feet ahead of us, the flesh puppet I'd summoned leaned against a storefront, smoking a cigarette. He was bigger than me, both in height and weight, and he radiated malice. Interesting how some evil humans have mastered the "don't fuck with me" vibe used by the nefarious. Or maybe we'd learned it from humans. Who knew? Like the boundaries between Land and Sin, at times it all seemed to blend. He smoked, his urge for violence rolling off of him in waves.

"Just another block," Virginia said, her voice tight.

I nodded, kept silent. Had nothing to do with the rather impressive air of intimidation around the man slouching against the building; I didn't want to engage Virginia in conversation. Step Two would work much better if she wasn't focused on me—if she understood the danger as it was happening, instead of acknowledging it after the fact.

We walked, and the human smoked. Waited.

Watching peripherally, I bit back a smile. He was the perfect flesh puppet for what I needed—he looked like he stomped on baby rabbits just to hear them squish. I could have been invisible, as far as he was concerned; he stared at Virginia, leering as he took a pull from his cigarette. In his mind he stripped her and had her spread-eagled over the hood of a car as he fucked her from behind. There was nothing remotely passionate about his gaze; for him, it was all about the power. He was a sexual predator, a rapist waiting for the right victim. Scum of the Earth, the sort of evil human that the nefarious come to blows over—did his soul belong to Wrath? Greed? Pride? As far as I was concerned, they could chop his soul into three and pull; Lust deserved better than the likes of him. Then again, I wasn't into power games.

Virginia noticed him. Wasn't her fault; he was dressed in his Bad Ass leather and spikes, and he was working mojo with his eyes. That's something even the mortal seducers knew: eye contact is crucial. Locking gazes isn't staring. It's far more intimate, and far more powerful. To do it properly, you can't blink. You pick one eye, and you lock onto it like a leech. And you don't stop. You sure as Hell don't look at the target's friend. Other things matter, too, if the mojo was really going to work—no smiling, no talking, or the spell would break. And I don't mean the sort of infernal magic I wield; I'm talking about the power of lust. Eyes are windows to the soul—and the soul is pure magic.

But this guy wasn't trying to make a move on Virginia. He'd sized her up a block ago, already knew how many positions he'd force her into before he sliced her and left her to die. Now he was just toying with her, seeing if she'd respond to him.

And she was. He'd caught her like a deer in the headlights—as we drew close, her gaze was riveted on his. She slowed her steps without being aware of it, or of how fast her heart was beating. I heard her breath catch in her throat.

The man exhaled smoke through his nostrils, like a dragon, and offered her a lazy smile. His teeth gleamed in white perfection. With a casual flick of his wrist, he tossed the cigarette to the pavement, stepped on it with his boot. Ground it into a smear like a bloodstain. Tobacco roadkill.

Either the smile or the crushed cigarette was enough for Virginia to snap her gaze away, look straight ahead. A muscle worked in her jaw as she picked up the pace, without trying to look like she wanted to bolt. A splash of citrus. I inhaled her fear as it spiked through her, kept my excitement in check as we passed the big man without slowing.

I felt his gaze on my back.

Come on, puppet. We're right here. Fresh meat—easy prey. Come to me.

We were maybe three feet away when I heard him push away from the wall, start to dog us. He was in no rush, but with those long legs, he didn't have to run to catch up.

Pitching my voice low, I asked, "How far to your car?" My words came out strangled, tense. Hard not to sound that way when I was feeling the equivalent of a demonic adrenaline rush and hard-pressed to act like I had a stick jammed up my ass.

Virginia must have picked up on my tension, because her reply was just as soft. "The lot's at the end of the block."

"Okay. You keep going. Don't stop till you get inside your car, lock the door. Don't look back."

"What—"

I pushed her forward and jumped to the side, landed in a crouch and pivoted. The man's hand swung out, slicing the space where I'd just been. The blade in his hand shone wickedly in the moonlight.

No powers, I reminded myself. Nothing remotely demonic. Just man to man.

And I wouldn't have it any other way.

Flexing my fists, I grinned broadly, feeling just as wicked as his knife. "Hey, chuckles, no cutting in."

He ignored my quip and lunged, his weapon aiming for my gut. I sidestepped, clamping onto his forearm as he stabbed empty air. Bringing my knee up, I slammed his arm down. A snap, like a twig breaking. And then the man roared in pain.

Mmm. Shivers.

The knife clattered to the pavement. I debated grabbing it, using it to introduce him to his intestines. Over the man's yells, I heard Virginia, who'd ignored my instructions (as I knew she would), talking to someone on her phone, sounding panicked. Gave our location, said we were being mugged. Probably called the police.

That clinched it: no knife for me. The authorities would give me a headache, and Virginia might think I was bloodthirsty. I wanted to impress her, not scare her. Gritting my teeth, I kicked the weapon away. Then I released the man's damaged limb and shoved my elbow into his stomach. His shout ended with an *oof* as he doubled over, staggered back.

Virginia said, "Police are on the way." Her voice was gruff, determined, even though I smelled her fear. Loyal, aren't you? You won't abandon someone, not after the way your asshole husband abandoned you.

The flesh puppet regained his footing and looked up at me, murder shining in his eyes. He growled, "You're so dead."

I smiled. "You're so cliché."

He roared again. "I'm going to gut you, then fuck your woman till she screams!"

Mortals: melodramatic as celestials, as easily goaded as Berserkers.

Snarling, the human launched himself at me, his broken arm cradled to his chest, his good arm straight out, hand curled into a fist. So freaking predictable. I blocked the blow with my left forearm while pushing up, knocking him off balance. Then I cocked my right arm back and slammed my fist into his jaw. Crunch.

His head snapped back, and he crashed to the ground, a flesh puppet with cut strings. And down he stayed.

Virginia's breathy voice: "Holy God."

Heh. Wrong direction, doll.

I turned to face Virginia, who was staring at the unconscious attacker like she was waiting for him to spring up and shout "Boo!" One of her hands covered her mouth; her eyes were wide, shocked. She tore her gaze from the man to look at me, search my face as if she were seeing me for the first time. Looking like she might bolt.

Quick—be vulnerable.

I shook out my hand, winced. "The movies make that look easy."

She lowered her hand from her mouth, and her smile was a work of art. "I take it back," she said. "You can be a super-hero."

I laughed softly, massaged out the pretend soreness from my hand. "I'll settle for being a spy. They seem to get the girl more than the superheroes do."

Amusement sparkled in her eyes—and maybe a hint of desire as well. "Is that what you want? The girl?"

This is it. Don't fuck it up, Daunuan. Easy, easy . . .

I managed a blush, then cleared my throat. "If I said yes, the girl might say no. So . . . no, I'm in it for the altruism."

She let out a laugh. "Tip for you: any female over seventeen is a woman."

"Noted."

"A girl might say no," she agreed, dimpling. "But a woman might say yes."

"Really." I couldn't help the hopeful tone; I felt like a demon asking for his first taste of a human soul. Please, Sire—I want some more.

She shrugged, laid-back. Her smile was playful. Inviting. Enticing. "One way to find out."

"Well then." I took a deep breath, then said in a rush, "Virginia, would you like to go to dinner with me tomorrow night?"

"Absolutely."

I grinned like I'd just discovered the entrance to a sultan's harem.

Bingo.

Chapter 11

Small Talk, Big Demon

"**I** can't believe it," Terri said, mouth agape. "You have a what?"

"A date," Virginia replied, prim and proper. And barely able to contain her smile. "Tonight. At seven."

Nice to know my lady was looking forward to our first Date later tonight. Grinning, I leaned back against Virginia's kitchen wall, invisible, eager for their conversation to continue. It wasn't every day a demon got to hear what his client really thought of him. I had to admit, I was curious. I'd followed her home last night, after the altercation in Albany, but her routine had barely changed. Other than smiling to herself more than usual, she still acted like a sleepwalker as she'd gone about her evening customs. Maybe more dazed than exhausted, but certainly nothing to really make note of.

"About time," Terri said. "So? Details!"

Virginia searched in the refrigerator before taking out a tub of cream cheese, an oily package, and a jar of capers. "What do you want to know?"

"His name, for starters."

"Don." Virginia didn't say anything else, but her smile stretched into a grin.

Heh. My lady was a tease.

Terri, seated at the kitchen table, let out a snort. "More,

damn it! What's he do? Is he a doctor? You should date a doctor."

"No, but he works in health services."

Terri took a sip from her coffee cup, grumbled, "You're enjoying this . . ."

"Don't know what you mean," Virginia practically sang.

"Quit stalling! Come on, what is he? Oh God, don't say he's a male nurse . . ."

"Nope." Virginia dropped her supplies on the counter, then went back to retrieve a tomato and an onion and placed them next to her stockpile of food. Glancing over her shoulder, she said, "He's a massage therapist."

"Ooh. Good with his hands."

"I wouldn't know."

Terri clucked her tongue. "Extrapolate, Vee. He's a masseur, thus, he works with his hands. On clients' bodies. Hee! I'm all sorts of giddy for you!"

I liked the way Terri thought.

"He's a nice guy," Virginia said, bringing the capers, cheese, and the package to the table, setting everything down. "Polite, and funny, and strong . . ."

"Strong?" Terri unwrapped the paper, revealing sliced lox. "Ooh. Did he use those strong hands on your shoulders? Give you a back massage?"

"Stop that. He beat up a mugger."

"You were *mugged?*"

I winced; Terri's voice had risen three octaves and probably had just deafened all the dogs in the area.

"Almost. Don stopped him. Disarmed him, knocked him out."

Terri almost fell out of her chair. "Holy God, the mugger was *armed?* As in, armed and dangerous?"

Not as dangerous as her voice. I shook my head to clear it. Bishop's balls, she could teach the banshees a thing or two.

"Yes, but Don took care of it." Virginia pulled out a small tray from under the counter, then took out a knife from the butcher's block. "You should've seen him. He knew exactly what to do. Me, I barely called the police without peeing myself, I was so scared. But him?" She let out a happy sigh, and my stomach tightened in pleasure from the sound. "He wasn't scared at all. He was so confident, so strong."

"What, a karate guy or something?"

"Guess so. It all happened so fast." Virginia pulled out a hair band from her jeans pocket, tied back her thick curls so they were out of her face. As much as I liked her hair loose, I enjoyed the unobstructed view of her eyes. She said, "One minute, this total biker from hell's coming at us with a knife. Then he's on the sidewalk, out cold, the knife's in the gutter, and Don's shaking out his hand from punching him."

Terri whistled her appreciation. "Nice! So did you meet when he rescued you? How romantic! I like the damsel-in-distress thing."

"No, we were locked in an elevator for a half hour." This said offhandedly as she started slicing the tomato.

Terri blinked. "Get out of here."

"Seriously. He'd come up to see Mel, an appointment, but Mel pulled a Mel and wasn't there. It was just me, locking up." She dumped the tomato wedges into a bowl, brought it to the table. "So we got into the elevator, and next thing you know, it stops around the tenth floor."

"Love in an elevator . . ."

Virginia grinned. "Nothing like that. We talked. Told really bad elevator stories."

"Yeah, *that* sets the mood."

"Please. He wasn't hitting on me."

"Then he's an idiot."

I smirked.

Terri eyed the rest of the breakfast fixings. "You sure you don't want me to help?"

Virginia shook her head and walked back to the counter. "Come on. Brunch in my house, you're the guest. I get to be the queen when it's your turn next Saturday."

"Yeah, and you always manage to help even when it's my turn to host. Nothing wrong with you sitting back once in a while, you know. Let others do some of the work for a change."

My lady smiled as she grabbed the onion, started peeling the outer skin. "I like doing the work."

"You're used to it."

"Same thing."

"Not really." Terri raised her cup, and for a moment, the only sounds were her sipping coffee and the steady chopping of Virginia's knife.

Look at her fingers move, how she holds the vegetable so carefully, the blade so deftly. This was the woman who was comfortable in her kitchen, who used her tools and worked her own kind of magic with food. I liked this side of her, which was so different from the shell-shocked person who lived in this big house without seeing anything around her. I liked this woman here, now, her wrist steady, her fingers strong, carving and preparing and taking part in life. Such a small thing, making a meal. But it meant so much in the scheme of things. She was so beautiful to watch as her eyes misted from the onion fumes, as she brushed away the tears with a careless stroke of her hand.

"So you guys were stuck," Terri prompted.

Virginia nodded. "At first, everything was fine. But after about twenty minutes or so, I saw that he was sweating. It wasn't hot in there, but he was getting pale, and there was this look in his eyes." She shook her head as she scraped the onions into a bowl. "Oh, he was still talking big, telling jokes and laughing. Acting like everything was fine. But he was getting anxious."

"He scream like a girly girl?"

She shot Terri a look laced with meaning that only a woman could possibly understand. "Come on, Ter. He started having an anxiety attack. I think he's claustrophobic."

"Oh," Terri said, relenting. "Ouch, stuck in a box for a half hour? Must have really sucked to be him."

"Yeah. But he tried to hold it off, tried not to make a big deal out of it. You know, ride it out."

"Sure. Must have been embarrassing." Terri shrugged. "Guys don't want to show women that they're weak."

"Nothing weak about this," Virginia said as she brought the onions to the table. "Being vulnerable isn't the same thing as being weak."

"Leave it to Vee to like her men average and vulnerable."

"Hey, he's like six feet tall."

Terri waved her hand dismissively, her huge grin conveying her mirth. "*Pfft*. Puny."

"Not even close. He's bulky. Enjoys a meal."

"So he's average and fat."

Virginia rolled her eyes, took out two bagels from a paper bag. "You're such a bad friend . . ."

"Sorry. I meant to say he's God's gift to women."

Hah!

Maybe I'd keep my eye on Terri after I seduced Virginia and took her to Hell. Blondes, so I've heard, know how to have fun . . .

"So your savior had an anxiety attack."

"Yeah. Poor guy." Virginia's eyes shone warmly, and her voice was soft as she said, "He was sitting on the floor, hyperventilating. Looking lost. And I talked him down, got him to take some deep breaths."

The playfulness bled out of Terri's face. Her eyes narrowed, and she leaned forward in her seat. "Vee."

"He was okay, and then the elevator started again."

"*Vee*. Don't go playing caregiver again."

Again? My ears perked up at the warning tone in Terri's voice. What was wrong with my lady playing angel of mercy?

Virginia shook her head. "Come on. This was nothing like that."

"Uh-huh." Terri leaned back again, but her face remained cautious. Skeptical.

"Hello? You miss the part about Don taking out a mugger? He's not the kind of guy who needs a nursemaid. He's strong."

"Yeah. I heard." Terri frowned. "Look, you're a big girl. I just don't want you to get stuck playing Mommy, that's all."

"Ter. We're going on one date."

"I know, I know. And I'm thrilled for you. Finally, my girl's getting out there again." She smiled, but it was tight, and filled with worry. "But Vee, please. Don't try to take care of him."

"I said—"

"I *know* what you said." Terri took a deep breath, then said in a rush: "You're finally moving past taking care of Chris. I don't want you shackled to another man you have to nurse. You deserve better than that."

Virginia's back stiffened. Without looking at her friend, she said, "Don't."

Terri bit her lip, held her tongue. Took a sip of coffee, her eyes reflecting her hurt, her concern. Virginia didn't see; she was fumbling with the bagels on the counter, her face dark, mouth set in a frown.

I thought about pushing Terri again, the way I did at the bar a few nights ago, but I didn't want to put a wrinkle in their friendship; I was getting way more information this way. So I settled back. Waited.

"Sorry," Terri finally said. "I can't help it. I worry about you."

"It's okay." The hard line of Virginia's shoulders softened, and she let out a tired sigh. Rotating her neck and left shoulder as if they were sore, she took out plates and napkins, forks and knives, and brought everything to the table. "You want your bagel toasted?"

"No thanks." Terri scanned my lady's face. "Vee, I'm really sorry. Really. I want you to have fun, God knows. And for once, it would be super if a man took care of *you*. Pampered *you*."

"I don't need to be pampered," Virginia said, yanking out a bread knife from the butcher block. "I don't need to be coddled. All I want is to be treated with respect."

"Honey, first get yourself right and properly fucked. Then go for the respect."

Virginia burst out laughing, then shook her head as she lined up the blade to the bagel. "I'm not jumping into bed with him."

Not yet, anyway. I smiled wistfully. Soon, soon, soon . . .

"You should," Terri said. "Let him run those masseur's hands over you, get you relaxed."

"I thought you wanted him to fuck me." She started cutting, holding the bottom of the bagel as the knife cut through the top, headed down.

"That too. Stop, stop, stop! I'll do the bagels," Terri said, standing.

Virginia blinked, looked down at the half-sliced circle of bread in her hand, the knife stuck midsaw. "What's the problem?"

"Same as always. No one's ever taught you how to cut a bagel properly. Safely." Terri shook her head, clearly disgusted by Virginia's cutting technique. "Way you're going, you're going to slice your hand off one of these days, die from blood loss or shock."

Hah. Not on *my* watch.

My lady smiled, rather sheepish. "Way I hold it, more like stab myself in the belly."

"Oh," Terri said, rolling her eyes. "That's much better. Give me the knife before I get violent."

They switched places.

"So what're you going to wear tonight?"

Virginia pouted. "I have no idea. God, what am I thinking? I can't do this . . ."

"Of course you can," Terri said, not looking up from the bagels.

"But . . . I won't fit into anything, I'm so overweight . . ."

"You're gorgeous, you're funny, you're smart."

"But . . ."

Terri said, "There's only one thing you need to do for tonight, Vee."

"What's that?"

Terri met Virginia's gaze. "Lose the wedding band."

"So," I said, struggling to keep the conversation away from sex, "have you always been in Saratoga Springs?"

Virginia blotted her mouth with her napkin before answering. She was so fucking genteel, it was killing me. Even her outfit was screamingly proper, from her gorgeous hair pulled back into a harsh bun to her cream-colored sweater, high cut and roomy, to her blue slacks, pressed. No-nonsense blue pumps on her feet. Makeup was at a minimum; even her plump lips seemed bland, toned down. All of her sensuality, masked with layers of plainness. I wanted to sweep away the plates and glasses and tablecloth and throw her down on the table and fuck her right there in the middle of the Thai restaurant, bring color to her cheeks, her made-to-be-kissed mouth. Make her forget about what was proper as I made her come.

But no. No sex. Not even a hint of sexual attraction. This Date . . . Screw that, this wasn't a Date at all, but a regular human date: just a guy eating dinner with a girl. Completely hands-off, and all talk. *Real* talk. With no promise of any sort of gratification later.

Satan spare me.

"I've been here for about ten years," she said, spreading the cloth napkin over her lap. "Originally from Brooklyn."

"What part?" Like I cared.

"Marine Park. Near Flatbush Avenue."

"Why'd you move upstate?"

"We wanted to get away from the city, find a place where a minute actually meant a minute, you know?"

I nodded, tried not to look bored. Toyed with the noodles on my plate.

"My best friend's been up here since college—she went to SUNY Albany, never came home. So we visited her a lot, most holiday weekends, that sort of thing. And after a while, it just made sense to come up here permanently."

"You moved with your family?"

A blush stained her cheeks, and she reached for her water glass, took a hasty sip. Looked like I'd hit a sore spot. Unholy Hell, a reaction! Emotion! Progress!

After she swallowed, she said, "With my husband." Solemn, like this declaration held great weight.

Oh, right. Good girls don't cheat. She's feeling me out. Okay, I can play along.

I glanced at her hand, noticeably bare of a wedding ring. Kudos for Terri. Nodding I said, "Ah." Not sure what else there was to say, I left it at that.

She fidgeted, nervous. When I didn't fill the silence, she added, "I'm not anymore."

Liar.

I coughed to hide my laugh, then said, "Sorry."

"It's okay." She covered her left hand with her right one, as if she wanted to hide a ring that wasn't on her finger. Her voice falsely chipper, she asked, "So what about you? Have you been in the area long?"

"Not very. I travel a lot. For the job." Best way to lie is to tell the truth and just twist the meaning.

Relaxing, she twirled some of the Pad Thai around her fork. After a mouthful, she asked, "Where are you from originally?"

I smiled. "Down South." Way, way down.

"You don't have an accent."

"No?" Laying it on thick, I put East Texas into my voice. "Figure that's because of all the travel. But I'm happy to oblige, if you want me to extend the Southern charm."

Grinning, she shook her head. "No need, unless you want to. That's so cool, how you can just turn it on and off like that."

Going back to my Northern voice, I said, "Lots of practice."

More food, for both of us. I was so out of my league with the small talk that I was happy to stall. Manipulation via mastication.

After a few more minutes of eating, Virginia asked, "You get around a lot?"

"Oh, yeah."

"You like it?"

"Depends." She obviously waited for me to say more, so I added, "I like my job, so I do what I have to do."

"You said you're a massage therapist, right?"

"I did." Oh, this was killing me . . .

"So are you, um, a traveling masseur?"

"Not exactly. I go to where my clients are."

"Oh," she said, like she understood. She dabbed at her mouth with her napkin again. Put down her utensils. "And Mr. Brook's one of your clients?"

"Maybe. If we can ever meet." I shrugged. "Recommendations," I said vaguely.

"I see." Smiling, but strained around the edges. Playing with her non-ring. She wasn't having a good time.

Neither was I.

If only I could find some way to get her to open up, tell me something I could use. How to steer this conversation into something I could work with? I couldn't loosen her up with my power. And as sure as angels are asses, talking sex would only scare her away.

What's an incubus to do?

I glanced at Virginia's bare finger. When all else fails, go for the obvious. Let's see if I can get her to admit how unhappy she is with her loser husband. "How long?"

She blinked, smiled. "Sorry?"

"Since you've been married."

"Oh." Blanching, she looked down at her hands. "Two years."

Huh. I'd expected her to make up something more believable. Wait, can good people actually lie? "Long time," I said evenly.

"I guess." She cleared her throat, but didn't look up at me. "Chris died."

Oh.

"I'm sorry." I couldn't hide the surprise in my voice; her revelation had hit me like a sucker punch. She was two years a widow? You'd never know from looking at her house. Even without any photographs or other pictures on the walls, her husband's clothing was in the closet, his pillows were on his side of the bed. Bloody Hell, she still wore his ring. Except for tonight. "Was it sudden?"

She shook her head. "Cancer."

Shit, she was shrinking in on herself. Walling me off. My fault for pushing. I reached out, put my hand on top of hers, showed her we had a connection. Voice soft, I said, "Must have been hard for you."

Virginia swallowed, didn't reply.

"And him," I added.

She said, "He fought it." Spoken like the words were choking her. "Fought it for a year. More. Fourteen months."

"Sounds like he was very strong."

That got her to meet my gaze. "He was. The doctors told him he had only a few weeks. He refused to believe them. Chris was stubborn," she said with a smile that must have broken her heart.

"And a fighter," I said.

She nodded. Her eyes shone, overly bright. "Yes. He was a fighter." She wasn't crying, but I heard the tears in her voice.

"Virginia. I'm so sorry." I squeezed her hand.

"Thanks. It's okay. I just . . ." She took a deep breath. "I just miss him sometimes."

Sometimes? Sure, if that was loosely defined as oh, always. She still pined for her husband. Still wanted him—that was clear from her dream, from how she could only remove his image from her home but not his physical belongings. How she still wore his ring.

Fuck me, she was still in love with him.

I reached for my scotch, resisted the urge to knock it back. Instead I took a measured sip. This did not bode well. It was one thing to make her forget about a jackass of a husband who'd loved her and left her . . . and something else entirely to compete with the memory of a loving husband. The dead take on mystical importance to the living—they could do no wrong, they were perfect. They were untouchable.

I asked, "How'd you meet him?"

"High school. We started dating in tenth grade, never stopped."

High school sweethearts? Barf. "Just knew you were right for each other?"

"Yeah." She was smiling now, and her voice was heavy with memory as she played with her ring finger. Grasping for a ring that wasn't there. "There's never been anyone else. It's always been Chris."

Hoo-boy. Her true love, her only love, was her dead husband. My assignment just got a shitload harder. Assuming I survived this, I'd have to think of some way to pay Pan back. Maybe something with starving hyenas and spleens.

After another swallow of scotch, I said, "Sounds like he made you very happy."

"He did." She looked at me suddenly, an unreadable smile on her lips. "Geez. Look at me, babbling about him when I'm out with you. You must think I'm an idiot."

Well, yeah. But mortals did so enjoy the notion of love. Bless me for an angel, I'd never understand it. "I think you love your husband. Nothing wrong with that."

"Thanks." Her smile eased into something warm, comfortable. Ah, look at her—those full lips, those rounded cheeks. Hers was a face meant for smiling. She stammered, "I, uh, I don't do this."

"What, eat Thai food?"

She was grinning now, big and unself-conscious. Beautiful. "No. You know. This." Motioning to the table. "I mean, you're the first man I've gone out with. I mean . . ." She blew out a breath, laughed at herself. "I'm really bad at this."

"No, you're not." I smiled my encouragement. "Why haven't you dated?"

An offhand shrug, burdened with the lie of casualness. "Haven't wanted to go out with anyone."

"So I'm your pity date?"

She chuckled. "I make exceptions for superheroes."

"And spies."

"Them too." A pause, a hint of a blush. "This is stupid, but I feel guilty. Like I'm cheating on Chris."

"Virginia . . ." I all but radiated sympathy, understanding. Shit like that. "Do you want to go home?"

"No!" Startled, vehement. She let out a laugh, again said, "No." Softer this time, but insistent. "I like being out with you."

"Me too."

"I'm sorry, I know I'm acting weird. I'm just nervous."

"No need to be."

"I know. Still."

We shared a smile, but I saw the tightness around her eyes.

"Tell you what," I said. "I promise I won't kill you on the first date."

She barked out a surprised laugh that made my heartbeat quicken. Muffling the sound with her hand, she laughed silently, shoulders moving, eyes sparkling. She smiled through her fingers, said, "I'm going to hold you to that, you know."

I winked. "Count on it."

Dessert: fried bananas with chocolate sauce and ice cream for her, pumpkin custard for me. When I was with a client, foods had real flavor and texture. But being with Virginia went beyond those meager senses; it was like the food exploded into new sensations, delights of smell and taste that went beyond description. She made the meal practically orgasmic.

For the first time in my existence, I understood why some humans chose to gorge themselves into insatiability. What would have made this treat even better would have been if I was smearing it all over Virginia's naked body, then lapping it off, inch by inch, nibbling along her limbs, my teeth grazing her curves. My lips gliding over every part of her . . .

"Sure you don't want to try some?" Virginia offered her fork to me.

As much as I wanted to—as easy as it would have been to

turn that simple gesture into a prelude of carnal activity—I said no. In this guise, I was laid-back, understanding. Easygoing. And not at all sexually aggressive. It was fucking killing me, but I would play the role.

And maybe, just maybe, my lady would reward me with a kiss when we got back to her place. And then the evening would take a very different turn.

"Your loss," she said.

I watched her lips move as she put the morsel into her mouth. Chewed. Swallowed, and oh, look at her throat work. My loss, indeed . . .

Somewhere behind me, I heard the sounds of someone eating. Unlike our fellow patrons, this particular person smacked his lips, grunted. And, unless my nose deceived me, farted. Charming. Some mortals turned the act of gluttony into an art form.

I heard snuffling laughter—wet chuckles, heavy with amusement and appetite. And pitched much too low for human ears.

Oh, fuck.

Turning in my seat as if I wanted to flag a waiter, I saw him, seated two tables down. Mountainous, he overflowed his chair as he gorged on a rack of lamb, jelly glistening from his thick lips. A hint of black hair glinted atop his head; his wide mouth was framed by a Fu Manchu mustache, the pointed tips dripping with gravy. His golden skin strained to contain his girth; overstuffed, it looked like a pastry inflated to the bursting point. Piles of food filled his table—roast chicken and whole fish, ham and brisket, dishes of steaming vegetables and baked potatoes and bowls of fruit, foods not limited to the Thai selection here at the restaurant. He wiped his mouth with the back of a hand that was large enough to dwarf a bear's paw. And then he met my gaze.

Belzebul, King of Gluttony, grinned at me. Pieces of meat were wedged between his teeth, speckling his smile like flies in a bowl of soup.

Sweat popped on my brow, and I commanded my heart to

get the fuck out of my throat and back in my chest where it belonged.

A waiter saw my outstretched hand, approached the table. Tearing my gaze from the Lord of Hunger, I picked up my cup with a clammy hand, pointed to it. The waiter nodded, dashed off to fetch me more coffee that I didn't need.

Virginia said something, a humorous comment that I didn't hear, so I smiled and nodded as I thought about Belzebul. I hadn't sensed him. Even when I'd been staring right at him, I hadn't sensed him; he was completely off my radar in a way that only the strongest of the Abyss and the Sky could manage. Unholy Hell, how powerful was he?

Powerful enough to rule the Gluttons. As strong as Pan, easily, but much older than my liege-lord. And much more cunning.

I tried not to listen to Belzebul reveling in his feast, but the sounds were deafening—his smacking grunts echoed in my ears. And now he's tearing away the meat with his teeth, and it's pulling, ripping, the flesh stretching and slowly giving way and, now he's chewing, slobbering . . .

The waiter returned, filled my cup, then retreated. I took a hasty sip, didn't taste the liquid as I swallowed.

Maybe he didn't recognize me.

GREETINGS, CHOSEN OF PAN.

Shit. **Greetings, Lord of Hunger.**

"Don?"

I blinked, smiled at Virginia, who cocked her head as she looked at me. "Everything okay?"

LET US TALK, LIBERTINE.

"Don?"

"Hmm? Oh, sorry. Just lost in thought, that's all." **As you wish, Sire.**

"Don, what's wrong?" Concern in her voice now, bordering on worry.

"Nothing, doll," I said, distracted by the entity two tables away. I could feel his piggy eyes staring at me, his hungry gaze boring into my back. He was probably wondering if I'd taste better with catsup.

AMUSING.

Whoops.

" 'Doll'? You didn't just call me 'doll,' did you?"

I ignored Belzebul's hiccoughing chortles, focused on Virginia. Was surprised to see the slight curl to her lip, the sardonic gleam in her eyes. "What?"

"What is this," she asked, "the nineteen-forties? 'Doll'? Really?"

Even with one of the seven Kings of Sin mocking me, I managed a smile. Couldn't help it; my lady was so fucking gorgeous when she was in a huff. The flush to her cheeks, the hint of darkness in her eyes . . ."Sorry. Old habit."

"I'm not a doll. I'm not some fragile toy that's going to break with the slightest touch."

Oh, Virginia, you have no idea just how easily you could break.

"Duly noted," I said, my thoughts churning. First the attacks from the nefarious. Then Eris's appearance at the opera. Now the ruler of physical appetite, here at the same restaurant as me.

Times like this, I could really use an Oracle.

Reaching for the sweetener, wondering what the King of Hunger wanted with me, I winked at Virginia. "So can I call you 'sugar'?"

She groaned around her mouthful of dessert, but I saw the smile she tried to hide with her fork. "You're a flatterer."

Every chance I got.

I BRING YOU TIDINGS, AS ONE CREATURE OF GLUTTONY TO ANOTHER.

I almost dropped my coffee. Me, one of the Hungry? I'd been called many things in my existence—most of them rather colorful. But never has anyone suggested that I was a creature of Gluttony. Sipping my drink, I answered the demon king. **Pardon, Sire, but I think you may be confusing me with another of the nefarious.**

NOT UNLESS THERE IS ANOTHER DAUNUAN, PRIN-CIPAL OF LUST AND CHOSEN OF PAN. He chortled, a wheezing sound fat with mischief. *YOU ARE HE?*

I have that pleasure, Sire.

YES, YOU AND YOUR PLEASURES. WE ALL HAVE THEM. MINE IS OVERINDULGENCE. THOUGHTLESS EXCESS. GLUTTONY. AND WHAT IS LUST, IF NOT AN OVERINDULGENCE OF SEX? A GORGING ON DESIRE?

I hadn't figured the King of Hunger to be one for philosophy.

YOU BELONG TO GLUTTONY, LIBERTINE, AS DO ALL OF YOUR KIND.

The memory of Eris: *What is lust, if not envy over another person's sexual prowess?*

Bloody Hell, all the elite were fucking insane.

YOU SHOULD KNOW, LIBERTINE, THAT GLUTTONY WILL NOT PARTICIPATE.

The sound of my heartbeat filled my ears; my blood roared through my body. Participate? In what?

AND NEITHER WILL SLOTH. WHICH IN ITSELF SHOULD BE OF LITTLE SURPRISE.

Of course, Sire. My throat constricted, and I forced myself to take a deep breath. As much as I wanted to, needed to, ask what he meant, to do so would show weakness. I hadn't survived this long by admitting to my superiors what I didn't know.

THE OTHERS, HOWEVER, HAVE ACCEPTED. SO YOU MAY WANT TO WATCH YOUR BACK. OR YOUR BACK-SIDE, AS IT WERE.

Sire, I thank you for your generous news. I sipped my coffee, fought off my growing panic. What could I ask that was acceptable? **But I do wonder why it is that one as powerful as yourself has decided to share this information with one such as me.**

AMONG OTHER THINGS, I PREFER AN OVERINDUL-GENCE OF FAVORS. His laughter burbled in my mind, voracious, dark. *YOU OWE ME ONE, DAUNUAN, CHOSEN OF PAN.*

Fuck.

Belzebul's presence winked out, leaving only the echo of his chortles, and the thick, soft feeling of cotton in my head. If I turned around, I knew his table would be empty, with no hint of either him or his meal.

"Don? Are you okay?"

I took another sip of coffee before I answered. "Fine. Why?"

"You've been so silent." Virginia paused, and something in her eyes softened. Her voice low, she said, "You're pale. And you're sweating."

She was right: I was sweating like a condemned man standing before a firing squad. An encounter with any of the Kings of Hell would do that to a demon. I took a deep breath, then let out a laugh. "Honest? I'm kind of nervous."

"I'm scarier than a mugger with a knife?"

Heh. "You know how you said you don't do this?" I motioned to the table, the restaurant, us. "Me, either. I haven't been on a date like this in . . . well, it feels like forever." True. All of my other Dates had less talking and a lot more foreplay.

We looked at each other, she with her issues, me with mine, and we shared a laugh.

She asked, "Aren't we the pair?"

"Oh, yeah . . ."

"So we'll go slow," she said, her eyes big and wide and trusting. "One day at a time."

Stretching my smile so wide that my cheeks should have cracked, I agreed.

If only Hell would let me take it that slow.

Chapter 12

Under Pressure

I glanced at my host's watch for the millionth time. Quarter after three in the morning. Still too early for me to call Virginia.

Fuck me, did time always go by this slowly, and I'd just never noticed it?

Sighing, I retreated back into my host's mind and let him take over for a while. The flesh puppet blinked, shook his head, then picked up his pace. Still had a half mile to go before he got home; the city bus hadn't shown, so he was stuck walking home, in the dark, down the deserted city streets, because he was too cheap to call a cab. His loss, my temporary gain. He was wrecked after a long shift at the local quickie mart, skimming the registers and backwashing into the cola bottles, so jumping into his body had been a cakewalk.

Killing time à la possession. Infernal equivalent of drinking on the job. Daunuan, how far you've fallen. Risen. Whatever.

It wasn't like I could slum at the Voodoo Café and grab a drink and a quickie with a passing demon; Belzebul's message had made that perfectly clear. I had no idea what he'd been referring to, but whatever was afoot was big enough to have the majority of the seven Sins play along. And that meant there was a good chance that it would be open season on everyone's favorite incubus.

No, strike "good chance"—he'd said flat-out that I should watch my back. They'd be coming after me—bloody Hell, had already been coming after me—and I just wasn't in the best frame of mind to fight. So no boozing between planes for me. And making a Pit stop was out for the same reason. Which meant the mortal coil for now. And keeping my infernal radar set on high. As long as I could sense them coming, I'd be okay.

As for the other thing . . .

I checked the time again. Sighed. Still too early. Kept walking, breathing in the stagnant city air, which even now was laced with the human remnants of pollution and desperation. Senses wide-open, I listened, making sure no infernal visitors paid an unexpected visit, but there was only the sound of the city itself, resting but not sleeping. And there was darkness, of course—at this time of night, in this particular part of Albany, no lights blazed from storefronts or domiciles, no car headlights broke the monotony of the long street.

Even though the nighttime stillness was nothing close to the absolute blackness of Pan's antechamber, it had the same effect on me: alone in the dark, all I had were my thoughts for company. (My host's thoughts, I'd quickly discovered, were as insipid as an angel's demeanor. Yawn.)

And so I thought. About Virginia. Specifically, about how dinner last night had ended. She'd given me her phone number, said I should call her. I'd grinned like an idiot and made all the right noises . . . and then she went home.

That was it: no kiss—not even a chaste peck on the cheek—no offer to go back to her place, no heartfelt declarations of adoration. Nothing. Just a phone number, with two words as instructions: *Call me*.

And I had no idea what the proper protocol was for following up.

Was I supposed to call her right away? Wait twenty-four hours? Call in the morning? At night? At all? Maybe I was just supposed to show up on her doorstep and seduce her? No, I'd already tried that.

A fucking phone number.

I already knew her number. Not that she knew I knew her number. But still.

My host paused to pull out a pack of cigarettes. A smoker, thank Gehenna! Just what I needed. He lit up, and I relished the taste of the tobacco going into his lungs. Secondhand smoke: nectar of the nefarious. We smoked; he walked. And I fumed.

By this point, my clients have always kissed me willingly. *Always.* And all I had to do for subsequent Dates was call them, whenever I wanted, or just knock on their doors. Once my clients kissed me, they were mine, body and mind. All that was left was the soul. (Which was reserved for Date Number Four.) I never had to worry about things like implications; my clients dropped everything for me. It was always at my convenience. None of this prior planning bullshit I had to contend with for Virginia.

Of course, none of my previous clients had ever been good. Not even remotely. Good people, apparently, didn't kiss on a first Date—pardon me, little *d date*. Good people didn't pick up on sexual innuendo, let alone know what to do with it. Good people sure as Hell didn't do what I wanted, when I wanted it.

In short, good people sucked. And not in the way that brought a smile to my face.

Through my dark thoughts, I heard mortals talking somewhere up ahead—their voices were hushed, urgent. I could have picked up their words if I really wanted to, but I was too busy trying to puzzle out the hidden meaning of the almighty phone number.

What did Virginia want me to do? If I called too soon, I might scare her away—maybe she'd think I was too aggressive. Or too desperate. Or, *pfaugh*, what if she thought I was a loser? After that insane display of mine at the restaurant, breaking into a cold sweat when Belzebul had taken me by surprise, Virginia probably thought I was leaning away from "vulnerable" and more toward "weak."

Acid churned in my host's stomach, and I clamped down on the cigarette with my teeth, nearly bit through the filter as I pictured Virginia, her kissable mouth pulled into a sneer, judgment shining in those emerald eyes and finding me wanting.

No, I couldn't call too soon. I'd already invested too much time in this particular form for me to start over with a new look, new backstory, new approach.

But if I waited too long, Virginia might think I wasn't interested in her—and then she would be reserved, even uninterested, when I actually did call.

So what was the balance between too soon and too long? Satan spare me, why didn't she just tell me *when* to call her?

Is this what mortals did when they liked each other? Or maybe when they *didn't* like each other? Was this a test?

Was Virginia fucking with me?

I smoked, pondered. No, she liked me, I could tell. She could have gone home when I'd given her the out, but she didn't. That meant she liked me.

Right?

My frustrated growl reverberated deep in my host's throat. Bishop's balls, I wanted to bang my head against a wall until my host's brains leaked out. Maybe I should go to the Abyss and take on whoever, or whatever, challenged me. At least that I could understand; in Hell, the strongest survived, and the weakest learned to kiss up or play dead.

But this Virginia thing? *Pfaugh!*

Relationships were fucking stupid. Screw that: *mortals* were fucking stupid. If people just gave into lust without assigning stupid meaning to everything, the stupid world would be a happier place. At least, I'd be a happier demon.

I pinched the bridge of my host's nose, tried to think. If this headache was what it meant to seduce someone who was good, I'd cheerfully stick with those who worshiped evil. Evil was straightforward. Uncomplicated. Better yet, my powers worked on evil people, so even if they weren't really into me, it didn't matter: I always got my client Hooked . . . And I always took their souls. Always.

Stupid, fucking good people and their stupid, fucking phone numbers.

I looked at my host's watch again. Sighed. Still too soon to call. Fuck me, this was going to be a long night.

As I passed an alley, I saw the sources of the voices I'd heard before: a guy was getting a blow job from someone; a gal, based on the skirt and thigh-high boots. Lucky prick. The rate I was going, Virginia would never even glance at my crotch, let alone . . .

. . . Wait a second.

My footfalls slowed. Stopped. I stared into the mouth of the alley, took in the man's outfit, from his cap to his jacket to his boots. That wasn't just any guy getting a hummer. I grinned, slow and big, chuckled softly.

Hellooo, officer.

I hated cops. They tended to be either stupidly noble or completely corrupt. The noble ones made me want to puke— they were all like Jezebel's meat pie, out to save the world. And the corrupt ones were so easy to take down that I barely broke a sweat. But they were so cute when they screamed.

After a last drag, I flicked the cigarette to the ground, cracked my host's knuckles. Walked into the alley.

Time to have some fun.

The woman was on her knees, slurping away, her purrs of encouragement ringing false to my ears; sounded like she wanted the cop to hurry up and blow his wad so she could get on with her life. Based on the fake fur coat, the leather boots, the barely there skirt, it was a working night for her. The officer had his head tilted back, his policeman's cap askew, his hands fisted in the woman's hair as she sucked his rod, maybe teabagged him. His gun holder smacked against his ass as he bucked his hips. He didn't hear me coming, probably because he was too busy thinking about coming himself. A good steak dinner will do that to a man.

Still grinning, I tapped him on the shoulder.

He started, jerked away from the woman. Pivoted to face me. One pistol sheathed, his other sticking out to say hello, he snarled a declaration that was probably supposed to scare me. His hand fell onto his gun belt.

I put my hands up in mock surrender, then leaned in close . . . and let my true form radiate from my host's body. Through a mouthful of fangs, I said, "Boo!"

The cop shrieked, high-pitched, musical, the sound almost as delectable as his sudden burst of citrus and sweat. Yum. Over his panic, a gasp, then a thud to his left. Peripherally, I saw a slumped form on the alley floor. The hooker, collapsed in a faint. My senses were awash in citrus and sex and the last clinging remains of vanilla. I inhaled deeply, let out a contented sigh. There's nothing like the smell of pure terror. Nothing.

Cowering in front of me, the cop kept shrieking. His erection had deflated, and with it came a stream of urine that hit my host's shoes. Right, time to slip into something more comfortable. I stared into his glazed eyes and . . .

Contact.

I hopped out of the clerk's body and into the cop's, settled down in my new digs. Flexed the arms, got used to the new size and packaging. Zipped up his/my fly. Grinned hugely at the clerk, who had staggered back and was blinking too fast as he stared at me, at the unconscious prostitute, back at me.

"Run away," I whispered, patting the gun holster at my hip. "Fast."

He didn't need to be told twice—he bolted like a hellhound was on his trail.

Well now. All dressed up—I pulled out a key ring from the cop's jacket pocket—with someplace to go. I was sure I could find a use for the gun and the handcuffs . . . and hellooo, Taser. Yes, this night was starting to look up.

Glancing at the crumpled form of the woman, I debated waking her, having her finish what she'd started. No, she probably needed the sleep.

I let my host skim the surface of his mind, for now. Come on, puppet. Let's go for a ride. With the siren on.

* * *

By eight twenty-three that morning, I'd played clerk (boring), cop (most excellent, especially when I interfered with a mugging and gave the criminal the scare of his life), gangbanger (fun, especially when beating up the same cop I'd just inhabited and then stealing his patrol car) and clergy member (which had given me the runs). I was feeling recharged. Confident. Ready to take on the world.

After depositing my latest host body in a pew, I put on my "Don" costume and walked outside into the Sunday-morning sunshine. I'd made sure to borrow a cell phone from the gang member. He probably didn't notice, as it was one of four on his person. Magicking up money was easy; using my powers to summon up a cell phone, complete with its own wireless sort of magic, was something else entirely. One of these years, I really was going to have to study up on recent technology. Maybe I could finagle a wizard into giving me a crash course, in exchange for a favor . . .

I called Virginia's number, and she picked up on the third ring.

"Hey, it's me. Don."

"Hi," she said, sounding pleased. "Surprised you're up so early."

"Actually, I haven't even gone to bed yet."

"Wow. Why the all-nighter?"

"Wasn't tired. Kept thinking about you."

A pause, then she asked, "Really?" Cautious, yes . . . but interested. Maybe it was despite herself, but she was interested. I wanted to cheer.

And I wanted to throttle the part of me that wanted to cheer. What the fuck was wrong with me lately? You'd think I'd just sprouted horns yesterday. Of *course* Virginia was interested in me. I was an incubus. She was a living, breathing woman. End of story.

"Had a great time with you last night," I said, aiming for honesty.

She smiled. I couldn't see it, but unholy Hell, I felt it, right there over the phone when she said, "Me too."

"Is this an okay time to call?"

"I'm actually on my way out," she said. "But I can talk for a few minutes."

We chatted for a bit—small talk, but the conversation was relaxed, easy. With every word she spoke, every time she let out a laugh, her voice betrayed her growing comfort with me, her growing attraction. Oh, how I enjoyed the sound of her voice, hearing those words, any words, spoken from her lips, that laughter bubbling from her mouth.

I did that to her. I made her forget her empty life, her gnawing loss.

And just listening to her voice made me smile. This was the woman who lived beneath the cold shell, the one who'd been abandoned when her husband had sickened and died. This was the real Virginia, full of mirth with hints of wickedness. This was the woman who made my heartbeat quicken, the one I wanted to bed. The one I wanted to pleasure like she'd never known before.

The one who made me smile in a way that only one other creature ever could.

My Virginia.

All too soon, she said, "Ah, jeez, look at the time. I really have to go. I'm late for church."

Well, to that end, a job well done for me. "I'd like to see you again."

For a long moment, there was only the sound of static over the phone line. Shit, did I push too much? Come on, doll. You know you want to see me. And I want to see you. All of you. Maybe with just that red scarf, and nothing else . . .

"What're you doing later?" Her words tumbled over themselves in their rush to escape her lips.

Feeling a huge grin unfurl on my face, feeling my chest loosen, I asked, "Today? Nothing, really."

"So . . . you want to come over?" A pause, then, in a rush: "Unless it's too much out of the way, I'm all the way in Wilton and you're near Albany, that's a good fifty minutes without traffic—"

"Stop," I said, laughing. "Too late to try to talk me out of it. I'm coming over."

"Really, you don't have to . . ."

"I want to. You just have to tell me when."

"Um . . . I'll make us dinner." That said like it was a lifeline, something she could cling to: dinner was safe.

The image of her in her kitchen, preparing a meal for her and Terri, bloomed in my mind—she had been so at ease, so very relaxed. "That sounds wonderful."

"So, you want to come over, what, around fiveish? Too early?"

"Just right." Remembering that I wasn't supposed to have her address, I asked her where she lived. She told me, and I pretended to write it down. "Should I bring anything?"

"Just yourself."

"Uh-uh," I said. "I have to bring something. And I don't know you well enough yet to just know what you like." What turns you on. What makes you melt.

"Well . . ." She laughed, said, "You can never go wrong with chocolate."

"Chocolate," I repeated, picturing me drizzling the thick liquid between her breasts, nuzzling my face between them as I lapped up the confection and sucked it from her nipples . . . Adjusting my pants, I said, "Noted. Anything else?"

"No, really," she said, sounding flustered. "Please don't go through the trouble."

"It's no trouble."

"Well then. See you tonight." That last said like she couldn't believe she'd actually made plans.

"I'm looking forward to it." Like you would not believe. "See you later."

I disconnected the call, barely catching the whiff of sulfur and the stink of a cat drowning in cologne before a voice hissed in my ear: "You're supposed to fuck her, not sweet-talk her."

Closing the phone, I turned around, smiled tightly at Callistus. He was riding a man's body—either a pimp or a wannabe, based on the purple velvet outfit and twenty pounds of gold jewelry on his neck and fingers—but the psychic connection between Seducers announced his presence, even without his telltale odor. No matter what human he possessed, Cal's nature always shadowed his face, gleamed in his eyes. Even after all this time, I didn't know if that was a sign of weakness on his part, or a hint of vanity that danced closely with the Arrogant.

Nonchalant, I put the phone into my back pocket. Acted like Callistus wasn't worth my attention. "I'm savoring the seduction."

"Don't make your excuses to me. I'm just the messenger." His red-rimmed eyes mocked me, but beneath their mirth I saw hints of rage.

Didn't like being an errand boy, did you? "Part-time job? Or a new role for you?"

"We all have to get used to new things," he said, baring his human's teeth in a feral grin. "You, for example. You'll have to tell the Boss why you haven't done what he's asked of you, *Prince* Daunuan."

A finger of ice touched my heart, pressed. Was I out of time? No, impossible. Not when I was so close. Not without a warning from Pan. Demons had rules, even demon kings. Unless I broke a rule myself, they had a decorum to follow. Pan had admitted as much to me, when he first told me about my new place in the scheme of things.

Keeping my voice neutral, I said, "If he was summoning me, he wouldn't bother doing it through you."

"I'll have to tell him you said so."

Callistus, posturing? He may be Pan's number two, but he didn't have our King's ear. I was willing to bet my life on that. "You do that," I said, calling Cal's bluff. Crossing my arms over my chest, I added, "I'll wait."

A pause, pregnant with tension. I sensed Cal tapping into his power, letting it fill him even with the risk to his human host. Mortal bodies weren't made to channel infernal magic— not mere glamours, but *real* magic, the sort that shattered human reality with the force of Hell and ripped their world asunder. Humans who tapped into that power tended to melt.

Plenty of time for me to "borrow" a car, drive to the local mall, and convince a chocolatier to give me the biggest box of goodies in the store.

Say what you will about me, but I could be a persuasive ol' demon.

Narrowing my eyes, I hissed, "Here, Callistus? D1
that? You're either insanely overconfident, or insane
Even if you win, the paperwork would bind you for
Not very princely, is it?"

His human's eyes regarded me for a moment befor
his power level drop. "Not very princely of you to tal
way out of a challenge."

"There was no official challenge. And I'm not Prince.

"Right," he said, rolling the word. "You're a principal. V
equals, Daunuan."

"We're many things. But equals will never be one of the1

Another strained silence as we locked gazes. Finally, he sa
"The Boss is getting impatient. Starting to think you do1
have what it takes to be his number one." He smirked h
agreement.

"Have to take it slow with good people," I said with a tight
smile. "I'm already influencing her actions."

"Yeah?" He arched an eyebrow. "She spreading her legs for
you?"

"Made her late for church just now."

Cal's smirk transformed into a hungry grin. "How impressive. Daunuan, Prince of the Seducers, on the same level as a
human telemarketer."

Asshole. "You have a message?"

Smiling his disdain, he said, "If you don't claim your good
girl's soul in the next two days, the Boss is going to decide that
you failed. And you know the price of failure."

Sure: imminent death.

"So the message is this: Two days, Daunuan. By all means,"
Cal chuckled, "take your time." He touched the brim of his
pimp's hat, then winked out of his host in a puff of brimstone.
The pimp swayed, then turned and retched on the church steps.

I knew the feeling. Two days until deadline. Emphasis on
the first syllable.

But more pressing at the moment: eight hours until dinner
tonight. Until Virginia. I smiled just thinking about her.

Chapter 13

Don Juan Comes to Dinner

Five o'clock on the dot, I rang Virginia's doorbell. Waited with gifts in my hands and a smile on my face.

Tonight, doll. Here, in your house, where you're most comfortable. Where you're safe. Tonight's the night you kiss me, Virginia. I just know it. You'll kiss me, and then I'll strip away your hesitations, your insecurities, your fears.

Tonight's the night I show you what it means to have your body worshiped like a goddess.

I smelled her before she appeared, breathed in her scent of jasmine and musk, of blackberries and chocolate. Or maybe the chocolate was from the box in my arms. No. No food could ever smell as delectable as Virginia did. Inhaling her sweetness, I held her aroma deep within me, felt drunk from her very presence. Yes, tonight.

Soon.

Virginia opened the door, and it was all I could do not to stare. Her black hair framed her face in loose waves instead of her usual wild curls, looked thick and lush and ready to have my fingers run through it. No makeup around her eyes, but she didn't need it: her eyes sparkled like spring grass wet with morning dew. And those lips . . . a whisper of red, like gloss, making me think of strawberries. Those lips moved into a soft smile, and something in me both tightened and relaxed at once—desire, yes, but more than just a physical urge. A want, a need, that I couldn't name, couldn't understand.

I didn't want this feeling, this sensation so completely foreign to everything I've ever known. And I couldn't imagine feeling any other way.

"Hi," she said, and her voice surged through me like magic.

"Hi." Oh, damn me, look at her. Instead of a bulky sweater or a screamingly proper blouse, she wore a two-tone jersey that was both casual and frustratingly enticing, outlining her shape with a wanton ease that hit me in a wave of jealousy—I wanted to be that fabric caressing her large breasts, her rounded belly, whispering over the indents of her waist. I wanted to wrap myself around her and squeeze her and feel her body move and ache and breathe beneath me . . . I hardly saw her loose jeans, her bare feet. Her curves hypnotized me, enslaved me. I looked at her, and I was lost.

Boom *boom*.

"Oh my God," she said, staring at my gifts, "is all that . . . for me?"

Oh, Virginia, just wait until you see what's in my pants.

Grinning, I offered her the bouquet of flowers. At the mall, I'd had the most enlightening conversations at a shoe store. Bored women with too much money and too much time were all too happy to tell me what tokens of appreciation they loved to receive from their men. All it had taken on my part was possessing the salesman (closet snuff-film freak) and nudging the customers (rich and shameless) with my gigolojo as I slipped designer shoes onto their feet. Flowers, by far, had been a favorite. No roses, though; roses, apparently, were too quaint for current standards. Bless me to Heaven, I'd never understand women.

"Really," Virginia said, "you didn't have to do all this. These are gorgeous." She buried her nose into the bouquet, smiled like someone had whispered promises of true love while dancing under the stars. "I love daisies."

"I saw them and I thought of you."

"Thank you. And wine? Don, really, this is too much."

Wine had been the second favorite of the shoe divas. "I was passing by the store, and I saw the brand. Had to get it." All too true. Not every day an incubus buys a bottle of Love My Goat red wine.

"I love Bully Hill wines," Virginia said, taking the bottle. "Ever try their Fusion? Terrific stuff. But only at room temperature. If you chill it, it tastes like cough syrup. God, and the chocolate! Look at this chocolate!"

That was for the two-pound gold box I'd just offered her. I couldn't not bring it; it was the one thing she'd asked for specifically.

Blushing, she said, "Don, thank you, but this is really too much." A whiff of citrus. A tic in her jaw.

Fuck me, I'd gone too far. She was uneasy. Battening down the hatches. Probably thinking I was trying to bribe her with sweetness to get some sweetness in return. I was, but that didn't mean I should advertise it.

Defuse it. Fast.

"I know, I went overboard," I said with a shrug, a sheepish smile. When pushed, offer the truth, or parts of it. Enough to sound sincere, enough to get them off guard. "But it's been so long since I've done something like this, I sort of didn't remember what girls like guys to bring."

She peered into my face, my eyes. My heart thudded in my ears as I awaited her judgment, and I smiled until it felt like my cheeks had frozen.

Finally, she shook her head and grinned. It was wry and sexy and absolutely perfect, and I released the breath I hadn't known I'd been holding.

"Women," she corrected, her eyes bright with silent laughter. "I have to tell you, Don, you're the worst thing for my diet."

"I thought that was Mickey D's."

Her smile broadened. "Mickey D's should be even half as good as this. This is all wonderful, thank you." She stepped aside, held open the door. "I have to find a vase for these. Please, come on in, take off your coat."

"Thanks." I walked in, looked around the living room, pretending that I'd never seen it before.

"You're sweet. Be right back." She darted into the kitchen, calling over her shoulder, "Throw your coat anywhere, have a seat."

Stripping off my jacket, I put it on the large suede chair in the corner, then sank down onto the loveseat. I heard her fumbling around in the kitchen, opening and closing things. Wondered if I should offer to help. Remembered Virginia telling Terri that she liked being busy, so I kept my seat. So what would a good guy do right now?

Gamely, I said, "I like your place."

"Thanks . . . ah, here we go." A cabinet slamming, the sound of running water. More kitchen-comfortable bangs and scrapings, and then Virginia emerged, holding two wineglasses. "Would you like red, or red?"

"I'll take the red." Even if there was another option, I'd have taken the red—it would be the only bright spot in this boring room with its tans and creams. I'd never seen Virginia come in here, not in all the time I'd been watching her. There was nothing physically wrong with the living room, other than being neutral to the point of dullness, but all the same it held the stale feeling of disuse, had an air of malaise. She'd probably insist on coasters so that we didn't ruin the finish on the table. Shame we weren't going to be in the kitchen—that room, at least, was peppered with remnants of activity, of emotion. Of life.

She hovered in the archway between the kitchen and the living room, cradling the glasses to her chest, and I watched as she thought something through, looking at me the whole time with a half smile on her lips. I asked, "Everything okay?"

"You know, I was going to do the wine in here. But then I'd be worried about spilling on the furniture or, God forbid, putting the glasses on the table without a coaster." She wetted her lips, said, "Mind if we just sit in the kitchen and let our hair down?"

Did I push my thought into your mind, Virginia?

Bloody Hell, did my power work on you after all?

Smiling, I said, "I'd like that a lot."

"The key to making tacos," Virginia instructed me, "is to prepare everything ahead of time."

"I'm learning about the importance of prior planning," I said, slicing a red pepper into strips. I had a small pile of vegetables going—peppers, tomatoes, onions, lettuce. That was my job: chopping the vegetables. I'd insisted on helping, just to see if Virginia would cave—I remembered how she'd refused to let Terri lift a finger until it was time to slice the bagels. After a token resistance, she'd handed me a knife and a cutting board. Maybe it was the glass of wine, loosening her up. Maybe it was just me.

It didn't matter, of course . . . but part of me hoped it was the latter.

Virginia dumped grated cheese into a serving bowl. "Once you have all the ingredients ready, all you have to do is brown the beef, heat the shells, add the seasonings, and voilà. Tacos." She smiled at me, crinkling her brow as she cocked her head. "You really never made tacos before?"

"I've led a very deprived life."

"Poor guy. Well, you're doing a wonderful job. Chopping like a pro."

"I know how to handle a knife," I said, smiling.

She tore open a packet and dumped its contents into another bowl: a chunky red sauce that brimmed with spices. "Because you're a spy?"

"That too."

After placing the vegetables onto a serving platter and arranging the taco shells onto a baking tray, she turned on her oven, put ground beef into a large pan, and turned on one of the burners. I was refilling the wine.

"So tell me more about your deprived life," she said, stirring the meat.

"Not much to tell." I handed her the refilled glass. She

looked so damn sexy, stirring spoon in one hand, a glass of wine in the other, her thick hair tied back in a haphazard ponytail at the nape of her neck so she wouldn't get it in the food. "The life of a traveling massage therapist isn't the thing of epic song."

"Have you been anywhere interesting?"

"Albany, New York . . ."

She chuckled, sipped her wine. "No, really. Anywhere . . . I don't know, glamorous?"

"I've been all over," I said sincerely. "Any place in particular?"

"Paris?"

I shrugged. "Overrated." I liked it much better prior to the Belle Époque, back when it was a city of rage over gods and kings, back when it was a city of blood.

"I've heard it's the most romantic city in the world."

"That's the spell of the *Tour Eiffel*, of Montmartre." And of the red-light district in and around Place Pigalle. But I didn't think Virginia would like to hear about the prostitutes and the sex shops. "It's got its ugly side, too, like any city."

"So tell me about some of the beautiful places you've been to."

Sounded like Virginia was a romantic at heart. "You know what's nice? Maui. Nothing like going to Haleakala, going up to the summit and watching the sun rise when you're ten thousand feet in the sky."

"That sounds wonderful."

"What about you? Where's your favorite place?"

"Me? Oh, I don't travel."

"Why?"

"Don't know," she said, shrugging. "Never really wanted to."

Never really wanted to do anything, did you, Virginia? Who are you, really? "So what do you like to do?"

She smiled at me over her shoulder. "Nope. We were talking about you."

"We were?"

"Don the superhero, man of mystery. I don't even know your last name."

I was tempted to say "Juan," just to see her reaction. Instead I replied, "Walker."

"Don Walker, Texas Ranger."

I arched a brow. "Sorry?"

"Old TV show," she said, grinning. "Bad joke."

"Oh, but I'm the one who shouldn't be a comedian?"

"I never said I was quitting my day job to do improv." She stirred, asked lightly, "So, if you travel that much, does this mean you'll be leaving the area soon?"

Ah. Abandonment issues. Smiling, I asked, "Getting rid of me already?"

Her blush was absolutely breathtaking. "Nothing like that, really."

"I'll be around for a while." For the next two days, at any rate. "I'm not planning on leaving anytime soon. And actually . . . I'm thinking about staying."

"That's good to know," she said, a smile playing on her face . . . and a whisper of pumpkin spice wafted from her, tickled my nose.

Yes. *Yes.*

Grinning, I drained my glass.

Soon we were seated at the kitchen table, and she was teaching me the correct way to stuff a taco shell.

"First you have to put in the sour cream," she said, demonstrating with her own shell. "Just a dab, but you spread it on with the spoon. Then the lettuce. Next, the beef, the sauce, and the cheese. Then you sprinkle on the rest of the veggies. And there you have it," she said with a triumphant grin. "A perfectly made beef taco."

"Who knew that eating was such an art form?"

"It's only if you don't want your taco to break when you take your first bite. If you don't do it right, it goes all over the place."

"Not exactly first-date food, huh?"

"This is our second date," she said primly, then giggled. "Third date's lobster."

"Okay, so like this, right?" I made my taco under her watchful gaze, and she nodded her encouragement as I stuffed the shell according to her specifications.

"And now," she said, "the taste test."

"We comparing shells?"

"No, you take a taste, and if the shell doesn't shatter, you pass the test."

"I love a challenge."

We lifted our shells and bit. A mouthwatering mix of foods . . . and a splatter of tortilla and toppings hit my plate.

Laughing, Virginia chewed. After she swallowed, she said, "You may be worldly, Don Walker, but you're no taco connoisseur."

"All too true," I said, enjoying the sight of Virginia at the table, smiling like she couldn't contain her happiness. Tendrils of hair had escaped her makeshift ponytail, and those curls framed her face, threatened to brush her taco. Her cheeks were slightly flushed, either from wine or from amusement, and her shoulders were loose. Relaxed. She was completely unself-conscious for the moment, and she'd never been more gorgeous in the short time that I'd known her.

More wine.

I did better with my second taco; nary a dollop of sauced beef dripped onto my plate. But Virginia didn't fare as well; her plate was still mess-free, but a runner of sauce dripped from the corner of her mouth. Her hands and mouth were full, so I reached over, wiped away the stray juice with the side of my hand.

Let my fingers brush against the outline of her mouth.

Her heartbeat quickened; I heard it, and her surprised gasp, as my touch stayed just a moment too long to be innocent. Eyes wide, she looked at me, her face frozen, her scent a heady mix of arousal and guilt and fear.

I smiled—just a good-guy smile, nothing seductive about it—and took another bite of my taco.

She released a shuddering breath and returned the smile. But as she ate the rest of her food, her bites were smaller. Neater. No messes for me to wipe away.

You want to kiss me, don't you, Virginia?

Gehenna knows, I want to kiss you.

We finished the meal and sat in our seats, sipped more wine. End of the bottle.

"So tell me more about you," I said. "What do you like to do?"

"Me? I'm very boring."

Yes, but you're also a little drunk. And there's a dark world of emotion inside of you, waiting to come out. "Come on. Besides getting stuck in elevators, how do you pass the time?"

"Well . . . I like to read. Watch TV. Listen to classical music. Draw."

"What do you draw?"

"Oh, I don't, not anymore. But I used to do charcoal portraits, some still-life paintings. Have a master's in studio art." She smiled wistfully. "Was a time when I thought I'd make a living as an artist."

"Yeah?"

"But what they don't teach you at school is *how* to actually make a living as an artist." She giggled, tipsy. "Bills to pay. Real life, meet daydream."

"I'd love to see your work."

"Told you, I haven't done anything with it in a while."

"Your old stuff, then."

"Oh, no. I put all that away when . . ." Her voice trailed off, and she took a deep breath. "When Chris died. I packed it all away. Locked it up."

"Why?"

She shook her head, shrugged. "Just couldn't look at it anymore. Couldn't be reminded of possibilities that'd never come to be."

"Virginia." I reached out, touched her hand, and she looked at me with the hint of tears in her eyes. "Art's a gift, like music. It's meant to be shared, to go on long after you've moved on."

She smiled, tight; her eyes betrayed a raw wound that hadn't scarred over, even after two years. "An art lover?"

"Among other things."

"Well, some things are meant to be put away."

"And some," I said, leaning in close, "are meant to be shared." And then I kissed her.

Even with her lips closed, I tasted red wine and spiced meat, smelled her soul nestled among the other aromas of confusion and pain, of desire and guilt. My gigolojo didn't kick in; she had to kiss me first, and kiss me willingly, for that to happen. But I had to kiss her now, show her that she could share that part of herself with me. It was a gentle kiss, a tender meeting of lips. And it ended much too soon.

She pulled away, flustered. "Don't."

"It's just a kiss." My voice was soft; my hand was still on top of hers. "I promise, I won't hurt you." Yet.

"Don." She sighed, looked away from me. "Please. I like you, but . . . I'm just not ready."

"It's okay." I squeezed her hand lightly, smiled. "We said we'd go slow, remember?" And so what if I had a deadline of less than forty-eight hours? Anything could happen in that amount of time.

"I know," she said to the wall. "But I don't think I can do this."

"Do what? We're just talking." Holding hands. For now.

"Be with you."

"Virginia."

"You don't understand. It . . . Losing Chris was hard. So very hard. I just can't go through that again."

"Virginia. I'm not dying on you." Hopefully.

"I know. But I keep feeling like I'm betraying him. When I look at you looking at me like this, when you touch me . . ." She wiggled her hand out of mine. "When you kissed me."

"It's been two years," I said. "You're allowed to have feelings for someone else."

"It's not about what I'm allowed. I can't help how I feel."

"Of course not. But being a widow doesn't mean being a martyr."

She whipped her head around to glare at me. The look of pure venom in her eyes cut me like diamonds. "You don't know anything about what being a widow means."

Shit. "You're right," I said softly. "I'm sorry."

"He was my husband, my best friend. My love." She swallowed, said, "The last fourteen months of my life with Chris were completely dedicated to him, you know? I was with him all day, every day. Taking care of him. Handling the family, who tried to help but wound up exhausting him with their visits, their tears, their anger over him dying. Like it was his fault. They didn't see how much they were hurting him. And God, he was in so much pain."

Like you, Virginia.

I said nothing, implored her with my eyes to go on, get it out—didn't mention how I saw her tightening up, her shoulders braced for battle, her mouth set in a rictus. The way she played with her wedding band, half-pulling, half-petting, as if she both loathed it and loved it.

Now her tears spilled freely down her cheeks, made trails around her mouth. "I saw it in his eyes, in the way he held himself. How he reacted when he thought I wasn't looking. He was in agony."

Ah, doll. Do you hear yourself? Don't you see you're talking about yourself?

"But he never complained. Never." Her eyes flashed, liquid fire. "He fought like hell against it. But he never once asked why him, or cursed at his luck. Not like his family. Not like me." Her breath hitched. "He took it all with good grace. God, that almost killed me," she whispered. "How he never complained."

"It sounds like he was a strong man."

"He was. Oh God, he was. But it didn't matter," she said, voice flat. "He still died."

"Yes. And you've mourned for two years. It's okay to live your life again."

She clasped her ring, twisted it. "I'm sorry. Chris was strong, but I'm not. I can't do this, Don."

Bishop's balls, she was angry at herself for living when her husband was dead. The way she just slept through her life, the way she didn't try to enjoy herself except when her friend Terri, or I, distracted her . . . She was punishing herself. Mortals did stupid shit like that: they blamed themselves for things they couldn't control. Having feelings could really suck. I'm damn glad I don't have any.

"You're stronger than you know, Virginia."

"Uh-huh." Dull. Vacant. She was wilting in front of me, like a flower starving for the sun. I was losing her.

My chest felt too fucking tight.

"You are strong," I insisted. "When we were trapped in an elevator, you didn't panic like me. When we were almost mugged, you didn't run away, even though I told you to."

The tears on her face glistened in the kitchen light, like angel's wings. "That was different."

"No, doll. It's not."

Her lips twitched, but she didn't reply.

"You *are* strong, Virginia," I said again. "But what you're doing now has nothing to do with strength. It has to do with holding on to pain."

"No—"

"If there's one thing I know about, it's pain. Look at you: your neck's practically screaming with tension. You've been rotating your shoulder since you started talking about Chris."

Frowning, she caught herself midshrug, lowered her shoulder. Winced.

"Come on," I said, holding my hand out to her.

She blinked at me, asked, "What?"

"You're hurting. I'm a massage therapist. Let me help you."

"I don't know . . ."

"Clothing on," I said with an easy smile. "And completely professional. Promise."

She worried her bottom lip as she debated, and oh, bloody Hell, how she reminded me of Jezebel.

"I don't think I want a massage. Not . . . you know. Lying down. I can't do that."

"Then just a small neck rub. We'll do it right here in the kitchen," I said.

"Don . . ."

"Trust me."

Virginia swallowed, closed her eyes. After five heartbeats, she whispered, "Okay."

I wanted to whoop for joy. Instead, I said, "Turn around in your chair, so you're facing the back."

She did so, slowly, as if in a daze, drifting in a miasma of wine-fueled emotion. Settling down on the chair, she asked, "What do I do with my arms?"

"Rest them by your sides, hands on your thighs." I stood up, walked behind her. "I'm going to touch you, now. Go with it, doll. Can you do that?"

"Yes . . ."

"Good." I placed my hands lightly on the middle of her back, stayed that way as she took a breath, a second, felt the rhythm of her breathing, felt her life in my hands. Without breaking contact, I slid my hands up toward her shoulders, right next to her neck. Gently squeezing the triangular muscles there, I moved my hands down over her shoulders. Repeated the movement, increasing the pressure as I went.

"Feels nice," she said, voice thick.

"It's supposed to." Placing one hand atop the other, I splayed my fingers wide and moved my hands in slow circles, starting at the top of her neck, working my way down to the top of her right shoulder, back up again. Three more times, and then I moved to her left side, repeating the same small circles, feeling her muscles respond to my touch. I massaged her slowly, deeply, taking my time. This was where she held her pain; I would take all the time in the world to help her set it free.

Her breathing gradually deepened, and now she was rolling her head as I worked, letting out sighs of pleasure.

Oh, Virginia. This is just a hint of the way I could make you feel . . .

I rubbed her neck, my hands swishing back and forth, stroking and lifting the muscles there. Moaning, she *mmmmed* and *ahhhed* as I moved my fingers and thumbs over her, coaxed her body into giving up its tension. Trailing my fingers up, I massaged the nape of her neck, her scalp, making tiny circles as if I were shampooing her hair.

"God, that feels so good . . ."

I smiled, moved my hands back down to rub her neck again. Enjoy this, Virginia. You're allowed to experience pleasure. You deserve it.

Let me be good to you.

With broad strokes, I swept my hands over her shoulders, down her back. And then I broke contact, knelt down by her side. Her eyes were closed, and a lazy smile was on her lips. How I wanted to kiss her again . . ."Feel better?"

"Oh my God, that was amazing," she said, sounding sleepy and content. "Thank you so much."

"Thank you for trusting me."

She opened her eyes then, and looked at me, embarrassed. "Don . . . I'm sorry I freaked out like that . . ."

"You didn't," I said, reaching over to clasp her hand. It was a gesture of friendship, of warmth . . . and it let me put my fingers on her inner thigh. "There's nothing to apologize for."

"Feel like I ruined our night."

"Aw, doll. You didn't. You told me something so very personal. And hey, you taught me how to make and eat a taco."

She smiled, rueful and so damn sexy. Closed her eyes again, sighed. Content. "Tacos for massages? That's a nice barter system."

Yes, but it's not enough. What would move her to the point of expressing her attraction, her desire?

Music.

"Hey," I said, squeezing her hand, "you mentioned you liked classical music, right?"

"Mmm. Yes."

"I have a couple tickets to the Music Festival tomorrow night, at the Center." Or I would, once I went to the Saratoga Civic Center later to work my magic and snag the tickets. "Would you like to go with me?"

"Oh . . ."

If not for the wine and the massage, she might have said no out of reflex. She might have come up with a ready excuse, a quick defense. Might have hidden away in her sheltered world where nothing happened and her life was slowly passing her by. But now she was relaxed, at ease. Pliable. Thinking about my offer.

"Yes. I'd love to."

I didn't realize I was smiling until my cheeks started to hurt. "Terrific."

She laughed. "Have to admit, I didn't take you to be a fan of classical music."

"Oh," I said idly, "I've always had a thing for Mozart."

Chapter 14

Amadè

The Hague, November 1765

The smell alone told me it was his room: it reeked of blood and sickness, of sweat and shit. And the boy, himself, awash in the clinging sweetness of delirium, accented with the orange tang of fear.

I slipped through the oak door. He lay there, in the canopied bed, nearly lost amid the thick patchwork quilt. The dancing light of a single candlestick—planted firmly in a copper stand next to his bed, atop a mahogany bureau—illuminated his round face, the hollows under his eyes, the shadow of his large nose. Fever consumed him, slowly, burning him from within as his own sweat drenched and chilled him without.

"Master Wolfgang."

He thrashed, beat his head against the feather pillow. With a groan, he opened his eyes to look at me.

I knelt at his side, turned down the quilt to his waist. His white bed shirt stuck to his wasted body in clumps. "Such heat, child, does not need the additional help."

"I must sweat out my fever," he said, his voice higher than that of children his age. But his voice held the magic of music, transformed all his words into light and beauty, his voice into a song.

"No, little one. Not unless you wish to meet your Creator that much sooner." Gently, I tugged down his loose shirt to smooth it over his torso, then fluffed his pillow.

He gazed at me with fever-glazed eyes. "Are you an angel, come to take me to God?"

I smiled, caressed his sweating brow. "That is not my designation, Wolfgangerl."

"You know me, sir?"

"Oh, yes. I was with the Prince of Orange two months gone, and heard you perform at Court."

"With Nannerl." He smiled, blissful. "She walked finally, you know. Across the bedroom floor by herself, just today. She's just a week out of bed."

"So I hear."

"I'm so happy that she is better. She suffered so. They bled her. Performed last rites."

"They were a bit early on that mark," I said. "You love your sister."

"I do." He took a wheezing breath, which shuddered through his slight frame. "Where is Papa?"

"He and the doctor are outside, taking the night air. Discussing the great grace of God, and how He has blessed the world with two young prodigies. And other things, perhaps."

"Papa lies," he whispered, his smile serene. "About my age. Says I'm not even eight."

"And that, child, is because humans are fickle in their adoration." I snored my derision. "What was amusing and entertaining when you were seven grows old and dull when you are nine. So say the idiots at Court."

The boy tried to shrug, but his body failed him. A flutter of movement by his right shoulder was all he could manage. I adored him for his effort. "Papa says they are fickle."

I rested my hand on his hot cheek. "They are fools, Wolfgangerl. All of them. Pay them no mind. You are meant for things far grander than their vision could ever perceive."

"You are most kind, sir." His eyelids slipped closed. "I am sorry, but I am so sleepy."

"I understand. It is the sickness, young master. It is eating away at you. Your papa's Grand Tour may end here, in Holland."

He sighed. "Papa will be so sad . . ."

"Oh, indeed."

"You sound like you are making fun."

"I? Why would I make fun of your papa?"

"Truly, I do not know." A flick of his lips, a slight twitch of a smile. "Papa loves me."

"Yes, I see how his love dictates his actions. You are too trusting, young Mozart."

A pause, and then he said, "There is a reason for everything."

"Oh? And what reason is there for your sickness?"

"A test . . ."

I snorted a laugh. "Of course. Your papa pushing you and your sister at a punishing pace that would cripple most adults has nothing to do with it. The fault is God's."

"What God sends . . . must be endured. Papa says."

"So wise, for one so young. And so talented. And so trusting. But for all your wisdom and talent and trust, you know little of human desire. Desire on all its levels." Smiling, I brushed a sweat-slick lock of golden hair away from his eyes. "But then, you're just a boy."

His breathing sounded more labored. The boy was failing, right here, in front of me. No, that cannot happen yet. He cannot die now.

A whisper of power licked over his skin, settled deep within him. Burned away a touch of his illness. His eyes snapped open and he gasped, then he released his breath, sighed. Smiled. "I feel stronger."

"It is temporary." Leaning close, I whispered in his ear, "You are supposed to die, Wolfgangerl. Your darling papa has bartered your soul for fame."

The boy blinked, then turned his head away. The pillow was damp with his perspiration from where his cheek had touched it. "You are wrong, sir." His light voice trembled with passion.

"Am I?" Ah, child, if you were allowed to grow, to channel that passion into your music, you would shake the very world.

"Next after God comes my father."

I laughed softly. "It is the nature of the good to trust, child. Trust in God, trust in your father, trust in the world to appreciate beauty when it is presented with it. But people are as quick to destroy beauty as they are to cut away ugliness. Some people," I said, "are evil."

"I am sick," he said. "You are a devil in my mind."

"You are sick, child, that is true. But I am not here to torture you. If anything, just the opposite."

Rolling his head to face me, he said, "I do not understand."

"When you played all those weeks ago, I was smitten." Just remembering the melodies he had created, the sounds that had ridden in the air, sent a rush of sensation through me—so different from sex, and yet so compelling. Climactic. "Such music, and from a child. You are proof of all that humanity can aspire to. You have a rare gift, young Mozart. One that I would see you keep."

The boy frowned. "What do you mean?"

"I can burn away your sickness, Wolfgangerl. It may return, and then I may choose to burn it away again. I can keep you alive to write your music. Alive to stun the world with the beauty you create. But there is a price."

He licked his dry lips. "What price, sir?"

"You were to go to Envy. A blood sacrifice. An eternity of freezing water, all so that your father could be the only Mozart people remembered." I stroked his face. "But if you were to declare yourself to me, I would mark you. Save you from the water. Make you mine. And you, child, would live a while longer. Long enough to compose such music that would long outlive you. Such music that would make you immortal."

"You want my soul."

I smiled. "What I want, Wolfgangerl, is for you to make music." The soul would be an additional benefit. "It is up to you. You do not have to accept. You do not even have to believe me. Perhaps I am lying."

He stared at me for a long moment before he replied. "What is very funny is that I do believe you." He sighed, mournful. "Papa lies."

"He is human," I said with a shrug. "Some would say it is simply his nature."

"Then the fault is God's. As you said."

"No, child. You said it. I was mocking your father."

"God the Father?"

"As you wish. Tell me, do you accept my offer?"

For a time, he said nothing. I listened to him breathe.

Finally, he said, "Last year, in London, Papa became sick. We moved to Chelsea for him to rest. I finally had time to play. Do you know what I did, sir?"

"Pray tell me."

"I created a symphony, for all the instruments of the orchestra. Especially the kettledrums."

"It must have been magnificent."

"No, I nearly forgot to give the horn anything to do." He sighed. "I do not know what it means to be a boy. All I know is God, and family, and music. And sickness. I am always sick, it seems."

"Yes."

"Tonight, Papa spoke to me of the vanity of the happy death of children. Of the will of God."

"Did you like what he had to say?"

"Not particularly. I don't believe there is any music in Heaven, except for hymns. And those are so boring."

I laughed softly. "Wise beyond your years. Tell me, Master Wolfgang, do you accept my offer?"

"I am sick," he said. "And I am sure I am dreaming." He met my gaze firmly. Determined. "But if you can take away my sickness, if you will let me live to make music, then how can I say no?"

"How indeed?"

"Sir, I accept. I am yours."

I pressed my lips to his clammy brow, kissed him.

Marked him.

None from Envy would touch him now, not unless they wished to declare a war of Sin. And although the Envious were jealous by their nature, they would not choose to act upon that jealousy. The boy was mine.

And his music would belong to the world.

"You have made me very happy, young Mozart. Close your eyes, child, and sleep. While you dream, I will burn away your disease."

I ran my finger over his forehead. His eyelids fluttered, closed. Before slumber took him, he whispered, "Who are you, sir?"

Smiling, I said, "Man proposes, God disposes . . . but a devil takes his due."

Vienna, July 1773

I smelled him before he arrived—the exhilarating aroma of ginger and cloves, of peppermint and rosemary. And something else, this time: the lemon scent of anticipation. He was looking forward to seeing me today far more than ever before.

Boom *boom*.

With a lazy grin, I sprawled on the narrow bed, stretched my form long, languid, just before he entered the room in a rush. His cheeks were flushed from exertion, and his lips were an enticing rose. Such beautiful lips. Expressive. Like his music.

Closing the door behind him, he smiled at me. "My lord, I do apologize for the delay. My father has been watching me like a hawk."

"I am used to waiting." I smiled my understanding, let my gaze crawl over him, caress him. He had filled out somewhat since we had last met, six months gone, though the full-sleeved shirt he wore did little to hide his narrow frame. His sleeveless waistcoat hung low, the hem dangling mid-thigh, but I saw how baggy his breeches were beneath it. I could not tell if that was by design or from lack of food. My own breeches fit quite snugly and, thanks to my own cutaway coat, revealed just how excited I was to see him.

"You are not eating enough," I chided. "You need to keep up your strength."

"I eat, I eat." Laughing, he stripped off his waistcoat, revealing how sorry a thing was his linen shirt—plain, and thin, it looked as if it would fall to pieces with the slightest touch. Delicate, like he was. He dropped the clothing to the floor, kicked off his leather shoes. "When I remember, I eat."

"Look, your stockings sag by your ankles. You're too thin."

"My lord, I already have a mother."

"And is that who you wish me to be today?" I asked, smiling toothily.

"I wish you to be you. My savior," he said, reverent. "My lord."

"Come," I said, opening my arms to him, "and give your lord a kiss."

He leapt into my embrace, sealed his mouth against mine. Wrapping my arms around him, I devoured his kiss, tasted the flowers and spices that were his soul.

My Wolfgang.

Pulling away to draw in a breath, he said, "I've missed you so." Planted tiny kisses on my cheeks, my nose.

"I know. And I, you." I untied the black ribbon that had clubbed his hair at the nape of his neck, ran my fingers through the fine golden-red tendrils. "How much time do we have before your darling papa misses you as well?"

"Forever and a day. He is at the house of Herr von Mesmer, stealing jealous looks at his glass instrument."

"Oh?" I asked, arching a brow. "I had thought your father's tastes lay with a different sort of pipe." For emphasis, I reached down and squeezed his own instrument, which tented the front of his ill-fitting breeches.

He laughed, high-pitched, childlike. Musical. "No, my lord. Not that. I speak of the harmonica."

"And I speak of time." I kissed his jaw, his neck, stroked him against the rough wool of his clothing. "How much?"

"Enough, Lord," he panted, rubbing against my hand. "Oh God, how I've missed you. How I love you."

"Show me."

His tongue attacked me with passion; his lips bruised me with adoration. His fingers, so long and dexterous, able to tease such unearthly melodies from mortal violins, now played over my chest, plucked at the curls nestled there as if they were strings.

As he explored my body, I tangled my hands in his fine hair, touched him far more intimately with a whisper of my power—just a soft *push*, and soon his body was moving next to mine, undulating in a fluid beat of desire. *Legato.* Every note of pleasure that rang from the lips of the young maestro was a song, *espressivo.*

"My lord," he groaned. "I need more time."

Ritardando, lento. "Is this better?"

"No, Lord, not that. I . . ." He stilled. *Fermata.*

I waited.

A burst of lemon, of orange. He licked his lips, said, "A few more years. Please."

Sighing, I stroked his soft hair. "My Wolfgang. I've told you before, my influence is greatly limited in that regard."

"I feel it in me again, my lord. Creeping through me, insidious. Dark. And so hungry." He shivered against me, so I held him until his quakes subsided, traced lines along his back. "It has teeth, my lord. Please," he whispered against my chest. "More time."

"My magicks can destroy only so much of your disease before it returns."

"Please."

"Even if I were to burn off this latest threat, it would only retaliate in what, a matter of months? Weeks?" My heart felt heavy. Such a loss for the world. For me. "You are dying, young Mozart. Again."

"I know, Lord."

"You've done so much with your borrowed time. Sonatas. Arias. Symphonies. Concertos. And the operas! *Mitridate, Rè di Ponto . . . Ascanio in Alba. Lucio Silla.*"

"That last was not so well received, my lord."

"Not to the extent of *Exsultate, jubilate*, no. But I admit a particular fondness for the operas." Smiling as I heard the overture to *Lucio Silla* in my mind, I stroked his back. "Perhaps it is finally time for your soul to be freed from its mortal shell."

He stiffened in my arms. "Please, Lord. No."

"Do not fear, Wolfgang. I will be with you until the end, with you until judgment. And your work will live on, for all time."

"I don't fear death, Lord."

A lie, that, but understandable. Mortals feared what they didn't understand.

His voice beseeching, he said, "But there's so much music left in me yet. I just need more time to learn how to express it, how to transpose it from my head to paper. Make it real."

I reached up to clasp his chin, tilted his face so that I could look deeply into his eyes. "Truly?"

"Yes, Lord. Even now I hear the sounds of an opera—*your* opera," he said, inspired. "My work has all been for you, but I have not yet given you something in return for my extra years. I will write you an opera."

"What are you saying, Wolfgang?"

"Give me more life yet, and I'll write you an opera like none has ever heard before. Dark and passionate, yes . . . and unrepentant." His eyes flashed, and I could almost hear music reverberating in his mind as he thought aloud: "Basso, maybe, even a baritone, but certainly not a tenor, not for him. A nobleman, of course. A libertine, who lives for love. Who will not change his nature, no matter that he would wind up in Hell."

"My Wolfgang," I whispered. "You would do this thing for me?"

He blinked away visions of the orchestra, focused on me. Smiled, *dolce*. "I am ashamed I have not offered it sooner. Yes, my lord, I will write your opera."

No one had ever given me such a gift. Sacrifices, yes. Offerings of virginity, of course. But music? For me? This was flattery at its finest.

It was intoxicating.

"Then you will have the time you need," I declared, "and then some."

"Oh, my lord, my lord," he cried, peppering my face with wet kisses. "Thank you!"

And then, desire. Our bodies, our voices, transformed into music—melody and harmony, twining, blending, *istesso tempo*. Faster now, *accelerando*. *Vivace* as he lost himself to the sensation of fleshly symphony. A triumphant *sforzando*.

And, at last, *fine*.

Lying together, our hands entwined, the maestro murmured, "I have never yet asked your name, my lord."

I smiled, already wondering what my opera would sound like. "I? I am Don Juan."

Chapter 15

When Sins Collide

"That was magnificent," Virginia said, eyes lit with passion. Her hand was clasped in mine as we walked out of the main auditorium to the lobby. "So powerful. Passionate. Utterly breathtaking."

Like her. Virginia had dolled up for the performance, forgoing her baggy shrouds for a formfitting cocktail dress. Cut low enough to emphasize her twin assets, and with a hem high enough to reveal more than a glimpse of thigh, the black velvet wrapped around her enticingly, seductively. Simple without being plain; elegant without being extravagant. She'd coiled her hair into a tight twist, but some of her curls had already fought their way free. Sooty lashes framed green eyes sparkling with delight; wine-colored lips curved into a contented smile.

She was easily the most gorgeous woman in the room.

"Mozart is definitely passionate," I said. "And prolific. And practical. He wrote the Twenty-second Piano Concerto four days after completing a sonata."

"So fast?"

"Vienna in the late eighteenth century was very Catholic, which means the theatres were closed during Advent and Lent. So the bored Viennese attended more concerts."

"So that's what people did before television . . ."

Heh. "Composers like Mozart wrote as many new pieces as they could, added them to their performances of favorites."

"You know so much about him."

"Told you, I'm a fan of his. This piece was a huge hit, almost from the very beginning. It was supposed to be an *intermezzo*, an intermission piece, but the audience loved it so much that he performed the andante as an encore."

Virginia laughed, shook her head. "You are a fascinating man, Don Walker. Do all superheroes know as much about classical music?"

"Only the extremely intelligent ones."

"That's good to know. Holy God, is that the line to the ladies' room? Ugh." She squeezed my hand, said, "If I'm not back in my seat before the next performance, send in a search party." Then she shrugged out of my grip and headed toward the long line of women.

I watched her walk, enjoyed the roll of her hips, the way the hem of her dress swished around her thighs. Her black heels were simple, almost plain, but they called attention to her full calves, her delicate ankles—transformed her walk into a seductive, swaying motion.

If you don't kiss me tonight, Virginia, I may combust from desire. Death by blue balls . . .

A scent of lilacs rimmed with frost.

Smiling lazily, I turned to face the cherub, swathed again in a Sky-white evening gown. Wondered how she'd look in red. Certainly not as untouchable as she appeared now: the haughty set to her mouth; the complex weave of her sun-kissed hair, which would have taken a mortal woman the better part of three days to mimic; the glacial look in her celestial baby blues. But her lithe body, even draped in pure white, was exquisite. "Feathers. What're you doing here? Shouldn't you be on line still, filing your first soul claim?"

"My lord, I bring you news."

"Oh?" I wrapped an arm over her shoulder, started walking us to a less-crowded part of the lobby. She accompanied me with a stiff gait, a tense back. Pitching my voice out of the human range of hearing, I said, "Do tell."

"I've been hearing things, Lord. Below. Horrific things."

"Sweetness, you work for Hell now. The water cooler chat isn't exactly about fluffy bunnies and babies' laughter."

"This is different." Looking at the floor, she said, "I think there's a price on your head."

Couldn't help it: I snorted. "Really."

She stopped walking, planted her feet on the floor. I released her, pivoted so that she was in front of me. Shoved my hands into my jacket pockets. Waited. Smiled at her discomfort. She might be beautiful, but she was still proud enough to turn the Arrogant into creatures of Envy. I couldn't say that I hated her—she wasn't worth such an investment of passion—but I admit that I liked getting under her skin.

And damn, how I'd love to get her under me, turn that haughtiness into heat. I remembered the sound of her groans as I'd suckled her. Teased her. Showed her how good I could make her feel . . .

I could make such a succubus out of you.

Her voice soft, she said, "You do not have to mock me, Lord."

"No," I agreed. "But it's so easy to do."

She slowly lifted her head and met my gaze. Her porcelain skin was clear, coldly perfect, except for a hint of pink on her cheeks. I'd pissed her off. Heh. She sniffed, and I grinned at that sound of contempt. "Truth hurt, Feathers?"

"Perhaps I shouldn't have come." Clipped. Angry.

"But you did."

Her lip trembled. "A mistake. One I won't repeat."

"Okay," I said, chuckling. "Okay. Don't go changing your helpful nature on account of me. Tell me, what've you been hearing?"

She lifted her chin, frowned her disdain. Such arrogance—so common to her kind. "Perhaps I should leave you to determine the truth of my words."

"Aw, don't get a halo up your ass."

"Charming, my lord."

I was having altogether too much fun with her. "Come on, sweetness. Tell me. I won't tease you."

"You're lying."

"But only a little."

I watched her internal struggle play out in her eyes, smiled as I waited. Whistled the andante to the Twenty-second Piano Concerto. Saw a handful of men, and a few women, check out the angel as she deliberated. Grinned over how oblivious she was. Her new role was as ill-fitting on her as mortality was on Jezebel.

Like an angel among the demons.

My breath caught as I heard my own voice, remembered touching Jezebel's soul—

. . . *such beauty unholy Hell such grace and power and damn me the light and*—

A stabbing pain, squarely between my eyes. Grunting, I pinched the bridge of my nose, rubbed. Fuck me, that hurt.

"My lord? Are you unwell?"

Blinking, I looked up to see the cherub frowning at me, her ice-blue eyes melting, overflowing with concern.

You really can't help yourself, can you, Feathers? No matter if you pluck the angel from the Sky and put her in the Pit, she's still an envoy of Heaven. "It must really suck to be you," I said, wondering how she hadn't lost her mind among the damned and the demons, how she was able to hold on to herself as she played the role she'd been assigned.

Her eyes narrowed. "Excuse me? Are you insulting me, Lord?"

Like Virginia, she was stronger than she knew. Poor angel, with your clipped wings—feathers singe so easily. They smell like ashes when they burn.

"My lord?" She tilted her head, regarded me closely. What are you looking for, angel? "You don't look well."

"I'm fine," I said, my voice ringing hollow in my ears. I sounded like I'd gotten hit by a truck. Twice. "Just have a headache."

Her frown deepened. "The infernal cannot get such mortal anomalies."

"When we wear mortal shells, we can." The discomfort had receded almost as quickly as it had come, but it echoed in my head. Remembered hurts, phantom pains.

"I am sorry to cause you such distress," she said.

"It wasn't you. It's . . ." My voice trailed off, and I frowned. Damn me, what in Hell had I been thinking about?

"My lord?" The angel's voice was a breathy whisper. "What is it?"

"Nothing," I said again, feeling cold. Feeling uneasy. *Feeling*.

Why was I feeling anything? Demons don't feel. We don't have emotions, not in the mortal sense. So I couldn't be experiencing a growing sense of dread, of nagging certainty that I wasn't seeing something, something important.

Except I was. No matter how much demons lie to humans, we can't lie to ourselves. I was feeling, fuck me raw, I was *feeling*: this pressure in my chest, this tightness in my throat, the staccato thumping of my heart.

I was afraid.

But not for my own survival; over my thousands of years in the Pit, I'd come to recognize that response well. This feeling had nothing to do with me, even with my faulty memory and my sudden headache, with my assignment and the consequences of failure. With the so-called price on my head.

I was afraid, yes . . . but for someone else.

An image flashed, one of emerald eyes sparkling with mirth, of curly black hair that hated to be tamed with a brush—or tied back in a haphazard ponytail.

No.

I clenched my teeth, growled. I'm a demon. I don't have feelings for others, be they human or infernal or neither. I *don't*. What I felt was nothing.

"Lord Daunuan?"

"It's nothing," I snarled. "Nothing." It had to be a physical reaction to the stress I was under. Constantly being on edge, looking to see if any nefarious were in the area, angling to get Virginia to kiss me willingly.

Thinking of Jezebel with her prude apostle, pretending she was in love.

"My lord? Your fist . . ."

I looked down, saw that I'd made a fist . . . and that my power was emanating from it in a cocoon of energy, crackling red, humming with the potential for destruction.

Shit.

Taking a deep breath, I dissipated the magic, shook out my hand until it was just a human hand, with no hints of other-worldly power radiating from it.

I needed a fucking vacation.

"I'm probably mistaken," the angel said quietly. "Or maybe they were speaking of another incubus."

Meeting her troubled gaze, I said, "Tell me. What did they say?"

"There's not much to tell, truly. When I was on line to file the claim . . ." Her face crinkled with consternation. "Ah, thank you for that, Lord . . ."

"It's nothing," I said.

She stared at me, those unreadable blue eyes searching for something that I couldn't give her, seeking something I couldn't understand.

With a shrug that showed how little the whole thing mattered, I said, "That particular client wouldn't shut up. Dumping her on you made it easier on me."

"Of course," she replied, nodding, her gaze so cold and yet so full of warmth. How beautiful she'd look when that gaze was laden with passion, with lust . . . She cleared her throat. "On line to file the claim, I heard others talking about . . . well, about the King of Lust's new favorite. And about what they would do if they found him before the elite. About how they'd use the boon."

Boon?

Only the Kings could grant a boon. Did one of the Kings of Sin or Land set a bounty on me? Was it against me personally, or a way of testing Pan's mettle as ruler of Lust?

YOU SHOULD KNOW, LIBERTINE, THAT GLUTTONY

WILL NOT PARTICIPATE, Belzebul had said. *AND NEITHER WILL SLOTH.*

Which one had set me up?

"Such horrible things they said." The angel rubbed her arms. "My lord, Hell is coming after you."

"Probably nothing so dramatic," I said, tapping my chin. "Which demons said what specifically?"

"I'm not sure, Lord. All the nefarious look alike to me."

"Cute."

"It is not meant as such."

"Even cuter. So tell me, Feathers," I said, eying her, "why'd you give me the heads-up?"

Her lips twitched—a sign of amusement? From her? Wonders would never cease. "Never let it be said that I never did anything for you. Clean slate, my lord."

The memory of Belzebul's words echoed in my mind, hungry and insatiable: *YOU OWE ME ONE, DAUNUAN, CHOSEN OF PAN.*

"You're learning, cherub."

"I'm trying, Lord."

With an angelic smile, she blinked out, leaving behind the tantalizing smell of winter lilacs.

In retrospect, the thing that really pissed me off was that I didn't sense the attack coming. Sure, I was occupied with thoughts of whether Virginia was going to do more than plant another chaste kiss on my cheek, but really, that was no excuse.

But damn, what a kiss—buffeted by the cold nighttime air so that her tendrils of hair whipped my face in a dominatrix's sign of affection, with the rest of the concert crowd milling around or near us as we left the Center and ambled through Saratoga Park to take the long way to get to the lot where my (borrowed) car was parked, just this: Virginia rising on her tiptoes, brushing her mouth against my cheek.

That moment, frozen forever in my mind, etched into my

heart—Virginia setting my blood on fire with that small move-ment of her lips, with that imprint of her mouth on my skin.

"Thank you," she'd said.

Just that, and the kiss—so innocent, so completely guile-less. So utterly tantalizing.

"Anytime." I'd squeezed her hand and grinned at her, felt almost drunk with anticipation. Other people strolled near us, maybe headed toward the same public lot, maybe headed else-where, but I hardly noticed them. Who cared about anyone else? Tonight would be the night. We'd go back to her place, and I'd hold her close and touch her face, tell her how much she meant to me, how she was the only good thing in my life, how she's tamed my inner demon . . . And then she'd look up at me with those soulful green eyes, and she'd smile, flattered and excited and more than a little aroused . . . And then she'd tilt her face up to mine and—

And it was right then, as I was vividly imagining the taste of jasmine and chocolate on my tongue, as we walked across a grassy lane, that my head screamed in warning. No buzz of an-ticipation, this; no subtle hint of wrongness. An urgent screech, insistent, overwhelming.

I barely had time to throw myself over Virginia and knock us to the ground before the bolt of energy sliced over us.

Virginia cried out beneath me, but I refused to let her go. Pinned, I knew where she was, even if she had her face pressed against the dirt and grass. I sensed the other humans around us, but I couldn't spare them my attention—could barely think because of Virginia, squirming beneath me, drenched in the citrus scent of stark terror, sending a fuck-me-now signal right to my brain, even with the threat of imminent destruction looming over us.

At times, being a creature of Lust had its disadvantages.

Over the sound of Virginia's frantic heartbeat, of her ragged breathing: a chortle of laughter.

I looked over my shoulder to see a giant of a man in a tuxedo grinning at me, a ball of power illuminating his left hand. His eyes gleamed gold, which marked him as a Coveter . . . And based on how I hadn't sensed him at all, he had to be one of the elite.

"Slippery, aren't you?" He took aim. "Probably from all the scented oil."

Shit.

I gestured behind me, coaxed the earth to rise up in a knoll between us. A moment later, the Coveter's magic struck, spraying chunks of dirt and roots everywhere.

"Don!" Beneath me, Virginia struggled. "My God, what's happening?"

Ignoring her, I shouted to the demon: "You can't do this— there are innocents here!"

"You mean the humans?" His grin broadened. "I summoned them, rake. They're here at my request. Such greedy things. They do so like shiny objects," he said, his golden eyes sparkling hypnotically, brighter than the street lamps illuminating the grassy path.

I risked a glance around, saw about twenty people standing in a loose circle around us, their faces blank, empty. Shit, shit, shit. Just because he was using his power didn't mean I could without consequence; if any mortal died by my hand, I'd have to fill out mounds of paperwork. Not to mention that Virginia would never understand self-defense that involved infernal magic. I was betting that was big on her list of turnoffs.

"Don, he's crazy," Virginia said, frantic.

Grimacing, I tried to think of a way to get Virginia out of here, ideally without her any the wiser of what was really happening. "You can't attack me here, like this," I called out. "The Kings will have your hide."

"Big talk for a little rake. But you're right." His power winked out, and he folded his arms across his chest. "I don't need to take you down personally. Not when I have my devoted followers all too ready to lay down their lives for the cause."

Virginia's breath tickled my neck as she twisted beneath me. "Don, what's going on? Do you know him?"

"Shhh. Don't speak. As soon as you can, run. Don't stop for me."

"I'm not leaving you here with a crazy man with a gun!"

A gun that shoots magic laser beams. "Don't argue, doll." To the Coveter I called, "There's an innocent here."

"A pretty one too," he said. "Wonder if there's any hint of greed in her soul."

"*Innocent*, chuckles. Maybe you should invest in a hearing aid."

"Maybe you should consider begging."

As if. "Let her go, or there'll be Hell to pay."

"Oh, Seducer, you're so droll. Who do you think had me come after you? But you're right. No need to get my hands dirty." Eyes gleaming like golden stars, he said, "Kill the man. If the woman interferes, kill her too."

As one, the humans surged forward.

Fuck.

I hissed in Virginia's ear: "Run!"

She might have said something, but I tuned her out as I scrambled up and lunged at the nearest person, a man in his late forties—out of shape, stuffed into an expensive suit. He swung at me, a pitiful blow that I ducked under. Grabbing his arm, I propelled him into three more people who were in a tight cluster and approaching fast. Annnnd . . . strike!

An arm hooked around my neck, pulled.

Grunting, I doubled over, flipped the person over my back. He flew over me, crashed in a heap. A quick kick to the head, and he was down for the count.

A sound like whistling, over my head.

I ducked, watched a rock bean another person in the chin. Spinning on my heel, I saw Virginia let loose with another large rock, this one smacking another person in the chest. Then a teenaged girl tried to scratch my eyes out, so I stopped gaping at the woman I'd been desperate to save.

"Told you to run," I shouted, shoving the girl into two more attackers.

"If you think I'm leaving you, you're as crazy as the crazy guy."

I turned Virginia's way again, watched her scrabble for more ammunition, narrowly avoiding a bear of a man as she scooped up earthly debris. "Now is not the time to show me how strong you are, doll!"

Pitching rocks, she said, "Don't call me doll!"

I didn't know if I was impressed or frustrated.

My head rocked back before I felt the actual punch on my jaw. Ow. I staggered backward, barely blocked a second hit. Felt that connection jolt up my arm. Guy in front of me knew how to fight. Rabbit punch to my gut, and suddenly I was doubled over.

Fuck this.

Tapping into my power, I slammed my fist into his jaw in a magically augmented uppercut. The guy went down, ate dirt. Two more people were on me before I could take a breath.

A woman's cry—Virginia.

Snarling, I lashed out with my power; no time for subtlety. Blasting my way through the human obstacles, I leapt to Virginia's side, shoved my fist into her assailant's nose. Crunch. Would have taken down anyone not zombified by infernal charm. Blood gushed from the ruins of his nose, must have made it hard for him to breathe, but he didn't stop, didn't even blink as he reached for me. A side kick to the groin took him out.

I grabbed Virginia by her shoulders, rougher than I'd intended. "He hurt you?"

"I'm fine," she said, but her breathing and her posture told me she was lying.

"Get out of here, call the police!"

"Not leaving you." Her tone brooked no argument; her eyes screamed fury.

More bespelled humans approached, some carrying makeshift weapons of tree limbs and rocks, others had stripped off their ties, their belts, came at us intent on choking the breath from our bodies.

I couldn't fight the humans and the Coveter while protecting Virginia.

"Please," I said, "run."

"No."

No time.

I released one of her shoulders to point toward the flood of mortals surging toward us. Aiming high, I cut loose with a flash of light. It cut through the dazzle from the Coveter, stopped them in their tracks, befuddled and blinking. The demon snarled curses, threw his power over the handful of mortals.

"Don," Virginia breathed.

We had maybe ten seconds before his magic took effect. Couldn't teleport out of the park with Virginia in tow; mortal bodies couldn't survive shifting between planes. We were trapped.

She whispered, "What did you—"

"Shhh." I touched her face, saw how wide her eyes were, glassy with confusion, with fear. "It's okay," I said, stroking her cheek. I had to keep her safe. "It's just a dream, Virginia. Go back to sleep."

Her mouth opened, the protest already forming, but I bathed her in my power, dragged my finger across her brow and told her once again: *Go to sleep.*

She crumpled in my arms, unconscious.

I lowered her to the ground, set her down gently. I didn't know how long she'd be under the influence of my magic— bloody Hell, she shouldn't be affected at all. But as long as she slept, I wouldn't have to worry about her safety. Touching her brow, I made her a silent promise that it would be okay.

And then I turned to face the onslaught.

They lurched forward—weapons in hand, or making weapons of their hands—their faces wiped clean of emotion, of thought. Nine men and women about to either kill me or die themselves, and they'd do either one without pause.

Summoning my power, I let it fill me until I must have glowed as brightly as the Coveter's eyes. I could have vaporized the humans, but because they weren't in their right minds, Hell would consider their demises wrongful. Which meant enough paperwork to tie me up until the turn of the next century.

Think, Daunuan. They're evil. You're a demon.

Influence them.

I released my magic in a wave, let it crash over them and pull them under, drowned them in lust. The Coveter screamed his rage, hit them again with his own power, demanding they bow to their greed. Caught between us, the humans rocked back, swayed from the torrent of two sins warring over their souls. One of them collapsed from the strain, her body jittering on the ground. No matter—they were flesh puppets, nothing more than toys.

And by Gehenna, I refused to share with a Greedy bastard like the Coveter.

Wincing from the effort, I summoned more infernal energy, more than I'd ever been able to handle before. I wasn't a second-level incubus, hovering just north of the elite; I was elite, first level, on par with the dukes and barons of the King's Court. A principal, soon to be Prince of Lust.

Second only to the great god Pan.

Power filled me, consumed me, ravaged my form and fucked me. My lips peeled back in a snarl, my teeth clenched from the pain, I channeled that power into the mortals. Grinned as I felt it seep into their bodies, seduce their minds.

The Coveter bellowed as he threw more magic over the people . . . and let out a strangled cry as I took that magic, altered its very essence until it, too, was lust. For what is greed if not lust for physical objects?

"You're mine," I whispered.

The humans fell upon one another with tongues and fingers and mouths—touching, groping, grunting like animals. Growling with passion.

I didn't realize I was on my knees until I tried to take a step forward. Fuck, no, that wouldn't do. But when I tried to stand, nausea rolled in my stomach. Blinking away black flecks—flecks that looked like the bits of food stuck between Belzebul's teeth—I commanded myself not to throw up. Maybe I'd overdone it with my display of power. My heart pounded in my chest, the sound filling my ears, my head.

From somewhere beyond my range of vision, the Coveter hissed, "Think you can steal from me, rake?"

"Finders keepers, chuckles." Sheer stubbornness kept me upright. That, and certain knowledge that if I collapsed, I'd never get up again.

Okay, so, overriding sin in a human wasn't as easy as it sounded. And doing it in nine humans simultaneously sort of took the oomph out of an entity. Duly noted.

Around us, the mortals fornicated. Sort of like Woodstock, minus the drugs and rock 'n' roll.

"I'm going to gut you," the demon hissed.

"No guts, no glory."

He stepped out of the darkness, his fists lit with infernal flame. "I'm going to bring him your head on a silver platter."

I wanted to ask, "Him who?" But I was too busy gaping at Eris, who'd appeared behind the Coveter—Eris with her broadsword, the blade gleaming as wickedly as the Coveter's eyes. She hefted it and swung, hit home.

The demon's head flew from his body, ichor and blood fountaining from his severed neck. It landed on the ground and rolled like a ball, coming to rest by three of the rutting humans. They didn't notice.

"Princess," I said with a tired smile. "Fancy meeting you here."

"Just spreading dissention," she said. "Coveters. *Pah!*" She spat on the decapitated body.

Good—if she saw this as an opportunity to take out one of her enemies, then I didn't owe her anything for helping me. That was my story, and I was sticking with it. Watching her through hooded eyes, I rested, let my body build up its strength. I didn't relax, though; Eris's sword would slice through me as easily as it had the Greedy. If she approached with the weapon in hand, I'd fight.

Well, I'd sweet-talk her. And if I had to, I'd fight. "What brings you here, Lady Envy?"

"Business. And, as it turned out, a bit of pleasure on the side." She toed the dead body, then glanced at the small orgy. "A little night music, eh?"

"Complete with magic flutes."

"Hmm." She spied Virginia, still fast asleep. "Poor thing's all tuckered out, isn't she?"

"I have that effect on women."

"So I've heard." Eris smiled, the bitterness pulling her lips into a sneer. "Why, Lord Libertine, you seem to have set your sights on the unattainable. A good girl for one such as you?"

"It passes the time."

"What an interesting hobby. Is that your mark on her?"

I shrugged. "If I don't write my name on my things, someone might try to steal my toys."

"I understand completely."

"Well then." I forced myself to stand, was pleasantly surprised to find I wasn't as depleted as I'd thought. If this was a perk of being elite, sign me up. I'd happily keep on ticking to take a licking. "Time for me to take my things and go."

Eris smirked at Virginia, then cast me a very knowing look. "When you tire of spending your efforts on one like her, give me a call. Perhaps I can alleviate any . . . frustration."

"Lady Envy, coming from you, that's quite the offer."

"Hard to be jealous over something like that," she said, motioning to Virginia. "Not a scrap of evil in her soul. You're wasting your time."

"It's mine to waste."

"You know what they say, Lord Libertine." She grinned, her jade eyes glinting. "Waste not, want not."

With that, she disappeared.

Chapter 16

Lies

"We're home, Virginia."

In the passenger seat, she kept sleeping. Either she'd been tired before I'd put her to sleep, or maybe my power had just been that strong. No complaints here; it had made it that much easier on me to just scoop her into my arms at the park, turn on my infernal "ignore me" signal, and carry her to my borrowed car.

Turning off the engine, I stepped out of the vehicle, went around to her side. Opened her door. Smiled as I watched her sleep. So peaceful, Virginia. Are you dreaming of me? I could have discovered that for myself, but I found I didn't want to invade her mind. Let her have her privacy; once she kissed me, all she'd think about would be me.

I could wait. For a little while longer, I could wait.

Lifting her up, I cradled her to my chest. Her weight felt good in my arms. She felt good—so soft, so comfortable. I could have carried her to the rim of Creation and back. I could carry her forever.

Shutting the car door with a kick, I carried her like a bride up her porch steps, used my power to unlock her front door.

Her cheek pressed against my shoulder as I held her. I breathed her in, from the floral scent of her shampoo to the faintest tang of sweat, down to the chocolate and musk, the jasmine and blackberries of her soul. Her hair tickled my nose.

Infuriating woman, staying in the park like that, when she should have run. Choosing to help me fight. Throwing rocks as if she had the skill of David with his slingshot. Refusing to leave me, scolding me for calling her "doll."

My Virginia.

I walked us through her dark living room, down the hallway and into her bedroom, where I sat her down on her bed to peel off her coat. She didn't wake. Laying her down gently on top of her comforter, I smoothed her hair away from her face. Her twist still fastened most of her tresses, but those curls that had pulled free were wild and messy. Untamable. And so very soft around my fingers.

Soft like her cheek, which I felt now as I ran my hand down the side of her face. Soft like her lips, which I traced so very lightly with my thumb.

"Virginia," I said, my voice as soft as her skin. "We're home."

When she didn't respond, I leaned over, brushed my lips against her cheek. Just returning her kiss from before, a hint of what was to come. I smiled against her face as I remembered her spontaneous kiss, so chaste yet so full of promise, remembered the feeling of my blood catching fire.

With a sigh, I pulled away. Saw Virginia looking at me, her big green eyes sleepy, dazed. But not afraid, no, not afraid.

"Don . . ."

"You fell asleep on the way home," I said, touching her hand. "Sorry, I shouldn't have woken you."

"I had the strangest dream."

"What was it?"

"You were there. With me." She smiled—oh, such a magnificent smile—and closed her eyes again. "You were a magician."

"But not a superhero?"

"You were that too." Her eyes opened, and her brow crinkled as she looked at me. "It felt so real."

"In your dream," I said, holding her hand, "did I get the girl?"

She laughed softly. "Woman."

"Woman," I repeated, smiling.

"You woke me up before that part of the dream."

Moving my thumb in small circles over her palm, I asked, "So, in the rest of the dream, what do you think happens next?"

A pause.

"I'm not sure," she said faintly.

"What would you like to happen?"

Her lip trembled. "Don . . . I can't."

"Can't what?"

"You know."

"Why?"

"It . . ." She blew out a sigh, turned her head away. "It feels like I'm cheating on him."

Oh, Virginia.

"You're allowed to enjoy yourself," I said.

"You don't understand . . ."

"I think I do."

"I love him."

Jezebel whispered, *I love him, Daun.*

"Your heart belongs to him," I said—either to Jezebel or to Virginia. It didn't matter. "But for tonight, for right now, can your body belong to me?"

"Don . . ."

The pleading in her voice made me shove away all thoughts of Jezebel. Tonight wasn't about Jezebel at all. Tonight was about the woman here before me, lying on her bed. "You don't have to be scared, Virginia. All I want to do is make you feel good. A massage," I said, "but not just on your back."

Her face was as blank as the Coveter's bespelled prey.

"All you have to do is say no," I said, "and I won't touch you."

I heard her heartbeat flutter in her chest, fast as a hummingbird's wings. Smelled her fear, her guilt. Her desire. "I don't know . . ."

"You'll be in control, Virginia." I increased the pressure of my thumb on her palm, just a little, and made the circular pattern a little bigger. "I'll touch you, I'll shower you with touches, and if you want me to stop, I promise I'll stop."

She swallowed thickly, said nothing. How I wanted to kiss her throat, feel her pulse between my lips . . .

No. This wasn't about what I wanted, what I needed. I had to convince her that it was okay for her to feel pleasure. That it was okay for her to still be alive, even though her husband was gone.

That it was okay to want, and to be wanted.

"Virginia? Will you let me please you? Will you let me make you feel good?"

"I . . . I don't think I could . . . you know. With you."

"You don't have to," I said softly, firmly. "I don't want you to. Tonight, I want it to be all for you. I don't want anything in return. Just the sound of you enjoying my touches. That's all."

And I meant it. I didn't want her to kiss me tonight, didn't want my gigolojo to kick in and wipe away her inhibitions. I wanted her to be in control, wanted to bring her to the breaking point because she let me.

I wanted her to orgasm because she trusted me, not because of my magic.

Tears shone in her eyes, and her lip trembled. But she didn't tell me no.

"Virginia," I said, my voice gentle, "may I touch you?"

She squeezed her eyes shut, and the tears seeped between her lids. I reached over, brushed away her fear, her sorrow.

Her voice a whisper, she asked, "You'll stop? If I tell you to, you'll stop?"

"I swear it."

Taking a hitching breath, she said, "Yes."

Yes.

For a moment that could have been an eternity, I just looked at her, at how her body lay upon the cover, the rise and fall of her chest as she breathed—so nervous, so skittish. Her cocktail dress outlined her form, black on black in the dark of the room. I ran my gaze over her body, from the curve of her shoulders to the large swells of her breasts, from the plump form of her arms to the rounded shape of her belly, the flair of her wide hips, the spread of her heavy thighs, the tapered length of her calves, her ankles, the iridescent shimmer of her stockings. The small points of her feet, still stuffed into their high-heeled shoes.

Sweet Sin, she was so damn beautiful.

I climbed onto her bed, eased my leg over her waist until I was straddling her. Her gaze locked onto mine, and I read the terror in her eyes.

"There's nothing to be afraid of," I promised.

"I know. It's just . . ." Her voice broke off, strangled by a sob.

"Do you trust me?"

"Yes."

"Then close your eyes, Virginia."

She screwed her lids tight. My poor frightened doll. As sweet as her fear should have been, it tasted sour on my tongue. I didn't want her to be afraid of my touch, of her response.

I'll show you, doll.

Reaching down, I stroked her face with the pads of my fingers, skimmed across her forehead, and back again, working my way up to her hairline. Lingered there, then moved down, tracing the delicate curve of her jaw, her neck. When my fingers dusted over the ridge of her collarbone, I began again, slower this time, letting my fingers play over the sensitive area just beneath her chin.

She lifted her head up, gave me more room to explore. Her eyes were still closed but not squeezed tight. A start.

I moved up the other side of her face, brushed the outer edge of her ear. Her breathing shifted as I skimmed my nails over the cartilage, flicked her lobe. When I skirted the tender area between her ear and her cheek, she let out a soft *mmm*.

"Feel good?"

"Yes . . ."

My fingers danced under her chin, up the other side of her face. Teased her other ear. "This too?"

"Yes."

I played there for a moment, listened to the change in her breathing as I rubbed the pads of my finger and thumb over the shell of her ear, gently squeezed the lobe. My hand brushed down her neck, skimmed over the hollow of her throat.

"May I kiss you, Virginia?"

She let out a dismayed sound—citrus stung my nostrils.

"It's okay," I said, running my fingers up and down her neck, tracing the line of her collarbone. "No kissing. Just touching. Okay?"

"Okay."

Using both hands, I pressed down on her shoulders, moved in slow, firm circles over the tops of her arms. Worked my way over her biceps, teased the insides of her elbows with my thumbs. Circled down her forearms. Lingered over her wrists, her palms. Slowly moved back up to her shoulders.

Her eyelids were lightly closed now, her lips parted. The musk of her scent strengthened with my every stroke.

Dragging my fingers, I trailed lines from her shoulders over the top of her chest and back across, inched my hands down until they were moving over the swells of her breasts. She tried to stifle a moan.

I whispered, "Okay?"

"Yes . . ."

My touch featherlight, I traced the outer part of her breasts. A shiver ran through her, and as I moved my hands back up, her nipples hardened. Her breathing was ragged, now, a counterpoint to the thumping of her heart. Brushing my hands over her mounds, I smoothed my palms over the erect buds. She cried out, arched her back as I moved my hands in tantalizingly slow circles.

"Okay?"

Voice thick, she said, "God, yes . . ."

Yes.

Splaying my fingers, I kneaded softly, rubbed her nipples with my thumbs. She moaned, started moving her hips beneath mine.

Oh, yes, Virginia. Let yourself go.

Rocking with her, I squeezed her breasts, pushed them together as I flicked my fingers over her sensitized peaks. She was groaning now, the sound caught between a whimper and a purr. My erection pressed against my pants, my cock throbbing with need as Virginia gave voice to her arousal.

How I wanted to suckle her, tease her with my tongue and lips until she screamed. But she'd said no kissing, so I held back. My balls ached for her.

Keeping one hand on her breast, I moved down with the other, grazing the outline of her side, the indent of her waist. I reached back and down, touched her inner ankle. "Okay?"

"Mmm."

I stroked up her leg, the outline of her calf, the dimple of her knee. Slowly caressed her inner thigh as I rocked my hips over hers, teased her nipple. A wet burst of pumpkin spice as my hand reached up. "Okay?"

She bit her lip, panted.

My fingers dusted between her thighs.

"Stop. Oh God, stop."

I froze, one hand dangling by her crotch, the other cupping her right breast. "What's wrong?"

Her breath hitched, and she turned her head away from me, but not before I saw her tears. "Please, just stop."

Oh, Virginia, don't cry.

Moving in slow motion, I eased myself off her and off the bed, knelt by her side. She rolled into a ball away from me, left me with only her back and her hair as her quiet sobs filled the space between us.

What did I do wrong? I know I didn't hurt her . . . "I didn't mean to make you cry."

Through her soft cries, she said, "I'm sorry, I can't do this."

"Virginia . . . doll, there's nothing for you to do but enjoy.

That's all I wanted," I said, stroking her hair, "just for you to enjoy. For me to pamper you. Make you feel good." Make you mine.

"I love him, Don. I still love him."

I love him, Daun.

A stab of pure rage, diamond sharp, sliced through my heart. Forcing my voice into a soothing blend of sympathy and chagrin, I said, "Of course you do."

"When you touch me," she whispered, "I see his face."

"If that's what you need, then that's okay."

"No, it's not." Voice stronger now. "It's not fair to you."

"Oh, Virginia, don't worry about me . . ." Not knowing what else to say, I stroked her hair. Not fair to me? There were rules, and there were ways to break them. It was never a question of what was fair.

She took a shuddering breath, and then a second, and soon her sobs began to subside. "It still hurts. There are days when I don't know how I'm still breathing without him."

"I understand," I said, my fingers twining in her hair, stroking her. Soothing her. Showing her that I cared.

Virginia quieted, said nothing as I glided my fingers down her neck, traced a pattern down her spine. After a moment, she asked, "You do, don't you?"

I brushed my fingers up, then back down.

"Who was she?"

And up. "Who?"

"The one who you see, when you look at me."

My hand froze. A tightness in my chest, a dull thudding in my head; her words echoed, boomed, overwhelmed me until all I heard was my own heartbeat, frantic, caught. I clenched my teeth in a smile that felt like a scream. "I don't know what you mean."

A moment stretched between us, laden with things unsaid.

When she finally spoke, her voice was as gentle as sleep, as certain as death. "I've seen it in your face, when you think I'm not looking. Earlier at the concert, yesterday during dinner. When we were at the restaurant, making small talk. I've seen

how sad you are, how sometimes you look at me and see someone else."

A vision of Jezebel, dancing onstage, the lights sparkling
over her body as she moved to the music.

"No, I don't."

"Someone hurt you." Not a question, yet charged with un-
certain surety. "Please. Tell me."

"Virginia . . ."

"Please." A whisper.

"You're wrong." I'd meant my words to be calm, soothing,
but they came out in a hiss. "There was no one."

Virginia stiffened beneath me. "Why won't you tell me?"

I saw the wicked gleam of Jezebel's eyes as she thought of
something particularly sinful.

"There's nothing to tell," I insisted, trying to believe my
words. Demons don't care about others. Jezebel can rot along
with her meat pie, for all that I cared.

Jezebel's silky laughter, rippling through me, squeezing me,
sucking me dry until there's nothing left and the finest drink in
the world is right there, bubbling between her lips . . .

By my side, my fist clenched. She meant nothing to me. *Nothing*.

"Don."

Jezebel's smoky voice in my mind, purring and coy, as she
said my name.

Across from me, Jezebel's mortal doppelganger sighed, low
and mournful, a sound like broken reeds blowing in a cruel
wind. "Either you've been lying to me this whole time, or
you're lying to me now."

What?

"Demons lie," I tell Jezebel. And she tells me to go fuck myself.

On the bed, Virginia started to cry again.

I shoved Jezebel out of my mind, touched Virginia's back.
Said her name, told her I was sorry. For what, I didn't know. It
didn't matter—as long as she stopped crying, I could help make
it better.

I could make her body sing.

In a breath full of tears, she said, "I think you should go."

No.

"I don't understand."

"I think you do." Her voice, taut with grief.

"Virginia—"

Wrapped in her tight fetal ball, she whispered, "Please, Don. Leave me alone."

Jezebel, wrapping her arms around herself as if she were cold, saying, "Go away, Daun. Leave me alone."

Rage sliced through me again, stabbed me. I dropped my hand away from her back before I broke it. "Virginia." A growl, a plea.

"Just go away."

Blindly, I stormed out of her room, out of her house, drowning in a torrent of emotion.

Demons don't feel.

I couldn't breathe.

Demons don't need to breathe.

My chest was too tight; something black and wet wrapped around my heart and squeezed.

Demons don't have hearts.

Burning—I was burning alive.

My face contorted in a snarl as I summoned my power to whisk me out of Wilton, New York. I said *her* name, the one who'd taken hold of me and seduced me and refused to let me go—the one who'd give me what I needed, right now, and by all that was unholy, nothing would stop me until I had her soul wrapped around my finger.

Jezebel.

I'm coming for you.

Chapter 17

Stripped

I paraded into Spice like I owned the place and everyone in it. Which really wasn't too far from the truth.

One of the bouncers tried to stop me, but I stared him down, radiating danger like a leaky power plant. Grinned around a mouthful of fangs as I let my true form wink through my shell. A smell of rotting grapefruits, of piss. Sweating, the bouncer held his palms up, backed away. Ran like the Devil was on his heels.

I inhaled his terror, relished the citrus tang, the ammonia tartness. No one was going to stop me from seeing a certain dancer. From having my wild, wicked way with her. From hearing her scream. Whether in agony or ecstasy remained to be seen. At the moment, I wasn't picky.

I'm here, Jezzie. And I'm hungry.

The main room of the club was sparsely crowded: just shy of midnight on Monday. A handful of flat-screen wall televisions displayed a football game, and even though a few patrons seemed to watch, everyone knew the only real sport here was a different sort of entertainment. A sound in my throat, either a purr or a growl, as I walked through the club, senses honed. Tasted the haze in the air, separated the odors of smoke and booze and sweat, latched onto the scent of sex that bound everything together in a pulsing web of desire tinged with bitterness—of wanting what you can never have. Lust, yes, but warped. A heart bleeding, blackened with envy.

I grimaced. Fucking morbid thoughts. Envy has nothing to do with lust, no matter what Eris might think. Envy was wanting something you couldn't have. Lust was wanting someone.

And I'd have her, all right. Let her try to tell me no. Let her throw her claim of love in my face. I'll rip away her protests and eat her love. I'll make you want me, and me alone, Virginia.

No. Jezebel. I'm here for Jezebel.

You're lying to me now.

Demons lie, doll. It's what we do.

Hot lights; loud music. Gorgeous women radiating sex. But not the one I wanted, needed. I know you're here, babes. You can't hide from me. Onstage, a redhead dry-humped the brass pole in time to the beat.

Frustrated and angry enough to set fire to the place with just a look, I strode to the bar. Ordered a shot of whiskey, had a seat on a stool. Asked the bartender where she was.

"Somewhere," he said with a shrug.

Helpful fuck, wasn't he? I put a twenty on the counter to aid his memory.

The bartender coughed, pocketed the money. Said, "Right, she just finished a set. She'll be on the floor soon."

"Thanks." Greedy bastard. Wait till you die, chuckles. There's a golden pot of oil waiting for you in Hell . . .

He handed me my drink, told me the price. I could have pushed, had him give me the alcohol for free, but he wasn't worth the effort. Besides, I had money to burn. I slid him another twenty, said, "Keep the change."

The bartender grinned like I'd just told him he'd won a prime role in a porn flick. "Surprised you knew she'd be here," he said. Maybe he felt obligated to earn the extra money. "She usually doesn't work Mondays, but she's in today. Covering Faith's shift."

I'd never doubted that she'd be here. Where else would she be—home with her prude apostle? As if he could satisfy her for long, or at all. As if any human truly understood the needs of a creature of Lust.

Who was she, the one you see when you look at me?

Shut up.

Bless me, Daun, the last thing I'd wanted was to fall in love.

Shut up! Demons don't love.

You have no idea what you're talking about.

It was a fucking conspiracy of Jezebels.

I knocked back my drink, ordered another. If I couldn't shut the voices up, I could drown them out.

The bartender offered me a sheepish smile along with the shot. "Women troubles?"

"Women *are* trouble," I growled.

"Damn straight."

Maybe he was greedy, but he was spot-on about the root of all evil.

About ten minutes and three drinks later, I saw her—saun-tering in her high heels like she didn't have a care in the world, smiling at her adoring fans. Basking in their attention. Teasing them with small touches, meaningless words. A wet dream sheathed in a gown of translucent black.

My Jezebel.

She worked the floor, rolling her hips like she was dying for a cock to fill the gap between her legs. Her curly hair bounced with her every step, taunting her customers with its easy move-ment, daring them to run their hands through it. Beneath her see-through dress, a red demi bra molded her tits into femi-nine perfection; the air-conditioning in the room ensured they stood at attention. A matching G-string hid her deepest trea-sure.

I'd go hunting for that treasure soon, plunge my fingers into her secret box and dig until I found liquid gold. She wouldn't tell me to stop. No, she'd beg me to fuck her raw, fuck her until Salvation Day. I'd split her wide and ride her, fill her, thrill her. Show her how much she missed me. Make her scream my name.

Make her want me more than anything, anyone.

I love him, Don.

I love him, Daun.

You'll love *me*. Me, Daunuan, Prince of Lust.

Me.

Jezebel laughed at something a flesh puppet said. I watched how her lipstick gleamed, so red and wet with promise. The man's hand touched hers, and my stomach clenched; the whiskey sloshed inside of me, ate away at me like acid.

I didn't feel like sharing my toys tonight. Time to collect what's mine.

A tight smile on my face, I let my power unfold. It snaked out, weaving around the other customers like a magic worm until it found a home in a very special apple and burrowed deep into its core.

Jezebel's wet, wet lips parted in a gasp as she teetered on her heels. Her cheeks flushed as red as her lingerie.

You like how I make you feel, don't you?

The flesh puppet steadied her, asked if she was all right.

She touched her chest, put her hand over her heart. Took a deep breath. Murmuring a reply, she smiled at the man in his cheap suit, but it couldn't quite disguise that she was flustered. Hot and bothered.

Oh, no, babes. I'm not done with you yet. I haven't even started.

Tapping into my magic, I *pushed* her again, nudged past her carefully developed social restraints and her stupid notions of love, touched her core. Stroked her once, twice. Whispered against the spot that weakened her knees.

She bit her lip, stifled a moan. Leaning heavily on the man's table, she closed her eyes, hung her head low as her body reacted to my touch. Her thick hair fell over her face in an ebony waterfall of curls. She quivered, her fists clenched.

I eased back my power, released her. Sipped my drink. Waited to see what she'd do.

When she looked up and cast a heated look around the room, I knew I had her. She spotted me, cocked her head. The man said something else to her, but she ignored him as she considered me, her gaze sliding over me like body lotion. Her blowjob lips curled into a smile. She liked what she saw.

Raising my glass in a salute, I grinned a Don Walker laid-back grin, flattered to be noticed by such a beautiful woman.

Without a parting look at the man in his shiny suit, she strolled toward me, lust already darkening her eyes.

Oh, Jezebel. The things I was going to do to you . . .

"Heya, sweetie," she purred as she stepped next to me at the bar. "May I join you?"

"I'd like that. A lot. But . . . do you think we could do it in private?"

She laughed, low and lush. "If that's your pleasure."

It certainly was a start.

The Champagne Room again, and Jezebel none the wiser. Full circle. But no more of the bubbly shit for me; there was only so much abuse I was willing to take tonight. A glass of angel piss would set me over the edge.

Jezebel shut the door behind us, then clasped my hand and led me to the sofa. I glanced around as if it were new to me—the plush seats, the wine-red carpet, the music filling the air with a sassy tune that made me think of foreplay. Or maybe that was from Jezebel holding my hand, her tapered thumbnail tickling my palm.

"First time here?"

I smiled, channeled more "aw shucks" good-natured bull-shit. "Does it show?"

She gently sat me down on the seat, nudged me back against the cushions. "Just a little. But hey, everyone has a first time." Laughter shining in her green eyes, she shrugged—an easy movement that jiggled her breasts. Veiled in translucent black, shaped by the red push-up bra, her mounds looked like they'd been created just for my hands, my mouth, my tongue. The thought of grazing my fangs over her nipples went straight to my dick. Inside my jeans, my erection throbbed, demanded release. Demanded Jezebel.

She used her knee to spread my thighs, then stepped in front
of my crotch, her body already moving playfully to the music.
She smiled at my hard-on like she was used to that particular
reception, then winked at me as she began to dance.

Folding my hands over my stomach, my legs open wide, I
feasted on her shape. I'd let her do the stripper routine for a
song, and then I'd throw her onto the floor and fuck her silly.
Grinning hugely, I thought about what I was going to do to
her in T-minus three minutes. And counting.

Rrrr.

"So tell me," she said, hands on her hips and inching their
way up, "who is she?"

"Who's who?"

"Who's the woman you're trying to forget?"

Unholy Hell, was it branded on my forehead?

"Don't know what you mean."

She smiled at my lie as she ran her hands up, over her waist,
the twin swells of her tits. "Okay."

*"Okay?" I ask Virginia, my hands on her breasts, and she says in
a voice thick with desire, "God, yes . . ."*

"Hey," Jezebel said, pausing in her dance, her hands hovering like birds over the nectar of her breasts. Concern in her
eyes, she asked, "What's got you looking so sad?"

I've seen how sad you are, Virginia whispers, *how sometimes you
look at me and see someone else.*

"I'm fine," I told Virginia and Jezebel both.

Someone hurt you.

Jezebel smiled sweetly, started dancing again. Her hands fluttered over her shoulders. "If you want," she said, lowering first
one dress strap and then the other, "I'm happy to listen."

"Nothing to talk about."

"Okay." She peeled her dress down to her waist, revealing
the scarlet demi bra that barely covered her nipples. Turning
her back to me, she shimmied out of the gown, wiggling her
ass and stepping out of the sheer outfit. I wanted to squeeze
those cheeks, run my fingers between her legs, get her sopping
wet . . .

Boom *boom*.

One song, Jezebel, and then you're mine.

Clad in her lingerie and stockings, she pivoted on her stilettos to face me, bent over and looped her arms around my neck. Pushed her cleavage a tongue's length away from my mouth.

I was going to suck her until her toes curled in pleasure, kiss her nipples until they were raw and aching.

"No kissing," I promise Virginia. "Just touching. Okay?" And she says, "Okay."

Fuck.

Jezebel lowered herself onto my lap, rubbed her crotch against mine. Smiled, gave me a look so full of sympathy that I wanted to puke. "Sweetie, as happy as I am to take your money, you really don't look like you're enjoying yourself."

I grinned to show her just how fucking much I was enjoying myself. So what that I couldn't get Virginia out of my head, even with a mostly naked former succubus straddling me, grinding me. "I'm fine," I said, my voice gruff. My teeth clenched, I kept grinning. Twined my arms around her waist.

She leaned into me, breathed on my neck. Whispered, "If you want, you can leave. No charge. Our little secret."

I closed my eyes as her compassion spread over me like a balm, blunted the edge of my rage. I wanted to fuck her until she screamed. I wanted to push her away and run like Hell.

Bishop's balls, what was wrong with me?

My voice hoarse, I asked, "Know what I really want?"

"What?"

"I want you to dance. Not on my lap. Stand up and dance. Slow. Sexy. That's what I want."

Her breath tickling my ear, she said, "Of course."

Moving in slow motion, she rubbed her breasts against my body as she stood. With a wink, she took two steps back and started to dance. Smiled at me like she wanted to hug me, tell me that everything would be okay.

Don't look at me, babes. The thoughts in your eyes are killing me. Swallowing thickly, I said, "Turn around so I can see your ass."

She did. Of course she did. The customer was always right. Oh, fuck me, look at how she moves, how her legs are spread wide and her cheeks are so perfect . . .

"This better, sweetie?"

"Oh, yeah."

The next song came on, a slower tune heavy with piano and drums and bass blending together in a sultry beat that reverberated through my body like a musical aphrodisiac. "I love this song," Jezebel said, swaying in time.

Now.

My magic rippled over her, soft, subtle, an invisible parasite that sucked away her self-restraint. It flowed through her, pulled her under, and she let out an *uhmm* and threw her head back and danced like she was making an offering to a god.

Or to an incubus.

As her fingers skimmed up her torso and traced the outline of her breasts, I stood up from the sofa. Her hands stretched up, past her face, reaching now for the sky, and I moved toward her.

Now, Jezebel. Now.

I encircled her waist from behind, moved my hands over her stomach, up to her breasts. Cupped her tits and squeezed.

Her arms raised high, she danced, lost in the music. In my magic.

My cock strained against my pants, pressed into her back. She moaned as I groped her, rocked her head as my power seduced her. The swells of her ass rubbed against the front of my thighs. Every muscle in my body sang with need, sang for Jezebel, here, now.

This was what I wanted. What I couldn't stop thinking about. Jezebel, my Jezebel, her body moving with mine.

But not like this.

Not when she's bespelled by my power and dancing to a tune that won't let her go, not even when I'm fondling her, pressing my dick against the curve of her spine.

My breathing ragged, I dropped my hands. I wanted to press

my fingers inside of her, stroke her, fuck her. But I wouldn't give in, no matter how much my body wanted her.

No, babes. Not like this.

She moaned, and desire pounded through me, filled my head and my cock and my balls with an urgent BOOM *BOOM*, made it impossible to think of anything but taking her, fucking her hard and fast until I exploded in her and seared her from inside and sucked her soul from her lips.

No.

I almost tripped over my feet as I backed away, sweat popping on my brow, my heartbeat frantic. Lost in my power, Jezebel danced.

No.

Squeezing my eyes shut, I forced my power back. It reared and slammed against me, demanded release, urged me and goaded me and coaxed me to set it free. But I shut it down, locked it away.

Drained, I sank onto the sofa, held my head in my hands. Felt like I couldn't breathe.

What's happening to me?

A soft touch on my shoulder made me peer up to see Jezebel staring at me, frowning with concern. "Are you okay?"

I couldn't answer at first; my mouth refused to work, my throat felt too tight. And my chest hurt as if I'd been stabbed. Panting, I said, "I don't know who I am anymore. And it's tearing me apart."

She sat next to me, took one of my hands in her own. "Tell me."

"I can't."

"Then tell her."

"I wouldn't know what to say."

"Oh, sweetie," she said, "I think you will. Just speak from the heart."

I barked out a strangled laugh. "What makes you think I have one?"

Smiling, Jezebel said, "Call it a hunch."

* * *

Virginia picked up on the third ring. Her voice thick with sleep, she said, "Hello."

"Hey. It's Don."

A pause, filled with the sound of my heart pounding in my chest, my throat, my head. Then she said, "It's one in the morning."

"I know. I had to call you."

"Don." My name, the name I'd given her as mine, spoken like a curse. "I'm going back to sleep now."

"Wait."

"Good-bye." A note of finality in her voice.

"Please."

I hated that word, and I despised begging. But it must be called the magic word for a reason, because even though she'd said she was hanging up on me, Virginia waited.

"I . . ." Want to hold you, stroke you, feel you pressed against my body. Need you, like I've never needed anything before. My words, tumbling in a rush: "I have to talk to you. About before."

Static over the line, and then she cleared her throat. "Call me tomorrow, after work."

"No!" No, don't shout, don't scare her away. Softer: "No. This can't wait. It has to be now." Now, before my words failed me. Now, before Callistus or some other from the Pit came after me with murder in their eyes.

I heard her let out a vexed sigh, and I imagined her hanging her head as she debated, her long curls shielding her, hiding the thoughts that flashed through her eyes. Clenching the phone tight enough to break it, I waited for her to pass judgment.

"Okay," she said. "Talk."

"Face-to-face."

"You're crazy. It's too late." Either about the time or for my words.

"I have to get this out. Tonight. Now."

Maybe she heard something in my voice, some sense of urgency, of desperation. Or maybe Good people just can't say no and mean it for very long. She said, "I must be out of my mind. Where are you?"

"Outside your front door."

The phone line went dead, and I thought that was the end. I'd lost my chance to understand what in Hell was happening to me. Lost my chance with Virginia. And after Pan was through with me, I'd never get another chance with Jezebel.

I closed my eyes, tried to think of options. Tried to think at all. But Jezebel's face filled my mind, or maybe it was Virginia's, or an amalgamation of the two; all I saw, heard, smelled was Virginia, the quintessential essence of the woman who had entered and altered my life, who made me question all I was, all I've been. I felt her there, in my mind, felt her so vividly that the world itself faded away and all there was in this life and beyond for now and forever was me and her. Those emerald green eyes. That laughter, rich and sinful and intoxicating. Her heady scent of jasmine and chocolate, of blackberries and musk.

And knowing it was only in my mind was enough to bring me to my knees. Gone—she was gone, and I was lost.

And then Virginia opened the door.

Chapter 18

This Pivotal Moment

Virginia stood in the doorway like a sentry, one hand on the jamb and the other on the doorknob, blocking passage. Her hair was sleep-tousled and wild, spiraling in corkscrews around her pale face, springing from her head in tangled clumps. Draped over her body like a shroud, her flannel nightshirt hung loosely, disguised the shape of her belly, her hips, her thighs. She frowned up at me, her full lips pulled into a pout, her eyes blazing with challenge and reddened from tears. She was utterly gorgeous.

"You look like hell," she said.

My lips twitched. "I'm sure."

"Have you been outside this whole time?"

"No. Went somewhere, did some thinking."

She said nothing, just stared at me with those angry green eyes that sparkled like gemstones. This was Virginia irate, Virginia awakened—and even though her fury was directed at me, I couldn't help but think that she was so much more alive when she was incensed than when she was dulled from resignation. No more sleepwalking through your days for you, Virginia. At least I'd accomplished that much.

A good deed from a demon. The very notion made me want to laugh.

"May I come in?"

Her eyes narrowed, but she relented, motioned for me to step inside. I walked into the living room, heard her close the door behind me. She didn't tell me to throw my coat anywhere, to have a seat. Instead, she stood by the door, arms crossed, hip thrust out, her face carefully blank. No matter how she masked her features, I still smelled her anger—a mustard scent, shot through with black pepper.

I held out my hands, palms up, as if begging her for something—forgiveness? understanding? I didn't know—then changed the motion and raked my fingers through the mop of my hair. I didn't know how to start. I didn't have the words.

Jezebel had told me to speak from the heart. But no matter what her so-called human hunch told her, I didn't have a heart, not like that. I was a demon, bred in the Pit and charged with seducing evil people. I killed them and took their souls to Hell for judgment and torture. And I enjoyed it.

More than that: my role defined me. It's who I was. All I was. Daunuan, creature of Lust. Incubus extraordinaire. I didn't have a heart. I didn't do feelings—that shit was for humans, for idiots like Jezebel who thought they were in love.

So what the fuck was I supposed to say to Virginia?

Daun, don't be such a guy.

Jezebel's voice stabbed me, diamond sharp.

"Don?" Virginia, tentative. Cautious. "Are you okay?"

I opened my mouth, and words tumbled out before I could call them back: "I lied. Before. When you asked who she was, and I said no one. I lied."

Virginia looked at me, a long, penetrating look that I felt boring into my skull.

"Her name is Jesse." Even here I lied, but I couldn't call her Jezebel. Not here, not to Virginia. "She's a dancer. She . . ." My breath caught, and I swallowed, tried again. "I've known her for forever, from before she chose that life. We were together for so long, through everything. I couldn't imagine it any other way."

My Jezebel, across the ages. Her form shifted over the long

years, but her true self remained the same—wicked, spirited, jubilant. My little succubus.

Virginia's gaze softened, and the thin line of her mouth eased. She waited for more.

"There were others through the years," I said, struggling to be honest because Virginia was good and no matter what happened she deserved, at the very least, some honesty. "She had her job, and I had mine. But we always managed to find each other. Always stole a moment to be together."

Virginia was still looking at me, but I didn't really see her—I was remembering the feel of Jezebel, our bodies slick with sweat and blood, slapping time in the symphony of sounds that was the orgy of the Red Light District, her talons raking across my back as she squealed her passion, my dick thrusting deep inside of her, filling her, completing her. Completing me.

"And then her job changed." Everything changed—the King, the Land, the very nature of Sin, if I believed Eris, and that was a toss-up because what was Eris if not the epitome of dissention? "It changed, and she couldn't handle it. So she quit. Gave up everything she'd ever known to be a dancer."

I see her, moving onstage, the spotlights splashing over her, the music riding her body as if it possessed her, men's hands on her thighs as they slide their bills into her garter and look at her with adoration and thoughts of fornication and she laps up their attention with a wet smile on her lips as they watch her and want her.

"I went after her," I said, speaking to someone I couldn't see, someone who needed to hear the truth, or a version of the truth. "Tried to help her."

"You keep your mouth shut," I say to Jezebel. "You don't want to come back to Hell, fine. But don't go telling the mortals about the Announcement. If you do, it'll go poorly for you."

"Tried to convince her to come home."

"It's not too late," I tell her, my voice as soft as a caress. "Come back with me now. Maybe claim the Rapture took you, or some celestial bullshit like that."

"But she said she'd fallen in love." That last word spat like a blessing.

I saw him, the prude Apostle of Shoulders, gazing at my Jezebel like a moonstruck idiot, his big hands cupping her face, roaming over her body as if it were his to explore, his to play with. His to have.

My jaw clenched, and I couldn't stop grinding my teeth. "He's wrong for her, doesn't understand her, could never give her what she really needs."

I'm dressed as her meat pie so that I can seduce her and kill her and take her to Hell, and because of my magic she believes the lie and is looking at me like I'm her everything. Why does that stab me? Why do I care that she wants her human lover and not me?

"But she says she loves him," I said, I growled, I sneered with all the disgust I could summon, "and that's all there is to it. She loves him, and all our history together gets washed away in a swapping of spit."

Bless me, Daun, the last thing I'd wanted was to fall in love.

You fucking liar.

A whisper, now, or maybe I didn't even say the words aloud and only imagined that I gave voice to my darkest thoughts. "And the thing that kills me, the thing that's making me insane, is that as much as I said I've washed my hands of her, that she's made her choice, I can't stop thinking about her."

Jezebel, dancing. Jezebel, laughing.

Jezebel.

My lips pulled back in a snarl. "It's like she's stolen a part of me, a part that I never knew I had. She's a thief and a liar and she left me. And she's invaded my mind, won't let me go. And bless it all to Heaven, I don't know how to make it stop."

My last word rang in my ears, echoed in the small living room, and that's when I realized I'd been shouting. I unclenched my hands, stared at them in wonder because I hadn't felt my nails cutting into my palms as I'd squeezed my fingers into fists. Blood on my hands. Blood from the heart I didn't have.

When Virginia spoke, her voice was low and soft, a contralto full of sympathy. "You still love her."

Love?

I sneered at her, at this human woman who dared to think that she knew me or understood me. My laugh was ugly, and it made her flinch. "I don't do love."

Virginia's lips quirked into a smile, and her eyes brimmed with compassion. "I think you do."

"You have no idea what you're talking about."

In my mind, Jezebel laughed.

Snarling, I turned away, squeezed my eyes shut. Tried to banish Jezebel from my mind, from my heart, but she spread through me like a disease, infected me. Suffocated me.

A hand on my shoulder, so light I shouldn't have felt it. "Don."

"I'm sick," I said, grasping at any explanation, no matter how pitiful, how weak. "That's what this is. I have a fever." Maybe from the other day, when that thrice-blessed Arrogant had sliced me. Something on the tines of the comb, poisoning me. A diamond chip from her ring, embedded in my skin. Under my skin. Killing me slowly with taunting flashes, with emotions I shouldn't be able to feel.

Demons don't feel.

"Tell me," Virginia said, speaking to me like a child. "Where does it hurt?"

"Here." I jabbed myself in the chest. "Maybe it's a heart attack." I'd magicked up a defective human shell. That's what this was. Faulty craftsmanship.

"Like there's a crushing weight in your chest." She placed her other hand over my heart.

"Yes," I said, my voice cracking. "Exactly."

"Where else does it hurt?"

I swallowed, said, "My throat's too tight."

"A feeling like you can't breathe."

My eyes snapped open and I saw Virginia standing in front of me, tears in her eyes and an understanding smile on her lips,

Virginia nodding like she'd known all along what was happening inside of me.

And so I asked her: "How do you know this?"

"Because that's how it felt when I lost Chris."

"That's not the same."

"It is." She took my hands, held them tight. "More than you know."

"It's completely different," I insisted. "He was your husband."

"And she was your other half."

Jezebel, looking at me like I was her everything.

"The other day," Virginia said, "you told me I was holding on to my pain. You were right. But you're doing the same thing."

Demons relish pain.

But this? This was a bleakness that scooped out my chest. Pain was hurt, and I knew that sensation intimately. This . . . feeling . . . I had wasn't hurt. What was it? "How do you make it stop? How do I stop thinking about her?"

"I don't know." She looked down, her thick hair shrouding her face. The mustard scent had dissipated, and now, standing before me, demure and compassionate and so very alive, Virginia smelled of sandalwood and peppermint—smelled of hope. She said, "Maybe it's not about stopping. Maybe it's about moving forward."

"Virginia . . ."

"Small steps. Baby steps. But maybe we could try. Maybe we could help each other." Her voice was a whisper, and she still wasn't looking at me. Maybe she was afraid I'd say no.

After all this, how could I say yes?

This moment, this pivotal moment, stretching on forever: my heart slamming in my chest, my blood roaring in my ears as she slowly looks up, shakes her curls away from her eyes, looks at me like she's seeing me for the first time and is surprised and sad and nervous and something else, something ineffable, something elusive and fickle and so damn fleeting that maybe it wasn't really there at all . . .

"Virginia, you don't know me."

"I'm learning more every day."

"Doll, you don't understand. This isn't who I really am. I'm—"

"I don't care what you think you are." Her eyes shone like the emeralds they mimicked, and she smiled, warm and wicked. "But for God's sake, stop calling me 'doll.'"

My mouth suddenly dry, I said, "Old habit."

"Well, Mr. Walker. I'm just going to have to break you of that nasty old habit, aren't I?"

I spoke her name, knowing what was coming and wanting it more than anything and wanting to tell her to run far and fast and never look back.

And then she stood up on her toes and clasped my face between her hands and kissed me.

As soon as her lips touch mine, my magic roars to life. She gasps in my mouth as my power shoots through her, fills her, breaks her objections and shatters her fears, sucks her down in a maelstrom of lust.

A man worth his salt would have pushed her away, would have fought against the power of the kiss. Would have sacrificed himself to save her soul.

Her gasp turns into a hungry growl and she attacks my mouth, ravenous. Insatiable.

Irresistible.

I'm not a man. I'm a demon, and lust is what I do.

Casting aside any pretense of humanity, I open my mouth wide and claim her.

My lips on hers, kissing deep, our tongues exploring, probing, playing.

Her aroma flooded me in jasmine and musk, stuffed me with chocolate and blackberries. Gorged on her scent, I moved away from her mouth, kissed her jaw, her neck. My tongue flicked over her skin, slid over the base of her throat. Her hands tangled in my hair and pulled.

Oh, Virginia, I'm going to make you feel so good. I'm going to cover every inch of you in hot kisses, wash every part of you with my tongue. Taste you and tantalize you until you beg me to let you come.

I slid one hand behind her back, used the other to trace the curve of her face, feeling the heat of her arousal blush her skin. Smelled her desire as it bathed her body in pumpkin spice. Mmm. Shivers, dancing through me like electric shocks, setting my blood to boil.

Mine, Virginia. You're mine.

Nibbling her neck, I worked my lips up to her ear. Lapped at her lobe. Grazed her with my teeth, and was rewarded with a gasp. Sucked the sensitive flesh, asked, "Feel good?"

"Yes," she said, her voice husky with want.

Kissing down her neck, tracing the area where her collar met her skin, I asked, "This too?"

"Yes . . ."

Lowering my hand, I brushed my fingers over her collarbone, unfastened the top button of her nightshirt. Kissed her mouth again, harder this time, as I released the second button. Her fingers found purchase on my shoulders, dug deeply when I opened her shirt even more and exposed her left breast. Leaving her clothing where it was, I cupped the full mound, then circled it with the pads of my fingers, moving concentrically, and so very slowly, toward its peak.

She was wild against my mouth, growling her frustration, her urgent need as she kissed me, her tongue slicing against mine, demanding, telling me what she wanted. When I dragged my thumb over her pert nipple, she groaned long and loud.

Breaking the kiss, I whispered, "Feel good?"

"God, yes . . ."

I squeezed her breast like it was the ripest of fruits, and then I took her in my mouth and drank. She cried out, a high *ahh-hhh*, scored my shoulders with her nails and arched against me.

Tonguing her nipple, I cupped her swell with one hand and used my other to unfasten another button. The shirt fell away from her shoulders, revealing her right breast, full and pebbled, her taut nub waiting for my attention.

Licking her areola, I laved my way between her mounds, rained kisses in the valley of her bosom. She was panting now, moving her hips and mewling soft sounds of pleasure as my saliva cooled on her heated skin. My lips on her right breast, kissing, tasting. Finding the nipple and giving suck while my fingers worked on its twin, teasing it with touches soft and touches not as soft.

My mouth on her, I looked up, past the large, soft swells on her chest to see her reaction, to let her see me sucking her. Virginia's head was tilted back, her eyes closed, her plump lips open as she gave voice to her pleasure, gasping and groaning from the things I was doing with my mouth, my lips, my tongue.

"Like this?"

"Yes . . ."

My hands on her breasts now, pressing them together as I kissed the crease between them. "Tell me what you want, Virginia."

"You."

I blew on her nipple, and she shivered.

"I'm going to go down on you," I said, my voice low and full of promise, "going to touch you and taste you and kiss you until you come."

My nostrils flared at the sudden burst of liquid heat between her thighs, and then I was drowning in the aroma of her desire. Her hands, clutching my hair; her hips, rocking as if I were already inside of her.

"Please," she whispered.

I had to be inside of her.

Snaking my hand down, I traced the rounded swell of her belly, dabbled with the indent of her navel. Ran along the top of her panties. Lingered there as I kissed my way between her breasts, and up, pausing to suck on the curve of her neck. My lips, on hers, feasting.

My hand, between her legs.

Her breath was a song of shuddering gasps, a melody of passionate cries. I splayed my fingers, felt the soft flesh of her inner thigh, brushed over her sex. Her knees buckled and I caught her before she could fall, lifted her, one hand sandwiched by her thighs, the other around her back, held her aloft as I nudged aside her underwear and fingered her.

Oh, doll, feel how wet you are . . .

She hooked her legs around my waist, clutched my shoulders and bucked against me, panting, her face flushed and hectic with need, her curls shimmering and her breasts bobbing as she moved, saying, *"Oh God Oh God Oh God,"* as if He were the one driving her to the brink.

Grinning as she lost herself to her building pleasure, I inched deeper, crooked my finger up and wiggled, and she threw her head back and screamed in wild abandon, grinding herself against me as the orgasm took her.

Yes, Virginia.

Yes.

Falling against me, shuddering from aftershocks, she said, "Thank you, oh, thank you . . ."

Heh.

"Doll, I haven't even tasted you yet."

I carried her to the sofa and set her down, gently pushed her shoulders until she was lying on her back. Her eyelids drooped, and a dreamy smile played on her face. *Ah, look at her, at the gentle sag of her heavy breasts, her nipples pearled and eager; at the relaxed swell of her belly, full and feminine; her damp cotton panties stretched over the mound of her sex, askew from my touches, her black pubic curls peeking through the edge of the material; her thighs, soft and white and expansive.*

"You're so gorgeous," I said, meaning it, stroking her with my gaze before I yanked off the scrap of clothing that hid her greatest treasure.

Climbing on top of her, I kissed her mouth, her chin, her ear. Whispered, "I promised to taste you and kiss you until you came."

"I already . . ." But her voice gave way to a tremulous gasp as I rubbed my hand over her sex, moistened my fingers with her juices.

"Ready, steady, go," I said with a grin, then pressed her clit.

A smaller climax this time, and as her body quivered I kissed my way down, attending to her breasts with my tongue before I moved to her belly. Breathed on the damp curls of her mons. Inhaled pumpkin spice. Exhaled over the divide of her outer lips.

Kissed her.

She moaned as I explored, writhed as I parted her with my fingers and licked. Arched wildly as I sucked her rosy bud, her hips bucking. Screamed in ecstasy as I took her between my lips and drank her down.

I lapped her with my tongue until her tremors subsided and even my deepest strokes resulted only with a contented *mmm*. I kissed the insides of her thighs, up over her hips, her stomach, her breasts. Kissed her swollen mouth, her heavy eyelids, her brow. She was bonelessly sated, grinning in delight.

"A man of your word," she murmured, reaching up to stroke my arm.

"Among other things."

My turn, doll.

I disintegrated my clothing with a thought. The smell of burned cotton tickled my nostrils, and my skin steamed.

Now, Virginia. Now.

She looked up at me, her eyes dark and filled with wonder and amusement and desire. "You *are* a magician." Soft laughter.

"No, doll." Poised over her, my cock eager and my balls tight and my magic surging through me, I told her the truth. I owed her that much. My voice husky, I said, "I'm a demon, Virginia."

She looked at me with her heavy, glazed eyes, smiled at me and said, "Okay."

"I'm going to fuck you and steal your soul."

"Okay."

The tip of my shaft touched her wet mound, nudged, and she cooed, closed her eyes.

"I'm going to take you to Hell."

"If we're together," she said, "I don't care." And I knew she meant it.

Virginia.

I couldn't hold back any longer: my magic poured over her as I slid into her, and oh sweet Sin she was so wet and willing and I slid out and back in, and she arched beneath me as I thrust deep, rocked her head back and forth, making music as she moaned.

Out and in, and her breathing quickened and her fingers clutched the cushions and she lifted her hips to take me deeper, deeper. Panting now, her face flushed and her nipples hard against my chest, and in a burst of pumpkin spice she came again, her muscles contracting around my cock, pulsing her pleasure, almost sending me over the edge.

Her mouth opened and I saw the shape of my name on her lips.

No.

I stopped her voice with a kiss, sealed my mouth over hers, devoured the sound. Kept my mouth on hers until she sighed and relaxed beneath me, and then I broke the kiss to look at her, to see the bliss on her face.

And I held myself back.

All I had to do was finish what I'd started. Explosive release inside of her, and my seed would take root and bloom into a poisonous flower of fire that would sear her from within and sicken her from without and would destroy her.

All I had to do to stop the agony of her death was have her call my name, my true name, have my magic bathe her, as it was now, and let her make me the master of her soul.

And still, I held myself back.

I couldn't kill her, couldn't subject her to an eternity of burning in the Heartlands of Lust, of torture and despair just because Pan had picked her as my assignment. She deserved the Sky, deserved eternal harmony. Deserved joy.

Virginia sighed, content.

Kissing her softly, I pulled out. She'd climaxed four times, more than enough for both of us. My erection didn't agree, but I brooked no argument. Not about this.

Her head lolled to the side, and her breathing slowed. I touched her hair, stroked her face. Enjoyed the way her lips had settled into a smile.

After watching her for a moment, I moved off the couch, scooped her into my arms. Held her close like I would never let her go. "Come on, doll," I said softly. "Let me put you to bed."

She cradled her head against my chest, wrapped her arms around my neck. Said, "Don't call me 'doll.'"

I laughed softly, kissed the top of her head. "Working on that."

And I took her to her room, pulled back the cover on her bed, set her down gently. Covered her with the blanket. Sat by her side for a moment, stroking her hair.

Her eyes opened, just a little. She murmured, "Stay with me."

Oh, Virginia.

Smiling, I said, "I'll stay until you're sleeping."

"Okay." Her eyes slipped closed.

I bent down, lightly kissed her brow. Whispered: "Go to sleep, Virginia. Dream of me."

She did the one immediately; as for the other, I wouldn't invade the privacy of her mind to check.

Time passed as I listened to her steady breathing, stroked the thick curls of her hair. Watched her as she slept, looking more peaceful than I'd ever seen her before.

She'd kissed me willingly and let me seduce her.

She'd let an incubus fuck her, and in doing so, she'd damned herself. All that was left was killing her and claiming her soul.

But even if I didn't kill her, even if I just walked away and never saw her again, Virginia was marked for Hell.

And as I sat beside her in the dark of her bedroom, I swore by all that was unholy that I would find a way to save her.

PART III

THE AFTERMATH

Chapter 19

Revelations

The Voodoo Café was almost empty, which was a welcome surprise. I kept my guard up and my radar honed, but at least I didn't have a sea of faces to watch as I sat in the corner and drank and tried to think of a solution to my situation.

Or drink of a solution. I sipped my scotch, and I wracked my brain, and hours later I was still as lost as I'd been sitting by Virginia's side, watching her sleep.

I couldn't undamn her.

I couldn't fail in my assignment.

And I also couldn't get a buzz, which, at the moment, was truly pissing me off. I'd told Randolph to leave me the bottle, and he had, smart boy. And now the container was nothing more than a glass paperweight, and all the alcohol had done was coat my tongue and warm my throat while it masterfully ignored the thousands of thoughts that rocketed through my mind, all of which came down to two conflicting truths: I had to kill Virginia, and I couldn't kill Virginia. A growing sense of urgency had confounded me with every swallow, left a metallic taste that the peaty, smoky flavor of the drink couldn't wipe away.

A waste of single malt if there ever was one.

And then she walked in, radiating chilly perfection and celestial purity, and the answer hit me like Armageddon as I watched her sidle up to the bar and smile at Randolph.

I'm straddling Jezebel, pinning her shoulders with my elbows and stroking the side of her face as she tells me she needs me to seduce her and kill her so I can lead her soul to Hell, and she tells the angel that she needs her to do the "Snow White thing" to her body so that she'll be able to return.

The angel could keep Virginia safe.

Randolph slid a glass to her, and she lay her small hand over his larger one, brushed his fingers with hers before she clasped the drink. He grinned, smitten, but more like a schoolboy crush than an unquenchable urge to throw her down on the bar and fuck her. She smiled, took a delicate sip. Said something, and he blushed, nodded. Still grinning like an idiot, he floated away to the other end of the bar to wait on another customer, stealing love-struck gazes at the cherub, who didn't notice; she'd turned in her seat to scan the room. Once again, blonde and blue, with measurements that would be impossible for a mortal woman to mimic without either magic or silicone. Shoulders back, her breasts thrust against the white silk of her dress. Fixing a smile on her porcelain face, she threw her sunkissed hair over a swany shoulder. Lifted her glass for another sip. Licked the taste from her lips with a pink tongue that hinted at other parts of her equally pink and wet.

The cherub was on the prowl. If not for the nervous swing of her long leg, she'd make a passable seductress. For a wannabe.

Angels as Seducers, succubi as Nightmares. I still didn't know if that was a brilliant move on the King's part, or if it was undeniable proof of His insanity.

Her gaze roamed, searching. Studying. *Still practicing, sweetness? Still trying to work up the courage to do it for real, to attempt to tempt an evil mortal into a night of wild abandon before taking his soul Downstairs? All you have to do is let yourself go. You'd enjoy it, if only you'd let yourself.*

I smiled as I remembered the feeling of her tit in my mouth, her nipple pearled against the white silk like some Heavenly gem; her scent of flowers and spice, and a splash of peppermint as I found the spot on her throat that made her forget herself . . .

. . . And then the memory shifted and I was suckling Virginia, caressing the swell of her magnificent breast as I worked my lips and tongue over her erect nub and she cried out with the sweetest *ahhh* as I drank from her and swam in jasmine and chocolate, in blackberries and musk.

Shit.

I shook my head, knocked back the dregs of my scotch. Slammed the glass on the table. Stood.

At the bar, the angel noticed me. She must have recognized my mortal costume from the concert last night or perhaps she saw my true form beneath it: her eyes widened in surprise, or maybe fear, before a cold mask settled over her features, turning her gaze frosty, and her lips pressed together in a tight line. The slightest hint of her nodding her head in acknowledgment. A sniff of disdain, which made me grin.

She'd missed me. I could tell.

I strode up to her, planted one hand on the bar and the other on the back of her chair, invaded her personal space. "Hey, Feathers. Come here often?"

"No, my lord. This is my second time visiting."

My grin widened. "You're supposed to say, 'Every chance I get.' That's how Seducers greet each other. Sometimes."

"My thanks, Lord."

"Glad to help."

Her eyes narrowed. "You want something."

"Am I that obvious?"

"You haven't tried to grope me, and you've given me information that will be to my benefit. Yes, my lord, you are that obvious."

I leaned forward until my mouth was a breath away from hers. "Don't you mean I haven't tried to grope you *yet?*"

She swallowed, and I enjoyed the sight of that pale throat working, that long neck looking so kissable, so lickable . . .

. . . And then my tongue is flicking over Virginia's neck,

sliding over the base of her throat, and her hands tangle in my hair and pull.

Fuck.

I squeezed my eyes shut, but I couldn't banish the image of Virginia's large emerald eyes, dark and filled with wonder and amusement and desire as she laughs softly and says, "You *are* a magician."

"My lord?"

I am your lord now, Virginia. You kissed me and now you can't tell me no, you kissed me and you won't be able to stop thinking about me. You kissed me and gave me your life.

So why am I the one who can't stop thinking about you?

"My lord, are you all right?"

The angel's voice, dangling like a lifeline. I grabbed on, pulled myself out of the maelstrom of my thoughts. Focused on the cherub's face, on her big blue eyes that shimmered with concern and danced with the memory of the Sky.

"I've been better," I said, my voice rasping.

"What is wrong?"

Her question was so absurd that I barked out a laugh, let the sound pour out of me in a rush until I was doubled over, chortling. After a time the laughter tapered off, and I shook my head, grinned. "I don't even know where to start."

"The beginning is usually a good place."

"That's a little before my time."

Humor lit her eyes, but she said nothing as she waited. It struck me how different her kind and mine were as she sat on her bar stool, legs crossed, hands folded as if she'd be content to sit like that until Salvation Day: while the infernal knew how to wait, the celestial were patient. Until now, I never appreciated the difference.

I sat next to her, took a deep breath. Fumbled for the right words. When I spoke, I pitched my voice low, although that would do nothing to ensure privacy; the nonhumans at the Voodoo Café would be able to hear us, if they wanted to. So I chose my words carefully. "Our King gave me an assignment."

The angel's voice, like a summer breeze in my mind: *The woman at the performance.*

I stared at her. We had a Seducer psychic connection after all. Maybe she was embracing her new role. *Yes.*

Virginia Reed. I must have reacted to hearing her say Virginia's name, because the cherub added: *When I found you there, I saw you with the woman. Her soul was pure.* "Which I thought was strange, considering your tastes."

My lips quirked into a smile.

So I went Skyward and checked her record.

"You can still do that? Even after changing sides?"

She shrugged. "I didn't change sides, my lord. I was reassigned. I didn't fall from Grace. More like I'm an exchange student." *I hope,* she added, and I wondered if she'd meant to let that slip. "So, yes, I can still go to the Sky. Although I cannot stay."

The haunted look in her face told me that her Heavenly sojourns cut her to the quick. I grinned, said, "We have better music."

"That is a matter of opinion."

Angels. No sense of humor. *So what did the record say?*

Slated for Heaven, like her husband. Her brow creased. *But her record had a notation that I didn't understand.*

Aloud, I asked, "What did it say?"

"I don't know."

That made me arch a brow. *I thought angels could read any language.*

She shot me a look that would have transformed the Arrogant into the Jealous. "We can," she said with a sniff. Then in my mind: *But this notation was in gibberish. And now,* she added as she nibbled her lip, *I don't remember what it said. Every time I try, it feels like something is pressing my head in a vice.*

Something about her words struck a chord. For a moment, I saw Jezebel dancing onstage, her body shimmering with the colors of the spotlights, and I almost remembered something. Then it slipped away.

"So you know," I said. *Virginia was meant for Heaven. Pan told me that if I seduced her and damned her to Hell, I'd become Prince of Lust.*

Something flashed across her eyes—disgust, despair, or some combination of the two. But she held her tongue, kept her face schooled to impassivity.

So I watched her, I said with part of my mind as another pictured Virginia next to me, Virginia in the elevator as we told each other stories true and false, Virginia staring at me in wonder as she called me a superhero. *I learned about her. And then after I studied her, I inserted myself into her life.* Virginia inviting me over for dinner. "And she let me in."

Virginia teaching me how to eat a taco. My fingers brushing away the runner of sauce that had dribbled from the corner of her mouth.

"Last night she kissed me," I said for all the café to hear if they cared to while my teeth clenched in a grin I didn't feel, "kissed me willingly and knowing I wasn't what I seemed. Kissed me and then she was mine. And I fucked her."

I'm inside her and she's so wet and willing and she comes with a scream and pulses around my cock and I'm about to let go and my name is on her lips . . .

And I stopped her from calling my name. Grinning like a shark because if I stopped grinning I would have shouted, I met the angel's gaze and admitted the truth, which twisted my stomach into a knot and clawed at my chest like Virginia's nails in my shoulders: *I couldn't kill her. Couldn't take her soul.* My hands were shaking. I forced them steady, but I couldn't unclench my teeth. *So now she's damned but not dead, marked for Hell but unclaimed.*

The angel's eyes had softened as I'd spoken, and now they glistened with tears that shone like stardust. "Oh, my lord . . ."

And I have to kill her today, before our King decides my time is up and destroys me for failing him.

With a sigh, the cherub shook her head. "A painful decision, my lord."

You're going to help me.

She squeaked, "I?"

The same way you helped Jezebel when her man had died. You're going to keep Virginia safe, body and soul.

Her eyes clouded, and she took a quick sip of her drink before she spoke. "I wish I could, my lord."

"You can't tell me no."

"I can't tell you yes." *There are rules, my lord, especially for ones such as me, who traffic between Heaven and Hell. I can preserve life, yes. But I cannot aid a soul that is damned.*

You did for Jezebel's man. The prude apostle, his shoulders bigger than his imagination.

His soul was pure, Lord. What had happened to him had been an anathema.

"And this isn't?"

"What I think of your assignment and what is officially decreed are two different things."

Cold. From the angel's mouth, cold words. From my mind, cold promise: *Virginia's meant for Heaven.*

"She was." *Until you led her away from that path.*

Lead her back.

I cannot, my lord. She's damned for her lust. "There's nothing that I can do."

I closed my eyes, let out my breath in a long hiss.

Perhaps, the angel ventured, *when she is in Hell, you could oversee her torture? Soothe her agony?*

"There's no respite from the Bonfire," I growled. *I won't let her suffer.*

"You love her," the angel said.

My eyes snapped open. "Watch your mouth."

She frowned, her pale brow creasing, her gaze riddled with confusion. "Why? What did I say?"

My body clenched, taut with rage. *Demons don't love.*

Of course they do. You've been in love with Jesse Harris since I first met you.

Jezebel, walking toward the mountain complex of Pandemonium, and I'm watching her move, and I'm fascinated by her every step, as always. I don't understand what it is about her that affects me.

No.

It's something uniquely her, something I can't put my finger on, yet it's there all the same, in everything she does, everything she says, every motion of her body. It's infuriating and intoxicating. It's her.

Jezebel.

By all that was unholy, no.

Jezebel, pleading with me to let her save her man, her prude apostle who'd seduced her with his humanity, telling me that she loves him.

White-hot fury, searing me now, bathing the world in blood.

My hands on the angel's white throat.

She struggled beneath me, batted at my arms, clutched my fingers. Her panic fueled my ire and I squeezed. **Demons don't love.**

Her face purpled. Which shouldn't have happened; angels didn't breathe.

Demons didn't love.

It was because she'd dressed in a mortal form, I decided as my fingers pressed into cold, soft flesh: it allowed the angel to experience human sensations, or an echo of those sensations. A design flaw, as far as I was concerned. A wardrobe malfunction. That's what this so-called feeling was: a design flaw.

I didn't love Virginia.

I didn't love Jezebel.

"And I'll prove it to you," I told the angel before I shoved her away from me. She fell heavily upon the bar, coughing, her hands fluttering by her throat.

I felt the gazes of the other Voodoo patrons upon me, smelled their appreciation and their indifference and, in some, their fear. Screw you all. None of you matters to me. Only the cherub's despicable accusation mattered.

The fallen angel looked up at me, waves of white-gold hair framing her beautiful face, her neck discolored, her blue eyes brimming with sadness. "My lord," she wheezed.

I'll show you that all she is to me is a flesh puppet. "A fragile human doll," I spat.

I'm sorry, my lord. But whether for herself or for me, she didn't say.

A snarl on my face, I let my magic surge through me, and then I teleported to Virginia's house.

Chapter 20

Too Late

I materialized in her kitchen—no need for subtlety anymore. No need for anything other than throwing my power over her and having her speak my name before I killed her. I'd watch those emerald eyes glaze with passion before I fucked the life out of her. She'd die with a smile on her face and my name on her lips. Her soul in my custody.

Just another client.

Almost eight thirty in the morning. She should already be at her office, but I'd known she'd be home instead, basking in the afterglow of our sex, stretched languidly in her rumpled bed, naked, waiting for my return. I always left my clients wanting more. She would be no different. She was just another human doll, no matter her nature. And dolls were meant to be broken. Even the good ones.

Especially the good ones.

"Have to take it slow with the good people," I tell Callistus with a tight smile. *"I'm already influencing her actions."*

"Yeah?" He arches an eyebrow. *"She spreading her legs for you?"*

Oh, yeah. Hell, yeah. I grinned, but my face was too tight and my teeth were too large and it feels instead like I'm screaming.

"Virginia," I called out, my voice trumpeting her name, "I'm here."

"Here," she replied, from somewhere in the house. "Over here."

Not surprised, are you? Of course not. You knew in your pretty human heart that I'd come back for you.

I strode down the long hallway, already summoning my power so all I had to do was unleash it as soon as she looked up at me and smiled her welcome, past the bathroom and guest bedroom—but instead of the bedroom where I'd assumed she awaited with open arms and open legs, the door on the left was open, exposing the plain room with all its closed boxes and stuffed bags.

Except the boxes weren't closed anymore—not all of them. Hovering in the doorway, my fist quivering with magic, I looked in, my gaze darting around the small room, flitted across the hundreds, thousands of photos littering every surface in haphazard piles. Framed and unframed; loose and in albums; color, black and white. From miniatures to poster size. Photos and pictures and, now that I looked closer, sketches. A whirlwind of snapshots and portraits, scattered like debris, used and now discarded.

And there in the middle of the room was Virginia herself, wrapped in a faded terrycloth white robe like a castoff from an angel, her rich curls tied away from her face into a sloppy ponytail at the nape of her neck, Virginia sitting tailor-fashion on the floor with a sketch pad on her lap and a charcoal pencil in her hand. It was her, down to her scent, but something about her had changed—it was the easy motions of her shoulder and neck, no longer holding her pain; it was the faraway look of contentment in her eyes, so different from the momentary bliss of sex. It was subtle and it was overwhelming. It was the way she breathed as she sketched, as she created, as she lived. It was her. Virginia.

And I faltered.

Sweet Sin, look at her now: smudges on her pale forehead,

as if she'd impatiently brushed her curls away from her eyes before resorting to the hair clip; her lips, so plump and kissable, pursed as she worked; her mouth open slightly as if she had to coax the blooming image in front of her with her very breath; her eyes, dazzling and vibrant, moonlight on spring grass, as they focused on her work.

My magic slipped away as I watched her move the pencil over the paper, saw how she held it with such grace and precision.

She murmured, "Just need one more moment . . ."

"Take your time," I said, enthralled by how she conducted her own sort of music that transcribed song into form. Virginia the maestro, Virginia the artiste.

I'd let her finish the drawing before I claimed her. It was the least I could do.

More to busy myself than out of curiosity, I scooped up a handful of photos. And I smiled as I looked at them one by one. Here are some of Virginia from her youth—sitting with other children to lap up ice cream with their perfect, innocent pink tongues; Virginia alone, riding on a bicycle, her face trapped forever in an expression of exquisite delight; there, more images of Virginia embraced with friends and showered with love, of Virginia pensive and serious, a study of the woman buried within the girl. Older, now—stretched out long on a beach to let the sun drink her even more intimately than I had last night; laughing with other teens, their arms dangling loosely around each other's necks in easy trust; Virginia curled with a book; Virginia at one with her art as she evokes an image on a canvas with her paints and brushes. And here, Virginia as a woman grown, her body lushly feminine, her smile relaxed.

Her life, flashing before my eyes in a series of snapshots.

I found a large portrait of a woman in white and a man in a tuxedo. I gave the husband a moment's attention—his arms crossed over his chest, a huge smile on his face—before I studied Virginia in her bridal gown. She was glancing up at her man, a wicked grin on her face and joy alight in her eyes, her black curls pulled back and fastened with a white band. Her dress outlined her hourglass figure, snuggled her curves without obfuscating them in tons of lace and puffery so common to such garments in modern times. Her small hands were holding up the hem of the gown over her right leg, revealing the enticing shape of her calf, the eager length of her thigh . . . and the sinfully red garter, with a toy pistol tucked inside.

My Virginia.

I laughed softly, reached over to stroke the photo as if I could touch the garter snuggled over her thigh. Wondered if the gun had been her idea. Probably—she had a dark side that I hadn't had the chance to explore.

And never would.

I thought of her red scarf, its tail dangling over her full breast as if it were copping a feel, and how I'd decided that I liked Virginia in red.

"Okay."

Her voice—pleased, breathless—nudged me away from her wedding picture, that and the sound of paper tearing. Casting aside the photo, I looked over at her, at the woman who was going to make me Prince of Lust, the woman who meant nothing to me and yet somehow had come to mean something to me, the woman who'd seduced me with her goodness even as I'd damned her with my evil. The woman I was going to kill and take to Hell. Right now.

Except my power slipped through my fingers, wouldn't obey me.

Virginia, smiling down at the piece of paper in her charcoal-darkened hands. Saying: "It's not nearly as good as I'd like, but I had to go from memory. And feeling. I think I got it right by the eyes."

I had to kill her.

I couldn't kill her.

My heart screaming in my chest, my blood pounding in my head, I grinned at her, forced myself to be Daunuan and not Don Walker, showed her my appetite for her body and only her body as I leered, and lusted, and pretended that I was just an incubus who was untouched by her compassion, her laughter. Her life. "What do you have there, doll?"

"It's for you."

"I have something for you too." Reaching for my power, raging silently as it once again slipped away. I'd have to get her to kiss me, then, and jump-start the magic. Nothing was going to stop me from getting Virginia to say my name and bonding her soul to me.

She looked up at me as she stood, her smile nervous, and handed me the paper. "I hope you like it."

My hand, brushing hers as I take the offering, and something electric crackles over our fingers as we touch. Now. I'd do it now.

Before I told her to kiss me, I looked at the image on the paper. And my breath caught in my throat and time slowed, stopped as I stared at the picture.

A face looked back at me: my face, or Don Walker's, angular in its charcoaled lines yet softened by the stubble along the full jaw; dark, choppy hair that was too long in the front; straight nose, a narrow mouth set in an easy smile. And wide hazel eyes, heavy-lidded and sleepy ... with a spark of mischief, a hint of sin that spoke of long nights and sweaty sheets.

"Virginia." I breathed her name like it was a prayer or a curse or some combination of the two.

"Do you like it?"

"I ... yes, very much. It's wonderful. But ... why? Why draw me?" There had to be a reason, a motive. She'd beg me for more time. She'd tell me she wanted to draw and paint and do that with her life and leave her mark on the world, if only I'd give her more time. And I'd tell her no, and I'd delight in her despair and fuck her until she screamed and would feast on her soul.

"Because you made me want to draw again."

Something in her voice arrested me, pulled my gaze away from my own image, and when I looked at her I saw something in her eyes that I couldn't identify, something close to desire, something softer than lust. She said, "I haven't done anything like this since before Chris died. I never wanted to draw again. Until you." Smiling, now, and her voice was like music: "I woke up thinking about you, about how you make me feel. And I had to do something to show you, give you something for you to have. To keep."

Oh, doll.

"You don't have to give me anything," I said, voice gruff. I was going to take something like a thief; I didn't deserve anything like this.

"Of course not," she said, laughing. "Gifts aren't have-to's. I wanted to."

"I . . ." Fumbling for words, for something that I didn't understand. "What do you want in return for it?"

Her brow creased. "In return? Nothing. I'm not selling it to you. I'm giving it to you."

Her words made no sense. She had to want something for it. That was the way of things. Mortals offered, for a price. Demons gave, for a price. There was always a price. "You have to want something for it."

"More chocolate and flowers?" She giggled, such a girl, rested her hand on my arm. "No, silly. I don't want anything from you but you. God, you'd think you'd never gotten a gift before. Another habit I'm going to have to break you of."

What's a demon supposed to do with altruism?

"Want coffee? Me, I want coffee. Come on. Coffee time." She pulled me up, led me from the room with its memories of her life half-spewed on the floor, walked us to the kitchen, where she sat me down at the large table and then busied herself with her coffeemaker. Hummed to herself, out of tune but heartfelt, as she worked.

I set aside the drawing, closed my eyes. Listened to her wordless song. Said: "Virginia. I came here for you."

She hummed a little more, then said, "Want breakfast too? Maybe eggs?" Kneeling, she opened a cabinet and took out a large frying pan.

"I'm here for your soul."

She threw me a look over her shoulder as she stood up, eyes

laughing. "What, you're not after my body?" Using two hands, she put the pan on the stovetop.

"I'm a demon."

"My demon lover." She chuckled as she walked to the re-frigerator, opened it and rummaged inside. "It's dentists who're demons, not massage therapists. I think you're more a tiger than a demon."

My teeth clenched, I said, "Virginia . . ."

"Maybe some bagels . . ."

Why didn't she hear my words? "I'm going to kill you."

"Wait until after breakfast. I need coffee first."

She tossed off the quip with the ease of the already damned. She'd kissed me, and she was mine. She'd kissed me, and lost her inhibition. Her caution. Her fear.

Herself.

Virginia eschewed the refrigerator for the pantry, took out a paper bag. Dumped out a bagel onto the counter near her block of knives. "Only one left. Lucky you, I'm willing to split it."

I remembered Virginia as I'd first seen her, out with her friends and yet a half step behind them—the smile a touch too late to be spontaneous, Virginia sitting with her arms folded and her legs crossed and her shoulders so slightly hunched, all but screaming "keep your distance." That Virginia had been burned away in the heat of our kiss last night.

That was the Virginia I could kill. The Virginia I didn't yet know. A stranger, scarred by grief.

She took a bread knife from her block, started slicing the bagel.

I'll make you afraid, doll. I'll shock you awake, show you what's happening to you. And when you understand that you're doomed, you'll be that stranger again, and when I see your fear and your sorrow shining in your eyes, I'll pour my magic into you and force you to say my name.

"You think I'm joking. You think I'm this sleepy-eyed man—you think I'm a *man*." I rose to my full height, strode up to her and grabbed her shoulders, loomed over her. She dropped the bagel and the knife, stared up at me, annoyed, yes, but not afraid.

"I'll show you the truth," I growled. And then I shed my costume.

Her mouth opened in a silent gasp—her heartbeat quickened, her eyes widened as she stared at my horns, my fangs, the yellow of my eyes, the blue skin of my face. I released her shoulders and she stepped back, bumped against the counter, her gaze locked onto my form, taking in my long golden hair, the talons on my fingers, the thick pelt that began just over my hips and swathed my legs and ass, covered me down to my hooves. She stared at me, the demon Daunuan, and her hand flew to her mouth as if to muffle a scream.

Except she wasn't afraid.

No whiff of citrus, of rotting grapefruit. All I smelled was her unique scent . . . and a hint of pumpkin spice.

She wasn't afraid of me.

I never wanted her more than I did right now, at this moment, as she's standing in her kitchen in her old white robe. My blood pounded through me, boom *boom*, boom *boom*, sending happy signals to my brain and my balls. My body was already primed just from looking at her.

"Holy God," she breathed.

My lips quirked. "Not even close."

"You're . . ." Her hand fluttered by her mouth, then hesitantly reached out like she wanted to touch me, see if I was real. "You're blue." She blinked, looked me over again, slower this time. "And blond. A natural blonde, I see."

"Virginia . . ." Fuck me, don't laugh . . .

"And happy to see me. Wow. You're huge."

Grinning wide, I stepped up to her, erection first, and grabbed her upper arms. Hoisted her onto the countertop. Forget the fear factor; all I wanted was her. Forget what would happen after I seduced her; all that mattered was us, here. Now. "I'm an incubus, doll. Built for pleasure. Your pleasure."

"Don't call me 'doll,'" she said, distracted by my most prominent feature. "I should be screaming right now. I should be running for a crucifix."

"Wouldn't work," I purred, working at the knot of her robe.

She licked her lips, met my golden gaze. "Why aren't I afraid?"

"You kissed me willingly last night." The sash fell away and her robe parted, revealing her full breasts, her nipples already pearled and waiting for my mouth. I spread her thighs with my hands, and the triangular patch of dark curls between her legs begged for my touch. "When a mortal woman kisses an incubus, it kick-starts my magic. Strips away your inhibitions. Makes you want me." I ran the tips of my talons above her knees, the lightest of grazes.

"So you really are a magician," she said thickly, her eyes darkening as my hands crept up toward the apex of her thighs.

"I eat magicians for breakfast. And I'm going to eat you," I promised. "I'm going to make you come more times than you can count." My hand, gliding over her sex.

Pumpkin spice, and then: "Don?"

"Yes, Virginia."

"I wanted you before I kissed you."

Oh, doll.

I leaned into her and kissed her lips—tender, so very gentle. And then I hit her with my magic, bathed her in it, drenched her until she was sopping with it. She gasped into my mouth, then sighed, a long, deep sound that made my balls ache. Stepping back, I looked at her, bespelled, her head thrown back and her eyes closed, her mouth open and fixed in a smile, her breathing heavy, pulse quick.

Virginia entranced. Virginia waiting for my touch.

I had to do it now, before I stopped myself. Now, before I lost myself to feelings I didn't understand and shouldn't possess. Make her body sing with pleasure and make her call my name.

Ready, steady. Go.

My mouth on her neck, sucking, tasting. Fast, do it fast, and never mind how she's arching beneath me, how I smell her liquid heat between her legs. My hands on her shoulders, moving down, sliding the robe down—

And then a stink like drowning cats.

"Time's up, Daunuan," Callistus hissed in my ear. "You lose."

And then he yanked me away from Virginia and stabbed me in my back.

Searing pain, burning through me.

Gritting my teeth, I reached over my shoulders and grabbed blindly, caught his shoulders in my hands. Dug in. With a snarl I pivoted and flipped him over my back. His weapon jerked up, cutting through me and tearing my skin and muscles until it pulled free, nearly slicing through my neck in the process. He crashed against the table with an *oof*, scrambled to his feet.

Oh, fuck me raw, this hurts! Where his weapon had cut me my flesh screamed. Over the gallons of cologne he wore, I smelled smoke and sizzling meat and sweat. It felt like my back had been thrown into the Lake of Fire to cauterize the wound. Grimacing, I took a step forward, but the sheer agony in my back made me stagger.

He grinned at me, fangs flashing, red goat's eyes shining ruby bright against the snow of his skin. With exaggerated slowness, he licked my blood off his curved dagger. "Special blade for you, *Prince* Daunuan. Erinyes blessed. I'm going to gut you in righteous fury."

Oh, shit.

I shot out my fist and blasted with my power, but he dodged. *KABOOM!* went the kitchen table, grenading chunks of wood through the far end of the kitchen. Panting, I moved away from Virginia, who sat on the counter, lost in my magic, unaware of both demon and damage to her home. Thank Gehenna for small favors.

Cal sidestepped right, his weapon tight in his hand, his

hooves crunching over wooden debris, ignoring the splinters lacerating his chest and littering his pelt. We circled, me biding time to recharge my power, even with my body throbbing from the magic-touched cuts, him looking for an easy target. Cal always took the easy way out. Lazy bastard.

"What's the matter, oh Prince? You're looking a little pale."

"You smell like a nunnery."

"And you smell like meat. I think I'll fuck your woman before I destroy you." He chuffed laughter, grabbed his dick and pumped. "Give her something to remember before I claim her for Hell."

"Your dick is so small, she'll never know when you're inside of her."

He roared and threw his weapon, aiming for my heart. I leapt to the left, dangerously close to Virginia perched upon the counter. Too slow—I felt the blade embed itself in my right shoulder a moment before the pain hit me.

A scream in my ears, in my throat, as my shoulder burned and I smelled myself frying like hamburger. I fell heavily against the stove, landed in a heap on the floor, the large frying pan clattering next to me. Fury magic scorching through me, cooking me alive.

Got to get the blade out.

Can't move my arm.

Can't move at all.

Callistus approached slowly, his grin wide and his swagger proud, and he kicked me in the ribs. I bit back a grunt, struggled to move.

"You're so fucking pathetic," he said, shaking his head. He loomed over me, his cock curving up almost like a question mark. "You've had all the time in the world, and instead of claiming her, you courted her like a love-struck human. You're weak, Daunuan."

His hand, on Virginia's thigh.

No.

I refuse. Do You hear me? I refuse to let this scum-sucking bottom-feeder best me.

My power surged in me, through me, filling me with the energy of Hell, filling me to the bursting point. More than I'd ever taken before, and then some. And it hurt, yes . . . but oh, it felt so right inside of me. The knife popped out of my flesh, disappeared in a puff of brimstone before it hit the floor. Demon, heal thyself.

My left hand, moving now, reaching. Grasping something.

"And now I'm going to fuck your woman while you watch. And you'll hear her call my name before I kill her."

I closed my fist, felt the weight of the handle. Solid.

"And then," Callistus said, "I'm going to cut out your heart and bring it to the Boss and offer it and her soul to him."

He was on a roll and in love with the sound of his own voice. He didn't see me cock back the frying pan, or notice me charging it with my magic.

"And then I'll be Prince, and you'll be gone. And maybe your woman will be my chew toy."

"Hey, Cal," I said, my voice thready as if I couldn't draw breath. "Know what?"

He smirked down at me, the beaten thing at his hooves. "What?"

"You talk too fucking much." I swung up, smashed the pan into his knees and grinned at the crunch of bone.

Screeching like the damned, he clutched his legs. "Bastard!"

On my knees now, I backhanded him with the magic-heavy fryer, connecting with his stomach. His scream cut off as he doubled over.

Another swing, and I rearranged his face. He was staggering, his mouth and nose and cheek in ruins. I lifted the pan back like a baseball bat and swung again, smashing it into the side of his head. The force of the blow sent him flying across the kitchen, the sound of shattering bone loitering in the space where he'd been. He crashed onto the floor near the hallway with all the grace of a fallen rhinoceros.

A glance at Virginia showed me she was still under my influence, oblivious to the fighting and how close she'd come to getting killed by someone other than me. Lost in pleasure, she smiled, her head back, her breasts heaving and heavy. Be right back, doll.

Frying pan in my fist, I approached the shattered form of Callistus. He'd landed poorly; his neck was broken, and his arms had snapped like twigs. Didn't know if he'd been allergic to the iron in the pan or if my magic had been just that strong. Maybe a combination of the two. Didn't matter. He was dead.

And gone: with a final swing of the frying pan, I banished his remains to Hell.

Good fucking riddance.

"Well done, Lord Libertine."

I spun, weapon raised, my magic at the ready. And again, I was too late.

Eris, Princess of Envy, grinned at me as she held a knife to Virginia's throat.

Chapter 21

The Libertine's Punishment

"Oh, how I'm enjoying this."

Well, that made one of us.

The two women stood by the kitchen counter, Virginia with glazed eyes and a defeated set to her shoulders, Eris just behind her, holding the bread knife under Virginia's chin. Still in human garb, the Envious dripped with power—more than enough to stay my hand. Especially after the beating I'd taken from Cal's thrice-blessed Fury blade, Eris could wipe the floor with me.

"Virginia," I said, trying to feel whether any of my influence remained, or whether she was under Eris's power completely.

"She can't hear you," Eris said idly. "And call back your magic before I slice her like a pig."

Fuck.

Forcing down my power, I glared at Eris. "You have no claim over her."

"From what I see, rake, neither do you."

"She bears my mark."

"But her soul's untouched. Damned, yes. But not beholden." Eris smiled, and there was nothing bitter about it—it was a thing of sublime evil. "She's not my type, and she's a little small. But I think I'll keep her."

To hurt me. That's the only reason why she was doing this. I knew it in my gut, but I didn't know why. Not that the Jealous need a reason for anything they did; their Sin was fucking stupid. "So what're you going to do with your latest catch, pray tell?"

She shrugged. "Who knows? In a few hundred years, maybe I'll tire of watching her drown in the Water, give her to you for the Bonfire. Oh," she said, "I'm sorry, I forgot. You won't be around anymore, will you? No, when Pan's through with you for failing, you'll be nothing but an unpleasant memory."

My fists clenched at my sides, I shook with impotent rage. "You played me."

Eris raised her brows in mock surprise. "Of course I did."

"Why?"

She smiled, her lipstick red like raw meat. "Why? I could say that I wanted the boon your King offered."

I hissed a startled breath before I could stop myself.

"You didn't know? Oh, how rich." She chuckled, an ugly sound that made my stomach clench. "Your King had approached his peers with his decision to name you Prince of Lust. And he issued his challenge, which each either refused or accepted. Guess which King Mormo did?"

Belzebul, chortling in the restaurant, telling me that neither Gluttony nor Sloth would participate.

Pan's words, reverberating in my mind: *There's a certain decorum to be followed. I've already made my choice known to all the elite, across the Sins and Land.*

Pan. All along, it had been Pan. My liege-lord. My King.

All the lower-downs of Hell know that the King of Lust wants the incubus Daunuan to be his Prince, First of Principals.

Even before he'd told me of his plans for me, he'd set events in motion. The Coveter in the park. The Arrogant outside the wine bar. The Berserker in my client's bedroom. Callistus for Lust, doubly bound as Pan's errand boy and stand-in for Prince.

And Eris, Lady Envy, here before me, with Virginia's life in her hands.

All you have to do is prove yourself. And then the rank, and the power that goes with it, are yours.

Pan had set the elite of Hell after me so that I could prove my worth. Or maybe my only test really had been whether I could lure a pure soul into an act of lust, and the additional challenge was part of the decorum even Pan had to follow. Or maybe he'd done it because it amused the fuck out of him.

I'd have to ask him myself.

"So what was the challenge, Princess? Bedding me? You certainly threw yourself at me last week in California."

She laughed, musical and light, completely at odds with the bitterness in her jade eyes. "That? That little charade was to get you to let down your guard, rake. You're as susceptible to flattery as any of your ilk."

And hers. "Maybe I just like flirting with beautiful women."

"Maybe I'll relish being the one who destroys you." She pressed the curved point of the knife under Virginia's chin, used it to tip up her head, expose her pale throat. "Funny to think that this sorry excuse of a mortal is going to give me a boon from Lust. She hardly seems worth all the fuss."

"Is that what you're getting out of this? A boon? From Pan?" I threw my head back and laughed. Through my chortles, I said, "A little advice, Princess. Pan lies."

"Of course he does. But some things are binding, even to one such as him. He swore on his name to give a boon to the designee of Sin who destroyed you before you completed his little assignment." She grinned. "And that honor belongs to me."

"And here I thought you liked me."

"Oh, Daunuan, I've despised you for so long. Waited for so long for things to fall into place. Centuries of waiting. And now, rake, all my patience has paid off."

I smiled, nonchalant, seeking any way to disarm her. "Don't know what you're babbling about, Princess."

"Of course you do." Eris, indignant. "You stole from me. And now I'm stealing from you." She pressed the knife closer to Virginia's throat.

"What did I steal?"

"A boy." Her jade eyes flashed hatred like heat lightning, and she spoke a name that left me breathless. "Wolfgang Mozart."

I remembered that night from so long ago, kneeling by the child's side and burning away his sickness so that he could continue to make his music, heard my own words as I told him why I was saving him: *"You were to go to Envy. A blood sacrifice. An eternity of freezing water, all so that your father could be the only Mozart people remembered."*

"You," I said to the Envious. "You were the one trucking with Leopold, bartering with him for the boy's soul."

"Indeed. Years of work, of watching him and tempting him on the sly, wasted. All because of you." Her eyes leaked red as she spoke, hissing her accusation. "Even after he and I reached our agreement, you put your mark on the boy. And he accepted your claim, so there was naught I could do. You *stole* him!"

Whoops.

"It wasn't against you personally," I said, holding out my hands, attempting to mimic supplication while I tried once again to push Virginia with my magic. "The boy's talent was too good to waste, just to appease the father's jealousy."

"You know nothing of jealousy!" Her hand trembled with either palsy or fury—and while I hoped for one I was certain it was the other—and the serrated edge of the knife bit into Virginia's throat. "Call it back, incubus, now! Unless you want her to have a second mouth!"

Shit.

Once again, I pulled back my magic. My face was sculpted to impassive perfection, but my thoughts were careening through my head as I reviewed my options. What few there were, that was. I had to do something, had to get the Envious away from Virginia. But bless me for an angel, I didn't know what to do. If I used my power, Eris would strike. And if I stood here and did nothing, Eris would strike. She loomed, cobralike, her blade as deadly as any snake's venom. Virginia's glazed eyes stared at me as if I'd betrayed her.

Which I had, hadn't I? All along, I'd betrayed her trust. I was a demon. What did I know of things like trust, like loyalty?

But I did know flattery.

"You're right," I said, voice soft. "I know nothing of jealousy."

Eris's eyes narrowed. "You admit this?"

"Of course. How could I even try to understand your Sin, which you know so intimately?" Slow, slow. Flatter her, yes, but don't be a sycophant. Seduce her with words, and hint at what could happen with our bodies. All she had to do was lower the knife, and then I'd show her what I could do with my body. "All I know is lust."

"Yes," she hissed. The knife gleamed.

"But are the two so very different? You said yourself, Princess, that lust is envy of another's sexual prowess."

"And you replied that envy is nothing more than lust for everything anyone else has."

Hands out, coaxing now. Appealing to her vanity. "Maybe our Sins are more alike than even we admit."

Her hand wavered, and I thought for a moment this would work. And then Eris laughed, and I knew that Virginia was a dead woman.

"This," Eris said. "This is what I was waiting for all this time. Finally, there's something that you value more than that cock of yours, something that is truly important to you. Something that you want, more than anything. You stole from me, rake. And now I'm going to steal from you."

My mind whirling, I asked, "Why steal, Princess? I'll buy you something. I know a terrific shoe store. You love shoes, don't you? Of course you do, you're a woman. Let me take you shopping. I'll get you something nice."

She arched an eyebrow. "Oh, really?"

"Anything you want."

"How considerate, Daunuan. What I want is this woman's life." She grinned, and I felt her magic roar. "So I'll take it now."

A reek of festering dandelions and burned coffee as Eris's power washed over Virginia and clung like freezing water.

"Virginia," Eris said, her voice sickly sweet. She inched the knife higher, pricked the delicate skin until a bead of blood welled up, began to dribble. "He lied to you, Virginia."

Held by the demon's magic, Virginia said nothing.

"He's going to leave you. Just like your husband left you."

"No," Virginia whispered. Her gaze pierced me even as Eris's knife pierced her, and I felt the cut sting just as much.

"Stop," I said, reaching out with my magic and getting slapped away. "Eris, stop!"

"After everything you've done," the Envious crooned, "everything you've given up for him, he's going to use you, just like everyone else. He'll take what he wants, and then he'll walk away. That's what they do, Virginia. They walk away and never look back. Never return. They leave you, alone. Forever."

"No—Virginia, don't listen to her! She lies!"

Eris, smiling at me, like I'm amusing. "He's a demon, Virginia. He lies. That's what he does. He tricks you and teases you and promises you the world. He promises you that he'll stay. But he's going to leave you. Just like your husband."

"Oh . . ." Tears in Virginia's eyes now, scalding me as they slowly dripped down her cheeks. "He's going to leave me."

"Like your husband."

"Like Chris." Her voice was a sigh, forlorn and small. And so very hurt.

"Virginia! Don't listen to her!"

"And you'll be alone. Forever alone. And it's his fault."

The tears streamed faster now, but Virginia's sobs were

silent. As she stared at me, the glaze in her eyes slowly turned to hatred.

"He made you betray your husband's memory, and for what? For him to leave you when he's done. Discarded," Eris said. "Abandoned."

"You lied to me," Virginia whispered.

I called her name, but she didn't hear me.

"So bitter, just like when your husband was dying and nothing you could do could stop his pain or stop him from leaving you. So bitter, just like when you had to pick up the pieces of your life, alone." Eris's voice, hypnotic, insistent. "You feel it, don't you, Virginia? The bitterness, spreading through you like frostbite?"

And her response, so very soft: "Yes."

"The bitterness that he caused."

"Yes."

"No!" I lunged forward, but Eris stopped me with a press of her knife. Slicing deeper, the bead stretched into a small, steady leak. Virginia's life began to ebb away in a red ribbon. I thought of how I'd wanted to see Virginia in red, and the memory sickened me. Snarling my frustration and my dread— and my fear, oh, bloody Hell, I was so afraid for her—I tried to think of an answer. I had to do something, anything.

"Do you want to show him how much he hurt you, Virginia? Do you want to hurt him too?"

"Yes . . ."

No, doll. No. You're stronger than this . . .

"Then take the knife, Virginia, and slice your wrists."

"No!" I hurled my magic over Virginia, but Eris's power covered her, had frozen over her and both shielded and consumed her. I couldn't reach her.

As if she were already floating in the freezing waters of Envy, Virginia slowly reached for the knife Eris held by her neck. Took the handle. Started to aim for her left wrist.

"Virginia," I shouted, "I'm not going to leave you!"

Down came the knife, slow, steady. Unerring in its path.

"Please, don't do this! Virginia! I won't leave you!"

"He's lying," Eris said with a triumphant grin.

And then I knew what to say, knew what I'd been fighting and what would save her, the only words possible to say: "I love you."

Three words, more powerful than the strongest magic. I felt it in my chest, on my tongue; three words that could topple mountains and launch wars and shake the very Firmament. Three words that touched the rim of Creation.

Three words that touched my heart.

Virginia paused. In her hand, the knife trembled bare inches above her wrist.

"He's lying," Eris hissed. "Slice your wrists. The long way, down to your elbow. No mistakes."

"I love you," I said again, because she needed to hear it and I needed to say it. "You've changed me, Virginia. You've given me something I could never repay, something precious. Fragile. Something completely you. Something no one's ever given me before. I love you," I said, and Gehenna help me, I meant it.

Three words that could damn a demon.

As if waking from a dream: "Don . . ."

"Virginia, he's lying! Demons don't love!"

Focusing on the woman I needed to save, not for my own advancement but because she deserved to be saved, I asked, "Do you believe me, doll?"

"I . . ."

"He's lying!"

Her hands shaking fiercely, Virginia lowered the knife. "I believe you."

"Then call my name and let me save you."

And I reached inside and summoned more power than I'd ever had before, summoned it and more, until I was on fire with the energy of Hell and I threw it all into Virginia, melted Eris's hold over her, touched Virginia's core, and basked in her scent of the sweetest jasmine and blackberries, the richest chocolate and musk.

A burst of pumpkin spice, and when Virginia opened her

mouth she didn't call me Don Walker, because in their souls all humans know the nefarious. With a voice as passionate as any of Mozart's concertos, Virginia called my name: "Daunuan!"

Yes.

I saw it now, clear and shining and bright as a song in the air: her soul, a dazzling white gold, with the faintest tinge of red like a blush on an angel's cheek. Breathtakingly beautiful. I touched it and branded it, and with that one word and that one touch, Virginia was mine.

And then Eris grabbed the knife and plunged it into Virginia's stomach.

The world, in slow motion:

I'm throwing a bolt of power into Eris, shrieking my rage and denial as my magic bursts through me and slams into her, staggering her, and the knife clatters to the floor, and—

Virginia, falling to her knees, her hands clutched to her stomach, the blood seeping between her fingers, and—

Eris laughing now as I lunge to Virginia's side to catch her before she falls to the ground, Eris laughing at my pain and Virginia's pain and laughing at the dissention she's caused because truly that's what she does, that's her nature, and—

My fingers over Virginia's, trying to stop the bleeding because I had to save her from me and from the Pit, but the blood's gushing out of her and she's crying from the pain and look how her body is covered in her blood how her white robe is stained red and oh sweet Sin not like this, and—

Hands on my shoulders and now ice is wrapping over me and Eris is leeching my magic, Eris is under my skin and inside of me, and—

Virginia slips from my fingers and rolls to the floor and her blood is leaking out of her and onto the wooden planks beneath her, lapping up her life as red merges with brown, so slick and wet.

The world, frozen and cracking, everything just about to break.

"Hurts, doesn't it?" Eris laughed, the sound bitter and so very cold. "Having your prize stolen from you. Hurts more than you've ever known."

"You bitch." I was on my knees, Eris's hands clawing into my shoulders as she ravaged me, pulled at my very essence. "Get off!"

"She's dead, Daunuan. So what that you claimed her? She's dead and damned. And if you didn't lie to her, if you really do love her, then it's going to eat at you how she's damned to Hell." She hissed in my ear, "I win."

No!

I had to stop her. Had to save Virginia. But Eris was draining me, stealing my power and my strength, and her magic was spreading through me and coating my heart.

"Like I told you, Libertine. Envy always triumphs over lust."

She'd told me something else, too, that night at the opera, that night forever ago before Virginia: *Love is beyond either of us.*

She'd been wrong then.

My hands reached up, covered hers.

She was wrong now.

Deep within, I felt my magic thrumming through me, magic that connected me to Hell and defined who and what I was, magic that was so different from that of the Envious, whose own power was spreading through me like poison. I touched my magic and drew on the essence of Lust and more, drew on the strength of Sin itself, the Central Transgression that bonded all seven Sins of the nefarious. It crashed over me in a tsunami of raw energy, sucked me under and I opened wide and welcomed the pain and the power and let it drown me, ravage me. And more than me: it grabbed onto Eris, connected to me as she siphoned my magic, grabbed onto her and twisted and pulled. For what is envy, at its core, but another name for lust?

Eris screamed, tried to pull her hands away. "What are you doing? Stop!"

"Hurts," I said through clenched teeth, "doesn't it?"

"Stop!"

"As you stopped for her, I stop for you now." The magic roared through me, through us, and I slowly leeched her power as she'd tried to leech mine.

She swayed and fell, but my hands were still locked onto hers, pinning them to my shoulders. Sagging against my back, she said, "Stop . . . give you anything . . ."

"Anything?"

"Yes . . . please . . ."

"Well then. I'll stop."

She sighed, and I thought I felt her smile.

"Lady Envy?"

"Yes . . . Lord. Libertine." Her voice a thready breath now.

"I lied."

And I sucked her dry until her shell crumpled in upon itself like a mummified corpse and I kept going until that, too, crumpled and disintegrated into nothing more than ashes. They blew in the updraft of my magic, until I forced it back and let myself be just Daunuan, and the ashes of Eris drifted down in spiraling patterns and landed one atop the other, as if jealous of the space they each tried to possess.

In my arms, Virginia lay dying.

I'd cauterized the wound, but she'd lost too much blood, and the knife had torn up her insides. Demons don't heal; all we can do is destroy. She groaned against her pain, her face sweat-slick.

It wasn't supposed to be like this, doll. I was supposed to please you, make you feel good. Supposed to give you a piece of Paradise before I took you to Hell.

She shuddered as her life bled out, drew in a labored breath. Her face creased with agony. Whispered a name that wasn't mine. His. The husband's.

A freezing pain in my heart. Eris would have laughed.

Oh, Virginia. You never were mine, were you?

Tears streamed from her eyes, and she cried out.

"Shhh," I said, holding her close. "It's okay."

A gift, then. In exchange for what she'd given me so freely. A ripple of power washed over me, altered my form.

Stroking her cheek, I said, "Vee. Open your eyes, honey."

Her eyelids fluttered, opened. She smiled, said, "Chris."

She was looking at me like I was her everything, and for a blinding moment it's Jezebel in my arms, Jezebel dying, and I'm trying to soothe her pain before I take her to Hell.

"Vee," I said, smiling at her like I loved her, for I did love her, I loved her and now she was leaving me. "It's okay, honey. I'm here."

"Miss you."

"But I'm here now. Here to take you home."

"Please. Don't leave me."

"Oh, my Virginia. Vee. I'm right here."

In my arms, she gasped as the pain ate her alive. Whispered, "Love you."

"I love you too. Sleep, Vee. I'll be here when you wake."

I kissed her brow and stole her pain. With a sigh and a smile, she fell asleep.

And then she died.

I held her, rocked her as her body cooled. Her soul beckoned to me, tucked within her broken mortal shell. All I had to do was call her, and she'd come. Even now, I saw the tie between us, the soul bond that we'd forged with my magic and her calling my name. Pulsing with white-gold brilliance, Virginia's soul slept.

At one point, her phone rang. Soon I heard Virginia's voice, sounding tinny and flat and nothing like, her yet sounding so very alive, Virginia's voice telling me that she's sorry that no one was home, but leave a message and she'd call back.

But that's a lie, doll. There's no coming back for you. I sighed, stroked her hair.

"Hey, Vee!" The friend, Terri, sounding disgustingly chipper and perky. "You didn't call after the concert, so I figured that your Romeo stayed over. Tried you at work, but they said you called in sick, which you and I both know is an utter lie, girl! Can't wait to hear the juicy details about last night! I hope you're in his arms right now, listening to this and laughing your ass off!"

In my arms, yes, but listening as only the dead can listen. I've killed you, as surely as if I'd been the one who'd plunged the knife into your belly.

"Call me!" A click, and Terri's voice was gone.

How could I take her to Hell? How could I let the fires of the Heartlands char her until she was as black as Sin itself? She was meant for Heaven. Just like angels were meant to dance in the Sky, not seduce mortals Below. It struck me, as I caressed Virginia's cold face, that life and the afterlife were grossly unfair.

But what did demons know of fairness? There were rules, and there were ways to break them. That was all.

Time to stop playing by the rules. Time to change the game.

Angel, I called, picturing the cherub in all her haughtiness and her innocence that the Abyss had not yet warped. We had a connection; she'd proven it at the Voodoo Café when she'd spoken to me, mind to mind. Seducer to Seducer. We had a link. She would answer. *You hear me, don't you?*

Like a beacon in my mind: *My lord Daunuan?*
Come.

I summoned her, called her presence to mine just as Pan had summoned me in his chamber. My magic reached out through our link, found her and embraced her, sank into her. Tugged. Reeled her in.

A ripple of wind, a winter breeze, heavy with snow, and then the angel stepped out of the nothingness between realities, first one long leg and then the other, the angel standing before me now, like a vision in white, from her hair to her gown to her bare feet, to the feathery wings I'd never seen before and had not had the imagination to picture them in their soft, snowy perfection. She was starkly beautiful, but it was the hint of heat beneath the white shell of her form, the heat of lust, that transformed her into something radiant. A creature of Paradise, a creature of the Pit, a walker of two worlds. And, perhaps, a guardian angel.

She saw me and Virginia, and she sighed as if it had been her heart that had broken. "Oh, my lord. I'm so sorry."

"Don't need your pity." My voice, rasping and cold. "Need a favor."

"I told you, my lord, I cannot help her. She's—"

"Damned. I know." Snarling, now, the venom spewing from my mouth and raining down on the cherub, scaring her, making her flinch. "I did it to her. She wears my brand."

"Did you . . . ?" Her gaze flicked to the blood, the wound that had stolen Virginia's life.

"No."

"Ah." She glanced around, took in the damage, inhaled deeply. "Another incubus. And . . . one of the Jealous?"

"Yes. On both counts."

"Two against one is hardly fair," she said.

That made me laugh, and once the sound erupted I couldn't call it back—my guffaws filled the deathly still air, a sound of strangled mirth, of desperate absurdity. When I could finally speak, I said, "News for you, Feathers: Hell isn't fair."

"So I'm learning."

My insane laughter quashed, I sighed, stroked Virginia's hair. "And I'm going to complain to management about just how unfair it is."

"My lord?"

I looked up at her, saw the puzzlement on her face. Grinned, even though I really wanted to scream. "I need you to hold on to her soul for me. Temporary storage. Keep her safe for a little while longer." I took a deep breath, said, "Please. Can you do this for her?"

Something passed behind her eyes, a thought I couldn't read, an emotion I didn't want to understand. "Of course, my lord."

"Then come here, you."

She knelt beside me, and I grabbed her, too roughly, but she didn't complain, and I pressed her lips to mine and I gave her Virginia's soul, felt the tie of blushing white-gold loosen and slip away.

It's just for now, doll. I promise you, I'm coming back.

"She's sleeping," I said when it was done, because I needed to hear my voice to fill the emptiness inside of me. "Don't wake her."

"I won't, my lord." The angel cleared her throat, asked, "Where are you going?"

"To speak to our King." I'd let my hands do the talking.

"Ah."

"I'll be back for her, angel. Mark me on that."

"I'll be waiting for you, my lord. And my lord Daunuan?"

"Yes."

"Good luck."

I smiled, and there was no hint of humor about it. "Good or evil, I'll take what I can get."

And with that, I went to Hell.

Chapter 22

The Great God Pan

Smells of sex and blood, smells of sweat and terror. The blackness of Pan's antechamber surrounded me, but instead of inspiring panic or memory, it fanned my rage.

I'm here, my lord King.

A snort in my mind, and then: *COME BACK TOMORROW.*

This won't wait.

YOU'RE SUCH A PAIN IN MY ASS, DAUN.

As if that's ever been a problem before, Lord.

FINE, COME IN. MIND YOUR HOOVES AND DON'T STEP ON THE WORSHIPERS.

I didn't wait for him to Summon me with his magic; I focused on his presence and blinked myself to his side, cutting through the blackness and the odors of rotting meat, charging through the crushing weight between rooms.

And found myself in the midst of an orgy.

The grotto, filthy with mud, smelled like bat shit and human sweat and sex of all varieties. Humidity clung to the air (quite the feat, considering we were in the center of the Earth); the sultry wetness weighed heavily against me, slowed my limbs as dampness crawled over my skin. Hundreds of bodies littered the floor and walls of the cave, demons and damned and other nefarious writhing in serpentine passion, the sounds of their fornication filling the space, reverberating over rocks and down stalactites, taunting, compelling. A backbeat to the music of sex were panpipes and flutes and fiddles, their satyr musicians stomping time with their hooves. The smells and the sounds and the sights all blended, weaving a spell of seduction that gorged my dick and made my balls throb and filled my head with the sound of my heartbeat in a demanding BOOM *BOOM!!!* And I clenched my teeth against the hypnotic pull of passion.

In the center of the cave was a bed, his bed, spilling over with harpies, dryads, fauns, and two sphinxes, and at the top of the pile of flesh lounged the King of Lust, grinning wickedly as at least three woman pleasured at least six parts of his body. Looked like he'd had his fill of angels.

The great god Pan looked down on me, his blue goat's eyes alight with mischief. "Dive in, Daun. The water's fine." He smacked someone's ass, the slap muffled by the sounds of sex and music.

"You set me up." My voice was soft, barely audible over the din of the room. He heard me, though, as I knew he would.

He rolled his eyes. "Shit, do we have to do this now? I finally got me some prime Queen candidates here." He chuffed the harpy next to him under the beak, and she squawked her glee.

"Now."

"You are such a fucking buzzkill."

"Clear the Court or keep them as witness. Makes no matter to me."

He stared at me, his eyes hot as blue fire, and then he snorted. "Fine, fine. You heard your Prince. Get the fuck out of here." With a carefree motion of his hand, he banished the audience, even the dryad working between his legs. He'd also transformed the grotto into an empty black room, windowless and doorless. Flaming torches held aloft by sconces provided the only light, reflecting off the polished obsidian walls and floor, slick and cold after the damp heat of the cave. The smell of sex lingered in the air, or maybe that was just Pan himself.

"Private enough for you?"

"Yes, Lord."

"So what's on your mind, Daunuan?" He grinned, slapped his thighs with his meaty hands. "I know you've succeeded. I smell her on you, like frozen chocolate. Delish!"

"You set me up."

"What, the elite? Please. Had to go through the motions. It's the way of things. Anything that keeps the Nameless Shit's eye on Hell and away from the mortal coil is fine by our Supreme Ruler." He spat, a red, wet glob that landed near my hooves.

I growled, "They almost killed me."

"Wah, wah, wah. Grenades and horseshoes, Daun. Besides, they didn't kill you, did they?"

Not me, no.

"Like I said, it's the way of things. You won, that's all that matters."

Maybe once, before I'd been told to lure a pure soul into committing an unforgivable act of lust. But no longer.

"So this is a complete win-win," he said, rubbing his hands. "I have me a Prince I'm proud to call my number one, and I didn't have to pay a boon to one of those loser Sins. So, where is she?"

Hands clenched, I said nothing.

"Okay, I get it. You want it official, right? Fine. I, Pan, King of Lust, do hereby name Daunuan as my Prince of Lust." He chortled, said, "You thought you had power before as a first level? Wait until you get a load of this." His magic hit me, faster than thought—it burrowed into me and found my core.

And I absorbed it like a sponge soaks up water.

"Huh." He stared at me, then smiled, shook his head. "And here I thought I'd be opening the door for you. But you already touched that power, didn't you? See, this is why the challenge was necessary. Whatever doesn't kill you really does make you stronger, Daunuan."

"So I'm learning."

"And now, the grand prize. Where's the dolly?"

I stared flatly into Pan's goat eyes, let my silence speak for me.

"Come on, Daun. Let me see her. I want a little taste."

No.

He blinked, smiled. "Excuse me?"

I said no.

He laughed, huge and loud and completely without humor. "Funny guy. Let me see her."

"No."

"You don't get to tell me no, Daunuan." Eyes narrowed, hands clenched, his power thrummed inside of him, malevolent, festering. I sensed it as easily as I'd sensed Virginia's soul, sensed it as lust calling to lust. "Hand her over."

My eyes narrowed. "No."

His lips peeled back into an obscene grin. "Holy fuck in Heaven, I don't believe it. My boy Daun's smitten! You've got the hots for your dolly!"

I said nothing as he chortled, said nothing as he wiped away tears from his eyes and shook his head and snorted. "My boy's in *lurve*. Oh, bless me, Daun, you've made my day. My year! You're just too fucking cute. What happened? Got one taste of her good snatch and suddenly you're changing your evil ways? We don't change, Daunuan." The humor bled out of his face. "No cunt out there can cure you of your ills."

Baring my fangs, I said, "She didn't *cure* me."

"No, but she's gotten under your skin all the same. Where is this dolly of yours? I want to see the one who's gotten you all fucked up." He smiled, said, "She had this effect on you, maybe she'll be worth a turn in the sack from me."

My stomach knotted as I pictured him showering his brand of affection on Virginia, warping her soul until it was charred and black and as empty as those angels had been in his bed.

No.

No fucking way was I letting him touch her.

"Maybe she'll keep me entertained long enough that I'll audition her for Queen. What do you say, Daun? Would you like your dolly to reign over the succubi? Give you a chance to get laid by her through eternity?"

"You can't have her."

YOU DON'T GET TO TELL ME NO!

His voice roared through my mind, and I staggered, pressed my hands to my head. His words echoed, clanging like death knells, deafening me. I sensed him approaching, but couldn't drop my hands from my head.

Couldn't stop him from gripping my neck and squeezing.

"I've opened you up to more power than you'd ever imagined!" His voice, like rabies—a thing of madness and teeth. "I've made you my number one! I even picked out a dolly for you that looked like the runaway slut you liked so much!"

His magic sizzled through me, but even as I strangled I sucked up that power, used it to keep him from crushing my throat.

"I did that for you, Daunuan, gave you the chance to fuck her and kill her and have your wicked way with her, because I knew how much you missed your little succubus! And this is how you repay me?"

He threw me to the floor. I skidded across the room, then scrambled to my hooves, my head still ringing from the impact of his voice in my mind. I pivoted my body sideways and held my hand in front of me like a sword, the magic already gathering there, turning my fist into scarlet fire. I snarled, "She's too good for you."

His eyes telegraphed his disgust, how little he thought of my power, of my defiance. Rage contorted his face into a mask of evil that would make the Seraphim piss their togas. I prepared myself to counter the blast that was surely coming, thinking that he'd lead with his left and attempt to sucker-punch me with his right.

Then Pan blinked, and his infernal fury slipped away, replaced by a sheepish smile. "Screw me senseless, you really do love her, don't you?" He sighed, bemused. "Love belongs to lust. So how can I be upset with you?"

Because love has no place in the Pit, and you're an evil bastard who gets his jollies by tormenting others.

Keeping my magic pointed at him, I asked, "What're you saying, Lord?"

"Unholy Hell, look at us fighting over a woman. A woman! As if between the two of us, we haven't fucked half of Creation!" He chuckled, shook his head. "You want to keep her? You got it. Here, I'll even swear on my name." He cleared his throat, then shouted, "I, Pan, King of Lust, swear that I won't touch Daunuan's dolly while she's under his protection. In return, Daunuan will serve faithfully as Prince of Lust." He spat into his hand, then offered it for a shake. "Deal?"

Too easy.

"Daun," he said, holding out his hand, "we go back since almost the Beginning. Let's not have a woman come between us." His face revealed nothing other than his rueful smile, his unreadable eyes.

Much too easy.

But he's my King.

Frowning, I lowered my hand, quenched the magical fire with a thought. "We do go back a ways." In my mind, I saw me and Pan, eons ago, charging over the rocks of a stream, water nymphs tucked under each arm as Poseidon reared up behind us with the force of a tidal wave, roaring his displeasure at us borrowing his daughters.

Good times.

"There you go," he said, grinning. "Come on. Let's shake on it, make it official . . . Prince Daunuan."

I spat into my palm, and the saliva sizzled from the heat I still emanated. I gripped his hand, pumped once. A tingle on my skin as the deal took effect.

And then excruciating pain in my gut.

I stared down at the blood gushing out of my stomach, at the end of a white blade sticking out of me, at the hilt of the dagger in Pan's hand. As I understood what was happening, the pain exploded into agony that ripped away the world.

"Can't protect her if you're dead, Daun."

He twisted the hilt and pulled up, and I screamed as the dagger sliced through me, grazed over my ribs.

Pulling me close, Pan whispered in my ear like a lover sharing sweet nothings. "I know your weakness, Daunuan. The pain you feel? That's a diamond blade. Had it made just for you."

Oh no no no not diamond not that . . .

"You're dead, incubus."

And he twisted the blade again and aimed for my heart.

. . . my insides are being ripped apart by a knife hotter than lightning hotter than the Lake of Fire hotter than anything in all of Creation and I feel it inside of me searing me melting me and I can't move can't think of anything other than the pain Satan spare me the pain and I'm screaming and I want to die if only the pain would stop stop stop please make it stop . . .

YOUR FAULT, DAUN. THIS IS ALL YOUR FAULT. ALL YOU HAD TO DO WAS GIVE ME YOUR DOLLY. AND NOW I HAVE TO KILL YOU BECAUSE YOU DISOBEYED. YOU FUCKING SELFISH ASS.

. . . all there is in all of existence is the pain in my body and Pan's words in my mind and I'm dying even as Virginia died I'm dying with a diamond blade in my gut and my insides are leaking out and . . .

I'M GOING TO ENJOY CHARRING HER SOUL OVER THE CENTURIES. SHE'S GOING TO WARM MY BED UNTIL SHE'S A SHELL OF WHAT SHE'D BEEN, UNTIL THE VERY THING YOU LOVED HER FOR ISN'T EVEN A MEMORY.

. . . no.

Not her.

I won't let him touch her.

I swim through the agony and grab his hand on the hilt of the knife and thinking of Virginia I open myself up to the power of Hell. It surges through me, the very essence of Sin that shapes us as creatures of Anger or Pride, of Greed or

Envy, of Sloth or Hunger, and of Lust, of course, of Lust, and, damn me, it's all lust, all of it—desire for another's belongings, desire for ambition, desire for anyone and anything. It's all desire; it's all lust. It's all me.

I am Hell.

Myself. Daunuan.

I burn with the power of a supernova—cleansing fire, healing fire, all consuming. Energy like I've never felt before sings inside of me, a cosmic symphony, and I take that energy and focus it on the diamond blade inching toward my heart and with a thought I transform diamond into coal, and because demons are creatures of coal I absorb it into myself with a bubbling hiss as my wounds heal.

And then I open my eyes and see the startled look on Pan's face.

And I grin.

Pan, confused and, dare I say it, on the verge of panic as he suddenly held only the hilt of a dagger. "What the fuck . . . ?"

"Hey, Boss," I said, feeling my grin stretch into something feral. "I quit."

Still clasping his hand, I inundated him with my power, Hell's power, poured it into him and poured and poured, filling him until his skin distended and he stumbled to his knees.

"No," he burbled, his lips thick and chins tripled and face as broad as Belzebul's.

You don't get to tell me no.

"Nooooooo—"

And then I opened the floodgates and unleashed the full force of Hell. The power surged through me, exquisitely agonizing, using my body as a focus and letting me use it in return as I funneled it all into Pan. His flesh bloated, ballooned and kept expanding, and he screeched as I kept flooding him with the power, *my* power . . .

. . . and then, *boom.*

Wet heat slapped me as my ears and head rang from the

combustion. Chunks of what had been my liege-lord rained down on me, smoking and blackened, dripping with ichor and blood. Over the smell of brimstone and sex was the stink of goat meat. Broiled.

The great god Pan was dead.

Gritting my teeth, I pulled back my power, harnessed it and forced it down, even as it reared and squirmed to be free. Down, down, diminishing its fire—and finally extinguishing it. The magic of Hell was back in the Firmament of the world, resting. Waiting for me to touch it again.

I collapsed to the floor in a boneless heap, panting, completely drained and possessed with an insane hunger for feta cheese. After I could stand again, I'd eat. In about twenty years. Fuck me raw, I hurt all over. My eyes closed, and I drew a shuddering breath. Sleep. I needed to sleep.

DAUNUAN.

I screamed as His voice boomed in my mind, the voice of the Lord of the Abyss—the one who ruled us all and destroyed us on a whim, His voice trumpeting my name in my mind like the horn announcing Judgment Day.

COME.

In a blink I was in a large room blazing with the light of crystal candelabras dangling from the ceiling and white candles glowing in their silver wall sconces, a room walled with mirrors and a pattern of ivory thorns. In front of me was a dais, bloodred, at the top of which was a large marble chair carved with lions and bulls and eagles, proud and fierce and violent. The throne of Abaddon.

Upon which sat the King of All Kings, in His white perfection.

Oh fuck oh fuck oh fuck oh—

I tore my gaze away before I truly saw Him, threw myself prostrate at the foot of His dais. My heart slammed in my chest as if it tried to burst free from my body; icy fingers crept up my back, insidious as Eris's magic, freezing me, leeching my last vestiges of strength. I sensed others around me, behind me, felt the malefic presence of their Sins, and I knew the eleven . . . no, ten, Kings of Sin and Land were here as well.

I was a dead demon.

His voice, deceptively soft: "Daunuan, incubus, Prince of Lust. You are here before My Court to tell Me why you slaughtered the King of Seduction."

Sweat trickled down my brow. I felt the gazes of the other Kings, some hot with hatred, others amused, but all terrified of the creature before us, the fickle Ruler of the Pit who could destroy us with a thought, who was slowly destroying Hell and hurtling us closer to Armageddon.

"Speak, incubus. Why did you destroy your lord?"

I wanted to say that I'd killed Pan in self-defense, that he'd set me up and betrayed me, that for the past two weeks I'd been fighting for my life against the chosen of the Kings of Sin all because my liege-lord had bribed them with the promise of a boon.

And I wanted to say that I'd killed him because he would have feasted on Virginia's soul and tortured her as cruelly as any of the damned have ever been tortured, that her suffering would have been unbearable.

Mostly, I wanted to say that I loved her, and that I had to kill the one who'd forced me to lead her away from Heaven. But what does Hell care about betrayal or love?

So I told the King of Hell the other truth, which no one could deny: "Because he was an evil fuck who deserved to be killed."

A pause as I felt His judgment, and I closed my eyes and steeled myself for the greatest pain I had ever imagined, pain that would make Pan's thrice-blessed diamond blade seem a pleasant memory.

And then He laughed—low and soft, and so very cold, like a dusting of snow. "You speak the truth, Daunuan of Lust. And you amuse Me. You shall serve."

I swallowed, didn't dare to look up. "Sire?"

"You, Daunuan, are now King of the Seducers, Lord of Lust and Ruler of Passion."

Oh . . . fuck me. "Thank you, Sire."

"We shall discuss your coronation later. Go now—and Daunuan?"

"Yes, Sire?"

"Do a better job than your predecessor."

He didn't have to add the "or else"; it was very strongly implied.

"Yes, Sire."

And then He banished me from his throne room.

Chapter 23

And This, At the End of Everything

Virginia's kitchen was clean—no demon stains on the wooden planks, no shattered table thrown into the corner. The only sign of what had happened was Virginia's body splayed on the floor, her stomach sliced open, her blood on the counter and on her and pooled beneath her, the white robe saturated with red. The bread knife lay by her bare feet, and the bagel she'd been cutting—the bagel that was to be breakfast—had rolled to the refrigerator.

It was just another body. Empty. She'd never again brush away her unruly curls from her eyes.

You were just another human doll, Virginia. So very fragile. So easy to break.

I tore my gaze away from the corpse on the floor. The angel was perched on the countertop, legs crossed tailor-fashion, the white-gold globe of Virginia's soul nestled on her lap.

Glancing away, I focused on the blinking red light on the phone. A message. Terri's message. She was never going to call you back, Terri. Not unless you have a Ouija board. "You've been busy."

"I needed something to do, my lord," the angel said, then added, "My King."

Word gets around. I would have smirked if I'd had the energy. "You know?"

"He told me."

No need for me to ask which "He" she referred to. "Aren't you special?"

"I assume He told all of us."

"Sarcasm, cherub. Learn it."

"Yes, Sire. And my congratulations on your new role."

I leaned heavily against the counter next to her. Stared at Virginia's body. "Don't really feel like celebrating."

"I understand, Sire."

Somehow, I doubted that. I stole a glance at the globe resting in her lap, then looked away to stare at the place where I'd destroyed Eris. Not a smudge of mummified Jealousy smeared the floor. I wondered what the cherub had done with Lady Envy's ashes, then decided I didn't care. Tried to look at Virginia again, found that I couldn't.

Bless me for an angel, it shouldn't hurt to look at her.

I cleared my throat, asked, "How's she doing?"

"Sleeping, as you requested." I heard the smile in the angel's voice. "Unaware."

"Good."

I couldn't bear to look at her, to see how her spirit pulsed with joy and laughter, to see the red tendrils of lust corrupting her. And Hell knew I couldn't wake her, see the globe expand and take on human form—couldn't look at the soft curves of her body, the swells of her breasts, her belly, her hips, knowing that the Bonfire of the Heartlands would soon char her and melt her and burn away her goodness.

I'd damned her. It was my fault she was doomed for Hell, my action that had led her away from the Sky.

My action. My Sin.

The Sin that I now ruled.

I thought of Virginia, of how her eyes had sparkled like dew on spring grass, how her laughter had sounded like music. Thinking of her, of her enticing scent, of how she'd felt in my arms, I reached over and put my hands on the globe in the lightest of caresses.

I am Daunuan, King of Lust. And I pardon Virginia Heather Reed.

Her soul flared blindingly white, then settled back to its white-gold glow . . . unblemished by the telltale stain of lust.

She was free.

"My lord King," the angel breathed. "You forgave her."

"Take her to Heaven." I pulled my hands away, clenched them into fists to keep me from grabbing her soul and taking her to Hell and making her mine. "Take her to the Sky and bring her to her husband."

"My lord . . ."

"I promised." I took a deep breath, let it out in a shuddering sigh. "I promised her that her man would be there when she woke. Don't make a liar out of me."

"You . . ." Her voice cracked, then she said, "You could have kept her, Sire. You could have let her be with you. Your Queen."

"Yes."

"You loved her."

I looked down at my hooves. "And she loves her husband. She's meant for Heaven, meant to be with the one she loves. Take her, angel."

The angel stared at me, her sky blue eyes brimming with tears. "Sire, you've changed. You've learned compassion."

"Demons don't have feelings," I said, knowing I was lying and that was okay, because demons lie. "I don't do compassion."

She smiled, and the tears flowed down her cheeks. I'd finally made the angel cry, but it gave me no pleasure. "But you *do* do love, Sire."

"That's just another four-letter word."

But she and I both knew better.

She wrapped her arms around Virginia's soul, cradling it like an infant. "Sire? Would you like to say good-bye?"

Virginia, slipping away from me, forever.

"No. Take her. Go now." Before I change my mind.

In a whisper like a winter breeze, the angel disappeared, taking Virginia's soul with her.

I knelt beside Virginia's body, clasped her hand. Brought it to my lips and kissed it, gently, remembering the feel of those hands on me, touching me, her nails scoring me as I helped her body remember bliss.

Good-bye, Virginia.

A smell like fresh snow in the sunlight. I didn't look up at the angel; my gaze was locked on the mound of papers on the desk in front of me—lists of mortals damned for their Lust, how long they'd been burning in the Bonfire, whether their sin had been burned away, blah, blah, blah. Oh, Gehenna, the paperwork! Why did Kings have paperwork? I needed an assistant.

"Sire? It is done."

"Already? I'd have thought there'd be a longer line."

"That pleasure is reserved for the Abyss."

"Noted." Keeping my gaze on my paperwork, I asked, "So . . . is she happy?"

When she answered, I heard the smile in her voice. "She is with her true love, Sire, in the gardens of Paradise. Yes, she is happy. And so is he."

My throat tight, I said, "Good."

"Indeed." She paused, and I felt her Heavenly stare on my brow. Maybe she was surprised I wasn't wearing a crown. I'd tried it on, but it clashed with the horns. Hats had never been my thing. She asked, "Sire?"

"Yeah."

"Are you well?"

At that I did look up, met her pacific gaze. To show her I was still Daunuan, I grinned wickedly, even though I wanted to shriek to do the banshees proud, or let my wings sprout from my back and launch myself into the skies of Hell and shit upon the Courtyard of Abaddon. I was so fucking far from "well" that I knew I'd never be content again, not even in the midst of mind-blowing sex. Although, to be fair, I'd be willing to give that my best shot.

"More than well, Feathers. Fucking terrific." I flashed my fangs. "It's good to be the King."

She frowned, but what she said was, "I'm glad for you, Sire."

I leaned back in my chair, steepled my fingers beneath my chin. "So tell me. Now that I'm royalty, maybe you'd like me to pop your celestial cherry."

She blanched, and for a moment, I felt like my old self again. "No thank you, Sire."

"I'd make you feel good like you've never known before."

"I've known good all of my existence, Sire."

"Not like this, angel. I can make your body feel things you can't even begin to imagine." I pitched my voice low, added a purr, put on my game face, even though it was just going through the motions. "I can make your breasts ache for my mouth. I can find the sweet spot between your legs and make you wet just with a touch. I can lick you and taste you and drink your juices and make you feel like you're back in the Sky."

Her eyes had darkened as I'd spoken, and beneath her scent of lilacs and frost, I caught a whiff of peppermint.

Heh. Gotcha, Feathers.

"What do you say, angel? Want me to make a real succubus out of you?"

She took a deep breath and schooled her face to chilly impassivity. The splash of peppermint wafted away, just another hot wind in the depths of Hell. "You realize, Sire, that you could command me to sleep with you."

"Sleep? Who said anything about sleep?"

"I couldn't tell you no."

Pan's voice, roaring: *You don't get to tell me no!*

I shrugged. "Yeah, well, I'm not into power games." Not much, anyway.

"I'll think on it, Sire."

"Which means 'no.'"

She coughed and hid her mouth with her hand, but not before I saw her smile. "You know me well, Sire."

"Not as well as I could. Well, invitation's open, if you change your mind." I shoved away the papers, swept my hair from my face. Looked up at the angel, an idea taking shape. Grinning, I said, "Hey. How about being my major domo?"

"Your . . ." She frowned prettily, glanced at the piles of paperwork on my desk. Licked her lips. "Would that mean I wouldn't have to seduce mortals, Sire?"

"Depends how good a job you do pushing the papers."

"Accepted." She smiled, and somewhere children laughed in delight. Puke. "Thank you, Sire."

"Don't thank me yet, Feathers. I didn't say I'd never fuck my secretary. By the way, you can start immediately." I stood up, stretched. I was going on a bender, and if I was particularly lucky, I'd make it last through the rest of the year. The decade, even.

"Sire? Please don't call me that."

I rolled my eyes, then chuckled. "What the Hell. So what should I call you?"

"I rather like the name 'Angel.' It's pretty."

Puke, again. "An angel named Angel. Whatever. It's your name tag."

"Thank you, Sire. And Sire?"

"Yeah."

"She gave me a message for you."

I froze, felt my heart lodge in my throat. When I could speak, I asked, "What was it?"

"She said you should tell her."

Tonight.

Tonight I was going to tell Jezebel all of it—Virginia, Eris, Pan. My new role. I was going to tell her and show her, and then, when she was properly amazed and impressed by the crown on my horny brow, I was going to tell her to return to Hell with me and be my Queen.

Well, I'd ask her, at any rate. And she'd say yes. And no prude apostle was going to get in my way.

Waiting at Spice for her turn in the spotlight, I sat at a table, alone, watching the dancer onstage. She was good—sexy, knew how to move. Certainly wouldn't throw her out of bed. But she wasn't the one I was meant to be with, the one who knew me like no other did. The one who'd captured my heart.

My heart? *Pfaugh!* Satan spare me, what was next? Love sonnets?

I rolled my eyes. What was truly horrific was that if Jezebel wanted a sonnet, I'd give her one. I was sure I could think of something suitable.

Tennyson, maybe.

Better to have love and lust, her voice whispered, *than never to have lust at all.*

Bishop's balls, I was a sad, sad demon. A demon with *feelings.* Shivers. I shook my head, knocked back my scotch. I didn't know if feelings humanized me or if they emasculated me, and out of the two I didn't know which was worse. Whoever had said that change was always for the best should be roasted over an open fire.

Ah, screw it. I was still Daunuan. Just more cuddly.

And King of the Seducers.

Another drink, as I thought of how to start the conversation, how to ask the question. She'd say yes. Of course she'd say yes. She had to. And if she played hard to get, I had my arguments ready. I wouldn't even threaten her, or her prude apostle. Bless me to Heaven, I was practically switching sides.

I smiled. The things I do for her.

I even had a token of my affection waiting in my pocket (no, not that, although that was waiting for her too). Mortals liked such things, and for the moment, Jezebel . . . Jesse Harris . . . was mortal. Like others of her sex, she was an idiot for jewelry, even though she had a tendency to lose it or give it away. But once she wore my ring, she'd never want to take it off. I just knew it. I'd have to be careful when I took it out of its box to present it to her, of course; the diamond in its center was as deadly to me as marriage was to men. But women loved that shit. And Jezebel was worth it.

My Jezebel.

I grinned, imagining her reaction. She'd make a perfect Queen of Lust.

Then I frowned. What if she said no?

Shit.

I downed my drink. Ordered another. Maybe getting drunk was the best way to proceed.

Twenty minutes and who knew how many drinks later, she strutted onstage, began to dance and break men's hearts with every careless smile, every grind of her hips.

My head swam as I watched her, but it had nothing to do with alcohol. It was something uniquely her, something elusive and exquisite. Something I would die for.

Off came the clothes. Out came the wallets. Soon she had a garter of money around her thigh, like something out of a Coveter's wet dream.

I watched her dance in the spotlight, her body a thing of red and yellow beauty. I stood, ready to approach the tip rail and request a private dance, and once I got her alone I'd floor her with my power. I'd even put on the crown, if she wanted; women loved a man in uniform. And then . . .

. . . *my power* . . .

And then . . .

. . . *my power doesn't* . . .

And it hit me, as I watched her, sucked the air out of me and slammed my ass back down into my chair.

My power doesn't work on her, I'd said to Jezebel so long ago, speaking of the one who'd teach me things about myself I didn't know I had to learn. And Jezebel had replied . . .

Of course it doesn't. She's meant for Heaven. Your magic can't touch her, not if it's with malice aforethought.

I thought of how I'd tempted Jezebel, freshly scrubbed in her Jesse Harris body—how she'd danced with me, how my power had swayed her. How malice had most definitely been in my mind as I made her body sing with pleasure. How I'd done almost everything I could to sabotage her so-called relationship with the prude apostle. How her voice sounded when she'd called my name.

She's meant for Heaven. Your magic can't touch her.

My magic had done more than touch Jezebel. It had seduced her.

Again and again.

Jezebel wasn't meant for Heaven.

A laugh bubbled in my chest, and I let it out in a loud chortle.

A waitress near my table turned to look at me. "Sir? Everything all right?"

"Definitely." I grinned, felt my fangs extend as the force of Hell rippled through my body. "All is right with the world."

When the mortal Jesse Harris died—for real, no rescue missions to the Pit, no near misses, but for-all-time dead—her soul was going to Hell.

And then Jezebel would be mine.

I toyed with the idea of going up to the tip rail and stuffing a fiver down her garter and flashing my fangs, just for the Hell of it. But no—I'd promised that if she helped me, I'd leave her alone. For now.

So instead I dug out the small box with the deadly ring and left it on the table. The waitress was going to get the best tip of her life.

Grinning like I owned the world, I marched out of Spice, ready for anything.

I don't have to steal you away from your meat pie, Jezebel. You go ahead and play at this love thing. You can even grow old with him for all I care. Live your life to the fullest, babes.

I can wait.

Author's Note

It's all about the story.

Ever since Jezebel mentioned her buddy—the sexy incubus who could make her sweet spot tingle without even touching her—Daunuan refused to be just a minor character. Originally, he was going to be the one who shot Jezebel in *Hell's Belles* and then he was going to get killed by Paul. But the book took a completely different direction from what I'd imagined, and next thing I knew, Daun was (shudder) helping Jezebel instead of hunting her.

And then in *The Road to Hell*, his feelings for her became quite clear—to me, if not to him and Jesse. Demons don't love, after all. So what he was feeling must have been nothing more than indigestion. (No one ever said demons were the smartest creatures out there.)

I knew that I wanted to write Daun's story, but it took a while for me to figure out what sort of story it would be. Daun's in Hell, and Jesse's with Paul, which doesn't do much for a happily ever after for him. Did Daun even deserve a happy ending? He's a demon—an evil creature who has sex on the brain pretty much all the time. What would he know of love?

What if he had to find out the hard way?

That's where Virginia came in.

Poor Daun. He never knew what hit him.

So if you skipped to the ending (and given that this is a book about demons, it's okay to cheat; demons expect that sort of thing), then you know that this is closer to a dark paranormal than a paranormal romance because the "happily ever after" here is much more of a "happily ever afterlife." Virginia is content and Daun is content (for the moment). And so am I.

But with Armageddon edging ever closer, no matter what the King of Hell does (or possibly because of it), the very notion of a happily ever *anything* may be up for grabs.

Smoke 'em if you got 'em.

Like I said, it's all about the story. And Daun's story includes a Saratoga Springs that has an indoor theatre in Saratoga Park instead of an amphitheatre in Congress Park. It also includes both Leopold and Wolfgang Mozart, as well as William Seymour, who led the Azusa Street Revival in Los Angeles in 1906. Not the real Mozarts or Seymour, of course; this is fiction. (The facts behind these topics make for fascinating reading, and I am deeply indebted to numerous sources. To learn more about my research, please visit www.jackiekessler.com.) I am not claiming that Wolfgang really sold his soul (for whatever reason) or that "holy laughter" is anything insidious. I'm just telling a story. Daun's story.

And at his core, he's an evil bastard. In a cuddly sort of way.

—Jackie Kessler